Praise for
THE MEMORY BOX

**The Memory Box is a Houston Writers Guild
Manuscript Award winner.**

"**The Memory Box is a literary rarity**—a story of high imagination cast with characters who seem as authentic as they are complex. From the moment Caroline Thompson dares to Google her own name, the stakes and suspense develop, treating the reader to a 'can't put it down' mystery."

—Sidney Offit, author of *Memoir of the Bookie's Son*

"**In her impressive first novel**, *The Memory Box*, Eva Lesko Natiello tells the fascinating story of a woman whose memories piece together a self-portrait she doesn't recognize—until those memories yield to the terrible secrets they conceal."

—John Biguenet, author of
The Torturer's Apprentice and *Oyster*

"**5-Stars . . . be p**  **fairy tale away, grab on to** : **that you get through this** ır **mental faculties.** Eva Lesko Natiello shows tremendous talent and courage in her creation of a powerful dichotomy, reaching beyond boundaries."

—*San Francisco Book Review*

"... this one comes along and **tears to shreds everything you thought you knew about the genre ... And just when you think the book may have hit the limits of its genre, another sinister twist pushes it into serious Gone Girl territory.**"

—Emma Oulton, *Bustle*

"**Epically creepy ... creepier than Gillian Flynn's Gone Girl. After the last word, I had to take a deep breath, and think of cute, comforting things, like kittens and baby hedgehogs to stop the chills running through me.**"

—Sally Allen, *Hamlethub*

"**Could not put this book down.**"

—Jessica Collins, *Books, Ink's*

"*The Memory Box* **left me feeling stunned ...**"

—*onlinebookclub.org*

THE MEMORY BOX

THE MEMORY BOX

EVA LESKO NATIELLO

FINE LINE
PUBLISHING

For Joe, Margaux & Mark
my inner circle

PROLOGUE

Saturday, April 21, 2007, 9:07 a.m.

The oddest sensation seized me that morning. At first it was subtle, nearly imperceptible, like the onset of a rolling fog. It crept over me with quiet, unsettling determination. I tried to shake it. But the feeling only grew stronger. It permeated my joyful veneer until it snuffed the thrill from my core. I'd never felt anything like it.

Things weren't going as planned. I didn't expect to feel doubt the day after I handed him my manuscript. I anticipated pride and celebration, joy. It was a triumph, for God's sake.

No. On second thought, it wasn't doubt that wormed its way into my giddy fever. It was something else entirely.

As a warm breeze leaked through the screened window over the sink, I shivered. And grappled with this feeling. It was foreign.

It was fear.

PART I

CHAPTER ONE

Friday, September 22, 2006, 2:38 p.m.

It's impossible to un-know a secret. Once you know it, you own it. It can't be returned like a borrowed book. Or burned like a love letter. The click of a mouse won't delete it from the conscious mind. It'll stick to the walls of your memory like dried oatmeal to a dish. The secrets you wish you never knew become a burden to lug. A bowling ball without holes.

Some people are great collectors of secrets. They roll around, like swine, in the muck of them. They gloat with pride to be the bearer of indelicate news.

I am not one of those people. I don't want to pry into the backstories of others with a crowbar and a meat hook. What's happened to privacy anymore? Nothing is private. Everything is knowable.

The thing about secrets is they're mostly regrets, aren't they? I mean, "good news" secrets aren't really meant to be kept. Just the embarrassing, shameful kind. Everyone's said or done something they wish they hadn't. Maybe they were young and immature, or drunk, with temporary poor judgment. Do these things need to be broadcast? Should mistakes be tattooed on forearms?

The latest gossip around town is about a man whose daughter is in Lilly's third-grade class. When he was young *and* drunk, he streaked through the dean's backyard on a dare. Unfortunately for him, he was unaware of a ditch being dug and fell into it, breaking his fibula in the process, which left him stranded to sober up in a dark hole, waiting to be rescued in his birthday suit. One of our neighborhood snoops discovered this by Googling his name. Now this mature adult is living the shame all over again, as the gossipmonger moms of Lincoln Elementary pass their babble baton down a line of eager recipients. I'm surprised by how prevalent this rumor-wielding type is. Even in a place like Farhaven.

Practically everyone in town has been Googled by these women, who in turn cast out their questionable findings like a fistful of feed at the zoo. I make sure to smile warmly whenever I see this dad or any of the other gossip victims at school. It could be any of us. I wouldn't want to be someone with something to hide in this town.

When they Googled my name—Caroline Thompson—a weeklong joke ensued at my expense. The search elicited only three hits. The skipper of the gossipistas, Gabrielle Callis, gave me the heads-up. "Caroline," she said, locking her gaze on mine. Unblinking. (She never blinks. Sometimes I want to blow in her eyes to see if that's physically possible. You'd think the weight of six coats of mascara and the law of gravity would collapse those lashes.) She placed a concerned hand to my forearm. "I wanted to be the first to tell you so you won't be embarrassed when you hear others talking about it." I swear she sips from a coffee mug with "Bomb-Dropper" written across it. What's more, she pays only occasional deference to the facts.

A shrill, nerve-splitting siren comes from the corner of my desk, nearly knocking me out of my chair. Everything on the desk vibrates. I grab the egg timer and silence it while I simultaneously contemplate throwing it out the window. I'm the one who sets the darn thing, then I'm always shocked when it goes off. Smarty Pants, who a moment ago was sleeping under the desk, sprawled across my foot on his back with his paws sticking into the air like an upside-down coffee table, flips over and rights himself on all fours. He barks and shoots me a look of annoyance. "I'm sorry, sweetie." I scoop him up and spill him into my lap. "I hate that thing, too." I kiss the top of his head and rake my fingers through his white, corn silk hair. I lift one of his ears and whisper, "Who's my best friend?" He follows, as always, with one certain bark. Sometimes I actually think he barks "Me!" which wouldn't be correct English, but I'd let it slide because he's so cute.

The time on my computer says 2:43 p.m. If I don't leave the house in the next three minutes to pick up the girls, the closest parking space I'll find at school will be in front of my own house.

Before I leave, I reread what I typed in the Google search box.

"Caroline Thompson."

I don't know why I haven't ever Googled myself. I've been so glued to my soapbox trashing this voyeuristic time-suck, I've brainwashed myself. I've got a right to know what people know about me. And I don't care if it *is* only three mentions. That's not embarrassing. Frankly, I'd be relieved.

It's a good thing I have no time to devote to this. I click

"search." If there are only three mentions, this isn't going to take very long, anyway. I check the time. I've got two minutes. I scan a few pages.

There's a strip of photos, running across the first page, of various Caroline Thompsons. I'm none of them. Once the esteemed potter from Colorado and the college professor from Pensacola are weeded out, as well as a few others I'm thankful I'm not, like the one who's incarcerated, I read the mentions that look like mine.

All three of them.

Well, at least Gabrielle didn't make that up.

The first is a review I wrote on Amazon for an electric tooth-brush. No wonder people have tons of Google hits if reviews count. The second is for the time I coordinated the used book collection for the Farhaven Public Library. The third—when I headed the Healthy Lunch Committee at Lincoln Elementary.

Dirt like that could land me in *Star Magazine*.

Who cares? At least I don't have any explaining to do.

I close the document, collect Smarty, and jump into the car to pick up the girls.

When I arrive at the school, I head toward the third-grade door where I find Vicki on her cell phone. There are clusters of moms and babysitters overlapping like a Venn diagram. Vicki's wearing head-to-toe moisture-wicking Lycra—her second skin—even on days she's not teaching a spinning class at the Y. Her head is tipped down and she's deep in conversation, unaware of my arrival. She repeatedly twirls the ends of her hair. I stand beside her, waiting for her to finish, when I feel a tug at my pant leg. Then a hand rifles through the pocket of my khakis like a crab in a paper bag. It belongs to a two-year-old.

My friend Meg's youngest. She's looking for a dog biscuit to give Smarty, who is curled up in my cardigan.

"Hiya, Sweetie!" I say. "Don't you look beautiful in that orange dress. Are those daisies on the pocket?" She nods with her whole body. "Where's your mommy?" She points behind her without looking. "Do you want to give Smarty Pants a biscuit?" This time she nods with such gusto her dress rocks back and forth like a church bell.

The phone remains pressed to Vicki's ear, though she hasn't said a word the entire time.

"You still on the phone?" I whisper.

"Not really." The words sift out of clenched teeth.

"On hold?"

Her head stays low while her eyes dart back and forth, then she snaps the phone shut. "I was faking a call." She leans into me. "I'm not gonna be a sitting goose for her anymore. What, do I have some sign on my head that says 'please, *please* accost me with your boring, senseless blabber?'" she hisses without taking a breath.

"That would be a large sign." I have no idea what she's talking about.

"I don't want to hear about how her daughter won first place, *again*, or her son the science genius, blah, blah, blah," she continues. "She's insufferable."

"Oh. Gabrielle?"

"Yes, *Gabrielle*. She ambushed me this morning."

I look around at the thick mass of moms. "I don't see her anywhere."

"Well, don't let that fool you—she can appear out of nowhere. Like the Wicked Witch of the West. I don't want to hear any more about that stupid crafts show she's having at her house. I'm not going."

"I'm not going, either." I shrug.

"Well, neither am I. I don't care that the wife of the pitcher of the Yankees is gonna be there. Or the Mets—" Vicki looks up at the sky for help, "who the hell knows. That's the only way she can get anybody there anyway. She claims she's raising money for the 'have-nots.' Do you believe she said that?"

"Sheesh. Altoid?" I flip the top open, trying to distract her.

She straightens up and ignores my offer. "And, I didn't want to tell you this, 'cause it's so ridiculous, but when I was volunteering at Field Day last week I heard her tell someone she saw you coming out of Weight Watchers." She yanks at her jogging top and scratches the skin on her forearm. "Not that anyone would believe it." Vicki's attention shifts for a moment to flake a gauzy piece of skin off her arm, post-sunburn. "You're thinner than your eight-year-olds," she adds before throwing her phone into her fringed handbag.

"What?" I balk.

The school doors sigh open, and 416 students scurry out like freed lab mice. I spot my girls racing over toward Meg, who's about twenty feet away clutching the hands of her toddlers as if they'd blow away in the wind.

"Hey, Meg, ready for tonight?" I shout over the heads of others. Expressionless, Meg nods. But not at me. Gabrielle is firing *news* at her. I think about retracting, but it's too late. A hand grasps my forearm.

"What a *shame*, Gabrielle. Did you hear that, Caroline?" Meg attempts to sound engaged as she now holds my arm for dear life, letting go of her daughter to do so. The little darling blasts off as fast as her tiny legs will take her until she trips on the bulging root of an old maple tree, then begins to wail. Meg's cue to bolt. Leaving me with the Wicked Witch of the West—who doesn't miss a beat. Gabrielle simply pivots on the heels of her powder-blue suede loafers to direct the news at me. I subconsciously cross my arms in front of my chest.

"Oh, Caroline, I may as well tell you, too, before you hear it from someone else, no doubt laced with falsehoods." She tightens the belt on her Burberry trench and takes a deep breath. The veins in her scrawny neck wiggle with excitement. "It's confirmed. You-know-whose husband took off with the au pair— back to England. They left yesterday."

My mouth drops open, and I shut it. No need to give Gabrielle free advertising. "Oh, God—that's terrible." I'm sick to my stomach. I was the last holdout to think that it was idle talk, that people were just jealous of the Norwegian au pair who has legs, like chopsticks, up to her ears.

"Well, yes, of course it's *terrible*, but if you ask me, it wouldn't hurt to pick yourself up a little. Having five children is no excuse for not keeping up on personal maintenance." She sweeps the flip of hair resting on her right shoulder, and her eyes pluck the crowd to see who she can apprehend next. This is her segue sign—she's about ready to move on. "Not that getting rid of the gray would have held onto him, but it was time to lose the baby fat at the very least. I'm sure you'd agree." She fixes back on me. "I hear Weight Watchers is quite successful."

Gabrielle's eyes throw a net over her next victim, thank God. She heaves her hand up over her head. "Oh, *Bern!*"

Bern is Gabrielle's chief disciple. In a twitch she's at Gabrielle's side, her springing curls still bouncing though her feet have come to a halt. She blows her nose and sticks the tissue up the cuff of her sweater, then gives Gabrielle her rapt attention.

"I've got the greatest news . . ." Gabrielle reports. I'm long gone by the time she spews her next package of poison.

The crowd around school is dwindling. Lilly and Tessa have appeared at my side, amid a tight braid of friends. They turn their heads toward me and call out in unison, "Hi Mom!"

"Hey, Caroline," Meg calls out as she walks in my direction, the kids dribbling behind. I wait for her to catch up. "Sure you can't stay for a drink tonight? Andy's still out of town, isn't he? Stay for a while," she says, and we resume walking toward our cars.

"Yeah, he doesn't come back till Sunday. But I've got class tonight. Let's do something next week. It'll be easier for me with Andy back. Hey, I heard you ordered a fancy cake for Delia, you want me to pick it up? I'm going into town."

"Mommy—" Tessa shouts from behind. "Smarty wants to go to the woods." I didn't even notice Smarty pulling the leash toward the wooded area behind the school. Tessa runs up and grabs my arm. "Can we let Smarty catch something so Delia can see, *please*."

"No, we cannot let him catch something. He's already been a bad boy once today," I whisper, "I'll tell you about that later."

Tessa turns to Delia and says, "Smarty Pants hunts mice! My mom says he has an identity crisis cause he thinks he's a bloodhound."

We silently pass Gabrielle and Bern, who are standing next to Gabrielle's gold Mercedes, still tangled up in a sticky glob of gossip. Two zoo lions at feeding time gnawing the same piece of slaughtered meat.

"Are you serious?" Bern exclaims. Her tiny stature forces her to look up at Gabrielle like she's gazing at the Statue of

Liberty. Occasionally she pops up on tippy toes with excitement. "Gabrielle—you can't be *serious*."

"I *am*. Allison doesn't *have* eighty-seven Google hits." Gabrielle reports this in a volume that benefits the far and wide, while her hands dance all over—shrieking-pink nail polish punctuating every word. "When she Googled herself, she didn't realize that there was another Allison Scotte—also with an 'e,' who's dead now but apparently led quite an interesting life back in the sixties—"

I think about my measly three Google hits as we walk by them, and I can't help but feel slightly inferior.

Meg and I don't say a word until we're well past them.

Once we're down the hill, she says, "Were they talking about that au pair again?" She shakes her head, "As if it isn't painful enough without their . . . going at it, like some—I don't know . . ."

Out of nowhere, my sister flashes through my mind. It's not the first time Meg has reminded me of JD. She'd say something like that. Both of them have an ability to soar above the clothesline of others' dirty laundry. They rarely engage in it. With JD living so far away, I'm lucky to have Meg to keep me grounded.

Since moving here nearly six years ago, making friends has brought along a certain amount of self-examination. It's like being a teenager all over again. No matter one's age, it's important to feel part of something. To feel like you belong. But the balancing act inevitably becomes how much of yourself are you willing to compromise in order to be part of a community? Which, in this case, is the very specific subculture of stay-at-home moms.

I'm in Meg's camp as far as choosing not to engage in dagger throwing with the likes of Gabrielle and Bern. It's one thing I will not conform to as an at-home mom who has put her career as a journalist and future novelist on hold to raise a family in the suburbs.

Apart from being a dagger thrower, Gabrielle is famous for talking about dinners she's had with "the Lesters" or "the Ferrneggis," or how, at her beach house, she's entertaining "the Pinnochets" or some such family with whom she's "*very* close." And somewhere after "we just got back from Vail with the Robsons," she'll stop midstream and say, "You do know the Robsons, don't you?"

I have no desire to wear my friends like charms on a bracelet. I have dear friends. We're *very* close, too.

I wave good-bye to Meg, who has crossed the street to her car. "No worries about the cake. I picked it up already. It's *huge*—you better take some home."

The girls and I hop in the car and drive into town to buy a birthday present for Delia.

"Hey, how was school?" I ask, as we stop at the corner for the crossing guard to sweep the streets clean of school children.

"Great," says Lilly.

"Great," says Tessa.

"Great." Who can argue with that?

"The car smells disgusting," says Lilly. "Smells like puke."

"That's gross, Lilly," says Tessa.

"Well, it does. I'm just tellin' it the way I'm smellin' it." Lilly clothespins her nose with her fingers.

"Smarty had a little accident this morning," I interject. "But it's all gone now, and I sprayed it with Lysol."

"Smarty pooped back here?" Lilly shrinks back in her seat, hoists her legs up, and draws her knees to her chin.

"No, he didn't poop. He threw up on the floor."

"Yuck. Did you have to tell us that?"

"Well, sorry, you thought he pooped. Anyway, he caught a chipmunk, and I guess he swallowed it because when I found it, it was kind of very disgusting."

"Mom!"

"Hey, go easy on me. I've had a tough morning. I couldn't just leave it there for Daddy to clean up."

"Did Smarty find it in the basement?" Tessa asks.

"Well . . . I don't know. Maybe, because when I walked him this morning, he was on a leash."

"Ha! Daddy was right!" Tessa exclaims. "Smarty knew something was down there. See Mom, Smarty *is* a dog detective. You have to let Daddy get him a job at the police department."

"Daddy's not serious. Anyway, I don't *think* he is. He can't possibly believe the police would hire a thirteen-pound Westie to be a search dog. Why don't we keep Sherlock Holmes to ourselves? Maybe you can train him to find stuff when we lose it. Like Daddy's car keys, Daddy's cell phone, Daddy's wallet . . ."

"I'm gonna tell Daddy you said that—" Tessa playfully slaps the back of my seat.

Once we finish in town, the girls pack for the sleepover, and we head to Meg's house, picking up another friend on the way.

By the time I get home from my writing class, I barely have the energy to inhale a few bites of Chinese before I undress, flop on my bed, and fall asleep. The next morning, despite it being Saturday, I resist the urge to hide under my comforter so I can instead be somewhat productive before I pick up the girls. A printout of today's schedule is on my nightstand. I swipe it and head to the shower.

The smell of brewed coffee meets me halfway down the stairs. The closest I'm ever going to get to someone waiting on me is my programmable coffeemaker. And the doggy door. I grab a mug from the cabinet and take my coffee and yogurt to the den to work on something for my writing class at Drewer University.

The house is quiet. It's just me and Smarty Pants. The only sound comes from Smarty chewing his toy mouse under the wing chair in the corner of the den. A wet rubber sound, a gummy-saliva squeak. Though I often crave quiet, this is not the welcomed kind—like a snowstorm that shuts the world down. Instead, it's a lonely, I-miss-my-family quiet.

I turn on the computer, and its hum comforts me. My right calf is pressed against the side of the CPU, which subtly vibrates. Smarty snuggles up to my left foot, using it as a pillow for his head.

Through the den window, above the mounds of pink rose bushes, the morning sun is cowering behind clouds. Every so often it bobs and weaves, in and out, but ultimately it's reluctant to reveal itself. The world is still. Or at least Brightwood Road is. No one is racing to work. No dogs are being walked. Nor are there any joggers jogging by. No sign of even a single grey squirrel scampering across any of the verdant lawns. All of the pristine center-hall colonials line up like toy soldiers, their American flags saluting at attention. The street looks like a vacant movie set.

There are a bunch of new emails to read. I check them first before I start to write. Chief among them is one from Andy. His arrival time tomorrow has changed to noon. After a quick glance at today's news headlines, I open the document with my work in progress.

I stare at the screen without really seeing anything. My mind keeps wandering to yesterday's conversation between Gabrielle and Bern. It was a stupid conversation between senseless, gossipy moms, and I'm angry that it's taking up space in my brain. If only I could type a few words, that might get me going. Time's ticking; I don't have all day. I need to pick up the girls at ten.

I'm an independent thinker, I remind myself. Just because I'm a stay-at-home mom doesn't mean I fill my days with vacuous activities, like *other* people.

My attention grows fickle. It's no longer on the screen at all. My eyes meander around the desk and stop on a framed photo of Andy and me at the beach, taken when we were dating, when I was still Caroline Spencer. Both of us are tanned a golden brown, the color of Andy's eyes, and I'm wearing a rather skimpy bathing suit, which I hold onto just in case my body ever looks like that again. As I stare at this photo, it occurs to me that the people in this town don't know my maiden name. Do they? When we moved here, I had already changed my name to *Thompson*. They would never Google *Caroline Spencer*. Not even Meg knows my maiden name.

I type *Caroline G. Spencer* into the Google search box. A visceral sense of promise gushes through me. Maybe I'm a somebody after all.

Smarty's now in the kitchen, nudging his metal bowl across the tile floor—dog speak for "I'm hungry." My mind strays to think about when I last filled the bowl while my finger clicks "search."

A tsunami of "Caroline G. Spencers" cascades before my eyes. Come *on*. My heart giggles. I click page two, then page three, then page four. "Yes!" Fist pump in the air. If only they could see me *now*. The Caroline Spencers don't stop. Is this juvenile? Am I acting like a teenager who's counting Prom Queen votes? No. Worse. I'm acting like a catty, immature gossipmonger mom. But I gloat for another minute. It's not like I'm going to count them and brag to everyone at school on Monday. I'm just having a private me-moment of reassurance: I too have been interesting, so *there.*

Before my head swells any more, I should verify that these "Caroline Spencers" are me. But I can't spend all day on this. I check the egg timer. Good, only a seventeen-minute diversion. My eyes sweep over the page. Midway down the screen, it's my sister's name, directly beneath mine, that catches my eye.

> Jane Dory **Spencer** *deceased at age 28 Lanstonville Press, April 21, 2000. She is survived by . . .*
>
> *www.lanstonvillepress.com/ . . ./*
> *jane-dory-spencer-deceased . . .*

What?

What is this?

I blink hard, once—twice—the third time pausing with my eyes squeezed closed to the count of five before I open them. I read again.

This can't be. This isn't my sister. My heart leaps up in my chest and goes cold. With flurries. Like it's a snow globe with a wind chill factor. Saliva floods my mouth. I try to gulp it down, hoping it'll push my heart back into place. I can't be reading what I'm reading. I let out a barking laugh to cut through my nerves. This is not *true, of course.* I just *spoke* to my sister. When was that? I struggle to remember. It seems like it was just . . . I don't know exactly. For some reason, I can't pinpoint it. But my sister is not *dead.* That's for certain. She didn't *die.* Oh my God, is this some kind of sick joke? Could someone have done this? People can't *plant* a Google, *can they?*

I convince myself to settle down. Take it easy. This must be *another* Jane Dory Spencer. Someone else's obituary. I can't wait to tell JD that I found another Jane Dory. She's gonna laugh her butt off over that—she's always hated her name. Hence the acronym. Oh, she's gonna *love* this.

I inhale with every muscle of my body, and the oxygen blow to my brain makes my head spin. I sit in a half-lotus, back in the chair, arch my back for strength, and click on the excerpt to read more:

> Jane Dory Spencer, 28
>
> Jane Dory Spencer 28, known as JD, a lifelong resident of Lanstonville, Pennsylvania, died on Friday, April 21, at Danielston Hospital in Danielston, Pennsylvania.
> Ms. Spencer received her undergraduate degree in Women's Studies at Barton College and a law degree from Stanton University in Hammond, New York. She recently worked as a law clerk for the Clarkston County Courthouse. She is survived by her mother and father, Elaine and Wally Spencer . . .

As I read my parents' names I become dizzy; small, white, slow-moving spots are now blocking my view of the computer screen. I press my eyes shut to get rid of the spots.

> . . . sister, Caroline Grace Spencer . . .

Oh my God. That's me.

CHAPTER TWO

Saturday, September 23, 2006, 10:12 a.m.

This time when I gasp, the air slashes my throat. I can't bear to read more, but I need to find the date of the obituary. My mind speeds in circles. I have to zero in. And forge an explanation. Any explanation. I think about those horrible hidden-camera game shows that I forbid the girls to watch because they're so mean-spirited—I wonder if those stupid school moms would ever do something so violating and evil. I look for the date of the article. I try to find the scroll key, but I can't. My fitful pecking is fruitless. *Shit.* I can't see the arrow key through the swarm of floating spots.

Finally. At the top of the page: *"April 23, 2000."*

What's *today's* date?

I reach for my desk calendar. I always keep my desk calendar right next to my mouse pad. But it's not there. It's *never* not there. I search my desk. On the right, the tissue box is perfectly parallel with my note pad. On the left, the lamp aligns with a stack of computer paper and a small cup of pencils (points up). Next to the tissue box is the egg timer. Everything's in its place. *Except for my calendar.* I thrust myself against the desk so hard that the wheels of my office chair hurl me backward, close to the door of the den where I leap up and spring toward the hallway.

"*April 23, 2000, April 23, 2000, April 23, 2000,*" becomes my chant, to remember it long enough to find yesterday's paper.

This is crazy—*beyond* crazy—like someone has kidnapped and drugged me. And—*and*—plopped me into a *cryogenics experiment.* How can this be? I've completely lost sense of the day—the *year?*

Not to mention—if this is true—*tragic life events.*

I rush from room to room, panicked, like a mom who's lost her toddler at the mall, tackling anything in my way. Poor Smarty, I trip over him twice, yet he continues to follow me underfoot with mirrored anxiety. He knows something's wrong. He always knows when something's up. Smarty has this sense. I don't know what to call it. He just senses stuff. He knows *me.* I'm getting crazy now. What am I talking about? I'm not in my right mind.

The sound of Smarty's nails on the wood floor is like the clicking keys of an old typewriter, a repeating staccato, a rhythm, a pulse. I can't stand it. It's creepy. But it's just Smarty. It's as if he's typing a note I don't want to read. He's right behind me, following. Or is he pushing? Crazy again.

I race around the corner of the den into the kitchen, and my left heel hydroplanes across a slick of oil. I skid with arms outstretched until I stub my small toe on the iron leg of a kitchen stool. My body jerks sideways from the shocking tremor that soars up my leg, causing my cheek to smack against the iron cut-out monkeys that line the back of the stool. My face singes from the contact. My body buckles. Determined not to lose ground, I clamber to my feet.

"April 23, 2000." The chant grows stronger and louder as if it's possible to ward off the unspeakable if the mantra is not broken. I have no idea what today's date is. Or the year. My memory is paralyzed. "Where's my goddamned calendar?"

Finally, on the bathroom floor, sits last week's *Sports Illustrated*. I collapse on the cold, hard tile and snatch it.

September, 2006.

Not until I hear the doorbell do I realize Smarty is licking my face and I'm lying on the bathroom floor. The sound bellows through the house again and again like a blow horn.

Who would ring the doorbell like that? It's insane. Paranoid that it's the police with horrific news, I peel myself off the bathroom floor, but misjudge the space and smack my forehead against the corner of the sink.

Voilá, the Macy's Fourth of July Fireworks Spectacular.

I wobble out of the bathroom and fumble for the closest wall to support me, down the foyer to the front door to kill the person on the other side of it. From the hall mirror, I catch a glimpse of myself. There's a bruise on my cheek in the shape of what appears to be a small monkey, the color of freshly burst blood vessels, a dark reddish-purple with a faint skinny monkey tail curving alongside my hairline. God, I'm a freak. The room spins. I steady myself on the cool brass of the doorknob just before opening it.

"Electrolux, ma'am. How are you today?"

Electrolux? Is he kidding me? He was doing Morse code on the bell like a soldier with Tourette's. The only people excused for ringing like that are cops and trick-or-treaters. Or a kid who has to pee.

His cell phone rings. He mouths "sorry" while he answers it. I'm in no mood for the vacuum man. Plus, he was just here, practically. Like four weeks ago. Who vacuums that much? I'm nauseous, and my head is splitting. Unease and confusion move through me like morning sickness. Looking at this guy makes me feel worse. Does he always look like this? He's wearing wrinkled grey. Pants, shirt, even his skin is lacking any discernible color. "Electrolux" is embroidered onto his right breast pocket, like he sewed it himself in the dark. His hair is pasted to his head—oil concealing its true color—though at this point I'd speculate grey.

Who am I to criticize?

He finishes his call and looks back at me tentatively. He starts his spiel, "Do . . . you . . . uh, need . . . some . . . bags, or *help* with anything?" He stutters and keeps staring at my cheek. "Uh, would you like me to call . . . somebody. A *doctor*?" His eyes zip back and forth as he sneaks glimpses of my cheek and my forehead while he repeatedly pats down the back of his hair.

Something warm slowly trickles over my eyebrow.

"No . . . not today." Vacuuming is the last thing on my mind.

"Uh, okay . . . I gotta go." He jerks backward down the steps.

I step back to close the door, then see him stop on the brick path to pick something up. He turns and hands me something. It's today's paper.

My eyes find the upper right hand corner where the date is printed.

September 23, 2006.

A sick feeling slides from my eyes to my throat and settles in my stomach.

Visions of the obituary sneak back to my consciousness like a whiff of something rotten. How could my sister be—? There's no way.

Just inside the house, an idea hits me.

I hurry back to the kitchen; Smarty chases behind.

My anxious finger presses the "Message" button on the dark grey box that listens to people when we can't. The automated voice starts, "You have two old messages in your mailbox."

"First message:"

"Hi, honey. I just got here." The minute I hear Andy's honey-roasted voice, my heart inflates. "I'm calling on the hotel phone because I think I lost my cell phone."

This would be the third time he's lost his phone this year. I can imagine him furrowing his brow as he talks into the phone, thinking he should be bummed out about losing it again. But down deep he isn't because "it's just a phone!" He often feels bad for not feeling bad. So he pouts to conjure self-condemnation.

"Why aren't you *home*." I yell at the answering machine, and my eyes begin to mist. I wouldn't be so vulnerable if he were home. I don't like feeling this way. It's not me.

What am I thinking? How exactly would this be better with Andy home? Would I really tell him JD's dead and has been for six years? And that I thought we spoke recently? No way. I need to sort this out first. My fingers fumble to find the stop button on the answering machine. He's getting to the part when he tells me he loves me. I don't want to hear that. I don't want any reminders of how great my life is. Was. Until this morning. Why don't we realize things are pretty damn good until they aren't?

There has to be a message on here from JD. I press the button again.

"Next message:"

"Oh hi, Mrs. Thompson. It's Rachel. I can't babysit on Thursday, the twenty-eighth, 'cause I have band practice. Sorry." Crap. "But I can do October eighteenth. Okay? Okay, 'bye."

Click. "Message erased. There are no more messages."

No messages from JD. That doesn't prove anything.

I'll just call her. Jeez, how long was it gonna take for me to come up with that?

Her number comes to me immediately. Like I dialed it an hour ago. My hands are trembling so badly that once I dial, I rest the phone in the crook of my neck and shove my hands in the back waistband of my pajamas. Why am I so nervous? She'll answer, and this charade will be over.

"Hello."

"Janie!" I jerk my head up, and the phone slips. I grab it just in time.

"No. This isn't Janie. Who's this?" says a guy.

"It's Caroline. Is, um, JD there?" My voice cracks.

"No. There's no JD here. What number are you looking for?"

I rattle it off, and he tells me it's the right number. My voice is shaking. "How long have you had this number?" I ask him, my teeth knocking against each other.

"About four years. Who are you looking for?"

"Uh, uh, my sister . . . JD Spencer. I know it sounds crazy . . . but, we're a little out of touch, um, I'm trying to track her down. . . . Do you know her?" My voice hiccups, and my eyes leak.

"Sorry."

I put the phone back, and it rings. I jump like a canned snake.

"*JD?*" A tear slides down my cheek.

"Hi, Caroline—no, it's Meg. Are you expecting a call?"

"Meg? Oh my God, *Meg.* What time is it?" The oven clock says ten-thirty. "I'm so sorry, is everything all right? Oh gosh, I'm really sorry."

"Don't worry, everything's fine. I was just going to ask you the same—only because you're never late. Hey, I feel like a jerk calling you, but I have to bring my kids to the dentist in fifteen minutes, and I'd drop Tessa and Lilly, but I can't fit them in my car."

"You should've called me sooner. I'm screwing up your whole morning." I barrel through the house looking for my car keys, trying not to pant into the phone. "If it wasn't for the vacuum guy . . ." In the mudroom I slide into flip flops. "Did everyone have fun?" I squeeze out a light, happy voice. It sounds breathless and psycho.

"Uh, yes and no. Or no and yes. Two left last night and one left at two in the morning. She had a nightmare, and I found her roaming around the house, crying. Poor thing. I hate sleepovers. You'll be happy to know your two fell asleep first."

"Oh, good. Listen, I'll be right there."

I hang up the phone. Smarty is sitting in front of me, his ears pointing to the moon. I can't go to Meg's in my current physical state, especially considering that I'm still in pajamas. There'll be questions. I could tell them I slipped on a lubed-up

piece of broccoli swimming in a puddle of oil and went flying into the kitchen stool, but that sounds ridiculous. Who'd
believe that? Wouldn't slipping on a piece of broccoli mean I
was running for my life through my kitchen? Why would I be
sprinting through my kitchen? Because I was freaked out of
my mind, that's why. I'm an open book, for Pete's sake. I don't
own a poker face. I own a scared-shitless face, an I-ate-the-
last-granola-bar face, an I-got-a-scratch-on-the-new-car face,
and an I-know-something-I-can't-tell-you face. Which means
I shouldn't face anyone. I strain to think. I need something
short and sweet. Short and sweet and neat. Not something
that will prompt questions. Meg will want to fuss over me and
be hyper-concerned, especially since Andy's in London. My
friends are like a SWAT team when he's on a business trip. In
a flash, they emerge from the nooks and crannies of their own
lives to swoop in and help me. Meg will ask if Andy knows.
If I've seen a doctor. And I'll just lose it. And I just can't.
Where would that get me? With the morning I've had, probably the psych ward of Mountainview General. I can't even
think about Andy getting *that* call. Thank goodness Meg has
a dentist appointment. She won't have time for me.

I arrive at Meg's house with a large Band-Aid stuck to
a swollen forehead and a good slathering of foundation that
fails to conceal the monkey. I look like a battered old lady.
Thank God I have my teeth. A stately Dutch Colonial stands
before me in a medium shade of putty, with a black lacquered
door on which hangs a pineapple doorknocker in weathered
verdigris. I'm embarrassed by its composure. I pick up my
shoulders, smooth down my shirt, and ring the doorbell. Then
I slip my hands in my back pockets to settle them.

"Oh, hi, Caroline. That was fast. . ." Meg barely turns

to look at me because she's on the phone. She motions with her head for me to come in, then whips back around, her eyes bulging. *"Caroline . . . what happened to you?"* The hand with the phone drops to her side. *"Are you okay?* Oh my God, what . . . *look* at you." She puts the phone back to her ear and says, "I gotta go. Call you back," then squints her eyes and peers back at me. "What happened?"

I finger my hair and mess it up so it falls on my face. I cup my chin in one hand and cross the other arm along my chest to support my elbow. "I fell, but it's okay. It looks worse than it is. I'm fine, really. Really, I am." My eyes find the floor. I become woozy. Then I inch my head up to look for Tessa and Lilly. I've got to get out of here.

"Fine? Caroline, my God . . . look at you."

I can tell this is not gonna be easy, and my emotions squirm and wrestle. *Let go, and tell her everything* is in a head-lock with *Beg her for help* at the hands of *Shut up and get the hell out of here.*

I practically vomit my explanation. "I slipped in the kitchen. There was food on the floor from dinner last night—Chinese—I ordered it steamed, but they put oil on it. Anyway, I slid and smacked into the stool by the island."

What should I have said? It was the truth. I was relieved not to lie. It's always the truth that sounds made-up. Which would explain the look on her face.

"What?!"

Meg puts her hands on her hips but says nothing. She tilts her head and gapes at my bruise. It must occur to her that her mouth is hanging open because she shuts it emphatically. In her silence, I call out for the girls, who are in the kitchen past the archway.

"What took you so long?" asks Lilly. I let it slide because she has her sneakers on—although not laced—just slid into with the back squashed down, but at least this will make for a quick exit. Their overnight bags are at the door.

When the girls look at me, I sweep my hair in front of my face and head toward the door. Over my shoulder, I thank Meg and promise to have them for dinner real soon. It sounds canned and glib.

"Did you call the doctor?" Meg asks again from her front door.

"Yes," I lie. "Thanks for having the girls—" I yell back to her without turning around, just a hand in the air. I'm the first in the car.

Lilly opens the back door and throws her bag in, then slides across the seat.

"Mom, what happened to you?" She grabs the front seat and pokes her head over. Tessa slinks into the car and melts into her seat; her eyes drop to the floor.

Tessa covers her ears, "La, la, la . . ."

Lilly smacks her on the arm. "Quiet, Tessa. What are you doing that for?"

"Tessa, Lilly . . ." I turn around to look at them. Lilly's face is only inches from mine since she's still leaning on the front seat. Her honey-colored freckles form constellations across her cheeks. Once she gets a good look at my bruise, her nose crinkles, causing the Big Dipper's handle to bludgeon Sagittarius.

"Listen, I'm okay. Don't worry. It's just a little bruise. It'll be gone by the time Daddy gets home. I did one of my klutz moves and slipped on a piece of broccoli in the kitchen and collided with the stools." I'm talking with my hands. I never do that. One hand forms a stop sign, the other does this lit-tle-itty-bitty thing, then both of them crisscross, and with fin-gers splayed, they create big, flashy fireworks. "And you know the monkeys? Look—one of them is bruised into my cheek. See it?" I point at it. "Is that hysterical, or what? A bruise in the shape of a monkey?" Lilly keeps following my hands like she's hypnotized. Tessa hasn't looked my way the entire time. "Who would believe something so ridiculous?" Tessa's eye-lashes pop up finally for a quick look. Both of their mouths drop open, and this is one of those rare moments when neither of them has anything to say. For ten seconds.

"Cute monkey." Lilly nods like an old man. "Good story." And pats me gently on the head.

"That's not funny, Lilly." Tessa hits Lilly in the arm, then looks out the window.

"Tess, it's okay, I'm fine—don't worry about me." I reach out to rest my hand on her knee and give it a little squeeze. I wish she would look at me, but she's staring out the window. The silhouette of her eyelashes in profile contrast against the bright light. "I'm a little worried about the stool—ha!" I fake chuckle. It sounds ridiculous. "By the way, let's not tell Daddy if he calls tonight, okay? He'll just worry, and he doesn't need any stress right now, especially when he's so far from home. He worries about us too much. Anyway, I'm sure it'll look better tomorrow."

I turn on the radio, and the car ride becomes normal. They launch into their chicken chatter, and I begin to chill out. This is good. I need the girls around me. I'll be okay.

A couple of times, I slide into preoccupations about JD but yank myself back in the moment. "How was Delia's?" I ask. They launch into a rapidly paced, immensely detailed rendition of their last eighteen hours—simultaneously, strangely unaware of their verbal collision: a story about a sports bra, someone having a crush on the boy from Germany, and something about blue tie-dyed soccer socks. They don't know it, but their innocent ramblings are creating a bubble-wrap afghan, unwittingly comforting and protecting me.

"Oh, Mom, guess what happened to Hannah? Mrs. Henry had to call her mom at two in the . . ."

"One in the morning."

"No, it was two in the morning . . ."

"No, it wasn't. It was one in the morning. *I know.*"

"How do you know, you weren't even awake?"

"I heard Mrs. Henry tell someone on the phone."

"Well, *whatever* . . . it doesn't matter anyway. Mom, Hannah's mother picked her up in the middle of the night. Can you believe that? She was crying and walking around the house—she was sleepwalking, actually, like a zombie, and Mrs. Henry found her in the kitchen by the stove. She almost caught on fire!"

"*She did not!* Mom, Lilly's making that up."

"No. No, I'm not . . . that's what Mrs. Henry was afraid she was going to do. Really."

"Are you smoking me?" I'm half listening.

"*What?*"

"What did you say, Mom?"

"I said, 'Are you smoking me?' You know, like 'Are you kidding?'"

"Mom!" Tessa gasps as if I just took my shirt off at the gas station.

"Mom, are you serious? Where did you get that from?" Lilly follows.

"From you girls. I heard you say it to somebody."

"It's not *'Are you smoking me,'* it's 'Are you *joking* me.'"

"Really, Mom, what *is* that?"

"Yeah, where did you get that from? You can't say that. Come on, it's embarrassing."

"Fine. I'm sorry I'm so offensive." Why is it kids are completely tuned in when you say something embarrassing but can't hear perfectly normal things like "Please put your dirty clothes in the hamper, not on the floor next to the hamper"?

They both break into ripples of laughter until they practically can't breathe. Tessa holds her stomach and falls to the side, where her head lands on Lilly's lap.

We're almost home, and I can't wait for this day to be over. The time on the dashboard says 10:57.

It's gonna be a long day.

I turn onto Brightwood Road and notice something I hadn't seen before. Beyond our front yard, tucked into the elbow of the road, the very first autumn leaf appears on Mr. Snedgar's oak tree; it's a blazing reddish-orange. The tree's widespread branches, like a hundred gnarled fingers, point in my direction. It's always this tree that portends the approaching fall. Though this time, it's far too early.

To SAY THAT I'm a little distracted once we arrive back home is the understatement of the century. The girls go upstairs to unpack their overnight bags and straighten their rooms while I retreat to the laundry room to deal with the mounds of clothes. I sit on the tile floor and sort the whites from darks while I try to sort my twisted emotions. I want to feel better.

Erase what's happened. Steal yesterday back. I want that typical Andy's-coming-home feeling.

The only way to move forward is to find JD.

Or find out about her.

I need a reliable source. That's not as easy as it sounds. First of all, my parents aren't alive—they died before Andy and I were married. In fact, Andy and the girls are all the family I have. But even if the pool of relatives were more plentiful, it's not as if I could call any of them and ask if JD died. How exactly would I phrase that? I'm afraid to ask anyone. Inasmuch as I'd stake my life on JD being alive, what if she isn't?

My mother would've been the perfect person to talk to. I could always get information from her without revealing my lack of it. Which was particularly handy when I was a teenager and wanted her opinion as to whether my father might ground me for one thing or another. Often you got a *lot more* from her than you were seeking. Some people like that trait in others—takes the pressure off of them to talk. That might explain why most of her friends were the quiet type. Including my dad. He seldom spoke. Perhaps he felt he didn't have ample opportunity, but I think he was relieved not to express himself. He definitely indulged my mother—not with fancy jewelry or a big house; those were beyond his reach. Instead, he was tolerant of her quirky ways. A perfect example of this was when my mother made a decidedly sudden and permanent change in the way she spoke, and my father never so much as flinched.

It happened when my sister and I were about six. My parents took a trip to London as a second honeymoon. It was their first trip abroad. While there, my mother "became" British.

She fell in love with "those charming, classy Brits." She was so transformed by the sound of their accent that she began speaking with one herself and never reverted back. Even in her final days.

She completely crossed over to the other side of the pond—linguistically, that is. The funny thing is that she never showed a bit of self-consciousness at the sheer craziness of it at all. I don't believe she ever thought, *How does a thirty-one-year-old woman, who's lived in the States all her American life, instantly become British after a seven-day "holiday" to London?* Believe me, everyone else did. Sometimes, now that time has distanced me from it, I think, *Bravo to her.* She didn't want to slip invisibly into a group of suburban housewives like a queen of diamonds into a stacked deck. It was harder for me to understand that back then, when my schoolmates (and their mothers) would impersonate her. Behind my back and to my face. JD and I were desperate for our mother to stop. But she didn't. She grabbed onto that accent like it saved her soul, and she wasn't letting go.

It was my father's reaction that had us dumbfounded. He never once gave Mom a hard time. He didn't seem at all embarrassed. He accepted it like it was her destiny. I think he was glad she was so happy. She'd finally found her voice (in a manner of speaking).

JD and I were mortified for a long time. We realized pretty fast that we should make friends with any new kids who moved into town. Those families just thought Mom was British. I remember that in first grade, I had a classmate named Cindy Bone. She was vicious—for a seven-year-old—and she had an equally vicious mother. One day, soon after my parents returned from England, I came home from school and was standing on my front porch when Mrs. Bone walked past our house with the evil Cindy. I don't think she saw me standing there, but she stopped in front of Mrs. Withers, our neighbor, who was weeding the flower bed in her front yard. With a mocking hand held up to the side of her mouth to feign discretion, she called out, "Has Elaine Spencer lost her mind, or has she landed a part in *My Fair Lady*?" That sent Mrs. Bone into an interminable horror-movie cackle that ended up in a half wheeze/half gag until she quickly stuck a newly lit cigarette between her shriveled lips. Thank goodness Mrs. Withers had the decency to turn away silently, start up her lawn mower, and drown out the rest of Mrs. Bone's insults, while dispensing grass clippings onto her perfectly white seersucker trousers.

By the time I left for college, I was used to it. I don't think very much about it anymore. But when I do, it reminds me to be aware of my own behavior—the emotional scars of children can take a lifetime to heal. If they do at all.

The laundry is separated, pockets checked for tissues and change, stains pretreated, and the washer filled with the first load. Once I close the lid, I head back downstairs to make lunch. The girls walk Smarty while I prepare three hummus and cucumber sandwiches.

Lilly and Tessa argue between bites about which craft project they'll do, and I'm relieved not to be needed for this conversation. They always want to do the same thing, though they never agree on what that is. The battle seems to be as important as the task. JD and I always wanted to do the same things when we were young. The difference was we never argued.

Together we clear away the table. My printout of today's

schedule is on the counter next to the blender, reminding me to do laundry, change bed linens, go to drycleaner, Clorox the shower drains, and return beach chairs to the crawl space. All that was supposed to happen before noon.

The girls decide on pom-pom puppets and start their project on the kitchen table. I go upstairs to finish the laundry and change the bed linens. At the top of the stairs I sigh deeply, trudge toward the laundry room, and lose momentum. Perhaps I never had it. I wander in and out of rooms; Smarty's my shadow. It's impossible for me to drum up enthusiasm for anything. I begin a task that should take five minutes, and fifteen minutes later I have to remind myself what it is I was there for in the first place.

Finally, Lilly and Tessa's sheets are changed and the laundry is half folded. I get to my room, and instead of stripping the bed I plop down in the middle of it. I cross-stitch my legs and coax positive energy to flow freely to my brain. Maybe something will kaleidoscope into clarity. I need time to think. I rack my brain—who would know about JD? If she were really *gone,* who would know?

Her college.

They'd want to know. They'd put it in the alumni magazine or directory or whatever that thing is that reports marriages and births and deaths.

I race down the stairs to find the main number for Barton College in my Rolodex. I know it's weird that I still have a Rolodex. I'll be one of those old ladies who holds onto ancient rusty hedge sheers when nifty, super-fast, super-sharp electric ones are available. And I'll never give up my corded phone— which hangs in the kitchen next to the fridge.

In the den, I unlock the bottom drawer of the credenza

and pull out my Rolodex and place it on top. Right next to my *desk calendar.* I pick up my desk calendar and squeeze it tight. Someone must have moved it. And closed it. I open it to the proper week and put it back on the desk next to the mouse pad. "Don't you move again." I jab my finger at it. A rush of hope waves over me. It's a sign. I know it. Everything's going to be okay.

I love my Rolodex—plucking at the soft indentation in the center of each card created by years of use where my finger pulled back on each one. The smell of the paper. I spin the Rolodex wheel and stop on J—where, over the years, I've kept all of JD's important information. There are several Barton phone numbers: her old dorm room numbers, the infirmary, and the Campus Center Information Desk, where she had a job junior year. I jot that one down.

I pass through the kitchen, waving and yelling, "Hi, girls—" Back upstairs, I use the phone on my nightstand. Smarty yelps and runs alongside me. It's amazing to feel cheerful and optimistic. Even when things are grim, when I have a plan I can tackle anything. Of course, things have never been this grim, so that theory will be tested. But being pragmatic, for me, is empowering. This is where I'm most comfortable. It also gives me a glimmer of hope. I could be on the brink of discovering this whole thing is some crazy mix-up, that *of course* my sister is alive. And very much living in Pennsylvania.

The Information Desk puts me in touch with the Alumni Office.

A moment later a voice says, "Alumni Office, can I help you?"

CHAPTER THREE

Saturday, September 23, 2006 1:28 p.m.

"**O**h, hi, great," I say to the Alumni Office lady. "This is, uh, Mary Jean uh, Crowe, class of '94." I clear my throat. "I'm, I have an unusual request, or question, really. Well, maybe it's not unusual, come to think of it, I bet a lot of people call with this kind of question. Anyway, um, I just happened to bump into a Barton alum on vacation in Bermuda, and well, I hadn't seen this person in, oh God, too long—you know how *that* is—we got to talking about the old days and what's happened to everyone, and, well, she heard that a roommate of ours died several years ago. Well, I just couldn't believe it—I mean, that would have made her twenty-eight. Anyway, I was hoping you could tell me if it's true or not."

There's a period of uncomfortable silence. I actually think maybe she's put the phone down and gone to the bathroom. Did I go on for too long? "Hello?"

Then her voice cuts back in, "You could go online and find out on Barton's website. Did you try that? Go online and type in your student ID number on the home page and look it up that way. Of course, it would only list a death if we received the information from someone. So if the name is not there, it doesn't necessarily mean she's not, well, dead. Not to be a downer, but I guess you're only going to know for sure if her name is there. Do you know any of her family members? Could you call one of them?"

"Uh, no. I wish I did." I pace my bedroom. Smarty watches me from the top of the bed.

"Well, you could try the website."

"Yes, but I don't have a Barton ID number because I went to the pharmacy school. I don't think those IDs work, even though it's technically part of the same school. We were room-mates off-campus. I was really hoping you could help me. I mean if it's in the alumni directory online, it's in the public domain, right? It's not restricted information, certainly, right? Is it possible for you to look it up for me? Please?"

I hear her breathing this time so I know she's still there. Someone else asks her something, and she covers the phone. There's distorted mumbling in the background.

"It's just that it's very busy around here with the semester just starting and everything," she exhales dramatically. "What's your friend's name and year? I'll see what I can do." Another reluctant huff. "You're going to have to wait a bit. I've got two other people on hold."

"Oh, no problem. I can wait all day!" I sit on the edge of my bed, then swing my legs up and crisscross them, tucking my toes under my bottom. Waiting for her to return, my knees bob quietly against my comforter. I start to whistle, then quickly stop. Off-key whistling has driven people who love me to hang up. Three lifetimes later, her "You still there?" makes my heart flip.

"Yes, yes, I'm still here . . ." I sit up on my knees like a begging dog.

"Unfortunately, your friend Jane Dory Spencer has passed away. I'm really sorry to confirm that. It happened in 2000. Too young." I could sense her shaking her head.

As the words leave her mouth and travel across the phone line, they grab me by the shoulders, dig deep into my skin, and thrust me back and forth, shaking me violently. They shake me to my core. My nerves vibrate en masse. I become light-headed. I sink back down, tuck my knees up to my chin, and wrap both arms tightly around them to keep myself together. The phone still rests on my shoulder, but is no longer pressed to my ear. I can't discern anything she's saying. "Wah wah-wah wah-wah"; she becomes Charlie Brown's schoolteacher. I'm gonna get sick. My head spins. The phone slips from my shoulder and drops to the bed with a soft thud. Muffled sounds levitate from it. Acids in my stomach slosh against themselves. The swells grow wild until my stomach's contents retch themselves out of me. When I slowly lift my limp head, all is still. A foul puddle remains on the fluffy white com-forter. Smarty is about to stick his nose in it. I grab him away, and he drops to the floor.

I return the phone to its cradle while sounds of the alumni lady still seep from the tiny holes on the receiver. When you discover you're losing your mind, you're excused of such rude-ness. JD's dead. I don't know how. I don't know why.

I'M NOT SURE how long I've been upstairs or how long Tessa

and Lilly's chorus of "*Swim meet! Swim meet! Swim meet!*" has gone on. Their shrieky, preadolescent voices pierce my state of shock. My gait down the stairs is catatonic, and I seem unconnected to my own legs. Once I reach the kitchen, Tessa and Lilly leap on me, still chanting "Swim meet." The weight of them collapses all three of us to the floor.

Lilly says, "Mom, it's almost two—I don't wanna be late. Are you driving us, or are we walking?"

"Mom, are you gonna *drive* us? Are you listening to me?" She springs up off the floor and reaches her hand out to help me. "Mom, did you forget about the meet?"

While I process what Lilly's saying, I survey the kitchen. It looks like a war zone. Pom-pom and pipe-cleaner soldiers have been left for dead on the stove top, under chairs, and in the sink.

I look back at the girls. "Wow, you guys have all your swim stuff together?" My voice sounds strange, like it's coming from another source. It's like I'm on cruise control, because I don't know how, exactly, I formed that thought and then sent it through my mouth. Even more surprising is that the girls are completely outfitted for their swim meet—bags packed and zipped.

"*Mom*—what's up? You look like you just saw a zombie. Are you ready? We're gonna be late." Lilly is jumping straight up and down, pogo-stick style. She's been waiting for this meet for over a month. The Farhaven Sea Lions are meeting their archrivals, the Locust Hill Barracudas.

"Are you okay, Mom? What's in your hair?" Tessa approaches to take a closer look and I shrink backward without thinking, pressing myself up against the sink to get the most distance between us. I turn to put the water on and look out the window. One of the girls from the swim team, who lives up the street, is already walking to the Y with her older sister, Rachel, our babysitter.

"Oh, there's Rachel. Honey, why don't you and Lilly go ahead of me? Rachel is walking with Olivia. They're right in front of the house." I knock on the window hoping she'll hear. "Go walk with them." I open the kitchen window that faces the side of the house and yell, "Rachel—Lilly and Tessa are going to walk with you guys. One sec!" I turn back around, "I don't want you guys to be late. Just stick together. And look both ways, left-right-left . . ." I pick up their gym bags and thrust them into their arms while walking toward the back of the kitchen as I try to coax the baby salmon upstream toward the door. "It'll give me time to freshen up. Hurry, girls, go now, Rachel just stopped on the sidewalk."

"Yeah, Mom. Fine." Lilly gets caught in the current and moves out the door. "But don't be late," she insists. The screen door snaps shut before she finishes her stipulation.

Lilly calls to Tessa, who's still in the kitchen. "I'm leaving, Tessie! I'm not going to be late. *I'm* not giving those Barracudas the psychological advantage." Lilly thrusts her arm in the air as she says this, pointing onward as if leading a crusade.

Tessa walks over to me. "I'll see ya at the pool, Mom. Right?" She squints. "You're coming, aren't you?" Tessa is fine-tuning her social antenna.

"Of course I'm coming. I just need five minutes. I won't miss anything. Just the warm-ups. I'll be there in five minutes." I pull away from her and blow her a kiss that feels ridiculous even as I do it, but I don't want her to smell the vomit on my hair.

She walks backward tentatively, giving me a strange look.

"Please don't bite your cuticles, Tessa. I'll be right there. Okay?"

She hesitates briefly to say, "Love you, Mom," before closing the door behind her.

At the front of our house, I look out the dining room window to watch them walk down the driveway toward the sidewalk where Rachel is waiting. While I silently pray the girls will be alert at the intersections, a non sequitur interrupts my thoughts, causing me to run to the den—my feet taking over for my brain.

I sit back down at the computer, and with *Caroline Spencer* typed into the Google search box, I press enter, and the hits ripple before my eyes. I scan them to find my sister's obituary again. I click on it.

> *She is survived by her mother and father, Elaine and Wally Spencer, sister, Caroline Grace Spencer, and by 2-year-old daughter, Lilliana.*
>
> *A funeral mass will be offered on Tuesday, April 25, at Our Lady of Lourdes Church. Burial will take place at St. Gertrude Cemetery in New Peak. The Dooley Funeral Home at 332 North Avenue in New Peak is in charge of the arrangements. Memorial donations may be made to the Lilliana Spencer Scholarship Fund, PO Box 721, Lanstonville, Pennsylvania.*

"*Daughter?!*" bursts out of me in a delayed reaction. My voice bounces off the walls.

My sister didn't have a daughter. I stop to think hard, but then my entire body involuntarily shudders when I realize my lack of credibility on the subject of my sister's—hell—my *own* life. My mind gallops through heavy mud. She was married? Who was her husband? It's like I'm squeezing my pitiful memory through cheesecloth, trying to separate the salient from the crap. How could I not know she had a *daughter*, and why would she name her *Lilliana*, when I have a daughter named Lilly? That's nuts. Why would she do that?

I know why she'd do that. For the same reason we always copied each other. We wanted to be identical. We prided ourselves on being the same, not different. We knew how lucky we were to have each other. All twins feel that way. Perhaps we should have drawn the line before giving our daughters practically the same name.

Where is this niece of mine now, now that my sister is gone? Why don't I have any contact with her?

My relationship with JD is—*was*—the most important relationship in my life. Just as I think those thoughts, my conscience twitches. How would Andy feel hearing that? How can a sibling relationship be more important than a spouse's? I feel suddenly ashamed. Should I be? I don't know. It's a twin thing. We had *unspoken* understanding. I don't think that happens in relationships with men. All women want their men to know what they're thinking. They think it's a sign of true connectedness; a phenomenon I'm convinced females invented. It only exists in romantic comedies. In real life, unless you tell your husband exactly what's on your mind, you'll be waiting a very long time. I've learned the hard way. After which Andy will inevitably say, "Why didn't you just tell me?"

I need to find JD's daughter.

Which means I need to find JD's husband.

My brain throbs when I strain to recall who JD was dating

back then. This is obviously a ludicrous task since twenty-four hours ago I didn't know my sister was dead or that she had a daughter. Now I'm supposed to remember who she was sleeping with back in the '90s?

JD had a baby in '98, the same year Tessa and Lilly were born.

It doesn't make sense. None of this makes sense.

Finding JD's husband is what I must do. It's crucial. It'll answer everything.

I think back to the obituary, which didn't mention a surviving spouse.

I return to the Google hits and scroll down. But this time I stop halfway down the page:

> *Hammond Gazette, Hammond, New York, December 10, 1993*
>
> *Milton Abner indicted for practicing medicine without a license. . . . One case, that of* **Caroline Spencer***, led to . . .*
>
> *www.hammondgazette.com/ . . ./ milton-abner-indicted-for-practicing-medicine___*

Hammond Gazette—I went to Hammond University, in New York. The *Gazette* was the town newspaper. My entire body tightens as I try to brace myself for another potential blow.

I click on it:

> *Hammond Gazette, Hammond, New York, December 10, 1993*

Milton Abner Indicted for Practicing Medicine Without a License

Milton Abner has been indicted by the Hammond County Grand Jury for practicing medicine without a license. He was arrested in October at the makeshift medical clinic he set up at the 527 Oak Street apartment he rented after several young women accused him of falsifying his credentials as an obstetrician and of performing illegal abortions. According to police, medical equipment and boxes of syringes, pills and other medical supplies were found at the apartment/clinic.

Abner came under suspicion when Caroline Spencer, 22, was brought to St. Barnabas Hospital in East Hammond, New York, in critical condition that necessitated emergency surgery. During a botched, illegal abortion, Ms. Spencer lost excessive blood and became unconscious. Mr. Abner called for an ambulance and then fled the scene, leaving Ms. Spencer for dead.

St. Barnabas Hospital immediately filed a police report, and after regaining consciousness, Ms. Spencer gave investigators the information needed to lead to Mr. Abner's apprehension.

Mr. Abner illegally posed as an obstetrician, advertising his services for "safe and certified abortions" in local newspapers. An initial investigation found that Mr. Abner has never held a medical license. His last

occupation was that of a television commercial actor.
One of his most recent roles was that of a doctor.

A second investigation was simultaneously conducted
by the State Education Department based on com-
plaints by several Hammond University students,
including Hilary Baldwin, regarding Abner's unortho-
dox medical techniques and procedures. Ms. Baldwin
has transferred to an out-of-state university.

When Ms. Spencer was asked how she found the
bogus doctor, she said her boyfriend, Timothy Hayes,
a pre-law student at Hammond University, found him
for her. Multiple calls placed to Mr. Hayes for comment
were not returned. Timothy Hayes is a senior and will
graduate at the end of this semester. Ms. Spencer has
since withdrawn from Hammond University.

The investigation led . . .

My eyes are frozen open. The numb feeling a foot gets
when it's sat on for too long has taken over my entire body.
I can't speak, think, breathe, blink. *Abortion?* It's as if I'm
reading about someone else, not me. But my name *is* Caroline
Spencer. At least back then it was. I *did* go to Hammond
University. I *had* a boyfriend named Timothy Hayes. I have
no recollection of an abortion, for God's sake.

I remember a girl named Hilary Baldwin. Everyone knew
her. Hyster Hilary. That's what they called her. Because of the
hysterectomy. She was one of the Hyster Sisters. God, that's
awful. Who'd call someone a Hyster Sister? She needed a hysterectomy and was on bed rest forever. She had to transfer
out of Hammond. Yes, I remember girls talking about her

abortion. She went to some guy who wasn't a doctor, and he screwed it up. Big time. She needed a hysterectomy because he butchered her. She wanted the hell out of Hammond.

What the hell was *I* doing there—getting an *abortion??* I wasn't pregnant in school! I can't seem to pull my gaze off the screen. It all feels like too much, too painful to recollect. But I can't pull myself away, either, even though I'm desperate to. Now that I think about it, there was another Hyster Sister. Another girl needed a hysterectomy because of that same fake doctor. Asshole. The other Hyster Sister, I just can't remember who that was.

I swallow hard. I *remember* parts of that. I do. So why don't I remember it all?

I look down at my stomach and my hand is resting on it. *Pregnant?* Me. It's just too much for me to process. It can't be true.

Well, *I* couldn't have had a hysterectomy. That's not something you forget. You just don't forget something like that. Not to mention, I have two daughters!

I unzip my pants and pull at the band of my underwear. Everything looks pretty normal down there. I exhale with relief. Nothing out of the ordinary. I pat my stomach and grab the zipper to pull it back up. Before I do, I take one more look. It's the faintest thing. It's probably nothing. But I think I see the subtlest pink line through my hair. *Subtle.* Except that it's kind of long. About three inches. Maybe four. That's if it's a line at all.

I did not have a hysterectomy. It's a no brainer. I have two beautiful daughters. Where did they come from? I didn't steal them from someone at the mall.

One click of the mouse gets rid of the screen. If only the

same could happen with my mind. Reading Timothy's name is like drinking a quadruple espresso. I scrunch my eyes closed to syphon my memory cells, demanding them to produce. I let the thoughts and images flood over me. Swatches of memories fly at me like frisbees. I don't slow them down or try to make sense of them. I don't want them to stop. The swatches are moments in time, not related to each other, like squares of fabric; different patterns, different colors. Timothy and I were crazy about each other. He was in love with me. And I with him. I try to piece the patches together, but the quilt is missing squares. He was brilliant. Just like his dad. His dad and his grandfather were partners in the prestigious law firm in New York, Hayes and Hayes, Ltd. A spot was waiting for Timothy to continue the family legacy.

Come to think of it, Timothy wasn't really brilliant. Not nearly as smart as his dad. But he had a knack for convincing people he was capable of just about anything. He was determined to finish law school and take the position that was "rightfully his."

Timothy's style was a bit strong for some people. I saw it as a sign of self-confidence. I was taken by how bold and self-assured he was. I'd never met anyone like that before. His detractors accused him of being all flash and no substance.

The light bulb on the desk lamp is flickering and is about to extinguish.

What ever happened to Timothy? Parts of my memory are clear, others are faded—like memory glaucoma.

If only my mind could close out of the *Hammond Gazette* article. But it's stuck there now. So is a heavy feeling in my chest. You don't need to be a rocket scientist to know you can't have a hysterectomy in 1993 and give birth to twins in 1998.

Jesus, *God*. I *couldn't* have been the other Hyster Sister. What kind of surgery did they do on me? I look at my desk calendar to see when I last had my period. I flip through August and July and June and May. Don't I write this stuff down? I can't remember having my period this month. Or last month. I can't remember having it.

I leave my desk and head to the bathroom to look for tampons. Wait. What about the girls? Why don't I hear them? They were doing arts and crafts in the kitchen. The house is too quiet. They're never this quiet.

"Girls! Are you in the kitchen?" I walk down the hall and stop right outside the den. "Girls—Tessa! Lilly! *Tessie?*" The house is silent except for the sound of gurgling bubbles from the fish tank. Smarty, who was curled up asleep under the leather wing chair in the den, pricks up his ears and launches into action.

My already threadbare nerves are too vulnerable. I pick up the pace, moving swiftly through the house, into the kitchen. Where can they be? I open the back door and yell, "Girls!" No answer. I turn back into the kitchen. They were just here—

In my socks, I slide across the wood floor toward the stairs. Smarty runs behind me, barking. I pass the kitchen table that has one of Lilly's swim caps resting next to some nose plugs while I grab the railing to hoist myself up the first two steps.

"Oh, my God," I say out loud, "they're at a swim meet." I exhale so completely that my entire body slumps over until my hands grasp my buckled knees.

I'm losing my mind . . . I must be. I said good-bye to them myself. They left five minutes—*shit*—thirty minutes ago.

I feel the little sacks of salty liquid stacking up behind my eyes like sandbags meant to hold back floodwaters. I need help. I can't go on like this. Andy's coming home in less than twenty-four hours. He won't even recognize me. How can I act normal? Look normal? I'm in over my head. This isn't about problem solving. That might work if it were someone else's life. Someone else's secrets.

If I had a hysterectomy, that would mean my girls are not mine.

It's incomprehensible that I'm thinking about this. This is nuts. How can the girls not be mine? I gave birth to them!

I need to cross this off my list. Nip it in the bud. I'm not having Andy come home to me in this state. No way. This is easy. I did not have a hysterectomy. And I am the mother of my daughters. Jesus.

I'm going to get them. Right now.

Lilly will be furious, but this is more important. Isn't it? The sanity of the mother? The mother is supposed to put the oxygen mask on herself first when the plane is crashing. Before she puts on her child's. The flight attendant says so. The mother is the caregiver. It's a known fact that she must be breathing to take care of her children.

I need Lilly and Tessa with me. I'll feel better having them near. We need to be together. Like some perverse interpretation of "Possession is nine-tenths of the law." I grab my car keys and handbag from the counter, and then a sweater from the mudroom, which I zip to my chin.

On the way to the Y, I attempt to devise my plan of action. What am I going to do once I get the girls? I don't have a single idea. The wheels in my mind gnash, and it's not pretty. They're fractured and rusty and broken and screeching. Though they try to catch at the right time, in the right place, they can't. What's the matter with me? I'm a natural-born strategist.

I yank open the front door to the Y. The dense smell of chlorine thickens the air and seeps into my pores, weighing me down, slowing my jog through a long hall on a rubbery black floor that's used to prevent the swimmers from slipping. The painted cinderblock walls boast photos of past swim teams dating back to the 1920s; the hall leads me straight to the big pool where the meets are held. I grab the railing and take the stairs down to where the team is seated. I pass the rows of bleachers where the other parents sit with legs crossed and hands clasped; moms are wearing quilted jackets in various tones of forest green and brown. It's one of those September days when autumn attempts to prematurely evict summer, and everyone's wearing their fall finest. You can smell the new suede of their boots and their big leather satchels. A very good-looking group. Swimming is a respectable sport; it attracts good kids and fine families.

Looking at these people, I remember how important it was for me to immerse myself in the community—to get a fresh start in a new town. I was willing to go the extra mile to make good, solid friendships for me and Andy and the girls. When we got married, we decided not to raise our children in either of our hometowns. So after a good deal of research, we chose Farhaven. Neither of us knew anyone who lived here, and that was part of the appeal. Clean slate. New friends. Friends that would be ours, not *just his* or *just mine*.

The demographics of Farhaven are pretty homogeneous, one could say. People like us. But then, that's the benefit (or drawback) of living in the suburbs. In fact, if you're willing to adopt the suburban code, it's very easy to be welcomed with open arms, to be readily accepted, exist without incident, blend in. Perhaps even go unnoticed. Just live like the suburbans and you'll be fine. Go to PTO meetings and join the book club, host bunco, watch each other's children, have a block party or two, join the country club (or try to), maintain a good lawn, and the hummingbirds are guaranteed to buzz around your front porch every morning.

I summon my typical composure. I decide to abandon Plan A, which was to take the girls immediately. Where I would have taken them, I don't know exactly, which makes Plan A seem rash. So I quickly shift to Plan B, which is to wait out the meet as best I can. It'll give me time to think. I clasp my hands, too, to borrow a sense of calm from these people. I stand in place for the count of five to center myself, and scan the benches to locate the girls.

I look over the sea of familiar faces. First, I spot Vicki, who puts her hand up halfway to wave, then crinkles her face, turns to Meg, and whispers something. Meg is sitting in the row behind Vicki. She waves, smiles warmly, and pats the spot on the bleacher next to her to offer me a seat. I feel a tug. I want to sit there and spill it. She's my closest friend in this town. Or anywhere, at this point. If I could tell anyone, it would be her. She's been loyal from the beginning. In fact, she was loyal when we were mere acquaintances.

We first met when the girls were in preschool together, and we discovered we were both new in town and decided to be each other's emergency contacts. Much to my surprise, the school secretary needed to call her the second week of school.

Smarty was a new puppy then and was keeping me up at nights, like a newborn baby. I was exhausted during the day. One afternoon, I had fallen asleep on the couch and slept right through the girls' pickup time. Even the nonstop calls from the school's office staff didn't stir me. To my utter embarrassment, Meg brought the girls home that day. The next day I found a small wrapped package at my front door. A lavender-scented sleep mask and an alarm clock with a note that read, *Sweet Dreams, Your friend, Meg.*

I'm not going to sit next to her. I don't trust myself. Let's see: a sister's death, a forgotten pregnancy and possible hysterectomy, two daughters with questionable parentage. I don't think so. No one is that unconditional. How would I react if she came to *me* with a story like that? I'm on my own. I'm not going to risk losing her. I can't chance this leaking out to anyone, especially Andy.

In reply to her seat offer, I do a lame job of sign language. I point at myself while mouthing "I need," then do a quacking motion with my hand (the international sign for "talk"). But I can't think of anything that will mean "the girls" so I just say "the girls" out loud. A bunch of heads swivel in my direction. I sidestep across the cement floor behind the Sea Lions bench, where Tessa is sitting, stretching her arms over her head. I sit quietly behind her. I can't tell if I've made it in time or whether they've already started, and I'm not sure the girls know I'm here.

I take a deep breath and collect myself. These are my daughters. And I am their mother. I'm not going to let some stupid, ancient newspaper article from some pokey town in upstate New York rattle my world.

I stick my head over Tessa's left shoulder and whisper in her ear, "Hi, Tessa!" She's so startled, she nearly takes a nosedive into the pool from the third row. "I'm here. See. I made it on time. Your mother is here," I say plainly while slapping my lap for emphasis. I spot Lilly, who is up on the platform waiting for the whistle, which is imminent. In an enunciated whisper,

I call out, "Lilly, Lilly! Mom's here! Your proud mother is here! To see her daughters!" I stand up and practically salute and then quickly sit down again. She's already squatting. Oh God, I'm glut with pride as I look at the two of them. They're gorgeous and strong. Lilly tilts her head slowly toward me, in millimeter increments, then her body leans subtly to one side and her arms start to swing in big, wide, propeller-like circles. Then she topples into the pool.

The entire team gasps, as well as the onlookers and me. The sound of our collective astonishment shakes my fragile composure. I'm horrified. I glance over at her coach, who is now on her feet, her head whipped to the side to glare at me with a big nasty puss. Lilly could get a false start for that.

I immediately look down at my feet, sit on my hands, cross my legs. All tucked in. And quiet.

Vicki nicknamed the coach "Coach Mouth Fart" because she has a habit of blowing air audibly through one inflated cheek like French people are famous for when they're absolutely disgusted with you. Which is exactly how she's feeling about me right now. She adds an exasperated arm thrust into the air (like an old Italian woman is likely to do if you turn down a fourth helping of her homemade gnocchi), while I try to envision *her* parents. Maybe she's picked up these mannerisms from them. They could be French. Or Italian. Who knows? Are mannerisms in our genes? Do the girls have any of mine?

Lilly doesn't know what to do with herself. She's typically expressive, but being under water from her neck down squelches any physical reaction she might have had. But you can see all you need to know in her eyes. A potent mix of anger and embarrassment. I dig my fingernails into my thighs so I don't start to cry, because if I do, Lilly will suffer permanent emotional scars. When she slithers up the wall of the pool and climbs out, the other girls are in ready position, so she immediately returns to the block with knitted fists. She doesn't look at me. The starting signal sounds, and Lilly's in the water again swimming freestyle, her strongest event. My heel is tapping rapidly on the cement floor while I look around at the other parents. I smile lavishly all over the place.

I look at my watch. If I don't come up with something soon, Tessa and Smarty—both PhDs in the sixth sense—will sniff something's wrong before the day is out. God, I used to be so sensible. I prided myself on being smart. All my life, I had a solution for anything. Until today.

I tap my thumbs together in syncopation with my foot.

The cogs in my mind get unstuck and almost groove. A spark of an idea starts to kindle.

After a good, hearty, fake sneeze, I drop my head toward the floor to pantomime rummaging through my handbag for a tissue long enough to make a quick discreet phone call.

I whisper into the phone with my head between my knees. I cup my hand over my mouth so no one can hear me. It's almost impossible to have a conversation in here because of how loud it becomes with clapping and hooting. It must be Tessa's event; she's no longer on the bench. The person I'm on the phone with puts me on hold. I look up briefly. Tessa's in the water. The lady comes back, and I tip my head down. I quickly end the call and sit up.

People are cheering, and I follow their lead. God forbid the girls look at me and I'm not celebrating like the rest of the parents.

I subconsciously rub my hands up and down my jeans and realize they are slick with sweat.

CHAPTER FOUR

Saturday, September 23, 2006, 3:37 p.m.

The swim meet is over. I spring off the bench, look down at my watch, and dash over to where the team has collected. I quickly snatch up everything that belongs to the girls, like a chicken pecking at bird feed. Thankfully, Tessa and Lilly are sitting next to each other, so after I swing their gym bags over my shoulders, it's easy to grab both of their arms and guide them off the bench and rush them up the stairs. "Hurry, we don't have time," I say out loud to no one in particular. I'm a woman with a mission. And a plan.

They protest the entire way. But I'm impervious to their clamor. The Red Cross is closing distressingly soon, so I have no time to indulge them. I must ignore what they're saying, partly because nothing else will fit in my brain right now. I'll listen to them later. Later, they'll have my undivided attention.

I turn on the ignition and put the car in reverse. "Great job, girls. Really, really great," I praise them as I look to the side mirrors. No one is backing up behind me. The car jolts backward like it did when I was learning to drive a stick shift.

"Mom, I'm not even in my seat!" one of them says.

"I don't have my belt on," the other blurts.

"What a meet—*whew*—you girls were something else." I'm just going to keep this all light and airy. Real casual and normal. They won't notice a thing. I look down at my watch again. It's going to be a miracle if we get there on time.

"*Mom*—where are we going? Are you listening?? We don't have our clothes—"

"Or even a *towel*—"

"I'm freezing!"

I look at them in the rearview mirror. I can't think clearly with them complaining and persisting. "Oh, magnificent. Great." I smack the steering wheel. "You're cold! You're wet! Super. Have you thought about me? I may be losing my mind!"

The girls look at me with frozen faces, disbelief twisted with fear. I realize I didn't say this to myself.

I thrust the gear into park and notice their gym bags on the front seat.

"Oh, gosh, I thought you had your things. Here—I'm sorry." I throw the two bags into the back seat. "I'm so sorry. You must be freezing—here, let me turn the heat on." I look down at their feet and silently thank God they're not barefoot.

Lilly's hand goes for the door handle. "I'm going to get our towels—"

"*Lilly*, where are you going? Don't open that door. Stay in the car—there's no time. We might not make it as it is. I took your towels. They're in your bags. Look in your bags." I put the gear back into drive and head out of the parking lot. I have one hand extended into the backseat to support Lilly in case she springs forward—she's still not strapped in. "Hold on, Lilly."

"Make it where?" Tessa asks, shivering while pulling stuff out of her gym bag. I can't look at them like this. Wet and cold. It's killing me. What am I doing? I'm acting like a lunatic. It's breaking my heart—but I can't stop. We need to do this. I'll make it better after this is all over. I really, really will.

If we do find out that I've lost my mind, it may not be such a terrible thing (for them) after all, since we may be on the edge of discovering that I'm not their mother. We'll find out something soon at the Red Cross.

"My towel isn't in my bag, Mommy," says Tessa.

"This isn't my towel," Lilly snaps, "It's Sophia's!"

"Well, just use Sophia's towel, for Pete's sake. You're soaking wet, what difference does it make?"

"Are you kidding? She picks her nose! I am not using a nose picker's towel!"

"I'll use it. I'm freezing." Tessa grabs the towel from Lilly.

"Fine. Don't be surprised if you get boogers all over you."

I can't listen to them anymore. They need to be quiet.

"Listen, girls," my voice is thick with desperation, "I haven't told you about the terrible thing that's happened to Ricky." I quickly try to concoct who "Ricky" is and what the "terrible thing" is that I haven't told them. This sucks.

"Who's Ricky, Mommy?" Tessa is already feeling selfish for complaining about not having a towel. She starts to nibble at her nails.

Then Lilly blurts, "I can't believe you made me fall in the pool. What was that about? Embarrassing me like that. I'm gonna hear about that for the rest of my life. I could have gotten a penalty! The least you could do is have my towel. I'm freezing my butt off."

I let Sassy Pants have a moment. I can't say I don't deserve it. She's just scared and confused and is protecting herself with anger. Thinking about genes, I actually feel better about her tirade.

"Where are we going that's so important? What's the family emergency?" Lilly's back on track.

Tessa starts to cry.

"By the way Mom, we lost. We *lost* that meet, ya know—the one you're so proud of," Lilly points out. "And next time, don't clap for the other team. You're supposed to clap for us. We saw you."

I pull the car over to the side of the road and shift into park. "Tessa, please don't cry. Everything's going to be all right. I guess I didn't realize you girls lost. Well, you know that never matters to me. You know that, winning or losing, I'm still proud of you. And yes, I was clapping because . . . because . . . do you know what it's like for a mother to see her daughters being so amazing? Working so hard at something and then doing that thing they worked hard at? I don't give a *damn* who won." The girls turn to look at each other with synchronized shock. I scan Lilly's features and swear her eyes and nose are right off my face. I can't believe I cheered for the other team. And I just cursed in front of them.

"Here, take these." I frantically yank tissues from a box I keep in the car and quickly pat Lilly's wet legs. "Take these tissues and blot your arms. What do you have in your bag, Lilly? Isn't there something you could use to dry off? We just have to make one quick stop, and then we'll go straight home. Don't worry. They'll have towels for you there. They're good people there. They'll help us. That's what they do. Help people in need. Okay? *Please.* We just need to get there before they close." I look at myself in the rearview mirror to make sure I don't look too berserk for the Red Cross. I can't give them a reason to refuse our blood.

"Listen, you two. I know I've been a little off today. I promise things will get better. I'll be back to normal in no time—don't worry—we just have to stop at the Red Cross. Okay? One quick stop, and everything will be fine." As I say this, I scramble for an explanation as to *why* we are going to the Red Cross, and why exactly I'm going to insist blood be drawn from their innocent veins.

So . . . I tell them . . . the terrible, *horrible* news . . . about their second-great cousin, "Ricky," who is related to my grandmother's sister's granddaughter (whom they've never met or heard of). He needs . . . surgery. Serious surgery. And even though he lives in . . . Argentina, everyone in the family is donating blood just in case.

They barrage me with questions about Ricky.

"Girls, I don't know all the details—we're not shipping blood to Argentina, he's . . . having . . . the surgery . . . here someplace, in the U.S. Or maybe they are shipping it. I don't know all the details. Hurry up and get dressed Lilly. Look in the back. There's a bag of old clothes that I was going to drop at the Salvation Army. Blot yourself off with something in there, and get dressed. We have no time to waste."

"What blood type does he have?" Tessa asks. "Shouldn't we know his blood type? We just talked about this in health class."

"Uh, well, it's the same as mine. I don't know what yours

are, that's why we're going to check first. They're not going to take blood from you unless you have the same type as Ricky."

"How do they do that?" they ask in unison.

"Oh, don't worry. It's a simple finger prick." I don't dare look in the rearview mirror. I can't bear to see them scared. I gulp a pool of saliva and wonder if it's audible to anyone but me. There is a long silence.

"There's a swim cap and goggles in here that are not mine. Neither are these nose plugs. I don't even use nose plugs, Mom. My shirt's not here," Lilly says in a quieter tone.

"Lilly, that's your fault, not Mommy's. Coach tells you all the time to put your clothes in your bag," says Tessa.

"Lilly, use one of those old tops from the Salvation Army bag." I pray to God there's nothing in there that she's made me promise not to give away. She wears clothes until they're way too small for her because of her attachment issues.

Lilly reaches her arm around to feel for the bag. There's the crinkle of plastic.

"What do you mean he could die? We've never even met him—he's our cousin—our *only* cousin." Lilly can't handle death in any form, fiction or nonfiction. I should've thought this whole story through before it left my mouth.

"Please, Lilly, I don't know. Of course he may not die. Of course I want him to live, especially so you girls can meet him, just not now, okay? I'm just too upset to talk about it. Let's just try to stay strong, and do what we need to do."

The girls rummage through the bag of old clothes as we pull into the Red Cross parking lot. Before I step out of the car, I flip the mirror down quickly to check the makeup on my bruise.

"Here, put that on," Tessa says to Lilly, tossing her something from the bag.

"I am not wearing a Dora vest! Are you crazy? I wore that when I was three! *You* put it on."

Great, *now* she's a clothes snob.

"I already have a shirt. What's the difference anyway? There's nothing else in here besides this winter coat. Fine, take the coat."

I sweep some bangs over the Band-Aid on my forehead. I feel myself coming unglued. I'm jittery, and the littlest straw could break me.

"What the hell."

I don't believe my eyes.

I brush my hand casually across my chin. It doesn't budge. That's because it's connected to my chin—*in the form of a chin hair!* And it's long enough to pick up signals from low-flying planes. I stare at it. I'm not going to flip out because of this. This is not going break me. I have no time for this. But how and when did I become a lady with chin hair? I'm thirty-five. I remember what Gabrielle said about the woman whose husband left her for the au pair.

My eyes dart to the dashboard clock. We've gotta get in there—*now*. I have to move beyond this hair, though it's long enough to hang laundry off of.

"I'll take care of it later." I flip the mirror closed. "I keep up with personal maintenance. My husband is not gonna leave *me*."

"Why would Daddy leave you?"

Oh God, not again?

"Give me the hat in that bag. Is Daddy's old golf hat in

there?" Tessa hands it over, and I tighten the strap and pull the hat down over my head. Snug enough to keep everything inside.

Out of the car, we all hold hands and walk solemnly up the marble stairs, between the gargantuan, round columns that flank a huge wooden door, into the main foyer of the Red Cross. A very respectable, distinguished place.

We try to fit in.

I stand between my daughters. The girls I've always known as my daughters. They stand tall; both in wet bathing suits and goose bumps—while I wear a long, wiry hair on my chin, a purple monkey on my cheek, and a Band-Aid above my right eyebrow. All is quiet—except for the thrashing of my heart.

"Good afternoon," I say in my most refined voice. The receptionist takes one look at us, and her eyebrows twitch upward almost imperceptibly. She clears her throat and looks around, to make sure the security guard hasn't gone for the day.

"May I help you?" she lies.

"We're here to have our blood type checked." I tell her the story about Ricky. She looks at her watch, and escorts us into a donor room without remarking.

The girls each receive a medical robe and blanket, and slipper socks that the nurse insists they keep. After I fill out some routine paperwork, the nurse draws my blood. She takes a pint. But from the girls, for now, she'll just prick their fingertip for a sample to test the type.

"You must love your cousin Ricky very much," the nurse offers, trying to relax them.

They clutch each other's hand, their eyes fixed on the ceiling. They're magnificently brave, and I'm so proud of them. They're mostly, uncharacteristically, quiet except for an occasional mention of Ricky's name and questions about his illness or his mother and father—the aunt and uncle they never knew existed.

Before the nurse leaves the room to check the girls' blood types and make up Red Cross blood cards for us, she offers apple juice and cookies and a Band-Aid for Tessa's thumb, which is bloody from her gnawing on it. We munch on the cookies, and I whisper to the girls, "We're not going to mention this to Daddy. He's under too much stress, and I don't want to worry him about Ricky. Let's keep this little mission to ourselves." I wink. "Okay?" They nod with their mouths full.

When the nurse returns, she hands me the three cards, one with each of our names and blood types and says something to me that I don't hear.

I fan the cards, poker style.

Come on, three-of-a-kind I silently pray to myself. I lower my eyes and read them. Lilly Thompson A+, Tessa Thompson B+, Caroline Thompson AB+.

I close my eyes. I need another plan.

Sunday, September 24, 2006, 9:12 a.m.

THE WOODEN BLINDS are not drawn all the way to the sill; they reveal a twelve-inch gap of dark sky. It looks like night, though I know it's not. The glass panes are teeming with swollen droplets. They descend the slippery window, picking up speed, taking others with them, engulfing them, capturing them, becoming bloated and heavy. The rain falls without sound. The only sound comes from the clock on my bedside table. I look over to check that it is indeed morning. The pills

I promised myself if I didn't fall asleep by 1:00 a.m. are still there. They wouldn't have helped anyway.

Yesterday, after we returned home from the Red Cross, the girls insisted on writing Ricky a "Get Well Soon" card. They each included photos of themselves and pictures they drew for him to hang on his wall. I was queasy from inventing that colossal lie and for the unsettled business of our blood test. I never considered the test might not be definitive. I was so sure it would be. And now I have to mail this letter to a fake address in Argentina.

Whoever said, "You can never tell just one lie" wasn't lying.

My secrets seem to snowball while my lies pile up.

I passed on dinner, and as we were all sapped, we went to bed on the early side. Tessa couldn't fall asleep right away, and after hours of tossing and turning in bed, thinking about Ricky, she came into my room to ask if she could bunk with me. I was never so happy to have one of the girls slink into my room in the middle of the night. So Tessa (in Andy's spot), Smarty Pants (in his usual spot at the foot of the bed), and I finally fell asleep.

Then, around 2:15 in the morning, Lilly began flailing in her bed. The squeaky wheels on her bed frame agitate when she flips around, and this always wakes me but for some reason, never wakes her. *She's just trying to get comfortable*, I attempted to convince myself. Then she started whimpering. I was sure her nightmares had come back. She hadn't had one in nearly a year. Before that, they were relentless. Always the same dream.

I climbed out of bed and tiptoed in my typical zigzag pattern toward her room through the minefield of creaky floorboards. Her nightlight (in the shape of a butterfly) cast a soft, rosy glow on her room. The entire room was designed around that butterfly, and almost nothing has changed in her room since she was three.

One would not figure Lilly to be sentimental, but try to buy new sheets for her bed or talk about changing the color of the walls from soft pink and yellow to something less nursery-looking, and prepare for an onslaught of hyper-emotional possession devotion.

"Mommy, how can you take away my stuffed animals and dolls? They're mine. I don't want to give them away. Not even to 'less-privileged' little girls who would love them to death. *I* love them to death."

Just a sampling.

So last night when I entered her room, I ventured with practiced finesse, navigating through baskets of old stuffed animals, boxes of hair accessories, and short stacks of clean clothes yet to see the inside of dresser drawers, and still managed to trip over the microphone to her karaoke machine and squash one of Smarty's rubber toy mice, which let out a sickly squeak. Lilly completely ignores the clean-up schedule I tape to her mirror every Saturday. I shared a bedroom with a sister just like her, and it still drives me crazy.

But even if you closed your eyes and were lucky enough to be lowered into Lilly's room by trapeze, you would still know exactly where you were. Lilly's room has the perpetual scent of strawberry and peppermint. Strawberry from her detangler, which she sprays on every night before combing her long, auburn hair, and peppermint from the boxes of Junior Mints she hoards behind her pink and yellow gingham dust ruffle (which will attract a real mouse one of these days).

When I entered her room, the nightlight did something to the color of her hair, that for a fleeting moment made me think of JD, but then it was gone.

Her writhing grew more intense as she clutched her steadfastly loyal teddy bear, Tunum. She received Tunum on her third birthday and decided immediately to remove the little tag from its back seam (which announced the bear's factory-given name as "Giggles") in order to give him a proper name. When she paused for all of five seconds, then declared that name would be "Tunum" (with an emphatic nod of her head), Andy and I thought she was speaking a foreign language. We quickly ran to get *What to Expect in the Toddler Years,* wondering if there was a chapter titled, "When Your Toddler Speaks a Foreign Language." In the end, we chalked it up to Lilly's burgeoning sense of originality.

The allegiance Lilly has to everything else in her universe pales in comparison to that which she has with Tunum, the attendant of all things safe and good.

To watch her squirm and babble in the thick of her nightmare was disturbing, and while I knew about the actual length of dreams, and that it would soon be over, I couldn't bear it.

"Lilly, sweetie . . ." I said softly while gently petting her arm and stroking her cheek with the back of my fingers. "It's Mommy . . . I'm here with you. Wake up, sweetie, you're having a bad dream . . ." Finally, she opened her eyes, and when she saw me, she sprang up, grabbed me, and cried with determination.

"That girl!" she blurted, "And the lady. They're *back*."

CHAPTER FIVE

Sunday, September 24, 2006, 2:18 a.m.

"Okay, slow down, Lilly, it's okay, it's not real."

She gasped big gulps of air and spewed huge drops of fear. Her arms were coiled tightly around my waist.

"This is real, look around, you're awake now." I stroked her hair and started my nightmare-consoling speech, knowing that it wouldn't erase anything. It wouldn't take away the fear or confusion, or stop it from ever returning. But for what it was worth, maybe more for me than for Lilly, I always said the same thing.

"Why don't you try to calm down, take three big, deep breaths, and then start from the beginning . . ." Then it occurred to me that maybe this time we shouldn't talk about it at all. What was the sense in that, anyway? She already experienced it once unwillingly. "Hey, why don't we talk about something else? You don't need to think about that dream again. Where should we go on vacation?" It sounded absurd when I said it. Why don't kids come with manuals?

"It was different this time." She pulled her head away from my chest, "I mean, kinda the same—but different."

"Sure you want to talk about this?"

"I saw her bedroom. The little girl was so scared." Panic grew in her eyes. "She's really cute, I wish I could help her . . ."

"I know, sweetie." Lilly looked like a mermaid; from her waist down she was swaddled in a twist of bed sheets, which I unraveled as she spoke.

"It started the same." Lilly looked at me imploringly, "She took her dolly—*doll*, with her in the stroller to the playground. But it's weird; I don't know how they got there. One minute they were at home, and then I heard the swings in the play-ground screeching and screeching. I hate that sound. But the girl was smiling and playing with her doll—lifting it up and pretending it was dancing." Lilly slid her forearm under her nose and snorted up any remaining secretions not already deposited on her arm.

"Okay." I reached for a tissue from her side table.

"The mom was with her, but then she turned into the other lady. Why does she have to do that? She starts out so nice and pretty, and then she turns into the creepy new mom!" Lilly's chest started to heave, and her voice accelerated. "The mom said it was time to leave the playground. Before the friends came! They're supposed to wait for the friends. The girl got scared." Lilly stopped as if she couldn't believe what she was about to say. "She didn't recognize her. She looked different. She had the same clothes, the same voice, the same hair, but a different face. A completely different *face*. The girl put her head down because she was scared to look at the mom."

Once Lilly's legs were free from the sheets, she readjusted

and brought her knees up to her chin, hugged her shins, and rocked herself back and forth.

"Lilly, I'm sure it was still her mom. You know how dreams are. Maybe you just didn't recognize her. Maybe she got a haircut or Botox or something." *Botox?* Was I *serious?*

Smarty stood at the side of Lilly's bed looking at us, wagging his tail, as nervous as Lilly. I picked him up, and he nuzzled his head under one of Lilly's arms.

She took a big gulp of air like she was about to dive under water. "The girl said, 'Who are you? Where is my mommy?' And the lady said 'I'm your mommy, silly.' Then they got home. But it wasn't really their home. Do you know what I mean? It didn't look like their house, but it was."

"Did the girl have her doll?"

"No!" Her arms sprang in to the air so fast that I thought Smarty would go flying. "She lost it!" She took the bed sheet and pulled it over her head.

"Honey—"

She dropped her hands in her lap and the sheet with them. "The mom didn't want to go back to look for it. She said the girl never brought it. That it was in her room. But that's not true. She *did* bring it! I wanted to scream at the mom!"

"I know, sweetie, you told me. You said she had her doll." I stroked the tops of her feet through the sheet.

Why was Lilly having this dream? *Why?* It's not fair to be so scared when you're supposed to be at peace in your sleep. Where on earth was this coming from? Over and over again.

"She raced to her room anyway to see if her doll was there, but she couldn't find her room. It wasn't anywhere. Can you believe that? She looked all over the house, but she just couldn't find her room. She started crying and ran back downstairs to the mom, and told her she lost her bedroom, too. The mom laughed and said, 'You didn't lose your room, it's upstairs. It's the only room up there so that you'll never get lost.' She went upstairs again. She looked and looked, but there were no doors, no rooms. She ran up and down all the halls—she was so scared because she thought the mom was playing tricks, and then she looked for the stairs because she wanted to get out of the house and back to the playground to find her friends—but the stairs were gone!" Lilly grabbed Tunum, who was stuck between the bed and the wall, and squeezed him with the crook of her arm and clenched my hand with her other one.

"You know what happened then, Mommy? You're not going to believe this."

"What, sweetie?"

"The mom was standing behind her the whole time. The girl never saw her, but she was just there. Just like that. How did she get there if there were no stairs? And just when she noticed the mom, she saw a door. For the first time. But that door wasn't there before. There were sounds coming from inside the room. A voice. The little girl looked at the mom. She was frightened. I just wanted the dream to end—I couldn't take it anymore. But I didn't know how to wake *up*. *I couldn't wake myself up—*"

"It's okay, Lilly. You're awake now, and it's over." I pulled her close to me and hugged her safely. At first she gave in to it, and I could feel her heart racing against my chest; then she pushed me away.

"No, Mommy. That's not the end. The mom opened the door. The girl stuck her head in. No one was in there. But there was a voice a minute ago—I even heard it. But the room was empty. Everything was dark and gray. No pictures, or books, or toys, or clothes. Definitely *not* her doll. There were only two beds. With no sheets or blankets or pillows. Just mattresses. And the little girl said, 'Where's my room? This isn't my room.' She was crying. 'This room has two beds—'

And the mom laughed, 'Of course it has two beds!'"

"Then I woke up."

This time Lilly practically tackled me. She wrapped her skinny arms around me and dove her head into my chest with such intensity that I nearly fell off the bed. I felt Smarty try to stick his nose between our tummies. I held Lilly tight. I had to remind myself that no matter what kind of game-face she wears, she's quite vulnerable. Her heart was racing, and her chest moved up and down against mine.

"Thank goodness it's over. What a terrible dream."

"Do you know the girl, Lilly? Did you recognize her?" I asked, like a thousand times before.

"No."

I held her as close as I could and thought about what to say to her to convince her that it would be okay to close her eyes again, to go to sleep again. But I knew this torturous cycle. We'd been through it before. And it would be days, probably more, until she'd sleep peacefully again.

I grabbed another tissue from her nightstand. "Sweetie, is something bothering you? Did something happen at Delia's house or at school last week to upset you?"

Hmm, let's see, in Lilly's last twenty-four hours, her mother has had a freaky head and face injury, caused her to fall in the pool at a swim meet, embarrassed her in front of her friends and their families, and she finds out about a cousin she never knew existed—because he doesn't, but she doesn't know that—who "lives" in Argentina with a terminal illness, for whom she may need to donate blood. Well, I don't know, what could be causing her repressed anxiety?

Something also happened at school on Thursday, in the cafeteria, which Tessa told me about after a little nudging. I wasn't sure it was enough to really bother Lilly like it bothered Tessa. However, you never know what kids carry around inside, bottled up, waiting to manifest into a disturbing dream that will seemingly have no relevance.

"No, Mommy. Delia's party was fun. I didn't have any nightmares at her house," she said, blowing her nose.

I was conflicted as to whether I should bring up the school incident, but maybe it would help to talk about it.

"How about school?" I prodded.

Tessa told me the story when she came home from swim practice on Thursday. Not that she offered it enthusiastically, but I'm familiar with the quiet preoccupation that accompanies her distress, and with the right lure, I was able to fish it out. Lilly was invited to have dinner that night with her new friend, Alexandra (whose family employs a live-in cook who will make any meal on request). So it was just Tessa and me.

Typically, when Tessa comes home from practice, she can eat a horse, but Thursday she would not even look at food. She dribbled into the kitchen and dropped her backpack and swim bag to the floor, causing the wine glasses in the upper cabinets to clank. Seeping like an amoeba, she moved through the room, eventually taking over a stool at the island.

"Hi," I offered, approaching with caution.

"Hi . . ."

After all my efforts to get the alien to communicate had

failed, I went to the pantry, to retrieve a bag of chocolate Kisses that I keep behind the kale chips for emergencies.

"How was school today?" As soon as I said it, I realized my mistake—don't ask a question that can be answered with one word (Parenting 101). "I mean, how was the math tes—uh, um, I mean, what was your best subject today—and why?"

It was all I could think of.

Tessa slowly raised her head and scrunched her eyes, "In 300 words or less?" She couldn't resist her own joke, which caused a reluctant smile to materialize across her face.

Once again, I'm a mockery.

I let her take two Kisses while she told me what happened in the cafeteria at lunchtime. When she reached for the chocolates, I noticed scabs on her left thumb around the nail bed.

"So, after I talked to my teacher about the homework, recess was practically over, so I got my lunch and went straight to the cafeteria. I looked around for Delia and Lilly and Jenna. At first I couldn't find them, but then I saw Lilly and Jenna sitting at a table in the back of the cafeteria, with Alexandra. They never sit there. I saw Lilly duck under the table like she dropped something, but when I got closer, I realized she was hiding. I thought she was hiding from the boy in her class who has a crush on her. There was one seat left at their table, so I pulled the chair out to sit down, and Lilly popped her head back up.

"'You can't sit there, Tessa!' She started yelling at me. So I asked, 'Why not? Is somebody sitting here?' I heard Jenna say no, but then Lilly went semi-ballistic, 'Yes, yes, someone is sitting there—Sarah. Sarah's sitting there.'

"I said, 'Oh, sorry, I didn't know . . .' Then Jenna turned

to Lilly and said, 'Sarah's not in school today, Lilly. She's sick.'
Lilly got even madder.

"Lilly said, 'Can't you just find another table, Tessa? Why
do you always have to sit with us, anyway? There are plenty of
other seats for you to pick from.'

"Jenna said to Lilly, 'Why can't she just sit *here?*', and Lilly
turned to Alexandra and said, 'Well, this is Alexandra's table.
So Alexandra, it's up to you. But we know how popular you
are and that you have tons of friends, so if Tessa can't sit here,
we completely understand.'

"And then Alexandra just kept saying, 'Well, uh, well,
uh—well,' and that's when I just couldn't take it anymore,
and I thought . . . I thought I was going to . . . cry, so I walked
fast to the other end of the cafeteria by the bathroom. It was
almost the end of lunch anyway, so I just found a seat far away
from them. Then Delia saw me. She was sitting with Hannah.
She waved me over to sit with them. But just as I pulled the
chair out, the bell rang.

"I brought my lunch home. I didn't have time to eat it—I
wasn't hungry anyway."

Here we go again. I really didn't know what to say to
Tessa. I wanted to be able to come up with that really pro-
found enlightenment that would make sense of her sister's
jealousy and rivalry and insecurity. But there was nothing.
And anyway, I know I can't always have a solution in my back
pocket. Still, there's nothing worse than when the girls hurt
each other.

Tessa was quiet for a while, chewing. I popped a chocolate
in my mouth and chewed along with her in silence. Our jaws
moved in unison as both of us look blankly at the same piece
of nothing in the air.

I placed my hand on hers.

"I don't get her, Mom. If other kids are being mean to me, Lilly always sticks up for me. One time last year, remember? She hit that boy who pulled up my skirt."

I knew I would have to talk to Andy about this. So on Thursday night when he called, I told him. And we decided together to give Lilly a warning, to put her "on probation." If she acts mean-spirited toward Tessa again, she's not allowed to participate in the next swim meet. "Get 'em where it hurts," we said in unison, and it sounded really macho at the time, but I'm gonna have to be the one to tell her and probably even impose the punishment and, well, I'm a wuss.

In retrospect, I wish disciplining Lilly were my biggest problem.

Andy and I decided that we'd wait for Lilly to fess up. Often, I'll admit, this tactic is absurd. But we never stop believing.

When I asked Lilly if anything happened at school to upset her, I gave her some time to think about it. It seemed like a very long time. Then finally, the door opened a sliver. Her head stayed down, and she didn't look at me.

I guess Lilly's nightmares aren't really that perplexing. She's a burier. She just pushes all that emotional stuff down deep, thinking that she's getting rid of it, or hiding it. But it all comes back to haunt her in her sleep.

"Well, there was something that happened last week at school with Tessa. But it's no big deal. Even Tessa said so."

"Really?"

"It was just this thing in the cafeteria—no biggie—Tessa was looking for a seat at lunch. and all the seats were filled up at my table. So—"

"Oh."

"That's pretty much it."

"Oh. Well, why do you think that would bother Tessa? That doesn't sound . . ."

"*Because*, Mom, she wanted to sit there." Lilly squirmed around; first she threw her fist into a small tasseled pillow, then turned around and clutched Tunum, slid down in her bed, pulled the blankets up to her chin, and became very still. "And she couldn't—and that's all."

"Well, there weren't any empty seats . . ." I allowed.

"*Mom*, it wasn't *my* table. It was Alexandra's table, so it wasn't up to me, okay?"

"Okay, Lilly, don't get upset—I didn't know kids have their own tables."

"They *don't* have their own tables—people can sit wherever they want. It's a free country, isn't it?"

"Yes. Yes, it is."

"And, anyway, Alexandra is *my* new friend—not Tessa's. And Tessa has her own friends, anyway, so why does she always have to sit with me . . . and Alexandra? Plus Alexandra is very popular and has tons of friends. And she doesn't have time for *another* new one, okay?"

"Uh-huh . . ."

"And just 'cause there was one empty seat, it doesn't have Tessa's name on it. Alexandra probably needed it for one of her other friends. Think about how many of her friends she was going to have to let down, Mom. After all, there was only one empty seat."

"Oh. So there was an empty seat."

"Only *one*."

"Well, if all of this was okay with Tessa, then . . . that's what you said, right?"

"How am I supposed to know if she just ran off? I'm not a mind reader. So, I guess it was fine." Then Lilly hung her head, and with it, her face sank, too. When she started to cry, I felt horrible for starting this stupid thing. She had gone through an awful night already. I was just hoping that talking about this would be cathartic. What exactly did I want to prove here?

I pulled her head into me and rubbed big circles on her back.

But I just couldn't let it go.

"Lilly, you hurt your sister's feelings. And you embarrassed her in front of the other girls—which is wrong. Now, if you had spoken to her at home about needing some space and needing to spend time with other girls without her, I think she would understand. But to humiliate her in public is just cruel. Not to mention, you know as well as I that Tessa would never do that to you.

"The next time you're mean to your sister, you miss a swim meet. And that's a directive from Daddy, who heard all about this."

It should have felt awful, lacing into her like this, especially since it was the middle of the night and she was scared senseless from her nightmare, which was on top of an already horrible day. I don't know how to explain why I kept at it—my heart was aching for Lilly, but I didn't stop. It was as if I'd been waiting forever to say this—to teach her a lesson about loyalty and friendship and sorority.

I moved farther back on the foot of the bed. "You know something, Lilly. If you continue to act this way to your sister, guess what's going to happen? She's not going to want to be around you anymore. She's not going to want to hang out with you, or play with you, or laugh with you, or go to the movies with you, or share secrets with you. She may even turn against you, if you hurt her badly enough. Because once someone's gone, they're gone. And there may not be any way of getting them back."

And then I was cleansed. And deeply ashamed of myself.

I looked at Lilly. There were tears in her eyes. And tears in mine. We both felt miserable. Did I have to go on like that? What was the point? If only I could take it all back.

After we stopped crying, we fell asleep.

Just before daybreak, I went back to my own bed, where Tessa was in a peaceful slumber, and I fell asleep deeply for about an hour.

Now I lay awake, staring at the ceiling and the fragile cobwebs hanging off the chandelier.

I long for my typical Sunday morning wakeup call—the smell of bacon, coffee, omelets—when Andy wears the apron and when my nose wakes up before any other body part. Today, it's my frazzled nerves. I reach over to my nightstand and shut off the alarm before it wails and wakes Tessa, and grab today's schedule, which I printed last night.

Halfway down the page, in bold, I read: **12:00 Andy's Coming Home!**

A wave of nausea breaks in my stomach. He'll be here in a few hours.

I indulge myself in the calm of the house and focus on my breathing, deep inhale, deep exhale. The house is breathing with me, like it's an enormous lung and I'm in the midst of it. The breathing becomes hypnotic. It's easy to surrender to it—my body and mind are lulled. A moment into this peaceful state, my brain crackles. Slowly at first, like a bag of microwave popcorn, kernels pop one at a time until the popping is random and riotous. One of the white puffs is different. I try to slow it down, to stop it. Expose it. I pin it against the wall of my mind. The frenzy halts. I examine it closely.

My breathing stops.

I sit with this thought for a moment, stricken. It makes me terribly uneasy. I know I don't have to act on it. I play out all the possible outcomes in my mind. But none of them matter; it's what I have to do. Apprehension is preempted by desperation. I reach for the phone on my nightstand and dial.

"Hello, Rosanne Kriete's office," says the voice on the other end.

"Hello. This is Caroline Thompson. I know she's not there, but I'd like to leave a message. I need to speak with her as soon as possible. I need to see her. It's very important."

CHAPTER SIX

Sunday, September 24, 2006, 12:41 p.m.

We've been standing at Baggage Claim carousel #3 (where Andy's luggage will end up) for almost forty minutes because the rain and wind have delayed his arrival. The girls run back from the monitor. His plane has finally landed. After they finish a ring-around-the-rosie dance, they grab their signs off the floor and spring back to the foot of the escalator. The signs, which feature green and pink glitter glue bubble letters, read, "Daddy," and "We missed you."

Andy's happy, boyish face finally descends the escalator, and the girls run to attack him. I breathe a sigh of relief as I always do. The tiny scar at the corner of his mouth twitches, signaling his exhaustion. His arms wrap around me, and I breathe into his soft polo shirt—still smelling of fabric softener—he must've just changed into a fresh shirt on the plane.

He whispers in my ear, "Looks like I got home just in time." He pulls away from me and moves my hair with his hand to reveal the side of my face. "Wow." He doesn't get alarmed; he just smiles at me, but there's concern in his eyes. It probably would've been a good idea for me to tell him about that beforehand.

Deep down I know everything will be okay. I won't feel so alone anymore. In that split second, it feels as if I've come home, too.

"Guys, I had the greatest idea when I was on the plane. You know how I've been away a lot lately and I missed a lot of the summer? So I was thinking—we should have a party! A really big one—with a band and dancing, and maybe a roast pig. What do you think? Wouldn't it be fun? We haven't had one in so long, and . . ." The girls are now jumping up and down at his side, pulling at his arms and yelling out the names of friends they want to invite. "We could have it next Sunday and call it an 'Indian summer' party . . ." The girls cheer at the suggestion. He could have called it a cow-milking party and they would've had the same reaction.

I'm instantly in a state of semi-shock. I'm not even remotely in the mood for a party. Let alone one that I'm destined to conceptualize, organize, troubleshoot, and execute.

He wants to have the party next Sunday. A week from today.

He looks over at me and says, "Caroline, what's the matter? I didn't suggest we move to Siberia."

"Andy, who do you think is going to be available on such short notice?"

"Don't worry. Lots of people—I'll take care of that. Okay? I'm gonna take care of this party. You've been running around like crazy with me out of town, Caroline. So, *I'm* going to throw this party. How does that sound?"

"Far-fetched?"

No one hears me over the girls' "Yippee!" and "Go Daddy!"

"You don't believe me, do you?" he says to me. "Well, it's time to be a little more confident about dear ol' Andy's mad party-throwing skills. I can do this. Probably not as good as you, Caroline. Okay, definitely not as good as you."

"Sweetie, you don't have to do this to . . . "

"I *want* to—it'll be fun." He spots his suitcase on the carousel. "Caroline, I really need this—" He turns to grab his luggage off the conveyer belt and then turns back to me and adds quietly, "I might need a *little* help." He pinches his fingers together to show me how little.

Maybe it's exactly what I need, too. To dive into a project—a big party. It could help distract me and make me feel useful instead of lobotomized. Plus, being surrounded by good friends can't hurt.

We load the luggage in the car and head home. I drive so Andy can concentrate on catching up with the girls. Tessa nearly self-combusts with excitement in relaying the minute details of the riding competition she was in last weekend. It's hard for me to believe it was only seven days ago. It feels like a month, at least.

He asks a hundred questions about her horse and the events, which has Tessa beaming.

Lilly comes at her reenactment of the week a little differently. She reports on who-did-what-to-whom, who started to cry, how so-and-so got a new whatchamacallit (the one she herself has wanted her entire life), and, well, how life is just plain unfair. Andy takes it all in stride, partly because he hasn't been around to hear all this ad infinitum. Then he actually says something to make her feel better. "Life is just plain unfair," he says. How he thinks of these things, I will never know.

Andy used to come home from a business trip only to get ready for the next one, never really touching ground in a sense. He used to look forward to the travel. It's what he did well. And it allowed him to stay on the periphery of family life. He felt comfortable there. I didn't mind it; I knew when I married him that he traveled a lot. It was what I expected. It became part of our lifestyle as a family. But now, he comes home with the need to feel connected. He wants to make plans and be social. In fact, he told me just before leaving for London that he plans on interviewing for a new position at Global—one with less travel.

It's been just over an hour since he's stepped off the plane, and my energy has shifted. I can't believe I'm even warming up to his party idea, and I begin to make a mental list of what should be done, people to call, things to buy. It actually feels good to think about something fun.

If he's thinking about a backyard barbeque, I need to get things in shape back there. The pool guy was scheduled to come next week to close it up, but I'll change that now. We hardly grilled at all this summer, partly because we ran out of propane last month, which I didn't bother to replace, and partly because Andy was out of town so much. So we need propane, citronella for the torches, and now that I think of it, grill tools. I have no idea what happens to them, but at the start of every grilling season I buy a new set, and as the days of summer trickle away, so do they.

After we eat a late lunch, the weather clears up, and Andy takes the girls on a bike ride. It's a perfect time for me to dash to the hardware store to get a few things done, and it'll be nice for the girls to have Andy to themselves.

The hardware store greets me with the combined musty smell of wet lumber and galvanized nails, and the sarcastic, perverted store manager who never saw a female or a cheeseburger he didn't like.

He's fully immersed in solving a dripping showerhead problem for the unfortunate woman who got here before me. "When was the last time you took a shower?" he asks her with a greasy smile, undoubtedly visualizing the experience. He's taking way too long with all his stupid questions, and I'm starting to lose my patience.

I take a quick scan of the store, thinking about what else I need, when I notice the woman keeps looking back at me. Perhaps I leaked an audible sigh, or maybe she wants to be rescued from this guy.

I clear my throat. "Uh, sorry to interrupt, but—" I say, with my hand slightly raised.

"Oh, no, we're finished," she says as she turns to face me; her eyes have now seized mine. "Sorry, but don't I know you from somewhere? I just moved here from Connecticut, but you look so familiar to me." Her face scrunches up; she's determined to figure it out.

"No, sorry, I've never lived in Connecticut." She makes me uncomfortable. She's standing way too close, and she's way too intense, like she's not going to leave until she gets to the bottom of it. She's planted herself between me and the sleazy store manager like a massive redwood. I'd even rather talk to him at this point.

"No, not from Connecticut." She's stuck like day-old peanut butter. "I don't know . . . Did you ever work for NBC in

New York?" The stranger does not let up. It always kills me when people are insensitive to other people's sense of urgency. "Were you in the Page Program there? Oh, wait, no," a finger tentatively goes up in the air, "you know what, I think it might have been school—"

I get as stiff as the paint stick I'm using to drum on a can. I realize I must look like a paralyzed freak, so I shove my head in my handbag to search for something. "Oh, was that *my* phone? Did you hear that?" I pull out my phone and look at it. "I could've sworn—oh my gosh, are you kidding me, it's almost five o'clock? Jeez, I've gotta get going, I'm so sorry, but I'm . . . do you mind? I don't mean to be rude—" I point over to the hardware guy to get his attention.

"Oh, no, not at all," she deflates, "Sorry," then sidesteps, looking embarrassed, and disappears into the plumbing aisle, which makes me feel terrible since I'm the one who should be embarrassed.

"Welcome to Farhaven!" I call out to her and quickly turn back to the guy to order the propane.

I close my eyes for a sec to get back on track, but now I can't help but try to remember her. I can almost swear I've never seen her before in my life. Definitely not at school. That I know. She's mistaken.

This normally wouldn't bother me. It happens to people all the time. Probably I just look like someone she once knew. *Normally* it wouldn't bother me. But what if she *did* go to Hammond? She could have been a friend of a friend. She could know about—*the incident*. Or maybe she knows I never finished school. For God's sake—*I* didn't even know these things until yesterday.

There could be other things—

I have to buy what I need and get out of here. I make eye contact with the guy. "What aisle can I find the thongs?"

He doesn't say a word, but his eyes pop like doorknobs. Then his mouth opens slightly.

What's his problem? "You know, for when I'm grilling." Now his jaw drops open completely, revealing a pool of saliva that's collected around his tongue. Yuck. I look away, but not before seeing his eyes canvas me from head to toe. That's when I realize what I just said. An instant visual image of me grilling, wearing a thong, flashes through my mind. And apparently, through his.

Crap. Why can't I get "tongs" and "thongs" straight? Of course, there's no shame in asking for "tongs" at Victoria's Secret, but I never make that mistake.

The sound of my phone ringing, this time for real, rescues me.

"Hi, Andy. You're back from your ride already?" I pick up a wooden paint stirrer from the counter and tap it nervously like a drumstick.

"I came back home for my wallet," he says. "We're going to stop for frozen yogurt. I just wanted to tell you the Red Cross called."

My heart drops into my stomach. "What?"

"You forgot your sunglasses there."

"Oh! Oh, golly. *That's* where they are." I stop tapping. "I've been looking all over—"

"What was going on at the Red Cross?"

"At the Red Cross?" I start tapping again. "Uh, I was bringing over bags of old clothes. I cleaned out some closets last week, and those bins outside the Red Cross were full, so—"

"Oh, gosh, I've got tons of stuff I could give you. Well, listen, I have to drop my dry cleaning later, so I can swing by the Red—"

"*I've* got your dry cleaning . . . in the car . . . I took it with me." I make a mental note to race home to grab his dry cleaning before he notices it's still in the mudroom. "I'll swing by and drop it off and pick up my sunglasses. No problem. Thanks anyway. Hey, you get back to that bike ride! And bring me some frozen yogurt, okay?"

I quickly gather my handbag and to-do list that are resting on a stack of paint cans. My legs are like rubber bands, and they struggle to support the weight of the rest of me. I need to get out of here and pull myself together.

I clutch my handbag close to my chest and jog to the car.

The image of that woman from Connecticut clings to the back of my mind. I need to forget about her.

I make a quick decision to cater our party, and head to the Red Cross to pick up my glasses.

Monday, September 25, 2006, 7:30 a.m.

WHEN MY EYES flicker open, it's Monday morning. I don't move. My limbs are leaden. I've gained weight overnight; everything's heavy—my heart, my stomach, my conscience. But I'll have to get up and press on and somehow maneuver through the twists and turns of being a mother and a caregiver, while I evade the potholes and booby traps that have recently become commonplace.

How could I be so naive? To think that fish tacos and homemade guacamole with my joyous intact family, a few rounds of Charades, and some belly laughs are all it would take to dissolve my dread. Talk about a charade. My hand reaches over to Andy's pillow; it's already cold. Smarty is asleep in his spot. Why should I be surprised that he went to work? It's Monday morning, for Pete's sake. He could've stayed home. He's entitled to a day off when he travels on the weekend. But "you can't be considered for upper management if you take off."

I swipe my schedule from the nightstand and drag my feet to the bathroom, sliding my perky pink slippers across the floor, not bothering to lift my legs, not in the mood for a shower. The girls will be off to school soon, and I'm already anticipating my loneliness. I thought that with Andy home, I'd feel better, and I did at first. But the truth is that now I feel more isolated. Since I'm deliberately keeping things from him, I'm uncomfortable to be anywhere near him. I'm afraid of his questions—and of my reactions. I find myself dodging any kind of engagement. I feel farther away from him now than I did when he was in London.

In the bathroom, the thought of removing my pajamas makes my entire body shrink. The thought of being naked. I reach my arm around the thick, white, terrycloth shower curtain to turn on the water, but instead my hand becomes tangled up in something hanging from the dial. I stick my head around the curtain and am smacked in the face by the memory of Saturday's events. My body perks to attention.

The girls' bathing suits are hanging there, a mirror of my craziness—how I lied to them and made them promise to keep all of it from Andy. I climb into the shower and hug the bathing suits—nestling my face into the wet spandex still smelling of chlorine. Standing there in the rush that's not yet hot—my skin is studded in goose bumps. Water leaks from my eyes and mixes with the stream surging around my neck as it ripples over my collar bone and hurries to the floor.

The gush of water comes out in force, purging me. I feel small in the charge of it. The dial is set way too high and my skin burns, but I don't move. I lather my body by rote, starting at my shoulders. Mounds of soapy bubbles slide down my legs and swirl around my ankles like the silk ruffles of an evening dress. Then in one last breath, the residue circles the drain, and in a flash, gets sucked in. I feel neither awake nor asleep. The lemon-and-mint shampoo fails to deliver the "enlivened spirit" that it promises on the bottle.

There's no point in procrastinating. Today I need to resolve the inconceivable du jour: am I or am I not the real mother of my children?

The children I think are my children.

Good *God*, I can't believe I'm even having these thoughts. This is actually on my to-do list? I don't want to be searching for the true maternity of my girls. I want to be planning the school fundraiser and playing Scrabble with my family. Baking brownies and doing laundry. I want to put summer clothes away and vacuum sand out of the car and pick up dry-cleaning and trim fat off chicken breasts. Plunge the upstairs toilet. Get that colonoscopy.

After the girls jump out of the car at school, I look down on the passenger seat at my schedule and check the address for Truly Scrumptious, the caterer I'm hiring for the party, with whom I have a 9:00 a.m. appointment.

The meeting is short, and just as we finish up the dessert selections, my cell phone rings from the bottom of my handbag.

My body tightens. I recognize the number.

"Hello?" I say anxiously.

"Hi, Mrs. Thompson, it's Dee Dee from Dr. Kriete's." Her voice is warm but anxious.

"Hi, Dee Dee, I'm so glad it's you—"

"I got your message. You said it's urgent that you see Dr. Kriete, but you didn't say why. Are you all right?"

"Oh, well, yes . . . I'm, well, no, not really." I look at the caterer and excuse myself into the hall for some privacy. "I mean, it *is* urgent, however, it's regarding a personal matter." There is an uncomfortable silence, so I clumsily continue.

"I—okay, I'll . . . tell you . . . uh, I guess there are a few things. First, I hit my head on the bathroom sink—"

Before I continue, she interrupts, "Did you go to the ER, have you had a CT scan?"

"Oh, no, nothing like that. I'm sure I don't need a CT scan . . . Um, unless it's causing the—uh, other problems."

"What other problems?" Dee Dee's impatient, like there are people standing in front of her and a couple on hold.

"Well, I prefer to not go into all of that right now. On the phone." Dee Dee is typing; then she stops and the successive flicking of a pencil against the desktop commences. She doesn't reply. "Um, let's call it confusion. Memory stuff."

People in the background are chatting. I'm not sure she's even listening to me anymore.

"And I'm pregnant."

"Pregnant?" Got her with that one.

I brace myself for her response, which could be *Go to the Emergency Room,* or *Go to your gynecologist.* But I'm not going anywhere. Because I'm not going to the emergency room. And I'm not going to my gynecologist. Why not? Well, I don't even remember the last time I was there. Or who my doctor is.

Which is scaring the crap out of me. I mean, I must go once a year, at least.

"Listen, Dee Dee, I'd go to my gynecologist, but I need to see Dr. Kriete for the . . . foggy thing. And while I'm there, she can do a blood test. I need to see her. It's very important. I'm free the entire day, and I'm not opposed to waiting."

Dee Dee interrupts my blathering, "Dr. Kriete leaves today at four-fifteen. She said she'd squeeze you in at four if it can't wait. But you must be on time."

"Oh, I will. Thank you, Dee Dee. I'll see you then. And thank you. Thank you very much."

This is it. Dr. Kriete will help me.

It occurs to me that Dee Dee never said "Congratulations" or "How wonderful."

Or even "Good-bye."

Dr. Kriete has been my internist for as long as I've lived in this town, and if anyone can tell me what's going on downstairs, or upstairs, she can. She's the voice of reason. She's calm, in control, and confident; you can tell by the way she walks, with long, slow strides, her chin slightly higher than everyone else's. Lipstick freshly applied (she must keep one in her lab coat). She has an ease about her, and sincere warmth. She looks you straight in the eye, giving you all the time in the world as if you're the only patient booked the entire day. I trust her implicitly.

I'm going to tell Dr. Kriete that I've taken an early pregnancy test, and it's positive. That I want a blood test to be sure. I'll tell her that my gynecologist is unavailable, and I needed to see someone right away. For all I know, I *am* pregnant. I can't remember the last time I had my period. Anyway, if she takes my blood, I'll know I still have the goods *and* that the article from the *Hammond Gazette* is a sham. She'd *know* if I had a hysterectomy. I'll know Lilly and Tessa are mine. If she won't do a blood test, well . . . then . . . well, I don't know what then. I'll figure that out then.

My mind quickly shifts to finding someone to watch the girls. I can pick them up from school and bring them home. It'll take me no time to get to Dr. Kriete's.

Meg would watch the girls in a heartbeat. And I only need an hour—I could just drop them at her house. The girls would play with Delia, and it would be a win-win. But I'm not calling Meg. I can't see her when I'm feeling vulnerable. I don't trust myself.

Generally speaking, in this town, the Mommy network can be brutally judgmental. The sheer number of categories you will be judged on by other women is mind-boggling: Do you exercise, volunteer, have cleaning people; let your kids eat McDonalds, watch PG-13; do you belong to the public pool, private pool, country club; do you have a weekend house, beach house, ski house? How about your hair: do you straighten, highlight, color; do you get facials, waxed, laid?

That's until they really get to know you.

With old friends, whether you drink Coke or Classic Coke, you can yuck it up either way. Once you're out of college and your single days are behind you, you're truly lucky if you've managed to hang on to any of those old friends—the ones you've handpicked by careful scrutiny and examination of their loyalty and judgment. Because if you do happen to lose those bosom buddies—due, say, to the rigorous, time-consuming, pay-your-dues career years, or the I-don't-have-time-for-you-because-of-my-new-boyfriend-and-*his*-friends years, or the I'm-so-fat-and-depressed-I-can't-see-anyone years—the next batch of friends you don't get to choose. Your kids do. Because they are the parents of your children's friends.

So good luck to you. Who you get is a crapshoot.

I've been truly blessed with my lot.

Mrs. Hildebrand. That's who I'll get to babysit.

Mrs. H, as we affectionately call her, is a dear woman. The girls refer to her as Mrs. Halitosis. They don't care for her for obvious reasons. If only she didn't hug them so tightly, and for so long, I think they might like her better. As soon as I leave the house, she locks the doors and lowers the blinds. She tells the girls, "No one needs to know your parents aren't home." Even though she's a bit of a fretter, I can deal with it. Better to be overly cautious. It's her napping on the job that's a little worrisome. When the girls first told me about the "shut-eyes," I thought it was their attempt to get their teenage babysitters instead of Mrs. H. But I called home one day to remind Mrs. H to give Tessa cough medicine, and Tessa had to wake her up to take my call. The naps are usually quickies, the girls tell me, so I haven't made a big deal over them. I guess I like the idea of having a grandmotherly figure around. With Andy's mother being on the agoraphobic side of normal in the Midwest, the girls barely have contact with a real grandmother. Mrs. H means well. And thankfully, she's nearly always available.

When I arrive at Dr. Kriete's office, Dee Dee is on the phone at the front desk. She nods at me without interrupting her conversation.

"Are you feeling chest pains now?" she says to the caller, and I manage to feel slightly better about her reaction to me this morning. She's busy. Dee Dee doesn't have time to say "Congratulations" to every Tom, Dick, and Harriet who claims she's pregnant. Anyway, I'm here to see Dr. Kriete. That's why I'm here. And Dr. Kriete is a beam of light reaching out across a dark, foggy inlet. She'll bring me home.

I borrow a pen from the cat cup on Dee Dee's desk and sign in.

In the waiting room, I sink into the overstuffed chintz couch and take the middle cushion since I'm the only one there. I've never really noticed the details before—the sunny, yellow walls and antique botanical prints framed in gold, the plump chair cushions filled with an abundance of feathers, upholstered in colorful, blooming florals. It's more like the setting for high tea in the English countryside. I pick up a magazine to give my hands something to do and rehearse in my mind what I'm going to say.

"Mrs. Thompson." Dee Dee is standing in front of me with my file in her hands. She ushers me down the hall and places my file in the box hanging on the outside of the door. She turns and smiles tentatively, then lowers her eyes and gestures with her arm for me to wait inside.

"Dr. Kriete will be with you shortly." She bows out, slowly closing the door. No eye contact. No "The nurse will be right with you." Not a word about my weight, temperature, blood pressure, or peeing in a cup.

Two beats later, Dr. Kriete comes in. She removes my chart from the door and holds it close to her chest without looking at it. Her face is uncharacteristically solemn. I check my watch to make sure I'm not late. I roll up the cuff on my white cotton shirt and undo a few of the buttons so as not to waste any of her time. She moves pensively, then sits in the wheeled chair and rolls over to the examining table, gently resting one hand on my knee. Warmth comes from her hand. She's wearing a plummy-colored lipstick that suits her pale skin tone and dark hair. Her white lab coat reveals the animal-print blouse and black pencil skirt she's wearing beneath it.

Her demeanor catches me off guard. Where's that spunky Dr. Kriete?

Before she says a word, I nervously jump in. "Dr. Kriete, I hit my head here." I point to the little Band-Aid over my eyebrow. "On the underneath of the sink, I was on the floor, and—"

She puts the clipboard down next to me on the table and removes the Band-Aid, placing it next to me.

"I'd usually shrug off something like this, but I guess I've been feeling a little odd lately."

"What do you mean by odd?" Dr. Kriete looks back at me while her hand rests on one of my knees.

"Well, forgetful," I gulp. It's hard for me to get the word out. "A little unsure of myself, like, not sharp."

She grabs an instrument from the wall and looks in my eyes, then asks me when this happened. "Did you get a headache, or vomit?" My answers lead her to suggest a CT scan at the hospital. "It's important that we rule out internal bleeding. Even though there was external bleeding, internal bleeding could still happen. You should go to the hospital today. And I'd like you to call me with the results." She stops talking and writes in my chart, then looks at me. And I at her. We look at each other in prolonged silence. I don't feel so good about this anymore.

"Well, there's another reason I'm here," I offer. "I'm pregnant." I wring out a smile to bring some levity.

Dr. Kriete collects her thoughts. Her words come out slowly and deliberately, like she's been planning this conversation and what she'd say. Her whole vibe is off-putting.

"Caroline," she starts, "when Dee Dee told me you wanted to see me because you thought you were pregnant, well, I gave it a lot of consideration. You've been my patient for almost six years—so I'm gonna give it to you straight."

CHAPTER SEVEN

Monday, September 25, 2006, 4:11p.m.

Dr. Kriete doesn't sound like her usual self. What's she talking about, "I'm gonna give it to you straight"?

All of a sudden, I'm aware of my heartbeat.

Dr. Kriete holds her gaze on mine. "Caroline, it's time we got another doctor involved. We've talked about this before . . ."

As she says this, I reach for the Band-Aid to put it back on my head. My fingers feel strange as they do this. Almost numb. Tingly. The sensation moves to my hands and feet. I try wiggling my toes, but I no longer feel their presence. The rest of my body feels like it's separating into millions of minuscule particles that are all drifting apart and away from where my body should be.

Dr. Kriete's face contorts; she becomes stern and rigid. "Caroline, you filled out a medical history form the day of your first visit, over five years ago. It's right here in your file. You wrote that you have two daughters who were delivered vaginally. You checked "no" for C-section and "no" for hysterectomy. Yet you have a scar. And you did then. I noted it during your first exam."

She keeps talking. Her words gently bump off my skin, against my eyelids . . . and cheeks . . . and my ears. They sneak into my mouth and fill up my lungs and throat and gag me—I start to cough spastically.

She reaches into her lab coat and pulls out a pair of frameless reading glasses. She opens the file. "June 17, 2001 . . ." she slides her finger down the page, "Hysterectomy scar noted—unremarkable."

I'm submerged in her words. I'm drowning in them. They're like bubbles in a fish tank, blub, blub, blub . . . I'm not sure I'm breathing, but I must be because every once in a while I hear her again. Bits and pieces of real words make their way inside my brain.

"Sometimes patients go through these medical history forms quickly and mark "no" without really thinking or reading. So I gave you the benefit of the doubt. But in November 2003," she looks down into the folder, "you complained of abdominal pain. 'Diagnostic laparoscopy ordered for possible adhesions,' is what I wrote. I sent you to a gynecologist, and you later had the adhesions surgically removed. They were caused by the hysterectomy. We talked about this, Caroline."

When? Where was *I?* I want to ask her these questions, but I can't gather the words.

"Your uterus and ovaries have been removed. I've asked you about this before, and when I did I got the sense you didn't want to talk about it. But now I get a sense that you truly don't remember. Is that it, Caroline? Do you remember that surgery?"

Her mouth stops moving, like she's waiting for something. Then she takes off her glasses and puts the folder to the side.

"The hysterectomy happened before your daughters were born. There's no way it could've happened after they were born and before you started as my patient. The scar would never have appeared that way. Now how could that be?"

Her words stop feeling like bubbles. Now, they're sharp and pointy and dangerous and accusatory. My head is spinning, thoughts whirl through my brain, but I'm muddled; my mind is swampy. I can't extract anything.

"There's one thing I can tell you beyond a shadow of a doubt: you're not pregnant, and unfortunately you won't be in the future."

I've got to get out. She's sitting too close—it's suffocating me. I need air. I can't breathe.

"Listen, Caroline, you have two beautiful girls who love you very much."

If they're not mine, whose are they? I wish I could say this, but my thoughts won't cooperate with my mouth.

"You have a wonderful husband. You know you can't get pregnant. Stop torturing yourself this way. It's time I recommend you talk to a psychologist about this. You deserve to sort this out and make sense of it all, and move on with your life."

She tilts her head, "Caroline? Are you okay?"

Her mouth stops moving. Her lips meet in a restful state, silencing her. Thank God. She's going to spare what's left of me and let me go. I try to slide myself off the examining table by swinging my dangling feet to get momentum.

She rolls her wheeled chair closer to me and quiets my legs with her hands. "Of course, if there's ever anything you'd like to talk about . . . Regardless, I strongly urge you see a psychologist. I'll have Dee Dee prepare a list of recommended doctors, and, of course, I would be available to speak with the one you choose."

In one move, I slide my legs to the side opposite Dr. Kriete and heave my calves with just enough strength to land my feet on the floor. But my knees give out. My legs buckle. Dr. Kriete catches me. And lowers me into a chair, which she's dragged over with her foot. She sits across from me and holds both my hands, talking gently in a friendly, sing-song way. Tilts her head and smiles. Asks something. Someone's age? Someone's birth date? She picks up one of her hands and snaps her fingers in my face. I smell peroxide or something nasty under my nose. She says something about "water" and "husband." "His number." Something about "driving." "Relax." She pats my knee. She walks backward toward the door. She opens it and yells. She looks back at me behaving nicely, and ducks out of the room.

I try to get up again. I hold onto the examining table. My eyes focus briefly on the box of hypodermic needles. In long strides, I get out the door and down the hall, but briefly wobble as my foot catches the rug at the entrance to the waiting room.

Not *mine?* They're mine!

The room is like the Tea Cup ride at Disney. There's a pregnant lady tidying up the waiting room, organizing the magazines, dusting. She extends her arm to help steady me. I imagine her on a lifeboat, reaching over the side to grab my hand, in vain, while I float slowly out to sea. Then my eyes fix on her rounded stomach.

"Are you okay?" she asks.

A moment later I'm out of there, in the hall, out of the building, and in my car.

The air is bracing against my face. I take in big gulps. She's going to call Andy. I finally piece it together. I check my watch to see how long it's been since I was sitting with her. No watch. I turn the key in the ignition for the dashboard clock to light up, but I hold the key forward too long and it grinds the engine and spews a grating, painful sound. An old man on the other side of the parking lot shoots an annoyed "Don't you know what you're doing?" look. How dare he judge me? I honk the horn, with all the weight of both hands so the sound wails endlessly. He hurries into his car and drives away—his tires screech around the turn.

They may not know I'm gone yet. I could be in the bathroom. It'll take a few minutes to find Andy's office number in my file. I dump the contents of my handbag on the passenger seat and grab my cell phone to call Dr. Kriete's office from the parking lot. The phone slips out of my sweaty, trembling hand; I snatch it from the seat beside me and hold it with both hands to my ear.

Dee Dee answers; she's flipped out. "Where are you, Mrs. Thompson? You shouldn't be alone, and no way should you drive—"

I take one hand off the phone to shift into reverse, then into drive, and swerve out of the parking lot, navigating my way home. "Listen, Dee Dee," I try to interrupt, but she's like a wind-up toy in the fully wound position, "Listen, Dee Dee . . . Dee Dee! . . . *listen to me*—I'm going to hang up unless you listen." Silence. "You tell Dr. Kriete not to call my husband. I can't have her call him and discuss—any of this—with him. Do you understand? *Please—I beg of you. Please.* I just need a little time. Plus, I'm her *patient*. Do you get that? This stuff is between us. You tell her that. If she discusses this with anyone, well, she can kiss her license good-bye. Got it? You go tell her right now before she calls him. Are you listening?"

"Yes, Mrs. Thompson." She then whispers to somebody.

"Besides, he's—under a lot of stress. I just can't—concern

him with any of this—stuff right now. Are you there, Dee Dee? Did you hear me?"

In a robotic, conciliatory way, she says, "Yes, Mrs. Thompson. I understand. But that doesn't change the fact that you're in no condition to drive."

"Dee Dee—"

"The cleaning lady told me you were unsteady in the waiting room."

"I wasn't unsteady. I was in a hurry."

"Whatever. You're not displaying the signs of—"

"Dee Dee—I'm hanging up. You get to Dr. Kriete before she makes a mistake."

I press "End" and throw the phone on the passenger seat as I veer onto Brightwood Road. I swerve up our driveway without slowing and nearly take out a boxwood at the edge of the house.

None of the keys work in the lock on the front door. I don't have the patience to wait until they do. I run around to the back of the house and try the key there. It opens. The house is remarkably quiet, except for giggling coming from upstairs. Where is Mrs. H? Smarty Pants meets me in the kitchen and cocks his head to one side. When I don't pick him up, he follows me.

Perhaps they've pinned Mrs. H to the bathroom floor, brushing and flossing her teeth against her will. Or she could be sleeping.

I give a sharp tug to my shirt hem and quickly fasten the remaining buttons. Then calmly leap the stairs by two. The bathroom door is closed, and their laughter grows more animated. Something's amiss.

I slowly push open the door.

When the girls see me in the doorway, they suddenly freeze mid-motion as if I had a gun.

They've rigged the shower curtain so it swoops down into one end of the bathtub, and they're using the hand-held shower sprayer to soak the curtain to create a water slide for their old Barbies, which haven't seen the light of day for years. Lilly is standing up on the ledge of the tub dropping the Barbies on the shower curtain from above, while Tessa is soaking the "slide." Where the hell is Mrs. H? The entire bathroom is a water park. But I don't concern myself with that right now. I just need to see them.

"Mom—" is all Tessa can come up with.

I take a deep breath to encourage my heart to slow. Okay. Lilly really, really looks like me. It's not my imagination—people often say so. Our brows and the shape of our eyes, even if they're not the same color. Our expressions. We resemble each other at the *very* least. Everyone always says Tessa looks more like Andy. I give them both a bear hug and kiss them a few hundred times. My reaction to their girl-induced disaster leaves them speechless with their mouths agape. I turn to leave the bathroom and yell, "You've got five minutes to make that place look like Phoenix in August! Where's Mrs. H? Tell her I'm home."

I need to collapse.

And I do, on my bed. Smarty jumps up and rests his chin on my stomach. I don't know what to think anymore. What to believe. *Who* to believe.

How much more of this can I stand with no one to turn to?

My body sinks lower and lower into the bed. The mattress and my body become indistinguishable. My eyes are gently closed, and I am, for a mere second, at rest.

There's something on the inside of my eyelids. My eyelids become miniature movie screens for an apparition that's being sent to me. An image so faint, I strain to make it out. It's a book.

One I haven't seen in years. There's a photo on the book's cover. The photo, of a newborn baby, is surrounded by pink bows that line up end to end, bordering its outer edges. The baby is naked, sleeping in a nest of feathers. I've seen it before. My eyes burst open. It's Lilly's baby book! Oh my God, of course—Lilly's baby book! Why didn't I think of that?

I spring off the bed. Smarty practically backflips onto the floor.

This is it—this is what I've been waiting for. Of course—it's all there in black and white. Lilly's baby book. The answers! The truth. Thank you, *thank you*—whoever sent this to me. I can't wait to see Dr. Kriete's face when I tell her. This ordeal may have sucked the life out of me, but it didn't take my uterus.

At once I'm alive with hope. I *knew* I wasn't going crazy. Of course these girls are *mine*. And now—finally—the truth is at my fingertips.

Now, where *is* that book? I dig deep to mentally retrace my steps. It should be on the bookshelf in the den—but I don't think it is. Though it's illogical to me, in my mind's eye, I see it in my bedroom closet.

I tear open the closet door. The closet is oversized thanks to an addition we built onto our house a year after we moved in. Actually, we had two walk-in closets built, his and hers, side by side. Andy keeps his the way he wants. I keep mine the way I want. It's an insurance policy on our marriage. A high percentage of divorces are due to vastly different levels of tidiness. Plus, old Colonials weren't built with enough closet space or big enough bathrooms for happy marriages. I race to the back of the closet, passing my fall/winter wardrobe to the right, spring/summer to the left, and a section of each side is dedicated to small cubbies for stacks of sweaters and jeans. The back wall is lined with shelves;

shoe boxes fill the lower ones. Something propels me to the top shelf, to a bunch of extra pillows and piles of old, faded linens. I pull a few of the pillows down and let them fall to the floor, but the shelves are extra deep so it takes a stepladder and a full torso stretch to reach behind the linens. Touching the back wall of the closet, there are two books standing up on their sides. Their bindings are facing away. They're Lilly *and* Tessa's baby books.

To reach the first, I need to tip my head so my arm will extend to its max. My fingertips feel the hard cover and I inch it out without seeing it. I'm finally able to yank it down. *The World Atlas.*

What the heck is this doing in my closet? I drop it to the floor, and the stepladder shifts from its weight. That's going to the den. My hand reaches back for the other book. My fingers, like a tweezers, pinch the book. An Anne Geddes photo of a fat, rippled newborn swathed in a bed of feathers is on the cover. It's not a photo of Lilly—but I kiss it anyway—I know what this is.

It's Lilly's baby book, and I'm higher than the moon. I'm leaping out of my skin with hope. God, I haven't seen this thing in too long. I fan through it quickly with my thumb, while still at the top of the stepladder. With my eyes closed, I hug it tightly and kiss it once more. I browse slower this time. I want to smell it. And breathe the air that dances from the flurry of pages. I sit down on the middle step of the ladder. From a quick glance, it looks like there are very few written entries and even fewer photos, which surprises me. I thought I did more with it. But I don't care. It doesn't look like anything is entered after her second birthday. Hmm, I guess that's life. You start with gusto—all enthusiastic and excited to capture every milestone, then days and weeks trickle by and you get caught up with mundane stuff.

If you have two kids, it's even harder to keep up these sorts of things.

The first page features a beautiful photo of Lilly on the day she was born wearing her blue and pink striped hat and swaddled in the hospital blanket.

I kiss her photo and wrap my arms around the book, my affection growing by the heartbeat. While it's close to my chest, I inhale the scent of the past and vow to add to it from now on. Tessa's baby book wasn't on the shelf. I make a mental note to look in the den. My eyes focus back to the photo of baby Lilly. Oh gosh, how could I forget? She was so long and skinny. Just like my mother told me I was as a baby. Not like those quintessential diaper-ad babies, with ripples of fat and huge round cheeks. My little lanky lollipop; she was beautiful.

The next page says: **Hospital: St. John's Hospital, Lanstonville, PA.** God, Lanstonville, *that* seems like a million years ago.

I finger through a few pages and come to where I've listed her first foods: **carrots, peas, bananas,** and there's a photo of her on the day she started eating them. The kitchen looks like it was devastated by a very large pumpkin bomb; every surface is coated in orange—except if you look closely, there appear to be two blue eyes peeking through the orange muck.

A photo of her wearing one of those hideous headbands is next, and I'm shocked that I actually put one on what's essentially a bald head. I must have been delirious from sleep deprivation. Pages later, a locket of hair from her first trim.

It's not until page nine—**First Spoken Words**—that it finally occurs to me. None of what's written is in my handwriting. Nor is it Andy's. Quickly, I fan through the book to examine the rest and notice something strange about the photos. There aren't many, and almost all of them are fragments of photos. Photos that have been cut or torn. Photos that have been violated. Heads cut off of bodies. I go back to the beginning and look at the pages I skipped. **My First Photo with Mommy**. I gasp. And cover my mouth with a trembling hand. Lilly is sitting in the lap of a decapitated body. How could someone cut my face out? That's *nuts*.

Goosebumps migrate up my arms; they raise wisps of hair as they crawl to the back of my neck. Does Andy know about this? Has he seen this? Everything else about the photo seems normal—I'm wearing my post-pregnancy uniform—T-shirt and jeans. But no head. I start to turn the page and stop. Something catches my eye. Something's not right. On the ring finger of my right hand is JD's college ring. Why am I wearing JD's college ring? It's the one my mother gave her when she graduated Barton. It was my mother's, given to her by my grandparents on her twenty-first birthday. JD always loved that ring when she was a young girl. She was so thrilled when Mom gave it to her. In fact, she never took it off. Ever. So what's it doing on my hand?

It hits me like a sucker punch. It's not *me*. In the photo. It's JD. Those are JD's *boots*. I hated those ugly freakin' lumberjack boots. I begged her to bury them in the fashion-sins graveyard along with oversized sweatshirts and scrunchies. I swear she wore those boots to make me crazy. Her peace-sign watch is on her left wrist. It's JD, all right. What the hell is she doing on *my* page? **My First Photo with Mommy**, not **My First Photo with Aunty**.

My heart pounds heavily, methodically, like a train speeding over broken tracks, bum-bum, bum-bum, bum-bum. With force it pounds up through my chest, making the back of my throat throb. But it doesn't stop there—it keeps going—pounding on my head until it gets through to my brain and asks, "Don't you get it? Don't you get it? Don't you get it?"

But I *don't* get it. I *can't* get it. I won't get it. Lilly is *not* JD's. She's mine. And Andy's. I gave birth to Lilly Thompson. *I* carried her in *my* body for nine bloated, gassy months. My rage and confusion twist like the fragile metal strands of steel wool.

I rip through the baby book to find every other picture guillotined. Then the pages go blank. Nothing for Lilly's third birthday or after that.

I search every page again from the beginning—meticulously reading every word—wiping each sentence with my fingertip—dusting them off for clues. Until I get to the end of the book. There's a pocket on the inside of the back cover. Something tucked into the bottom of the pocket creates a bulge, a small square. After all these years, it's made an impression in the pocket that hides it. I look inside. It's a piece of paper folded so small. If you didn't go looking for it, you'd never know it was there. I reach my hand in.

"Jesus Christ!"

My finger is pierced by something sharp. Next to the square of paper is a tiny gold cross adorned with the skinniest pink satin ribbon tied in a bow around it. *"Jeez,* I'm bleeding." A tiny spot of blood has formed at the tip of my finger. It slowly grows. With my other fingers I retrieve the carefully folded paper and open it, pressing out the creases with the back of my hand.

CHAPTER EIGHT

Monday, September 25, 2006, 4:53 p.m.

t's a birth certificate. I read the words through a smudge of blood:

LILLIANA SPENCER
BORN FEBRUARY 10, 1998.
7 LBS. 3 OZ.
21INCHES
ST. JOHN'S HOSPITAL, LANSTONVILLE,
PENNSYLVANIA
MOTHER: JANE DORY SPENCER
FATHER:
DATE ISSUED: FEBRUARY 23, 1998

I gasp. So violently that my tongue is sucked up against the back of my mouth. Shutting out oxygen, blocking my airway. I panic. I try to breathe—but nothing gets through. I can't get air.

I'm suffocating myself.

My hysteria escalates. The anxiety is paralyzing. I flail my arms like a shipwrecked survivor. I can't move my legs. I start to convulse. I collapse doubled over.

Smarty barrels into the room and barks like mad.

Lilly rushes in screaming, "Tessa! Tessa! Mrs. H! Help! Mommy's . . . choking!"

Lilly pleads, *"Mommy*, please, *please* don't die . . . **Help! Mrs. H!** *Oh my God, Mommy . . . oh my God. Don't die."* Lilly throws her arms around me from behind and pulls me up. "Don't worry, I know the Heimlich maneuver, remember, I learned it in Girl Scouts, don't worry, Mom, I know what I'm doing."

The problem is I'm not choking on a foreign body; I'm choking on my own body. But I can't tell her this. Lilly swiftly and deftly thrusts her fist up and under my rib cage. She's sucking in noisy gasps of air, and I wish I could get some.

"Mommy, please don't die. *Please* don't . . ."

I manage to simultaneously rip her arms off me and gasp my first breath of air in an eternity. The momentum springs me backward. I collapse on top of Lilly, pinning her under me. Her head slams against the wood floor. A horrendous wail gushes from her. I clumsily roll over onto my knees. Lilly doesn't move except for tears streaming down the sides of her face, dropping off her cheeks onto the rug. Even her mouth doesn't move—it's frozen open, an agonizing sound pouring out of her.

"Oh, *God.*" My chest heaves for its first few lungsful of air.

I'm hunched over in a doggy position when Mrs. Hildebrand comes stumbling into the room, followed by Tessa.

"Mrs. *Thompson—Jesus, Mary, and Joseph*, I must have—what's—" Mrs. Hildebrand is flitting back and forth between me and Lilly, "Lilly, *dear, oh my*—" she reaches out for Lilly.

"*Don't* . . . **touch** *her*—" I spatter, gasping. I can't lift my head. "Call . . . nine . . .one-one . . . Missus . . . I . . . think she . . . brok—" My arms give in and I collapse again—this time forward, onto the rug.

Smarty scampers five feet one way, five feet another. Mrs. Hildebrand makes a U-turn out of the room, mumbling, "*911, Jesus, Mary and Joseph*," and pulls Tessa into the hall with her. She hurries down the stairs, breathless, the stairs thumping under her weigh "*Tessa,* sweetheart—where does your mother keep the brandy, dear?"

"*Stay put—Lilly . . . okay?*" I pant, "Someone's . . . coming . . . to help . . ." I cough between each word. I look over at her. Her eyes are leaking. A steady stream flows down her ears, wetting her hair. Silent now. Her body frozen. Her arms outstretched—perpendicular to her body—like a cross. I reach my hand over her cheek to wipe the tears. When I pull away a streak of red is left behind across her face. Her tears dilute the stain, and it gets carried away in the stream before I can wipe it. "Can you move your fingers? Your toes?" She wiggles both. "Where does it hurt, Lilly? Your head?" She points to her collarbone. "Okay. Rest your arm. Don't move, sweetie."

Slowly, I move my head toward her hand and softly kiss her palm without moving it, "Lilly," I whisper, "I love you . . . I love you so much—do you know that?" My heart chokes up, and for the first time I'm afraid of all the love I have for her. It scares me. "No matter what—I love you. No matter what—I'm your mother."

I curl into a fetal position next to her, outstretching my

arm across her legs. My head is throbbing. My cheek gingerly touches her jeans—soaked from the shower. I take in every inch of her. Her feathery breath flows faintly in and out of her mouth. Mrs. H's voice floats in and out of my awareness. But all I can think about is Lilly. Something flashes across my mind. A memory of when the girls were about five and we were shopping for school clothes. The thought of it thrills me. A real memory. Clear as a blue sky. I want to cling to every detail of it.

It was the end of summer the year the girls were to start kindergarten. We were in a dressing room of a store in town, trying on fall clothes. Nothing fit right. Everything was too big. I wanted to go grab the smaller sizes, and because the rack was so close to the dressing room, I wanted Lilly and Tessa to stay put. "Sit on the bench with the door closed," I told them. The door was only eight feet away from the toddler section. I should've just left the door open. Why didn't I just leave the door open? But I closed it and told them to wait there while I went to get the right size. "Don't open the door for anyone but me," I said to them, "I'll be right back, I'm just going right there, see?" I pointed. Before I closed the door, Lilly said, "No problem, Mom-*my!*" while saluting me with her left hand. Tessa slumped on the bench, her bottom lip curled. She stuck her pinky in her mouth to suck on. Not a minute later I returned and knocked softly on the door, "It's Mommy, I'm back. Open up, please." One of them twisted the knob. Grabbed and twisted. Grabbed and twisted. But they couldn't open it. It was locked and stuck.

The manager of the store came over to "help." She put her nose very close to the door, nearly touching it, and scolded, shouting into the door, "What do you girls think you're doing?

This is not a playground; this is not a game you know. Open this door!" Then she turned to me and said, "Do you have *any* control over your girls, ma'am?"

I couldn't believe the way she was talking to them—or me. I thought I could possibly hit her. She was standing uncomfortably close to me, and Tessa was crying behind the door.

"Don't talk to my girls that way—" I grabbed the door knob and shook it. "There's something wrong with this door! Do I have to call the police, or will you do the responsible thing and get my girls out of there?!"

Another store employee came over and was somehow able to open the door. Tessa was curled up on the floor like a slug. Lilly, however, was standing up on the bench with her feet a yardstick apart, hands on her hips wearing nothing but her panties and a shirt tied around her neck as a cape. She splayed her arms triumphantly above her head, Rocky-style.

"I did it!" Lilly yelped in sheer disbelief. "I did it—I got the door to open!" She crouched down to tell her sister, "Tessa, Tessa, I did it—I got the door open. Look! Come on, Tessa—pick up your head. Open your eyes—see, Mommy's here—see, it's okay—lift your head, Tessie. Mommy, you should have seen me, I climbed up onto this thing with my Super Girl cape on and said 'I huff and I puff and I blow the door down!' And look what happened, I blew it open! Can you believe it? Tessa, don't cry—we're *freeeeee!*" she said as she sailed off the bench with her arms outstretched, believing she could fly. She didn't even mind when it didn't work; she brushed herself off and said, "The cape is new, it needs some practice." She knelt on the floor and hugged Tessa and said, "It's okay, Tessa, I saved us . . . and Mommy's here. You can stop sucking your finger."

The siren of the ambulance pierces through everything. I can't stand that sound. I clutch my ears to shut it out. But these people are here to help Lilly. The siren stops as they pull up to our house.

I reach down to Lilly's feet and caress the tops of them. I'm careful not to touch her toes, painted sparkly blue, because of how ticklish she is. I love her so much, so incredibly, with every ounce of my being. The vision of the baby book and birth certificate in my mind repulses me. A rancid wave turns over in my stomach. I don't give a damn if it's true. If my sister gave birth to her . . . I don't care. She's *my* daughter. And I love her. Nothing will change that.

Nothing can change that.

My sister is dead.

Monday, September 25, 2006, 9:42 p.m.

WHEN WE GET home from the emergency room, where it's confirmed that Lilly fractured her collarbone—or more correctly, I fractured Lilly's collarbone, we sit without sound, weary, hunched over at the kitchen table eating cold pizza. Andy is by my side sweeping his hand in big circles on my back, staring off into space. He has no idea the kind of hell that's scorched me today. Singed my soul. The weight of it is smothering.

I wish I could tell him.

I need to tell someone.

I need my sister.

She would know what to do. JD is—*was*—the kind of girl, who, if you told her a piece of the sky had fallen, would help you look for it and then figure out how to get it back where it came from. No questions asked.

"Today really, really stunk, guys," Andy breaks the silence, shaking his head, his shoulders slumped.

Multiply that by infinity.

Then he claps his hands and jumps out of his chair. His display of energy is painful. "Who's up for one of my world-famous, obscenely gigantic hot fudge sundaes? Extra whipped cream." He looks over at me for approval.

Great. Pizza and whipped cream. I'm too tired to argue. We haven't had this much saturated fat in a month. We own whipped cream?

"I'm too tired, Daddy," Tessa mumbles, her eyes swollen and pink. She barely lifts her head.

"How 'bout you Lilly?" He's still trying, hands on hips, urging his team to get pumped up for the second half of the game.

Ever since the nurse in the emergency room gave Lilly a painkiller, she has said nothing. Not one word. Her head is tipped forward, hovering over a slice of congealed cheese; strands of hair rest in a patch of oil on top of it. Lilly's one arm is crossed in front of her chest, Pledge-of-Allegiance style, held in an arm sling to take stress off her collarbone. Her eyes have a codeine glaze. Her skin is so pale that her freckles looked bleached. She's done.

"Lilly?" Andy bends down and gets his face up close to hers to see if that'll do the trick. "I'm gonna help you upstairs, okay? It's time for you to call it a day. Tessa, why don't you take a quick shower, or at least wash up, and brush your teeth? You can take a shower in the morning. Okay?"

"All right, Daddy." Tessa slides her chair back from the table and heads upstairs.

It's hard for me to look at Lilly now and not see JD. Her freckles are JD's, and so are her long eyelashes. It's unsettling. Lilly asked me a question in the hospital, and I thought for a split second that she was JD. It was bizarre. I know I'm exhausted and terrified. My nerves are splintered.

Why is Lilly with *me?* What happened to JD? And her husband? What about Tessa? I've been glued to Tessa's every move, every word, for the last five hours. Searching her face like it's a map. Looking for leads—something. Where does she come out in all of this? Her name wasn't in JD's obituary.

While Andy helps Lilly up the stairs, I wait for the bathroom door to close, and become a burglar in my own home, sneaking into the den to steal five minutes at the computer.

I type my name and hit the Google search box. I can't stop myself. I need five minutes.

I scroll down the screen to find JD's obituary. It could have information I overlooked. There's no time to browse, so I scan the page quickly.

Even with the best of intentions, something new snags me.

When there are no signs of suicide. The clear-cut signs of someone planning suicide aren't always there. When Psychology Review spoke to Elaine Spencer regarding the suicide of her daughter, JD Spencer . . .

www.pschologyreview.com/week962/suicide/ . . ./ when-there-are-no-signs . . .

What. The. Hell?

I gawk at the screen. Then close my mouth and skim the page quickly and try to pluck out the main parts.

A noise comes from the doorway of the den. My trigger finger fires at the "x" to shut down the document. I freeze. Trepidation creeps through me like an ant army. I shouldn't be doing this. I should be upstairs helping my hurt, fragile girls.

I spin around.

Smarty slips under the wing chair with something in his mouth. His jaws are shut, cheeks full, and a long, skinny tail hangs out of clenched teeth.

"Smarty Pants, no! Where'd—" A tiny squeak stops my rant, and he pushes the rubber mouse from his mouth.

"You and those freakin' mice—you scared the crap out of me." He looks at me in confusion. I forgot about those damn toy mice. The girls hide them around to see if he'll find them. I wag my finger at him, "No more real mice for you." I turn back to the screen.

A new document is open. It's not the suicide article. I must've clicked on it by mistake:

> *Lanstonville Press, August 14, 2000. CAROLINE SPENCER IS AWARDED CUSTODY OF LILLIANA SPENCER.*
>
> *I fall into my chair.*
>
> *After the shocking turn of events, Caroline Spencer, the sister of the deceased, Jane Dory Spencer, is awarded legal custody of her niece, Lilliana Spencer, says the ruling by Judge William Lenox.*
>
> *When asked to comment on the ruling, Ms. Spencer said, "I've always had faith in our legal system. My*

sister wanted it this way, and justice prevailed. Clearly, her Will and Testament is, and should be, the last and only word. I will see to it that my niece is raised in a loving home. I will surround her with the memories and goodness of her mother, Jane Dory Spencer, the warmest, most generous, and loyal person that has ever touched my life, and without question the closest and most important relationship in my life. Until now. I will miss her immensely."

When asked about the girl's father and if he will have a role in the girl's life, Ms. Spencer had this to say, "For me and for Lilly, he does not exist."

Ms. Spencer refused to comment on the bizarre circumstances that shocked the tight-knit commu-nity of Lanstonville for months. When Ms. Spencer was asked to comment, her lawyer, Matthew Bickley, raised his hand to discourage Ms. Spencer from speaking and simply said, "We have no comment."

Ms. Spencer's plans for the near future are to move out of state with her niece and to '"start anew." She has not indicated where or when—

"**Caroline!**" Andy barks. He's so close to me that the ends of my hair fly in the air from the rush of his voice.

I spring from the chair. "Oh my *God!*" I shriek back, "Andy—*my God!* What's the *matter* with you?" My heart is racing. "Sneaking up on me like that! *Jesus. Are you crazy?* I nearly had a heart attack . . ." I stand with my back to the computer, obscuring it with my body. How long has he been standing there, and what has he seen? My mouth goes dry.

"*Caroline*—what the hell are you talking about, *sneaking*

up on you?" His voice is controlled and measured. A blood vessel bulges alongside his left temple. *"I've been calling your name all over the house. From the top of the stairs. From the kitchen. From the hallway. Hell—I was standing in the doorway of the den—ten feet away—"* he thrusts his arm back toward the door, *"calling your name, for Christ's sake. You didn't answer me once? What's the matter with you?"* He puts his hands on his hips. "My God, I seriously thought you were passed out somewhere. You scared the shit out of me. What the *hell* is going on?" Puffy crescents of skin beneath his eyes crop up, aging him.

"*Nothing's* going . . ."

Smarty is on his feet and anchored between us, his head bullets back and forth, ricochets off every word.

"I *thought* you were upstairs getting ready for bed . . ." he demanded.

"Well, I was *going* . . ."

"What are you doing in here, anyway? You're scaring me, Caroline, really—you just ignore me when I'm yelling like *crazy*, and Lilly is upstairs needing help, Tessa's practically a zombie from shock—did you forget about them—and you're on the computer? He's pacing the floor from the bookcase to the couch and back again, the width of the room. Waving his arms around. Like a spastic conductor. I pivot my body to mirror his so the computer screen isn't left exposed. Smarty follows Andy's every footstep. Which is weird, come to think of it. I've never seen Smarty do that.

"What's going on? And while we're on the subject of crazy, can you explain the bruise on your face? And the cut on your forehead?" He tilts his head, and his eyebrows creep up and meet at a peak.

I open my mouth again, but he keeps going.

"I asked you last night, and you said you'd tell me later. Well? It's later. I don't know, I've been home for twenty-four hours, and everybody seems to be falling apart. Can you help me out here?"

He's unraveling like a ball of twine down the Swiss Alps. I want to reach out to him and hold him. Hold him together. But there's not enough of me for both of us. I need to hold *myself* together. A lifetime of concern is pouring out of him—like it's been bottled up forever. I've never seen him like this.

"I couldn't find clean clothes for the girls . . ."

If he'd stop for a second, I could tell him I just washed the clothes.

" . . .so I went to throw some clothes in the machine and *jeez—Caroline*, how long have those clothes been in there? *They stink from mold.* It's disgusting!" His shoulders are up around his ears while his hands and eyes implore me.

I never put them in the dryer.

Who is this guy? "*I went to throw clothes in the machine?*" Huh? I didn't think he knew where the laundry room was. And his accusatory tone?

"Andy, *gosh*, I can't believe I—"

"You said you were *exhausted*. Then I hear *clicking* from the keyboard?"

"All right already, I'm . . ." My body is quaking. I wonder if he notices.

"I mean, Jesus, *Caroline*, I really don't want to get angry, really, I don't. But what are you doing in here, anyway? Writing? Shopping? What? What is it?" He doesn't wait for an answer. His head flops forward in defeat. He pauses briefly and lets out a gush of air. "Listen, I understand you're excited to be writing again, and all that stuff, but really—now?"

He continues almost talking to himself. I need to put a stop to this.

"I guess I should have checked here first. It seems like you're stuck to the damn computer these days." He throws his hands in the air. Then he looks back at me and says in a softer tone, "But really, do you think this is a good time?" His eyes are so sad. "I'm sorry I'm angry—I got scared. For Christ's sake." He puts his head down, and I think he's finished and that maybe he'll leave. A moment passes, his head pops up, and he comes alive again. I have an urgency to pee. I squeeze my thighs together.

"This day has been *crazy*—with Lilly and everything. We haven't even talked about what happened to *you . . . Jesus.*" Andy's running his fingers through his hair, creating parallel train tracks. He does this repeatedly and then stops, resting his hand on the crown of his head like a guy modeling under-wear, his bicep peeking out of his T-shirt.

"You do know Mrs. Hildebrand called me at the office, don't you? She got Margaret hysterical, which I'll admit isn't hard to do. She came running into my office saying Mrs. H was on the phone and that you were choking and that Lilly was trying to give you the Heimlich, and you fell backward on top of her and that an ambulance was taking both of you to the hospital . . . so of course, I didn't go to the meeting with Loughner and Sparks . . ."

"Oh, no . . . you missed the meeting?" The cinderblock at the bottom of my stomach stops my shaking. "But you're gonna reschedule, right?"

"Nah. They're on their way to Brazil tomorrow. I'll just

send them a report, I guess." He shrugs. "By the time they get back, it'll be old news." Andy's bottom lip is extra pudgy in the middle, giving him a perpetual pout that makes it difficult to discern when he's truly pouting.

"Well . . . don't be modest, Andy, in the report. You have every right to brag, honey. Come on. You did some great stuff over there." He doesn't look at me. My shoulders slump forward, and heavy throbbing starts in my head.

He starts talking to the carpet. "Then I rushed to the hospital and found Tessa crying in the waiting room with Mrs. Hildebrand, who looked like the next candidate for a gurney. They told me that you and Lilly were getting an x-ray."

His eyes peer up to meet mine. "And there's Tessa, rocking back and forth, crying, eating the skin on her fingers to the bone. I sat down and put my arm around her. She just kept mumbling, 'Is she going to die, Daddy? Is Mommy going to die?' It was awful. I'll never get that picture out of my mind—I can't stand the thought of it. Tessa told me they had to give you oxygen in the ambulance." His voice quiets, and it appears that his fire is extinguished. He's quiet and calm. An iced pond. I'm careful not to say anything. Not to move.

"Then I spoke to your doctor."

What? What did he just say? "*What?*" Every hair follicle on my scalp prickles with heat. "What do you mean?" I sputter, "Why would Dr. Kriete call you?"

CHAPTER NINE

Monday, September 25, 2006, 10:20 p.m.

I can't believe Dr. Kriete would defy me. My anxiety is trumped only by rage. Heads are gonna roll.

I'm a hum of nerves.

"What are you talking about?" Andy looks confused. "Dr. Kriete? Why would *she* call me?"

"Because—I don't know—I don't *know*. How would I know?"

"Caroline—your bozo doctor at the hospital, remember? We just came from Mountainview. Ring a bell?" He knocks the side of his head.

"Yes. Of course I remember." I totally forgot about him. I need to pull myself together and veer back into the right lane of this conversation.

"*Yeah*, I spoke to the doctor—of *course*. I find out you stopped breathing and need to be rushed to the emergency room—I wanna know what's going on. Right?" He looks to me for agreement. "All this on top of the bruise and the

cut . . ." He takes a step closer to get a good look, and I involuntarily shrink back. "It's concerning. I was bracing myself,
believe me, for what he was gonna say. Thank God your CT
scan came out clean. I was worried about that. Weren't you?"

"Yeah. I was worried." Unfortunately, I'm no less worried
now. No bleeding in my skull. No sign of fractures or brain
injury. Where does that leave me? "Well, I'm fine." I brush
imaginary dirt off my hands. "There's nothing going on . . ."
I wish he'd leave already. I can't look at his face any longer.
Pretending I'm fine is a joke.

"Sweetie, really, I know you had a really tough day."
He stands in the middle of the room. Footprints still in the
carpet, a trail from wall to wall. His energy shifts, and he
becomes subdued. The air feels lighter immediately. Even my
bladder relaxes.

"Of course I don't want to scare you, but you could have
died." His voice slows and becomes weightless; his words are
soft and filled with goose down, fluffy and cushiony. "You
couldn't breathe. That could've caused brain damage. You
can't sweep this one under the rug. I won't let you."

"Andy, I hate doctors."

"I know, and frankly I can see why—if you keep getting
these assholes who tell you anything that pops into their head.
'Vocal Cord Dysfunction'? Do you believe it—is that what
he told you, too? Come on. I mean, since when do your vocal
cords have to do with breathing—am I an idiot? You're getting a second opinion. I hope you know that. You do know
that, don't you?" His hands are back on his hips.

God, now he's fixated on the diagnosis. He would never
challenge a doctor's diagnosis. This is crazy. Tessa's got to get

him out of here before I have a real heart attack. Why aren't they looking for him by now?

"Yes—I mean, *no*." I finally interject something. "I *don't* need a second opinion. I most certainly do not need a second opinion. *Andy, it's Vocal Cord Dysfunction,* it makes perfect sense—the EMT told me that too, and anyway, you don't go to the experts and then argue with what they tell you. I'm not doing that. I'm not going there. If you're goin' there—you're goin' on that sad, cynical train all alone."

I can do without all this attention right now.

"And anyway," I add, "they gave me a chest x-ray, checked my vital signs, and gave me an EKG to see if I had a heart attack—which I clearly did *not*. They told me Vocal Cord Dysfunction paralyzes your ability to breathe, temporarily. And that once your body relaxes enough, it can take in oxygen. And that's it, Andy, *case closed*, I'm not discussing this anymore—with *anyone*."

"Caroline, it doesn't make 'perfect' sense, the doctor said it happens to asthmatics—you don't *have* asthma."

"**Or** *to people who have experienced sudden trauma or witnessed something shocking—like a murder!*"

Can the need to have the last word be encoded in one's DNA?

Andy surrenders, his hands in the air, then he lets them droop to his side. "So now you've witnessed a murder." He studies me. "That's a good one, Caroline. What the hell is it gonna be next? It's almost like I don't know you. You're acting nuts. And you're exhausting me. Why are we arguing about this?" he drops his head in his hands, and he collapses on the couch. A rip lacerates my heart.

"No, sweetie, please, of course you're right—I don't know

what I'm saying, of course I need a second opinion . . ." I want to reach out to him and touch him, hug him, but I can't move. Why the hell didn't it occur to me sooner that all I had to do was agree with him? That's all he wanted to hear.

"Thank *God.*" He searches my face and sees the woman he knows and is allayed of his fears. His eyes are tired and heavy. "My God—I thought I lost you there for a second." He stands up and steps toward me. "Sweetie, really, I'm on your side, for Pete's sake. Don't you know that? I just want you to have the best doctors and all that stuff.

"Why does it seem to get turned upside down, sometimes, with us? I love you, Caroline." He moves in to embrace me, his arms are outstretched, but I can't risk the gesture, it will put his head over my shoulder, and the computer screen will be in full view. Instead, I pick up Smarty and hold him with one arm and pat Andy on the chest with the other, hoping he doesn't notice how weird this is.

"I know. I love you, too."

He drops his arms. "We just need to find out that you're okay. Okay?"

"Okay." He turns around. He's finally going to leave. I hold my breath.

He looks over his shoulder at me. "Please, just don't get crazy on me, all right? I have to help the girls, unless they're already asleep." He crosses his fingers and smiles. Then he points at me, "No more writing tonight." On his way out of the room he glances down at the floor. "Hey, when do I get to read your story?" Before I can make out what he's looking at, he bends down to pick up a piece of paper directly under the printer.

"This must've come from the printer. Are you missing a—"

I snatch the paper from his hand with a quick snap of my wrist before he reads it.

He jerks back and recoils. *"Ah—shit! Son of a—"* He pulls his hands into his chest, wincing and swearing. "Caroline, man! What the *hell*—you just gave me a paper cut!" I look at his hand. The cut is nearly two inches long, right down the center of his right palm, the blood beading up at half-inch intervals. He cradles his right hand with his left one, grimacing.

"Oh, God, Andy, I'm so *sorry*. I can't believe it. Let me take a look . . ." I reach out to him.

Why didn't he leave before this happened? Why couldn't he leave well enough alone?

He pulls away from me. "No, it's okay, Caroline. It's *fine*," he snaps. He can't even look at me.

"But it's bleeding." I think about getting him a Band-Aid, but I can't leave him in here, alone. I didn't close out of the *Lanstonsville Press* article.

"You should get a Band-Aid for that—and some Neosporin." I have a firm grip on the paper behind my back, with both hands. I want to cry, but I'm afraid of losing it while the screen is open with my secret life hanging out.

I'm scared to let go of the dagger. Afraid that next time, it'll cut me.

He turns and leaves, slouched over, deflated and defeated, his head swaying from side to side. I can't remember the last time he raised his voice at me—or lost his patience, or got hysterical, or cursed at me, or cared so much. He mumbles on his way out of the den, "I just wanted to check that you were okay . . . I thought you passed out . . ." As he turns the corner and heads down the hall, and before his voice trails off, I hear him say that he'll tell the girls I'm all right.

My cheeks are wet, and my head slumps forward as if my puppeteer has let go of the string sewn to my scalp. I'm dizzy from holding my breath. But most of all, it's my heart that aches. A deep cavernous ache. It's that feeling you get when you've betrayed someone. And you've lost them, and you know it will never be the same because they will always question everything you do. And your chest has shriveled to accommodate the new size of your heart. Which is as small as a prune, dried up and deeply wrinkled from being sapped of life and joy.

The printout quivers in my clammy hands. He was so close to seeing it. My teeth bang like psycho cymbals. I turn it over.

Both sides are blank.

Tuesday, September 26, 2006, 7:30 a.m.

I THINK IT's Tuesday morning . . . and I think I'm awake. Voices leak out of another room. Tessa's room. That is, if I'm in my room, which I'm not entirely certain of since I can't seem to pry my eyelids apart. My head is filled with nine cups of firmly packed brown sugar.

So this is what a Percocet hangover feels like. I just wanted a sleeping pill, but I couldn't find them. I don't have much experience with this genre of drugs. They were in the medicine cabinet from when Andy had knee surgery. And though I don't remember taking one before, I know I've never taken two.

Slowly, the coma dissolves. First, muffled sounds turn to

voices, then words. Light seeps into the slivers between my leaded eyelids. It hurts at first. I wet my lips with saliva to help slide them apart, enabling me to take air through my mouth instead of my nose. The air that touches the insides of my cheeks feels odd but invigorating. The oxygen flows through me and sends out the wakeup call, announcing that life exists outside my body.

The girls are getting ready for school. Tessa yells across the hall "Mom, don't forget you're helping in the library today!"

Shit. I reach my hand to grab today's schedule off my nightstand. I need proof. But there's no printout. That's odd. Nothing's on the floor. If my head wasn't killing me, I'd look under the bed, but that ain't happening. It's not a big deal if I have to wait to get downstairs to find out what's on tap for the day. I can survive ten minutes without knowing today's events.

Lilly beats me to the kitchen and is in surprisingly good spirits. Andy's decided to go into work late so we can eat breakfast as a family, and he can accompany us to school.

"Are you sure you don't want to stay home, Lilly?" Andy asks as he rinses out his cereal bowl. "You don't have to go. If it hurts you, you should stay home."

Lilly's looking through the junk drawer under the toaster oven, pulling out all the colored Sharpies she can find. "I feel great. Tessa, you can sign it in purple if you want." She hands Tessa a marker to draw on the sling holding up her left arm.

"Lilly, you can go to school under one condition: if you feel any pain, you go straight to the nurse and have her call Mom to pick you up." He kisses the top of her head.

The girls want to walk to school today. We even bring Smarty. It's a beautiful Indian-summer day. I always feel lucky on a day like this—like it's a gift from the gods. What could go wrong on a day stolen from summer—possibly the last one before sweater weather arrives for good.

Farhaven is a beautiful town. Perfectly manicured lawns are edged with buxom annuals still in full, colorful glory. The mature elm trees that line the sidewalks create leafy canopies over the wide streets. Moms push strollers while walking their little ones to kindergarten. People wave hello to each other, to us. Andy looks over at me and smiles as he holds Lilly's hand, and I hold Tessa's. He's chatty this morning, filling in any moments of quiet. His fleeting episode as vigilant daddy/hubby has passed like a page in a calendar. Today he seems to be filled with the spirit of a young man realizing all that life has to offer, and he's walking with a lightness I don't know whether to be jealous of or inspired by.

The soft, warm air lilts along, lifting the ends of my hair so I feel it on my neck like a silk scarf. Even the birds are jubilant, playing tag through the hemlocks. I feel the warmth coming from Tessa's hand, and I'm overcome with happiness. Something that feels almost foreign.

Then it dawns on me. This is my life. It's everything I've worked so hard for. It's everything I've planned for. If I give it up, I'm the one to blame.

I'm not giving up a single blissful thing. I was happy before. I can be happy again.

After all, it was only four days ago.

By the time we get to the third-grade door, I've made up my mind. It's my fault that my world is coming undone. I uncorked the torment. I'm simply going to bottle it back up. Shove the cork in and toss it out to sea. Nothing else in my life has changed—*I'm in control here.*

If I forgot it once, I can forget it again. From this day on, no more Googling. That's a promise. Not even if my life depends on it.

"Good morning, Gabrielle!" I call across the street to work on my karma by singing salutations to the bad seed that grew the ugly tree, which up until six minutes ago shaded my back porch. *I'm in charge now.*

After kisses and hugs, Andy takes off with Smarty for home, and then to work. I stop by the nurse's office to give her a note from the doctor excusing Lilly from gym. Then I make my way to the library while humming "I Got the Sun in the Morning" from *Annie Get Your Gun.*

I love walking through the halls of Lincoln Elementary. Or any school. But especially an old one like this. The halls are lined with crayon self-portraits and postcards from the far reaches of the globe where the students and faculty have vacationed during the summer. There are friendly reminders posted along the walls, like, "Be kind to one another," "Expect amazing things to come from your brain," "Be inspired—read a book," and "Smile and say hello to people you know."

The painted cinderblock walls help the halls stay cool, even during a heat wave. I stroll with an ease I haven't felt in days. The sound of children's voices waft through the air like ribbons, weaving around my head and sliding down my shoulders. Laughing, singing, asking, shouting, at once muffled and distinct, winding around my arms and fingertips, in figure eights around my legs, alive and vivid, pushing me down the hall, guiding me to where I have to go. The voices, so enthusiastic, have an energy, a rhythm, and they're everywhere, surrounding everything, filling up all the empty space like Styrofoam peanuts.

When I get to the library, I breathe deeply through my nose to take in that musty smell of old books. It's so stimulating to be among the combined creative genius of Seuss, Carle, Sendak and Rowling, among others. I close my eyes and think of all the great authors toiling away long ago, not knowing at the time if their work would ever be read.

"Hello, Mrs. Thompson, I'm glad you could join us today," says Mrs. Wormstock, the librarian, who has an ample spray of dandruff on each broad shoulder.

"Oh, my pleasure. I'm all set for my marching orders. What can I help with?" I'm as cheery as a bowl full of rainbow-colored jelly beans.

"Well, let's see, we have some returns to shelve." She walks over to a rolling rack; the books have been placed on all of its four shelves in size order from tallest to shortest, bringing to mind the von Trapp family. As she walks to the rack, the floor reverberates with each step.

"I'm expecting Miss Leland's kindergarten class at nine-thirty. Perhaps you can read them a book?"

"Oh, I would love to."

"Very good, then, I'll let you get busy."

Before I start shelving, I snatch my pressed powder compact from my handbag to take a quick peek at my bruise and powder it liberally. I don't want to scare the kiddies.

The mindless work is so gratifying. I hum "These are a few of my favorite things . . . " as I contently return books to their proper place in the Dewey Decimal System.

Miss Leland's class should be arriving in about five minutes. Mrs. Stanton, the principal, walks in and waves Mrs. Wormstock over. In the midst of their conversation, Mrs. Stanton looks over in my direction and points at me. Mrs.

Stanton is old-school and all business. She could benefit from a teaspoon of warm and fuzzy in her morning coffee. I finish up the last row of books, which has me squatting close to the floor; my thigh muscles are burning. I'm dwarfed by the bookcases that seem to stack up to the moon, and now by Mrs. Stanton, who is a woman of significant stature.

"Mrs. Thompson!" she says, determined. The library's carpet silenced her approach, and so I am quite surprised and startled to find my face so uncomfortably close to her knees. I'm instantly reminded of why I, too, am a little intimidated by her. It's her leg. One of them is prosthetic, and I've never been this close to a fake leg before. She almost never wears pants in order to teach the children that handicaps are not something to be ashamed of or scared of. The kids haven't fully embraced that concept yet.

"Oh, hi, Mrs. Stanton, how are you?"

"Fine, fine, thank you for volunteering today. Mrs. Thompson, there was something I wanted to speak to you about . . ." Children's voices start to fill the library, and I know the librarian will be looking for me soon.

I stand and clap the dust off my hands, and take a step back to put a more comfortable distance between us as Mrs. Stanton tries again. "I wanted to tell you that while I was searching on Google last night—"

I snap to attention. And freeze. My bulging eyes freeze, my muscles freeze, my breathing and heartbeat freeze. Did she just say she was searching for me on Google? What the hell is that about? That's *outrageous*. That's an invasion of privacy. Isn't it? Maybe not. I don't care—it's—it's—peeping-Tomian! And she's not the slightest bit uncomfortable admitting it.

My eyes gloss over hers, careful not to meet them exactly.

I don't want to egg her on. Her mouth is still moving, but I don't listen. I sheepishly bring my hands up to my ears and nervously scratch my scalp while I think about how to slip away without bringing additional attention to myself.

"Uh, Mrs. Stanton," I start to talk on top of her, which I'm hoping will discourage her from continuing. However, she doesn't stop talking, and so I don't either; in fact, my own voice grows louder. "Sorry to interrupt you—um, it's just that—" What if she's read something on Google that I haven't? That I don't know about? My shirt sticks to my underarms. My ghosts are haunting me everywhere. They're not just in my house, in my den, but now in the hardware store, the doctor's office, the school library. Where next? I get that hot, prickly sensation again of pins and needles; they start behind my ears and slowly inch down to the lobes, at the same time crawling across my cheeks. They even prick the wet part of my eyes. She says "Lilly" and "custodian." It nearly paralyzes me. Could she know I'm not Lilly's real mother? Jesus Christ. She could have seen *that newspaper article.* My heart is no longer frozen; in fact, it's now like the Little Drummer Boy on speed. *Lilly* doesn't even know, for Christ's sake. I need get out of here before she says another word, before anyone hears her, or before she asks me to explain. In the reflection of a computer screen to her left, her disapproving face is scrunched up like used wrapping paper. Her mouth is still moving. My nerves get the best of me, and I hear myself humming, "When the dog bites, hmm, hmm, hmm, hmm, when the bee stings, hmm, hmm . . ." Mrs. Wormstock waves me over from the front of the room. Thank *God.* She holds up the book she wants me to read.

Mrs. Wormstock, who's standing next to Miss Leland, is

in front of the students, who are sitting cross-legged on the rug in the middle of the library floor.

"I'm coming, Mrs. Wormstock! Excuse me, Mrs. Stanton," I yell in a voice far too loud, then dip into a row of books, walking in the opposite direction. I'm panicking, and I keep walking. It's a long row of books, and I'm alone in it and hidden from view by the nonfiction section—books on nature, flowers, the ocean. I can't go read that book. I can't. I need to get out of here.

Mrs. Wormstock can't see me now from where she's standing. She calls again louder, "*Mrs. Thompson*, are you coming?"

I'm at the end of the aisle and out of ideas. There's a fire alarm in front of me on the wall. Don't even *think* about it. My heart is racing at a staggering speed. Mrs. Wormstock will need to read the book herself, I'm done with library duty. I can't believe Mrs. Stanton, the principal for God's sake, doesn't have more important things to do than interrogate a parent. One who's volunteering her valuable, personal time? To think of all the taxes we pay in this town! If it gets out that I'm not Lilly's mother, Gabrielle will have a field day. She'll see to it that I'm branded a fraud and a liar. How will my friends react?

Oh my *God*—what if someone tells Lilly? I can't have that happen. I'm not prepared for any of this.

I take a long step forward to look beyond the bookcase to judge how far I am from the door. My rubber sole clings to the rug. I hobble and attempt to gain my footing. Instead I lose my balance. I fall into a shelf loaded with books. Scores of books nosedive off the shelf. Books on planes, trains, and automobiles crash in waves to the floor. One after the other, open and splattered, their spines crack as they pile on top of each other—it seems endless.

The children spring to their feet, fumbling over each other to witness what has happened. Miss Leland claps wildly, booming, "Children! Children! Stay seated! One-two-three, eyes-on-me! One-two-three, eyes-on-me!"

They all stop dead in their tracks and answer back in perfect unison, "One-two, eyes-on-you."

Mrs. Wormstock gasps, "Oh, my, what's happened? Mrs. Thompson, are you all right?"

Through the now-empty shelves, I see that the library door is directly across from where Mrs. Stanton is standing; my escape would be in full view. The floor lifts and settles, lifts and settles, and I know Mrs. Wormstock is getting closer. I'm a cornered lab rat. I just won't be exposed like this, not here at the school library, in front of all these children, *my children*. No way. Not to mention the eyes and ears and judgment of the *non*-children.

"*Mrs. Thompson??*" Mrs. Wormstock's voice is even closer.

No one can see me. My legs are shaking. I have to pee.

"*Mrs. Thompson??*"

The fire alarm is right there. My right hand reaches out and pulls.

Instant camouflage. Hysteria builds like wild fire. The alarm's ear-piercing wail incites immediate panic. Miss Leland is flustered as she tries to encourage order while leading her class of scared five-year-olds out of the library. "Grab a buddy!" Mrs. Wormstock and Mrs. Stanton hurry to the aid of Miss Leland, who cries out, "Buddies everyone! No talking! Follow Mrs. Wormstock!"

I stay low to the ground until the last little sneaker evacuates and joins the commotion in the hall, which I scan from my vantage point. The fifth graders are pouring down the stairs from the second floor, and the teachers are pushing students outside with their collective "This is not a drill, folks." Tessa's teacher walks past the library door. There's Tessa. Anxiety is written all over her face. I can't bear to look at her. She's eating the skin off the side of her thumb. I withdraw into the library to think. But there's no time to think—so I insert myself into the stream of kids, keeping my head low.

I turn into a short stairwell leading to the exit. A placard is nailed into the cinderblock right beside the fire alarm at the first grade door. "It is unlawful for any person to willfully pull the lever of any fire alarm except in case of a fire." I swallow hard. I'm completely humiliated by my behavior.

CHAPTER TEN

Tuesday, September 26, 2006, 9:53 a.m.

I run the entire way home, my tears blowing off the side of my face like rain off a windshield.

I'm *not* in control. Who am I kidding? I can't just have my old life back because I stop Googling myself.

I don't slow down when my neighbor appears, walking her dog. I dart across the street diagonally and pretend I don't see her. I must look insane, panting, crying, my handbag bouncing off my hip. I don't care.

What's to come of me? How many people can I avoid?

Why is this happening *now?* These articles are old. Any number of people could have read these things for years. That damn Gabrielle. She had to start this Googling thing. I despise her. And her busybody bimbos. They disgust me. "Mind your own damn business!" I yell out loud to no one, but the UPS man crossing the street whips his head around, then jumps in his truck. My cheeks flush, and I drop my head and round the corner. I'm nearly home.

I need Andy. I need to tell him. That's okay. He loves me. We're in this together. He has stuck with me and all my shortcomings all these years. He's tolerated a lot from me. My need to have the last word, the little control thing I have, my inner neat freak. Let's face it; my stuff doesn't always dovetail with his. Even after I limited the "bad fats" from our diet (that wasn't pretty), he stuck with me. I know men who've left their wives for stupider reasons. Andy's not going to leave me after all we've been through. Actually, we haven't been through all that much. By all accounts, we have a great life together. This will test us. I have to trust him. For better or worse. Or, far worse than anything I ever thought worse meant.

I'm scared out of my mind.

At the house, in the kitchen, I grab the phone and dial his number. I review in my mind what I'm going to say. JD died—six years ago, and Lilly is not really my daughter but actually my sister's. Back in college I had an abortion and a hysterectomy.

"Global Enterprises, Andrew Thompson's office—" Margaret waits for a reply. "Hello? Global Enterprises—?"

Click.

Wait a second.

The phone is back on the wall; my hand is stuck to it. I don't move. Andy already knows about Lilly. I was awarded custody of Lilly when I was single. When I married him, I already had her. We were a package deal. Of course he knows that Lilly isn't his. But does he know Lilly isn't mine?

What did I tell him?

God, I need a Sno Ball right now. Do they make them anymore? Of course I wouldn't normally condone seven grams of saturated fats in a processed confection, but this situation clearly merits a bite. All I'd need is one bite, and I wouldn't need another for the rest of my life. I imagine the prickles of sugar touching my lips and the sticky marshmallow, the moist chocolate cake and luxurious cream. Oh my God. My eyes roll back in my head thinking about it.

I make a U-turn to the pantry. This is a waste of time, improbable to say the least. Up on the third step of the kitchen stool, I use my hand to search over my head into the cookie jar that our neighbors gave us when we moved in. I wasn't going to put it out in the kitchen. Who keeps cookies on the counter? Recipe for disaster. My hand finds something in the cookie jar that crinkles of plastic. Oh my God. Could it be? I grab ahold of it. *Yes.* I can't believe it. Seeing the pink balls of perfection in my hand makes me teary. I rip the sucker open and stuff as much of the ball as I can into my mouth and bite down. One bite. I place the remaining skinny crescent back in the plastic and fold the cardboard sheet so I can roll the plastic tight to keep it fresh. Before I return it to the cookie jar, I see the expiration date: 6/2002. Over four years ago.

I let the bite sit in my mouth. Saliva slides down the insides of my cheeks and dissolves the sugar. It trickles into my throat. The taste transports me. My tongue wiggles through the fluffy cake to the cream. A grin germinates in my stomach and sprouts across my lips.

I can handle anything now.

The sugar must have gone straight to my head because eighty-seven independent thoughts spin around in there. First they meander aimlessly, then hasten like a mound of leaves getting kicked up by a breeze. They move too fast to decipher. I snatch one and hold onto it for dear life. An image forms in my mind. It's the *Psychology Now* article on JD's suicide.

The doctor who wrote the article talked about the importance of "bereavement therapy" for close family and friends. He said it was crucial to "work through the emotional stages." Something like that. One of the initial stages for loved ones is self-blame—for not seeing the signs.

My mother was interviewed for the article. She admitted how difficult it was for the family to believe that JD took her own life, and how she urged her surviving daughter, me, JD's only sibling, to see a therapist to help sort things out. At the end of the article, it said that the sister of the deceased would not agree to an interview because she didn't believe her sister killed herself.

In the den I unlock the lower drawer of the credenza and pull out my Rolodex. Under "D," I flip through a surprising number of doctors. I find dentists, dermatologists, and general physicians until I get to a business card of a psychologist. It's stapled to a Rolodex card and has a handwritten note from my mother at the bottom of it.

Dr. Francis Sullivan, PhD

Licensed Psychologist

Specializing in Anxiety, Depression, Trauma

My mother's note says, "Lovie, Do ring the Dr." Next to that there's an arrow, so I lift it away from the card and flip it over; "It's been bloody hell for all of us; you'd do better to talk to someone who can help." I wonder if she ever spoke to the psychologist herself. My mother died in November 2000, right before Thanksgiving, so if she did, it was before November.

I pick up the phone on my desk and stare at the numbers. This doctor is probably not even around anymore—it's been six years. If so, she's not going to remember my mother. Smarty is sitting on the rug, looking up at me, watching my every move. His ears are pulled back. "What's the matter, Smarty?" He's always with me, through thick and thin. I whisper to him while I wait for someone to answer. "Who's my best friend?" He barks on cue.

I scratch between his ears, "Everything's gonna be—"

"Dr. Sullivan's office," says a woman on the other end.

"Oh." I wasn't expecting anyone to answer. At that moment I realize I don't know why I'm calling or what I'm going to say. "I-I, uh . . ."

"Who is this, please?"

"Oh, me? Well. My name—"

A phone rings in the background. "Can you hold a moment, please?"

She puts me on hold before I'm able to say anything.

A second later she says, "Still there?"

"Yes, yes I'm still there—*here*."

"Okay. Good. I'm sorry, what was your name again?" "Caroline Thomp . . . *Spencer*. I . . ."

"Did you say Caroline Spencer?"

"Yes."

"Hmm," she says while typing. "Uh huh. Well, let's see; are you still at the same number?"

"Do you mean my *mother?*"

"Is her name Caroline Spencer, too?"

"No. It's Elaine. Was Elaine."

"Well, I'm asking about *your* number. Is it the same as the one we have on file?"

"I don't understand."

"Are you Caroline Spencer from Cumberland Drive? Dr. Sullivan's patient?" She begins to type again.

"Yes, Cumberland Drive," I repeat, my voice hardly audible. "That's me." I lived at 16 Cumberland Drive.

"Okay. Wonderful. Are your calling for an appointment?"

"Uh. Well, yes. That's a good idea." Yes, I should meet this woman. She knows me. And didn't Dr. Kriete say this was the next step, "to talk to a psychologist to sort things out." A feeling of being rescued charges through me.

"Let's see, we have regular patients, you know, weeklies, bi-weeklies, et cetera. In fact, we're not taking new patients at this time. Technically, you're not new, however it's been a while." There's a swoop of pages being turned. All of a sudden, I'm desperate to see her. This is good news. I was her *patient*.

"I'm very flexible, whenever she's available—" I add.

"*She?* You mean he. Right? We're talking about Dr. Sullivan? Aren't we?"

"Yes. Of course, he. Did I say she? I don't think I said she. I mean, it's okay, I—he . . ." I sound insane. I'm sure she's making giant neon asterisks next to my name, secret code for psycho. A tear falls onto my desk calendar, which is open and eager in front of me, splattering the week.

"The next appointment he has is October twenty-sixth." She waits for me to respond, but I don't say anything. October twenty-sixth is a month away. *A month.* I could have a nervous breakdown by then. Actually, that may not be a bad thing. It might get me in sooner.

"Ms. Spencer?"

"Yes. I'll take it. Thank you."

"Keep in mind, his regular patient is on vacation—so you

can have that one appointment, but we can't make it a weekly. Do you understand?"

"Yes, I understand."

I give her my cell number and jot the time into my desk calendar under "Francis" and type it into my online schedule.

I lean back in the desk chair. I don't know if I'll make it till then.

ONCE I CLEAN up the kitchen from breakfast, I go upstairs to my bedroom. My closet door is ajar. I never leave it like that. Or things in disarray. The pillows are scattered on the floor. It's been like this since yesterday. Since before the emergency room. I never put them back.

Quickly, I gather up the pillows to return them to the top shelf. Lilly's baby book is sprawled on the floor where I dropped it last night. Her birth certificate is under it. My blood pressure soars just thinking about what would've happened if Andy found it. I stop suddenly. In a flash, I'm back up the stepladder. One more look for Tessa's book.

Even at the top of the stepladder I'm only high enough to see whatever's at the edge of the shelf. No book. I tear down some old blankets and reach a stack of linens and yank at the corner of the bottom-most sheet, allowing them to tumble to the floor. Nothing. Not a book anywhere. I take my arm and sweep it across the shelf, then stand on my tippy toes to get a look at the back. No book. A fire extinguisher. A down comforter. An emergency ladder to escape from a second-floor window in case of a fire. Unless, of course, the fire is in the closet. And a large, taped-up moving box in the corner of the shelf. "Bedroom Closet" is written across it. Why would I still have an unpacked box? With my fingertips over my head, I push at the corner of the box; maybe it's empty. But it hardly budges. I get a wooden hanger and nudge the corner of the box to get it a little closer to me.

The box has rotated. Another word appears on the side of the box in my handwriting, "ETAVIRP."

My heart skips a beat.

I'm as still as stone with my arm extended and the hanger at the end of it. Etavirp is a made-up word that JD and I invented when we were kids. We only used it with each other. It meant "secret" or "private." In fact, it's the word "private" backward. We were little when we made it up. We thought it was clever at the time.

I reposition the stepladder to get a better angle and climb back up. If only it was a step higher. The hanger begs the box from the back in tiny increments. Nausea creeps into my stomach.

Finally the box is far enough that I can grasp it with both hands. The box bulges at the bottom, testing the strength of its seams. Like a fat lady in a girdle. It feels like a fat lady could be in there. Carefully, I walk backward off the ladder with the unwieldy box in my arms; my chin rests on top. It's caked in dust, which wafts up my nose. An urgent sneeze forces the box to slip a little from my grip. The box is big enough that only my fingertips curl around the far edges.

On the floor I kneel next to the box and run my hand over the top to sweep the dust away. Several layers of tape have attempted to secure the contents within. Or shut the world out. There are strips of clear tape, now yellowed, that run along the narrow crevice where the two flaps meet to close the box. They're no longer sticky and simply mark a moment in time. Masking tape runs in the opposite direction and is also ineffective in securing the box like it once did. Three strips of blue painter's tape look like bandages, placed perpendicularly again. All three are sliced through at the box's opening. Silver electric tape seals the circumference, and there's one piece of shiny black tape about a foot long running down the middle that unites the flaps. It looks like it's sealing a mouth shut. I rip off the black tape with ease and pry my fingers under the heavy, veined electrical tape inch by inch around the box until it is unbound. When I lift the cardboard flap from one side, a gush of air spews out. As if the box is exhaling. It smells of age. That air has not seen the light of day for years. The mustiness finds its way to my lungs and forces a cough. Once I pull back the other flap, the contents are exposed. Staring into it, I get dizzy. Maybe it's the dust, or the weight of the box, or a sense of claustrophobia in the closet. I look down at my wrist for my watch, but I'm not wearing it. It's probably time to pick the girls up from school, or close to it. This is not a good time to get involved in an old box of junk. I flip the two sides down to close it and pat the black tape into place, but the tape has no sticking power left. I step out of the closet. The clock on my nightstand says 11:49.

What seems like days since I've seen the girls has only been three hours.

I have other things to do. Errands and other things. Enough with the closet and old crap. I need to move on. But first, I'll tidy up.

Instead of lifting the box back up on the shelf, I push it with my foot under hanging clothes as far back as it will go, leaning against the wall with both hands for support. There are shoe boxes in the way, so the box sticks out too far. I squat down and heave it an inch off the ground and guide it to the right, where there's space. With the side of my arm and shoulder, I shove it with all my strength. This is taking way too much of my time. With clenched teeth, I sit on the floor and drive the box with both feet, ramming it into the corner of the closet, and tears wet my cheeks.

Keepsakes are supposed to fill you with warmth and nostalgia. Sweet things, like newspaper clippings of your stage performances in high school, old love letters from teenage boyfriends. Special gifts that marked important occasions, like graduation day. My peeks-into-the-past track record of late has been odious at best.

I don't care what's in the box. If I haven't seen this stuff in years, I'm obviously not missing anything. It's going straight into the trash. Sight unseen.

I curl my fingers under the two flaps, clench my teeth, and yank the box back toward me. Everything is going in the garbage. I'm getting rid of it all. I stare at the taped-up mouth. It's ridiculous to be scared of a box. I had a good childhood. I had the most wonderful sister in the world, and we were an awesome pair. Like a lock and key. One useless without the other. My heart starts to pine for my youth. I kneel on the floor and drop my head in my hands, and beg myself to remember anything. Where do memories go when you lose them?

Without thinking I throw the sides open and look back inside the box. My heart flutters in gales. At the top is a thick stack of newspaper clippings. A proud smile grows across my face. I knew these would be in here. When I was a kid, I was in all the plays at school. I loved acting and singing. As a high school senior, I had the lead in the musical *Anything Goes*. My picture was in the newspaper. JD clipped it out and saved it for me. All our neighbors gave us their copies. I had to style my hair in pin curls for the role. These are my things.

With care I remove the newspaper clippings and place them on my lap. My legs are folded underneath me. I stop for a second to take in how wonderful this feels. Smarty saunters in the room and finds me in the closet. He licks the side of the box and jumps up so his legs rest on top of it, allowing him to peer inside while he sniffs obsessively. "Don't lick that, Smarty!" I clap my hands. "Come on down from there. Shoo! Don't drool on my things!"

He backs out of the closet and lies on the floor, watching me.

I can't wait to tell the girls about my days in the theater and show them these clips of me on stage. These were some of the greatest times of my childhood. I gently lift the newspapers one by one to find my photo.

The only problem is that all of the clips are obituaries.

One after the other. Dead people announcements. I turn them over to where the "local happenings" column is usually printed. No, only classifieds. I thumb through the stack. There are pages and pages of obituaries. Tons of them. Could these be JD's obituary—in quantity?

I crane my neck to look back in the box for something to jump out at me. The dried corsage from my prom. The handlebar fringe from my purple bike. My softball mitt from the sixth grade. What is this crap? Why am I doing this? Why didn't I heave the entire box with its contents into the nearest dumpster?

I grab the newspapers and throw them in the box. It doesn't matter that they're not neatly stacked with lined up corners. I'm chucking them. The one on top has an obit circled in red marker. Maybe these are JD's. I read it quickly: it's not JD's. I have no idea whose it is. I've never heard the name before in my life. Out of curiosity, I look to see if the others are the same. They aren't. They're all different. Different people, different towns. Even different states. None of them are from Lanstonville or anywhere else in Pennsylvania. There must be fifteen to twenty newspapers in the pile, all from other states: Maryland, Delaware, Connecticut, and New Jersey, and a couple from New York. The dates span from September to December 2000. All the pages are peppered with bold red circles drawn around select obituaries. I read each one. I've never heard of these people. None of them.

They all have something in common. All the obituaries are for young women who died in their twenties. Tragic premature deaths. All of the young women were married. They all were mothers of one surviving daughter. Coincidentally, or maybe not, the daughters were all two years old. The date, time, and location of the wakes and funerals are highlighted in yellow. In the margins of the newspapers are handwritten notes. In red marker. In my handwriting. Many of the margins have just one word: "No." Some notes elaborate: "not right," or "works in family business," or "doesn't speak English," or "too ugly." Or "too smart." A couple say "maybe." The "maybes" have a sheet of lined notebook paper stapled to them with more notes, like, "Coping without Partners meeting on Wednesday," or "Met for coffee—too curious."

The thoughts oozing into my mind are uncomfortable.

This can't be what I think it is. What it appears to be. There's an odd sensation in my stomach, like the jiggling of cold marbles tumbling over each other.

Out loud I remind myself, "Don't get distracted. You were getting rid of junk." I systematically stack the newspaper clippings into a pile and return them to the box.

Just before I silence the past for good and place the flaps down, my eyes inadvertently saunter back to the newspaper on top. This one has a beefy red asterisk on it. Written across the top margin of the newspaper in red block letters is: "Mr. Right!" I lower my gaze without moving anything else. My head and my eyes adamantly disagree on reading a single word more. My eyes win. The obituary that's captured in a blazing red noose from Spellington, Delaware reads:

> *Debra Thompson, 29. Debra Anne Thompson,*
> *beloved wife and mother. Leaves husband, Andrew,*
> *2-year-old daughter, Tessa . . .*

There is a note on lined paper in my handwriting attached to the newspaper clipping:

"Andy is perfect. Handsome and charming. Not very bright or inquisitive. Attentive but unobservant. Perfect in every way. Grieves for his wife but he'll need to quickly fill her shoes. Admits that he's scared to death to be Tessa's only parent. 'Needs a mother for Tessa.' Empathetic toward me and my role as a single parent. Barely asks anything about my 'deceased husband.' Tessa will be turning three next July— the perfect twin for Lilly. Andy's the one!"

CHAPTER ELEVEN

Tuesday, September 26, 2006, 2:07 p.m.

Behind the wheel of my car, I sit, parked under a sweeping elm in front of our house. I look at the place where I live. At the life I premeditated. I want to die, but I can't leave the girls at school, waiting in front of the third-grade door, watching all the kids and parents dribble away. Alone and abandoned.

But I can't pick them up either. I can't do it. I've spent the last half hour scanning the pages of the school directory, which lists the kids in Lilly and Tessa's third-grade classes. Dialing numbers to find someone who can bring them home from school. A real mom. I'm not fit for, or deserving of, motherhood. I'm a liar. And a sham. They don't know me. And I don't know me.

But it seems that all the real mothers are getting manicures. Or pedicures. I didn't even do that right. I never get my nails done.

I look at our lawn, which I dragged myself across to get to

the car; every step crushed the perky, stand-at-attention blades of grass. A lawn that says: *a respectable, privileged, and decent family lives here.* I've made a liar of it, too.

My grip on the steering wheel transforms my knuckles into a range of mountaintops with little peaks of snow at the summit. The car is idling, waiting for me. I pull away from the curb and drive. I don't know where, and I don't care. My head tips forward twice; I can't focus on the road. I pull the car over to the curb. My eyelids lose the battle to stay open. They are so heavy. My eyes bear the weight of all the evil they've seen. How can I blame them for shutting?

I reach around the floor of the car for a bottle of water, to splash my face.

Suicide attempts are actually a cry for help, aren't they? Those people don't really want to die, they want to be found and helped and hoisted up and out of the muck of misery. It's the classic cry for help, isn't that what they say? I wonder if JD really wanted to be saved but no one came to her aid. No one read the signs. Where the hell was I? Maybe she wanted to die.

I know the feeling.

With closed eyes, I reach down to the cup holder and feel around for a bottled water. There's always a bottled water in my cup holder. Water, vitamins, dental floss, and hand lotion are car staples. JD gave me that idea. She was always getting on me for not drinking enough water. She was a diabetic most of her life and could drink enough to drown herself.

My hand finds a bottle in the glove compartment. It's empty.

I love the sound that comes from blowing into an empty water bottle. If your lips are just right. A lonely foghorn sound.

It's so comforting—a fog horn. Calling you home when you're lost. Or foggy. Droning on, tirelessly, to show you the way.

This is the beginning of the end, I know that now.

I want to die.

But I don't want to die—

My chest collapses on the steering wheel. I let myself go. Screw the horn.

This time, I don't muffle it, or silence it; it's not a polite quivering cry, or the kind that seeps out like the air of a pierced balloon. It's painful and tragic and steals all my strength.

I think about the girls and Andy. Like a Super 8 film, images flash in my mind: our party on Sunday, the trip he and I are planning to Aruba, dinner with Sylvie and George, the winter and Christmas, decorating the house, Lilly's dance recital—The Nutcracker. At the end of the film, my family is weeping, wearing somber attire. Lilly and Tessa are wearing grey or black—I can't make it out—but they look awful, weary. They clutch each other's hand. I'm not with them. Andy's hand is in a fist, pounding his knee repeatedly. Lilly and Tessa are hunched and trembling and fragile—I can't bear to look at them.

The demons can't stay. It's time for them to go. I'm not ready to throw in the towel.

I return my hands to the steering wheel; my eyes are open; my seat vibrates from the engine humming softly.

So what if it *is* true? So what if I *did* try to find a suitable partner for myself, who could be a father for Lilly? *And* I had the strength of mind to think about a sibling for my forsaken niece. After all, I was incapable of having my own children. And she needed a sister. Everyone does.

I had a responsibility to Lilly, the daughter of my deceased sister.

Is that so wrong?

I'll tell you what it is—it's practically *brilliant*. Not to mention utterly responsible. I was grieving, for God's sake. My beloved sister—had just been taken from me. She chose me to be her daughter's custodian; if that doesn't say something, what does? She trusted me to make the right decisions.

Overnight, the weight of the world had fallen on my shoulders. I must have been scared out of my mind. One day, a carefree young woman in her prime dating years, on a thrilling career path, and the next, unwittingly, the surrogate mother of my sister's two-year-old daughter, stripped of my former life. On top of that, my mother and father were gone. How much tragedy could I take? How was I to raise Lilly? I was so young myself and ill-prepared for motherhood.

So that's what I did. I went shopping for a husband. With the utmost of practicality. I've done it a million times before—flats, heels, suede, leather, pumps, slingbacks. I know what I'm doing. I'm a scientist, and the mall is my laboratory. Maybe more women should go about it like that. After all, look at us now; we've been married for . . . six-ish years.

That doesn't make me a criminal. Is what I did illegal? Did I kill anyone? I had to do what I had to do. I'm not ashamed of that. It's very Darwinian if you think about it. And for that, I should be proud.

I grab the gear and put the car in drive. Wipe my face with my sleeve and sail smoothly through the streets of town, weaving in and out of familiar territory. I find myself in the parking lot of the grocery store near school without a conscious decision to be there, causing me to think about the last thing I ate.

It wasn't lunch. Or breakfast.

Amazingly, it has been twenty-four hours since I last ate. Yesterday, lunch. Frittata with asparagus. A cup of coffee this morning and a bite of a Sno Ball certainly don't count. No wonder I can't keep it together. I look at my watch—twenty-six minutes until I need to pick up the girls. I'll just get a couple of things. It's food I need, protein and something to get my blood sugar up. Something to drink.

Into the grocery store I walk with decisive strides. I have a plan. To eat. It's small, but it's something. I grab a cart. The Bee Gees are singing, "If I Can't Have You," and contentment washes over me when I see the young mothers with toddlers shopping for bananas and strawberries. It's all so normal. I become intoxicated by the smell of fresh baking bread.

I, too, grab a banana and strawberries, as if normalcy will infuse me by association. The apples are stacked in a pyramid next to bags of caramels—good and evil all in one square foot of grocery space. I pass them by and proceed to the yogurt section on the way to the deli and grab a peach smoothie, then order some turkey, just a couple of slices to eat in the car.

It's just lacking romance. Is that it? Is that what's making me feel so badly. I think about the way Andy and I met; it's depressing. Does he even know . . . I . . . how it really was? It doesn't matter anyway. We've passed the test. We're in love and have a wonderful marriage; I'm not going to beat myself up over this. So I went about it a little unconventionally. If it weren't so disturbing (and was someone else's life), it would make a great book idea. I file it away in my mind for my next class. I guess we *are* supposed to draw from real life, right?

On my way to the front of the store, I pass through the greeting-card aisle. There are birthday cards for "wife" and "husband." I read a few, hoping to identify with the sentiments. These couples met like normal people do. Starting with a crush, until death do us part. My eyes amble over to birthday cards for "daughter." Cards I've been buying for years dishonestly. Or deceptively? I don't have daughters. They are not mine. I have no children. That thought slams against my brain pretty hard and gets stuck in my throat like a Lego. The first card I pick up says, "Daughter, the day you were born, it seemed as if the sun shone a little brighter, the sky was a little clearer, the . . ." I can't bear it. I ram it back into the plastic holster it came from. Who writes this crap? I check the time on my watch. Oh my gosh, the dismissal bell is about to ring.

As I speed walk to the register, my grocery cart screeches madly and veers to the left. I always get this one. It takes all my might to wrangle the carriage to the right, just to stay straight. I dip in and out of three lanes until I find one with no line.

My hand explores the bottom of my handbag for my wallet. It's not there. Shoot. I open my handbag as wide as it will go, and this time I stick my head in. How can I not have my wallet? I never don't have my wallet. I empty the contents of my bag into the grocery cart, a stupid idea; half of it falls through the holes to the floor. Shit. No wallet. My belongings scatter every which way. On my knees, I struggle to reclaim my lipsticks and loose change, chasing down every last coin, praying it will amount to something.

Twenty-seven cents. That won't even buy me a banana. I swerve the carriage around. I *need* something to eat now. It's a matter of medical necessity. *I cannot leave without food.*

My feet take over as if they have a mind of their own.

The damn grocery cart keeps veering to the left—to keep this thing on track is like wrestling an alligator. My feet stop in the middle of aisle eleven: the automotive department.

No one's ever in the automotive aisle. God only knows why they have one. Midway—between floor mats and air fresheners—I stand intimately close to the motor oil, scratch the back of my neck, and look behind me. No one's there. Nor is there anyone to the left or right. I rip open the plastic deli envelope and stuff all three pieces of turkey in my mouth while I pop open the yogurt smoothie, and guzzle it down without stopping until my lips make a sucking sound when they get nothing but air.

This is *not* shoplifting. This is an act of survival. And child welfare. I poke the deli plastic through the neck of the empty smoothie bottle and tuck it behind a can of Pennzoil 10W40, wiping a trickle off my chin with the back of my hand.

Before I abandon the cart, I see a pack of Sno Balls at the bottom of it. How did those get in there? Did I do that? That's disturbing. But now that I see them, I can't resist a bite. Just one. I rip the plastic and stick a Sno Ball in my mouth as far as it will go. But not the whole thing. Just a bite. I put the rest in the plastic and stick it behind a can of oil, and make a beeline for the parking lot.

I'm almost at the car, and my cell rings. I grab my phone from the outside pocket of my handbag. I don't recognize the number.

"Hello?" I answer the phone.

"Mrs. Thompson?"

"Who's this?"

I look around the parking lot. It's empty. Except for the grocery cart cowboy who's herding the shopping carts. He looks up and sees me watching him push the snake of carts back to the store.

"This is Tina Wiggins, from Lincoln Elementary."

Tina Wiggins? Oh God. This is about the fire alarm.

"Yes . . ." I say tentatively. If I hang up on her, they'll just call again. Or send the police.

"I'm the substitute nurse. Mrs. Robin is not here today, so I'm filling in."

"Oh. That's great."

"I don't want to upset you, but Tessa had an accident."

"*Tessa?*"

"She's gonna be fine—really. It's been pretty hectic here today. They wanted the kids to have a normal afternoon, so they went outside for gym. She was running back into school and tripped. The brick stairs broke her fall. Unfortunately, she must have been biting her lip when she was running, and her front teeth, well, they've punctured through the other side of her lip."

"*What*—?"

"Don't worry. We're en route to the emergency room at Mountainview General. Could you meet us there?"

"What do you mean? Are you in an ambulance?" Oh God, no, not Tessa in an ambulance. She must be freaking out. At least if it were Lilly, she'd think it was cool. "Is Tessa okay? How is she doing?" I have a very low threshold for my children's pain. "Can I speak with her?"

"It's hard for her to speak right now. Her lip is packed up pretty good to stop the bleeding. We'll be at the hospital in a few minutes. She's doing good . . ." She whispers, " . . .sort of."

I start walking quickly toward the car. "Just tell her I'll

be right there, I'm not far—I'm on my way." The one time I'd be okay with her biting her cuticles, it's physically impossible.

"Thanks, Mrs. Thompson. Don't worry, she's in good hands, the EMTs are great. I won't leave her until you get here."

"I'll be *right* there . . . Oh, no, I have to get Lilly—"

"Oh, don't worry about that. She's going home with Delia Henry. We couldn't reach you at home or on your cell, so we called Mrs. Henry. She's on your emergency card in the office."

I've had my cell phone with me the entire time. It never rang.

"Mrs. Henry said Lilly can stay with them. I called your husband at work when I didn't get you on your cell. He was in a meeting, so I left a message with his assistant.

"By the way, before I forget, you should know, Tessa chipped a tooth—"

"Oh my God—"

"No, really, it's not bad. You can hardly notice. I'm sure you could leave it alone and no one would ever—"

"No, no, it can't be left that way. We'll have the dentist file it—it can't be left like that."

"Whatever. I just didn't want you to be surprised and react in front of Tessa. She's a little worried about it."

"I'm on my way. It won't be five minutes. I'm practically in the car." I hang up the phone, but before I put it back in my handbag I look at my recent calls. Two missed calls from Tina Wiggins. Damn phone.

I pull into the emergency room parking lot, for the second day in a row, slipping my car into a signed spot which reads: "Emergency Room Parking Only, 15 Minute Limit." I hurry toward the sliding doors. Hopefully, we can get Tessa taken care of quickly so I can pick up Lilly at Meg's and get home for a "normal" evening. Maybe we can even be home before Andy, so it will seem like a typical Tuesday night. I'll make one of our favorite dinners. That's what we need. To hunker down with a good meal and our routine. Normalcy. I promise myself to concentrate on Lilly and Tessa and Andy and everything that makes us a happy family. And no computer.

Tessa is in a wheelchair in the pediatric ER being guided into a room. "Tessa!" As she turns the corner into the room, her head spins around, and I catch a glimpse of her frightened eyes. The rest of her face is concealed by a bloody, white cloth and what looks like an ice pack. I hurry down the hall.

"Mommy." Her voice is muffled.

"It's okay, Tessa. You're going to be fine." I take a peek under the ice pack and try to conceal the shock in my eyes. Her two top teeth severed the skin right below her bottom lip. It's swollen and bloody. And alarming and gruesome. "Can you open your mouth and show me your teeth?" She attempts to open her mouth and winces. I find myself stroking my own, gliding my finger back and forth across my top teeth. "Okay, Tessa, you just rest. The doctor is coming right away. Before you know it, we'll be home. Okay, sweetie?"

She shakes her head and clutches my fingers with her free hand.

"Mrs. Thompson? I'm Tina Wiggins." A young girl who looks scarcely older than Tessa pops her head around from a conversation with a staffer.

"Oh, Tina," I'm stunned by how young this girl looks. Should I call her Ms. Wiggins? "Thanks for taking care of Tessa." Is this how school nurses dress these days?

My phone rings. "Excuse me." I pinch it from the inside

pocket of my handbag and pray no one else is hurt. Tessa grabs my hand again.

"Ms. Spencer?"

My head jerks up. I look around the room. Did anyone hear that? "*Who?*" I say without moving my mouth. I release Tessa's hand and give her the "one minute" finger as I slip into the hall.

"Who *is* this?" My heart has just gone from zero to ninety. I keep my voice down so Tessa and Tina Wiggins don't hear me. "Are you looking for JD? How did you get this number?" I focus on the caller's number.

"No. I'm looking for Caroline Spencer. This is Dr. Sullivan's office—she called here earlier today."

Dr. Sullivan . . . "Oh—yes," I pull the phone away from my mouth for a sec to slow my breathing, and say in a hushed tone, "This is Caroline Spencer. I'm sorry about the confusion." I say to Dr. Sullivan's assistant, "It's just that I'm having about four conversations at once—I don't know how in the world kids expect you to hear them when you're talking to the gas station attendant and you're on the phone at the same time." I pull the phone away from my mouth again, and wag my finger at an invisible child, "Sweetie, I'm on the phone now—wait until I get off, and then we'll call Delia for a playdate." Tina Wiggins is standing in the doorway of Tessa's room, looking at me.

"Everything okay?" Tina mouths.

"Oh, yes, with me? Fine. Sorry—had to take this. I'll be right off."

Tina points at her wrist, which doesn't have a watch, and mouths that she's leaving. I give her the okay sign.

Back to my call, "Sorry 'bout that."

"Ms. Spencer, if this isn't a good time, you can call me back—"

"No, no, this is a fine time, no, please—" I look into Tessa's room and give her a big smile and a thumbs-up.

"Well, here it is. Dr. Sullivan reviewed his calls from this morning, and he was very surprised to see you called. Bottom line, he's eager to see you. He'd like to make some time available right away. So you can scratch that date in October. He's willing to stay after his appointments tonight or tomorrow night, or any evening that works best for you. That's him talking, not me. I, of course, won't be here. I clock out at five. You'll have to let yourself in and sit in the waiting room until he comes out to get you. You know the drill, you've been here before."

This is weird. Five hours ago I was the pursuer, now I'm the pursuee. Something about this feels bad.

"Ms. Spencer?"

"Yes . . ."

"Is there an evening that works for you?"

We agree on tomorrow. I slip the phone into my jeans and return to Tessa. I pull a chair next to the bed and hold her hand. We wait together silently for the doctor to come. It would be a good idea for me to relax and transfer a sense of calm to her. But my secrets are multiplying by the hour. The ones I uncover, and the ones I conceive. They're like nesting dolls. Just as certain as one reveals itself, there's another lurking not far behind.

A nurse arrives to clean the blood away from Tessa's face. I'm preoccupied and don't say a thing to the nurse. Wait. Tomorrow is Wednesday. I planned to go to New York to a bookstore where my writing professor is reading from his newly published memoir. I had it planned for weeks. Actually, that's good. I already have Mrs. H booked to watch the girls (God help us all), and Andy expects me to be out. I won't have to lie. Sort of. He might expect me to cancel now, in light of this week's family injuries, but there's no way he'll remember, and I won't remind him.

It's worrisome how easily lying comes to me these days. I'm sure I'd worry about that more if I had nothing else to worry about.

When all is said and done at the emergency room, Tessa gets thirty-nine stitches through three layers of tissue—muscle, nerves, and skin—done at the hand of a plastic surgeon who takes forever to arrive. Tessa is a true champ. Silent and stoic the whole way. Our fingers in a tight scrum for the duration. We get home after eight. Tessa barely gets down a bowl of frozen yogurt before going to bed and falling into a thick sleep. I wish I could say the same for myself.

By the time the morning arrives, I'm almost eager to get out of bed. Lilly goes to school with a neighbor, and Tessa keeps me company at home for the day, she convalescing, and I cooking, cleaning, and doing anything that keeps me busy and not thinking about my meeting with Dr. Sullivan, which is in a matter of hours. I want to stay positive. I try. But ultimately, common sense tells me I'm just leaving one haunted house for another.

CHAPTER TWELVE

Wednesday, September 27, 2006, 6:19 p.m.

Dr. Sullivan's office is paneled in dark wood—reminiscent of the seventies, when Dr. Sullivan started practicing psychology. Let's hope he's had enough practice.

Framed photos line the paneled walls—pictures of him with his cronies, presumably, fishing mostly. There's a plump, stuffed fish mounted on one of the walls. A trout, I think . . . or a bass. It might be a shark. The scales are an iridescent bluish-grey. Its eyes stare down at me. Moving to the couch to see if they'll follow is probably an ill-advised idea moments before meeting with a psychologist.

But for the sign in the window, I'd think this was an old yacht club. If the office door opens and Gilligan appears—I won't even flinch.

The waiting room smells like an empty refrigerator, and the ancient Glade air freshener is not fooling anyone—they stopped making that style years ago. A deep ochre glow is suffocated behind a heavy nubby burlap lampshade, and the couch is as cushy as sitting on burnt toast.

I don't recall ever being here. And I'm getting used to that.

In the corner of the room, under a bulky wooden end table, is a white-noise machine impersonating the sound of soft rainfall. However, a muffled voice coming from behind the closed door is still audible.

Dr. Sullivan's assistant has gone for the day, as she informed me she would. The room is very still, and I'm somewhat calm under the circumstances. I'm hugely relieved that I'm minutes away from confiding in someone. And by doing so, enlisting an ally. Someone who'll help me bear the burden of these absurdities.

The array of magazines—*National Geographic*, *Outdoor Life*, *Sports Illustrated*—does nothing to arouse my curiosity. I wrestle with what I'm going to say to him. The sole reason I'm here, really, is for *him* to do the talking. There are blanks to be filled in. The fact that I've been here before is both frightening and fortuitous. There is nothing about this room or these photos that are familiar to me. But if I've been here before, he may have notes. I must be entitled to them. At the very least, he has to tell me what's in them.

The door opens, and who—to my amazement—appears? The Skipper. A dead ringer, anyway. Sans the hat. His smile is sincere as he takes my hand with both of his. He stands so close to me that, for a second, I'm not sure if he's expecting a hug. Making it more uncomfortable is that we're practically the same height. He's not short, but I, on the other hand, pack some longitude. A gift from my parents. His face looks somewhat familiar to me. But that may be because of the photos on the walls.

His hands are warm but not strong, more enveloping than anything. Padded.

"It's good to see you, Caroline. You look wonderful." He jerks his head back to get his overgrown bangs out of his eyes, and motions into the office. I look around for the other person with whom Dr. Sullivan was speaking, but the room appears empty.

"Likewise." As soon as the word passes my lips, I realize it's not my word. It belongs to my mother. I hate when I do this. When I'm feeling anxious I use words that don't belong in my mouth. He can probably tell when someone is not being genuine.

Then I remind myself he's not a psychic; he's a psychologist. "Thank you for seeing me on such short notice," I say, and sit down on a tweed chair with pale, wooden arms and coerce my throat to force down a wad of saliva. My calm must have stayed in the waiting room.

His face is kind, fleshy and round; his eyes sparkle with interest and warmth, though they're tired; the whites are somewhat yellowed and his skin a bit dry. It's hard not to notice his heavily veined nose—tiny burst blood vessels smother the entire thing. It's unsightly, actually. All of those hours fishing in the hot sun with no sunscreen. All those happy hours. It's a pity, really.

"How's Lilly?" he asks as earnestly as an uncle, while clasping his hands. The pained look on my face forces him to ask a quick follow-up, "She's okay, isn't she?"

Again that feeling of being in the dark. It's so frightening.

Not to know people who know me. About me. I have no idea how much he knows. Suffice it to say, it's more than I do.

I came here for help. It's time to shed the armor.

"Dr. Sullivan, I don't know exactly how to say this. How to explain what's going on with me." Any amount of preparation was a big waste of time; nothing could prepare me for how stripped I feel. "I need to tell you something before we begin." I grip the arms of the chair and squeeze, like I do when I'm about to get a root canal. "I don't recall ever coming here. I don't remember you being my therapist or ever meeting you."

He listens without interruption. Without even blinking. A long moment of silence transpires. I think about saying more, to help him, but I have nothing more. I need for him to take the ball. "I see." He shifts in his seat. The crunch of the naugahyde under his large frame is the only sound in the room. He rests his head back and lifts his chin slightly. "Hmm," he says, though I think it's meant only for him. The twinkle in his eyes is gone. It's been replaced with something else.

"Why don't you just forget about that for a bit, Caroline. Why don't you just catch me up on the last few years—how long has it been?" He forces a smile and looks down at the manila folder with a pink sticker on the tab, color-coded, no doubt, for "nuts."

"Oh, my, it's been six years? Can you believe that—I wouldn't have guessed that long. Well then, catch me up on six years. Give me some of the highlights. They've been happy, mostly?"

"Yes, they have been." It's good to realize this.

At the end of my account of the last six years—my parents passing away, marrying Andy, et cetera—I matter-of-factly tell him that I've discovered through "various sources" that there are pieces of my past—memories of important, sometimes upsetting, even tragic life events—that I don't recall.

"How did you first come upon these memory lapses, Caroline?"

I think about that for a second. This is embarrassing.

Screw the embarrassment. I've got real problems here. And if I'm not gonna tell Andy or Meg, I've got to tell someone. Someone who can't tell anyone. The ultimate secret keeper, right? That's the guy sitting across from me right now. He can't divorce me or gossip about me to all the women in town. That's why I'm here. Because I can be vulnerable with no consequences.

"I Googled myself."

At first our conversation, his and mine, is all very matter-of-fact, levelheaded, no emotion. Then the probing begins. Questions for which I don't have answers. He offers me a box of tissues, and I attempt to gather myself. I want to continue. He asks me about my relationship with Andy, a typical day, my physical health.

We decide the best way to proceed will be to review some of the pertinent old taped transcripts. Hearing there are *audio* tapes is incredible. I was expecting something written. Actually, I was praying there'd be anything at all, knowing that some psychologists will just sit there with you, not a pen or pad in sight, nothing to record the sessions beyond their own memory. No paper trail. I'm relieved he's not one of them or the note-taker type, either, for that matter. Audio tapes are an unbiased portal to the past.

He'll need some time to collect them and review their

contents to determine whether or not I'm emotionally ready for them. What on earth does that mean?

It feels like he's ending the session, but I just got here. "What about tonight, Doctor, isn't there anything we could start with . . . I . . ." My voice cracks.

He searches my face for something. What is it? His head cocks to one side and then the other, like a chicken. He flips through some papers in my file—which is rather thin. I convince myself that that's a good sign.

Dr. Sullivan closes the folder, smooths his sandy-colored bangs off his forehead, then clasps his hands on top of the file and looks at me. His tired, gentle eyes, along with his pudgy jowls, give him the appearance of a pug.

"Caroline, as we go forward with our sessions together, I want you to keep in mind that at times, listening to some of these transcripts won't be easy. By that, I mean the events of your past, they were . . . trying times. You may have difficulty listening to . . . the contents. Your demeanor, even. It was quite different from the way you appear today. I'm so pleased to see you now, much calmer and less . . . well . . . I'll be interested to see how you'd describe your old self. It's your well-being I'm concerned about."

What the *heck?* Okay, so he says this all without a hint of condescension or disapproval. But come on, I sound like a lunatic. A long, controlled exhale seeps out of my mouth. This doesn't feel good. Like when the music changes in a horror movie. Something's coming. Only it's not a movie, it's real life. Mine.

This could get a lot worse before it gets better.

Somehow, though, I'm confident it was the right decision to come here. I trust this guy. I don't know why, but I do.

Who else do I have?

"On that note, I'll require you be examined by a medical doctor. We need to get to the bottom of the memory loss, first by ruling out physical maladies. Once you have a physical work-up, I'll consult with your physician—so I'll need his or her contact information." He jots something down.

"Well, I *have* been checked by a doctor. A CT scan was taken of my head." He looks at me curiously. "Last week, in fact. I had this breathing thing, and an accident with the kitchen stool. They checked everything. A CT scan for internal bleeding and trauma, and an EKG. All that stuff. Everything's clean." I throw my hands up in the air like a magician.

"I see. That must have been quite a fall. That's good news. I'd like a copy of that report, Caroline. Could you have that sent to me?" He jots something in my file. "Looks like you bruised your face as well?" He lifts his head for a second and peers over his reading glasses, "Something here . . ." he points to his own forehead, and then head down again to make note. With his eyes fixed to my file, he continues, "So you've discussed the memory loss with your physician, then?"

"Well . . . *yes*. She recommended I see a psychologist." I completely forgot about Dr. Kriete.

"Did she recommend you see a neurologist?"

"For the pregnancy?"

"You're pregnant?" He removes his glasses.

"Oh, the memory loss! No, she didn't." My cheeks burn with embarrassment. I look at the floor. I need a flow chart. Literally. When I get home, I need to draw up a chart to sort my doctors, symptoms, diagnoses. A separate one for lies.

"Caroline, do you think you're pregnant?"

"Who me? No." I shake my head a few dozen times.

He slips his glasses back on and writes a few things I never want to read. "I would definitely suggest a neurologist. Do you have one?"

My head and my foot shake in unison.

"Don't worry," a reassuring smile brings pause, "as soon as that's done—"

"*But—wait, I—*"

He puts his pen down and sits back, pulls his glasses off. "I understand your eagerness, Caroline, I do. However, I need time to review your file and tapes. Which I'm happy to do right away. In fact, tonight after you leave I'll have a little time to go through some."

My clasped hands rest in my lap, and I sit up tall in my seat. "Please understand how grateful I am—you must know that—that after all this time you would see me on such short notice—not to mention even remember me—and I'm sure you have a procedure that you follow when old patients—a system—"

"Caroline—"

"—*many* of your patients are suffering—of course I know that, you have other patients with problems, and believe me, I would never minimize their distress, but I—I—" I slide forward and sit at the edge of my seat and take a deep breath—it gets caught for a second in my throat.

"Caroline—"

"I—I—don't want preferential treatment, Doctor, that's not what I'm suggesting—I would never suggest that. I just—I just—" My shoulders slump forward. "I can't go *home*—" It's like I'm punched in the stomach by my own thoughts. The severity cuts me in the middle; any façade of strength I had crumbles.

I reach out and grab the edge of his desk; he jerks back in his chair. "I can't go back there—I can't look at my husband—or my girls. I just can't pretend anymore—"

"Caroline, please—" He puts his hand up to silence me.

My eyes avert his. "I'm, I'm falling apart. I'm completely falling apart, and I don't know what to—" My face drops into my hands.

"Please, Caroline, please, just give me a minute to—*please.*"

He looks down again into the folder and slides his finger across the page, squinting. Without looking, he feels around the desk for his glasses, puts them on, and reads some more. He stands up slowly, pushing his chair away with his foot, then he hunches over the desk, leaning on it with his two hands. I can't tell if he's reading or thinking. He stretches back upright and places one hand on the round of his stomach, as if he's waiting for the kick of a fetus.

I grab a magazine from the side table and embrace it, *Bait and Tackle*, crisscrossing my arms around it to muffle my heartbeat.

Still immersed in his thoughts, Dr. Sullivan walks toward the door and tilts his head in my direction while keeping his eyes on the hallway outside. "Cold?"

Another door closes. Until tiny white dots appear in front of my eyes, I don't notice I'm holding my breath. The other door opens and shuts, and he returns with something in his hand, which I can't make out because his fingers are curled around it. Back at his desk, he pulls something out of a top draw. A mini-tape recorder.

I close my eyes and sit on my hands, aiming to center myself. He's changed his mind. He's going to play one of the tapes.

"Caroline, I'm willing to try something," he says with

trepidation. "During the course of your visits, I asked your mother and father to come in for a session, one at a time, with your approval, of course. You and I had already met several times. I explained to you that it would be helpful to your treatment if I were able to piece together some family background from the perspective of other family members. Your mother came in for one visit, but unfortunately I never met your father."

I can't believe we even entertained the thought that my father would come. And to talk to a psychologist, of all people. Surely I must have told Dr. Sullivan my father spoke only in emergencies. My mother, on the other hand, surely jumped at the chance to talk virtually uninterrupted for an hour.

"I think we can start with your mother's session. She agreed to the disclosure of its contents to you. Whatever I thought would be helpful. I never had a chance to play this for you because, well . . . you ended your treatment earlier . . . than expected. It provides background information that may—well, a breakthrough of some kind would be extremely ambitious, but let's agree it may help." He pauses and looks at me thoughtfully, searching. "Of course, we can stop at any time, Caroline. As soon as anything makes you the slightest bit uncomfortable."

Thank you, Mom. Gratitude courses through me. Maybe she did care about me. She's going to help. I guess I never believed, like some people do, that once people die and leave the world in a physical sense, they remain in a spiritual one and appear, like an angel, to support you in your darkest hour. I do now.

He slips the mini-cassette into the tiny recorder atop his desk and presses the play button with a pudgy index finger. As he waits for it to begin, he leans on the desk and taps the fingers of his left hand in quick succession. They look like breakfast sausages, and they make a dull thud on the leather desktop. I stick a finger between my teeth to stop their rattling, cross my legs, and squeeze my thighs together. I should have gone to the bathroom when I was in the waiting room.

When the voice begins, he sits down heavily in his chair; gushes of air seep from the seams of the cushions.

> **Dr. Sullivan:** Tell me, Mrs. Spencer; tell me something memorable about Caroline's childhood. Can you remember a story from her early childhood that you can share with me? Anything at all, it need not be profound or telling, just anything that pops into your head.
>
> **Elaine:** Oh, my goodness, Doctor, that's uh . . . well, hmm, let's see, my daughter Caroline, what can I say, she's . . .

What the—*hell?* I immediately clutch the wooden armrests and snap my head at Dr. Sullivan. *He's got to be screwing with me.*

He stops the tape. "What's the matter, Caroline? Are you all right?"

"Who *is* that? *Who's* speaking on the tape?" My body is straight as an arrow; my voice quivers.

He looks at me with complete confusion. "It's your mother. Don't you recognize her voice?"

"*No. I don't—*" The words taste curdled as I speak them. "Because—" I stab a finger at the tape recorder, "that's not my *mother—my mother's British.*"

"Your mother's British?" He tilts his head in bewilderment.

"*No.*" I shake my head impatiently, "*She's* not British. Her *voice,* I mean. *She has an English accent.* A *fake* English accent," I say through clenched teeth. I'm sick, sick with disgust; how could she do this to me? After all those years of embarrassing us, and then to drop the phony accent on the day she meets with Dr. Sullivan.

"I'm sorry, Caroline. I don't follow."

I tell him the infamous story, how it started when she was in her thirties, and all the while I feel like I've told him before, or he already knows, or he doesn't believe me. This sucks. I taste the bile in my stomach. Why would she tell me to come here, knowing she'd betray me like this? *She* didn't want Dr. Sullivan to think *she* was crazy. A nutcase with an overactive imagination. No. She saved that for me and JD and my father. To humiliate us. She wasn't going to take the rap for the way I turned out. I breathe heavily through my nose; my nostrils flare, my eyes fix on Dr. Sullivan without seeing him. Suddenly the thought that this guy was ever going to rescue me is fleeing so fast, it already feels like tomorrow.

He gives me a proper sprinkling of "uh-huhs" along with the neck action of a dashboard dog, while my mind races; I can't endure this. Is he testing me?

"When was the last time you spoke to your mother?"

"She's—gone, she–died."

"Oh, yes, that's right. I'm sorry, Caroline."

"But I can tell you this," I say as I prop myself at the cliff of my seat, my resolve stiff with fury. "Her accent was as thick as clotted cream until the day she died."

My mother's words still cling to the air, polluting Dr. Sullivan's office, each one veiled in deception.

"This must be very confusing, Caroline—"

He *must* have known about her. I must have told him about the ridiculous British thing. Didn't he know what this would do to me—hearing her like that? I was already barely hanging on. *What am I supposed to do now?* He was my last hope. How can I trust any of this?

I bolt out of my chair and grab my handbag. *"Confused?* I will not be patronized like this. Confused. *I'll tell you what I'm feeling*: hoodwinked! Manipulated! I will not subject myself to this duplicitous *crap,"* I holler at him, the blood vessels in my temples bulging. "Are you in on this, too?" I stab my finger at him.

"Did people judge your mother, for this . . . accent of hers?" He speaks calmly, not reacting whatsoever to my outburst, which incenses me. Calm as a summer breeze. The only thing showing signs of stress are the little white buttons on his blue Brooks Brothers shirt—creating little ellipses, revealing glimpses of his white undershirt.

He's talking to me as if I'm sipping lemonade with my feet propped on his desk.

"Yes, you're goddamn right they judged her, for good reason. It was nuts! Did she ever think how it would affect her kids?" My face is hot. My chest is seething.

I'm getting the hell out of here. I turn abruptly toward the door, swinging my handbag in an orbit around me, knocking the table lamp to the floor. The sound of the crash is startling, but my nerves are already on overdrive. I pivot back to him, jabbing the air with my finger. "This is a *sham*! I can't believe I fell for this!" I shout through my tears, "Is this the 'slightest bit uncomfortable' you were looking for? *You should be ashamed of yourself."*

I turn to face the door and put my hand on the knob for stability. I can leave, but I don't. The only thing standing in the way of escaping this torture and entering the torture on the other side is this thin slab of cracked wood. My head is hung low; I shout at the door just inches from my nose, "I'm *desperate* here. Don't you know that? Do you get it? I'm desperate." With clenched eyes I turn back to him, "I trusted you—I need help. I don't know where else to *go* . . or who to . . . talk to . . ." I drop my face into trembling hands. "What's happening to me?" I've all but lost the energy and will to leave. "To think my own mother . . . would do this. It was her idea for me to come here when JD died," I mutter "I trusted her—"

I lean against the door to support my feeble body. "And you pretended to care . . . that after all this time . . . you would be able to help . . . you were my last hope . . . what a sap . . ."

There's nothing more to say. I'm spent. I can't hold up my own weight. My knees give in, and my body settles to the floor. I shrivel up inside myself, weeping.

Dr. Sullivan is sitting next to me on the musty shag carpet. Time has passed. His back rests against the wall, and legs are outstretched. His two Docksiders form the letter "v." I sit in the same position. A box of tissues with a crocheted cover, embroidered with "Dr. Sullivan" in forest green, rests between us.

Quietly, he says, "I have absolutely no reason not to believe everything you tell me. You're my patient, Caroline, and I didn't invite your mother to speak with me to discredit you. Your mother chose not to share that side of herself, for whatever reason. But that need not concern us."

I can't imagine feeling worse. And if I stay, I know I will. But I know I can't go.

I stand up slowly and look at the door. I pull at the cuffs of my shirtsleeves and clear my throat. I sit back down on the burnt-orange tweed chair with the pale wooden arms, and without looking at Dr. Sullivan, I decide. "I want to hear what she has to say."

CHAPTER THIRTEEN

Wednesday, September 27, 2006, 7:21 p.m.

> **Elaine:** Well, Caroline was an intensely loyal sister, you
> know. She would do anything for JD.

I conjure an image of my mother in my mind. Like a poodle
in a dog show. Sitting there on Dr. Sullivan's couch primped
in a skirt suit, panty hose, and navy leather shoes, the ones
with a bow at the toe and a slight heel, to "accentuate the calf;
a woman with good legs should not keep them hidden in trousers," fresh lipstick, and her "day jewelry," like she was coming from somewhere. But she wasn't coming from somewhere.
And she wasn't going anywhere, either. "There's no harm in
keeping up appearances."

> **Elaine:** I think part of her loyalty came from what I always
> told them:

"Friends will come and go, but sisters are forever." I did like to pass on some moral fiber whenever I could.

That fiber's about to come up all over Dr. Sullivan's rug.

Elaine: I'm sure the rest stemmed out of her fantasy that she and JD were twins. I don't know if she told you this story—of course it would be a different version, because even to this day, she asserts that she and JD were twins and that I've lied about it all these years.

I turn, wide-eyed, to Dr. Sullivan. My mouth has dropped open, but I quickly close it. He looks over at me; neither of us says anything. He keeps playing the tape, though he makes a note in my file.

Dr. Sullivan: So the girls are not twins?

Elaine: Heaven's, no. They were born one year apart—to the day—which I suppose for some people is mad enough as it is. (Laugh.) Even I was rather shocked when I found out I was pregnant with JD. It was more than shock, really. I suppose you could say I was . . . not as excited as I should've been. Caroline was all of three months old. And she, after all, was an accident herself. Walter and I really didn't plan on having a family so early; we were newlyweds. Honeymooners, actually.

I can't believe she's calling him Walter. She never called him Walter. Nobody did.

Elaine: I was barely accustomed to being a mum and then—*that* news. But I can assure you, they are certainly not twins. God knows I would've gained a lot more weight than twenty-one kilos. That was one thing I promised myself: I was not going to be one of those fatties, eating everything in the cupboard and then taking years to run off the baby fat.

Nevertheless, no matter how many times I explained, or showed Caroline the birth certificates, which she accused me of doctoring, she was adamant, claiming that I'd left JD in the hospital with some such illness for all those months, embarrassed because she was not developing properly, and that finally Walter and I brought JD home at the insistence of the medical staff. It's really quite a story she's made up— and at such a young age—she was about four or five when she started telling people this ridiculous tale. Caroline had a very active imagination. She could convince herself of anything.

I even showed her photographs of the day her sister came home from the hospital. It's clear to see that next to Caroline, who was exactly one, JD was a newborn, all tiny and wrinkled like a peanut.

Dr. Sullivan: Why do you think Caroline felt so strongly about this?

Elaine: Oh, I couldn't tell you, doctor. At first, I just thought it was child's play. Like an imaginary friend? But, Caroline was obsessed with twins, and it wasn't a fleeting interest. She'd write school book reports on the subject— you know, over the course of her grade-school education. She must've read nearly twenty books about twins, perhaps more.

She had a deep need for JD to be just like her. At first, JD was happy to oblige, you know, when she was quite young. What little girl doesn't want to be like her big sister? In those days, they wore the same clothes, had the same interests, same friends. I dressed them alike. I thought it was sweet. Everyone thought they were so darling in their matching outfits. But when Caroline started to tell everyone they were twins, I had to put a stop to the matching clothes. It became quite embarrassing for me. She should've known better. Sometimes we'd quarrel about it in public.

When JD was young, she went along with it. But then, JD began to come into her own—personality and style and friends—oh, I shouldn't forget to say, the thing that made all of this more complicated was an illness Caroline had at about five. Midway through kindergarten, she caught pneumonia. She was very sick for several months. We hired a live-in nurse, a student nurse, actually. Walter couldn't afford a real one. I was just petrified of catching pneumonia. You can die from it, you know.

Dr. Sullivan: Yes. Unfortunately that's true.

Elaine: So, Caroline's teachers and Walter and I agreed that the right thing to do was to have her repeat kindergarten. In doing so, Caroline and JD were in the same school grade, and they had the same exact birth date. Well, that was enough for Caroline.

Dr. Sullivan: You started to say something about when JD got to a certain age, she "came into her own personality." What do you mean by that?

Elaine: Oh, yes, that's true. She was in . . . probably . . . first grade when it started, at the end of that year, if I remember correctly. She had a friend who was just mad about sports. Suzie something or other. The girl was a tomboy for sure, and let's just say her choice of clothes reflected that. JD didn't want to wear dresses anymore. She wanted jeans and trousers and plain, boyish-looking shirts—no flowers or hearts. She never cared too much for the frilly things anyway—it was always Caroline who did. Well, this Suzie girl was a lovely child, but let's be honest, her clothes were ghastly. At first I thought, there is no way on God's green earth I will dress my daughter in those clothes, but then, I must say, doctor, I've always prided myself with supporting my children's journey in finding themselves. Believe *me*, I was never expecting them to want to be exactly like *me*. And even if they did, I realized they might not realize it until they were much older. So, I decided to indulge JD and let her explore this new stage of her childhood.

I wouldn't have imagined Caroline to take it so badly. She was destroyed by JD's change in tune. She was personally offended, she felt betrayed. She couldn't understand why her sister wouldn't want to be just like her. She was doubly horrified that JD would want to be like someone *else*.

That was a difficult period for Caroline, especially because of her weight problem. She was plumping up by the cheese doodle. That was nothing I endorsed, believe me—I put her on a strict diet. She must've been sneaking food somehow. Sometimes I'd find her with her mouth rimmed in pink sugar from those *hideous* balls. You know the ones. Cream and sponge cake and food coloring. She'd inhale them before I could even detect what they were. I don't know how she got her hands on those. They were *not* allowed in our house. You could buy them at the gas station! Poor people ate them for breakfast!

Frankly, I don't understand fat people. How they can just let themselves go. Of course, Caroline was a child, and I was responsible for her. I told her that I wouldn't sit by and watch her blow up like some Goodyear blimp. I believe she didn't have friends because of how big she was. Kids don't like the chubby girl. Fat people are invisible, you know. Isn't that the irony of all ironies? The bigger people become, the more invisible they are. I told her, if she didn't stop gorging herself, she'd never have a single friend. Perhaps that's why it was crucial for her to hang onto JD.

Dr. Sullivan: How did Caroline's reaction manifest?

Elaine: Well . . . let's just say she became . . . desperate.

I could hear my mother turning the word "desperate" over in her mouth, like a hard candy, thinking that with enough manipulation of the tongue, the edges might soften.

Dr. Sullivan: What do you mean?

Elaine: Uh, how can I explain this? . . . Well . . . she must have thought to herself, of course she never told me this, mind you, but I did always try to be perceptive about my children. I could see by her behavior that she must have thought, "If you can't beat 'em, join 'em." And that's exactly what Caroline did. At first, it was innocent. She'd dress exactly like JD—no skirts, flowers, headbands—none of those girlie things she was accustomed to wearing. She cleared out her closet and drawers of those things and packed them into bags for the Salvation Army. That was always important to me—to pass on to my children a sense of obligation to help the have-nots. One should teach these things early on in life, don't you think? Anyway, Caroline now wanted clothes like JD.

Dr. Sullivan: Would you say Caroline believed she was changing her identity, of sorts?

Elaine: Well . . . maybe . . . I suppose you could explain it that way. But to me, that would mean Caroline would've felt she lost something of herself by doing so, and I don't believe she ever felt that way. I think if you asked Caroline, she believed her identity was being a twin no matter what form it took. It really didn't matter to her if she was in a dress or in shorts. And I guess, in retrospect, she didn't have an emotional attachment to any of those things. The real attachment was to her sister. She was a very determined young girl.

You know, that reminds me of the girls' high school yearbook. You know how everyone is given some sort of title, like "Most likely to . . ."? Well, JD was voted "Most likely to do the right thing," and Caroline was voted "Mostly likely to get what she wants."

Mine was "Most likely to be voted homecoming queen." Which I was, by the way.

Dr. Sullivan: Very nice. Congratulations.

Elaine: Thank you. It was a splendid evening. I remember it like it was yesterday. My gown was sapphire blue. It was said that I looked like Audrey Hepburn. A *young* Audrey Hepburn.

Dr. Sullivan: Very nice. Very nice.

Elaine: Anyway, JD's friendship with the tomboy didn't

last very long. There was a misunderstanding at school—
JD was blamed for something she didn't do, and we all
decided it was best for JD to keep her distance from the
girl.

Dr. Sullivan: You said that Caroline became "desperate."
Is that what you meant, when she threw her clothes away?

Elaine: Gave them to the needy.

Dr. Sullivan: Oh, yes, of course–my mistake.

Elaine: Well, there is one thing in particular I was thinking about . . . but . . . I'm not sure I need to go into all of
this . . . now . . .

My mother starts to sound uncomfortable for the first
time. I can imagine her crossing her legs and uncrossing them,
and re-crossing them. I can almost hear the soft swoosh of her
nylons sweeping in opposition as she obsessively picks invisible lint off her suit jacket.

Dr. Sullivan: Mrs. Spencer, we—you and I, and your husband, of course, want to help Caroline. Holding back information regarding her behavior or state of mind may at first
feel protective, but could in fact have the opposite effect.

Elaine: Well, I don't know. Maybe she should tell you
this story. It doesn't seem right for me to be the one. I'm
not going—she was not in a good place, you see—and
maybe . . . well, it was, anyway, some of this, I mean. I'm
not *perfect*, you know, though I may seem so to others. I . . .
perhaps I . . . should have paid more attention or something, but I . . .

Walter and I scraped together everything we had to

show them a good life. Certainly better than we ever had, and better than we could really afford, if you must know. I tried to fit in . . . to . . . this expected lifestyle . . . of these people around us. I was unfamiliar with these hoity-toity types. We thought we could fit in, that we could change, and I tried, you *must* know that, you can ask Caroline. It wasn't always easy for the girls, but I tried. Not Walter. I mean, he'd go along with my ideas sometimes if he thought it would help our standing. But he wasn't going out on any limb. He just didn't have the spine—or any other body part, for that matter—for what it took. And, well, I . . . I couldn't do it all myself. I couldn't be everything to everybody. I didn't even know who *I* was, or what *I* wanted. What if I didn't want children? I mean, I was so . . . I don't know what I'm talking about . . . I think maybe I should go. I think I'd better leave.

There's silence for a rather long time—but the tape is still rolling. Neither one of them says anything. The soft buzz continues and what sounds like Dr. Sullivan shifting papers on his desk. The conversation has stopped, yet I don't hear my mother get up and leave the room. I don't hear the door open or close; no one is saying "'Bye," "Have a nice week-end," "Good luck catchin' the big one," or anything. I can only imagine that they are both just sitting there silently. I look over at Dr. Sullivan for some kind of explanation, but his head is tilted upward; he's staring in front of him at the inter-section where the ceiling meets the wall. I turn to see what he's looking at, but there's nothing there. He doesn't shift his attention.

I'm about to say something just as the tape resumes. My mother's voice starts up again. She hasn't left.

> **Elaine:** Of course I want to help her, Dr. Sullivan. It's just that—(crying begins) that she loved JD so much. Maybe even too much, if that's possible. That probably sounds crazy to you. The irony of it all is that Caroline thought JD didn't love her back. She saw JD's need to be an individual as a personal affront—but JD just wanted to be her own person. It never had anything to do with Caroline. In fact, she loved Caroline more than Caroline would ever believe, but it would never be good enough. JD thought she'd have to prove herself to Caroline for the rest of her life. That Caroline would forever judge her and never believe her allegiance. Caroline is just an incredibly sensitive and needy girl. I just think she's going to be lost without JD. I'm really . . . afraid . . . (crying again).
>
> If she wanted to be like someone, why couldn't she have chosen *me* instead? I would've shown her how to be exactly like me . . . I would have . . . Didn't they want to be like me . . . either of them?

Whoa. I feel light-headed. I try to gather myself during their silence. I don't want him to stop the tape. I stare at the floor. She blows her nose. Dr. Sullivan doesn't say anything to her. He waits. She resumes a moment later.

> **Elaine:** It doesn't matter anymore. You've got to help her. She's complicated. You must have sensed that by now? You *have* sensed that by now?

Dr. Sullivan: She's . . . multilayered.

Elaine: Yes, multilayered, *yes*, indeed. Excellent.

Dr. Sullivan: And with each layer that's uncovered we're able to understand her more, and, in so doing, help her.

Elaine: Of course.

She sniffles. There is another period of silence. Then she clears her throat.

Elaine: When JD was about eight, I believe, she hurt herself on her bike. Actually, she was racing with some friends on the asphalt in the parking area of the middle school, which is across the street from our house. Our neighbors, the Krakows, their son and daughter were there, and Caroline of course, and the lot of them were playing across the street on their bikes. They made some kind of obstacle course or some such nonsense as children do. They needed to ride with speed—that was the point. JD was athletic. Make no mistake about that. She got that from me. I was on the track team—varsity—of course you may have suspected with my long legs.

Dr. Sullivan: Is that so?

Elaine: Anyway, JD wasn't competitive in any way. She liked sports for the sake of sports. Not so much for the competition—to beat someone or to win. I don't see the sense in that, but that was JD. It was JD's turn. There was a makeshift ramp they concocted. First she had to build up speed by biking in circles, which I suppose got JD a little dizzy, and when she got to the ramp, she lost her equilibrium. Because she was going fast, she was thrown in the air and came down on her face. JD broke her nose and chipped a tooth.

Caroline was screaming, that I remember distinctly because I could hear her from the kitchen window, clear across the street. I knew something ghastly had happened. There was blood everywhere, and Caroline bounded back to the house, panicked, to get me. She was distraught.

For days after the incident, Caroline was uncharacteristically quiet, pensive. She kept to herself, spent a good deal of time in the basement.

Several days later, I called the girls for dinner. JD was upstairs in her room doing homework. Caroline was in the basement. There was a playroom down there when the girls were little, with their toys and what not. So, I didn't think anything strange about it. But after I yelled downstairs several times to get her for dinner, and she didn't respond, I started to get annoyed. Mostly because I needed the girls to eat early. It was mah-jong night at our house. Dinner had to be cleared before I could set up. The ladies were coming at seven. I was already running late. I must have called her three or four times. I sent JD down to get her, and the next thing I knew, JD was screaming, "Caroline's dead!"

I hurried down the stairs. I thought I could have a heart attack. That's when it occurred to me—what if I *do* have a heart attack? What'll happen then? How will I get to the hospital? Would JD know to call an ambulance?

Well, thankfully, I didn't have a heart attack. Though looking back on it, it's astonishing I didn't. I found Caroline in the workroom, passed out on the cement floor in a pool of blood. She'd taken one of Walter's hammers and struck herself in the teeth. I still can't believe she could do something like that. But children do the darnedest things, don't they? She must've took more than one whack at her tooth, or else the one whack was mighty hard, because, as she told me later, while her intention was to chip one, she ended up knocking two teeth clear out of her head. We found them in the blood next to her nose. Caroline lost so much blood. She must have passed out from the shock of it all.

I'm not sure how I survived that.

We didn't have mah-jong that night, of course. I had to clean up the mess in the basement when we came back from the hospital. The blood and the teeth. The E.R. doctor said we should've brought the teeth with us. They could have stuck them back in if we were fast enough. But I didn't bring them. Didn't even think of it. That night I tossed the teeth in the garbage. Only to find Caroline rummaging through the pail to dig them out the next morning. Strange, don't you think, that she wanted to keep the teeth?

We had to reschedule mah-jong for the following month. All that good food gone to waste.

I always made a smashing party, you know. It was said that my parties were the best in town. I was known for my deviled eggs. It was my signature dish—though Caroline hated when I made them. She couldn't stand the smell of hard-boiled eggs. They were like none other because of a certain ingredient . . . no one's ever been able to figure it out. But . . . well, I'll tell you—if you'd like. Now that I've got you curious. Chili paste. The Orientals had it. They had a market a few towns away from us. You could find the oddest things there. Well . . . I guess the secret's out now!

She slaps her hands on her lap and chuckles.

Dr. Sullivan: And Caroline?

Elaine: Hmm? Oh, Caroline. Well, she's got two fake teeth in there now. But that didn't happen for a while. The gums needed to heal first. That next day when she woke up, she sprang out of bed like it was Christmas morning. I was putting laundry away when she ran to the bathroom. She got up close to the mirror and opened her mouth real wide—I don't know how she could look at herself that way. With her eyes as big as saucers, she thrust her fists in the air like runners do when they cross the finish line. She said, "I did it. Just like JD's." She was beaming. Blood on her cheeks and nightgown. The thought of her bloody, toothless mouth still makes me cringe. She walked out of the bathroom saying, "Twins forever."

Sure enough, she chipped a third tooth. Cheeky, don't you think?

The school guidance counselor suggested we take her to talk to someone, you know, a psychologist. But we never did.

Wally wouldn't have it.

CHAPTER FOURTEEN

Wednesday, September 27, 2006, 7:51 p.m.

The first thing I do in the car is smack down the sun visor. I slide my finger across my top teeth. They look like the rest of them. It's impossible to tell if they're implants. I give them a tug. Solid. I'd remember something like that, wouldn't I? I shut the visor and my mouth, which has been hanging open for the last thirty minutes. Maybe it's my imagination, but I start to taste blood in my mouth. I swipe my tongue around my upper teeth. My gums are throbbing. And I taste blood.

The little girl my mom spoke of—I desperately want to protect her. But I can't. It's too late. She needed . . . something. Why couldn't anyone see that? It didn't seem like anyone understood her or took the time to try.

This much I know. She's not little anymore.

My childhood was screwed up. Thinking about my mother's story makes my chest hurt. Or maybe it's my heart. It feels bruised. Or hollow. Something. I can't quite identify it.

It wouldn't really surprise me if someday someone told me a part of my heart was missing. Like if it showed up on an x-ray or a sonogram not fully formed or developed. A heart with holes. Maybe a heart grows only when it feels love. And when pain replaces love, holes replace heart.

How was it not clear to my mother that intervention was imperative? Overriding my father's denial was a no-brainer. "Cheeky?" That's *it?*

Dr. Sullivan knew better than to ask me anything once the tape stopped. He slotted me into a cancelled appointment on Friday. He said we'd talk about it then. It would give me an opportunity to process. Or not come back.

The truth is I remember some of the things she said. I didn't walk in remembering them, but as my mother told those stories, snippets of memories emerged. Like mushrooms pushing through wet grass.

The entire way home, I drive in a fog. I don't even remember what I went there seeking. But it wasn't this. I never considered that seeing Dr. Sullivan would be a process and I'd be putting myself in the eye of the storm. He said this would happen, but I didn't believe him. I never considered there'd be session*s*. Plural. How stupid. Moving one step forward and five steps back was not on my radar.

The fog from the car follows me into the house. Lilly and Tessa are already asleep. Andy isn't home yet. After I pay Mrs. H, I go straight upstairs and rinse the bloody taste out of my mouth, then crawl into bed.

Thursday, September 28, 2006, 7:30 a.m.

I'M GRATEFUL ANDY has already left for work and I don't have to lie about my night. Lying over the phone will be marginally easier. Anyway, it's only one innocent lie to help me keep my eye on the goal until I get my life back on track. I'm doing this for us.

In the middle of the afternoon, he calls and wakes me out of a sleep on the couch. After I dropped the girls at school this morning, I made a concerted effort to stay out of the den and off the computer. I sat on the couch to put my head down for a minute. Now half the day is gone. Andy called to remind me about tonight's event for the Children's Hospital. Nothing could've been further from my mind. The thought of having to take a shower, dress in nice clothes, and socialize with Sylvie and George is almost revolting. I wish I could muster the energy for a shower. But I can't, and I don't care that I can't. No one will notice anyway—I'll just pull my hair into a ponytail and sweep my bangs over my forehead.

Thursday, September 28, 2006, 7:05 p.m.

SYLVIE WALKS THROUGH our front door looking fantastic as always. Her husband, George, and Andy are old college friends. They hadn't seen each other in years, and three years ago Andy saw him at the grocery store. George and Sylvie had coincidentally settled in Farhaven too. That's when Andy and George rekindled their friendship and have been like two tines on a fork ever since.

"You look great, Sylvie." It's true. Her long, prematurely silver-grey hair doesn't detract from her youthful features—clear eyes, a streamlined nose, Chiclets smile. She doesn't need a speck of makeup, and only wears a slick of raspberry gloss over her lips.

"I'm sorry I can't say the same about you. What the hell happened? What's with the hair? Looks like you're gonna clean out the garage." She has a wonderful ability of saying exactly what's on her mind—almost like a five-year-old. It must be incredibly liberating.

She glides like an eel through the foyer toward the kitchen. "Please get me a drink, that man is a maniac," she says. "Fifty miles per hour on the side streets! The entire time I'm in that car, I pray a cop will pull us over. Andy's driving tonight, sorry, or I'm not going. I don't even care at this point if I miss the fortune-teller—even if she did save Patrice's life. I told you that story, didn't I? You know, the premonition about her ex. Remember?"

My face scrunches.

"I'll just send the Children's Hospital a check and call it a day. I don't need to go to this thing that badly," she says emphatically over her shoulder toward George. George steps inside when Sylvie adds, "And I'll take a *cab* home. Really, George, take that thing to Germany, will you. I think I'm going to get sick." She heads to the powder room.

Andy comes from behind me, chuckling, and gives Sylvie a quick kiss on the cheek as she walks by. Then he extends his hand to George. "Haven't changed a bit, have ya, George? Thank God for that, or I wouldn't recognize anyone around here."

Maybe he would recognize someone around here if he could string two straight days together at home in the last month. He knows I don't want to go tonight. I have a terrible headache, and I'm spent. And I didn't want to leave the girls with a sitter again. We're all hanging by a very loose thread, and what we need is family time. In a place other than the Emergency Room.

But the wife of one of Andy's customers is chairing the hospital fundraiser, and he thought "it would not be favorably looked upon" if we miss it.

Sylvie emerges from the bathroom and meets me in the hall. We walk toward the kitchen together. "I'm sorry we're late, hun, but I had to squeeze in a bikini wax, and my regular girl in New York is on vacation so I went to that place in town. Do yourself a favor, never get a wax in the suburbs—you'll be walking like a cowboy for a week." Her eyes lock on mine, as she peers over red framed glasses that she lets slide down her nose, then they sweep up and down. "You gonna change?"

"Who, me? I . . . was gonna wear this." I look down to see what I have on.

"Really? It's . . . a little . . ." Sylvie looks as though her nose has come too close to a wedge of Roquefort. "You okay?" she asks as I hand her a glass of wine. Now she's eyeing the side of my face. She brushes away the hair that's fallen out of my ponytail with her fingers. "Did someone hit you?" she asks quietly.

"Hit me? *No.*" At first I think she's crazy. Then I remember the monkey. I forgot all about that thing. It seems like months ago. "Of course no one hit me." Well, that's something to be thankful for, I guess. "I just fell."

"Sheesh, Caroline, you're a mess," she says quietly.

"I'm *fine.* How are you doing?"

She pauses for a second and checks out my face, then takes her finger and gently smooths out the makeup around my bruise. "Apart from my crotch, I'm okay," she says. "I'm just glad to see you guys. I *think*." Her eyebrows go up. She squeezes my hand and turns the corner into the breakfast nook where the girls are finishing up dinner with Rachel, their babysitter.

"Hiya girls! Oh my *God*, what the hell—*heck* happened to you two? Sheesh, have you all taken up roller derby?"

"Sylvie!" The girls say in unison, running over to smother her with affection.

Tessa's lip is still swollen. I need to call her doctor about that.

"Are you two all right? Good grief, you all look horrible," she says, pulling away from a bear hug to take a closer look at them.

"*Sylvie*—the girls look *fine*," I correct her.

"Do you want to sign my sling, Sylvie, or you can draw something if you want?"

"Sure, Lilligans, but why don't you work on that chicken first."

"You girls go finish your dinner. Sylvie will sign it later, when we get home."

Tessa looks at me, "Are you going to change, Mommy?"

I wish everyone would stop asking me that. "Go finish dinner, Tessa."

Sylvie pats Lilly on her bottom and says, "We'll chat later, okay?" She turns to me. "We should probably go—I'm not missing Madame Troia." She fingers through her handbag looking for something. She swipes on some lip gloss without a mirror and holds it out to me. "Want some? Might help."

"All right . . ."

"I told you that it's the same psychic that Patrice saw, right?"

I hope Andy doesn't expect me to be social tonight.

"I *told* you that, right, Caroline?"

"Huh?"

"Are you even listening to me?"

"What? Yes. Of course I'm listening."

"This is the *one*—*the* Psychic to the Stars. Patrice met her at a movie premiere at the Tribeca Film Festival. All of them were getting read, DeNiro, DiCaprio, all of them. Tad was there, too, with his new girlfriend, LuLu, who j'adore! Thank God he got rid of that frigid Sinclair. Gimme a break with that name."

What is she talking about? I nod generously. I seldom know who she's referring to. I've never met, nor heard of Patrice, Tad, LuLu, or Sinclair. I used to think I was supposed to know them, like they were people she'd introduced me to, or worse, celebrities that I should know from *People* magazine. But then I got to know Sylvie. These are people in her various circles who I've never met and probably never will. But that doesn't stop her from talking about them, sometimes quite intimately. It seems she rarely brings up the same people twice.

"Listen, Sylvie, I need to tell you something. I know we haven't seen you guys in a while, but Andy and I have to make tonight a cameo."

"How come?"

"We had a hellish week. The girls are banged up, and Andy's just home from London, and he's been working late . . ."

"And?"

"And what?"

"Honey, really? If I can't tell you, no one will. You look like a homeless person. Who just escaped an asylum."

I look down again to see myself below the chin. I didn't think I looked that bad. I'd be offended if I had the energy. But, I gotta hand it to her, she's getting warm with crazy hobo. She continues without waiting for a response, "I'm being nice. Believe me. Listen, I'm just concerned, that's all. I've never seen you so—like this. Your hair, your face, your . . . this thing you're wearing. What *is* this thing you're wearing?"

"Caroline, you girls ready to go?" Andy calls from the living room where the guys are smoking the putrid-smelling Cubans he squirrels away.

"Shit—that means separate cars." Sylvie looks at me nervously and then chugs the rest of her wine. "I swear he'll end up killing me some day in that car. If he needed a mid-life crisis, I would've preferred a girlfriend."

"Why don't I drive us? Let them go together. We have to take two cars anyway," I suggest.

"Brilliant." She grabs both of my arms. "You may not be a looker tonight, but you still got it upstairs."

She's as cold as tundra now.

I walk over to the table to kiss the girls good-bye.

"Rachel, we're only going to stay an hour, so we'll be home before the girls go to bed.

"Okay, Mrs. Thompson. Is it okay for them to watch TV after they finish their homework?"

"Um, sure."

"TV on a Thursday?" Lilly pops out of her seat.

"Shush, Lilly," Tessa grabs her arm and pulls her back down.

"Today's Thursday?" I say, while I walk out of the kitchen. I grab my handbag from the bench in the front hall. Andy puts his arm around me and whispers in my ear.

"You okay?"

"Why does everyone keep asking me that?"

"Well, you don't look like yourself."

"I have a headache. I'm beat, and all I want to do is put my pajamas on and take a bath."

"In that order?" He squeezes me and says, "Come on, Caroline, we have to go, we've been through this."

"All right then, let's go. One drink and we're out of there. Sylvie is coming with me. I'm going to take your car. You guys meet us there."

"Are you sure you want to drive with Sylvie? I mean, we haven't been out together in a while."

"She hates driving in the Porsche. You can catch up with George."

He kisses me on the cheek.

Sylvie slides onto the leather seat of Andy's car. "Did you hear what happened to George's niece Emma? She's in kindergarten at Lincoln School—oh, wait, don't Tessa and Lilly go there?"

"Yes . . ." I say tentatively.

"Oh, then you know about the lockdown. Well, it's because of Emma, can you believe that? Emma's the girl they were looking for."

"What do you mean, *looking for*? The girls didn't tell me about a lock down. When was *that*?"

"Uh . . . I think it was Tuesday? I don't know for sure— maybe George remembers. Ask the girls. They'll know.

"It started with a fire—*alleged* fire. Let's just say all the alarms were blaring, but it wasn't a drill, so they thought it was real."

That's the day I volunteered at the library. My stomach muscles tighten. "Oh, yeah," I offer, "the girls told me about a fire drill. They didn't mention a lock down." I coax a tennis ball down my throat.

"By the way, I got this story from George's sister, Donna, and you know how she is."

I have no idea how she is.

"You might have to fill in the blanks with someone less sketchy." Sylvie turns her head to look out the window and points to the restaurant on the corner of Mountain Avenue, "They have great fondue. You should bring Lilly and Tessa, they'd love it . . .

"Anyway, where was I . . . oh yeah, so all the kids were gushing out of the building." Sylvie turns to me and says, "I can't believe your girls didn't tell you about this, it was a very big deal according to Donna. All the teachers were freaking, telling the kids it wasn't a drill, that it was real. *Totally* calm and collected." At a red light, I look over at Sylvie rolling her eyes. "So, of course, Emma, who, don't forget, is still trauma-tized by the fire they had in their house last year, was petrified. Instead of leaving the building with the rest of her class, she hid under a desk in the library. But her teacher didn't notice she was missing until she got the kids outside and counted them. That's when Mrs. Asshole Teacher went into panic mode because she couldn't go back to look for Emma until the fire-men got there and searched the building for the fire. She knew her ass was grass. Once they got the thumbs up to return to the building there was a lockdown so the building could be searched for Emma. In the meantime, they alerted the police to search the neighborhood in case she walked off the school grounds, or worse—was taken. Do you love this? That's when they called Donna.

"After all that, they found that poor kid trembling under a desk in the library. And get this one—George told me that the principal called Donna yesterday to tell her there was no actual fire. That the alarm was pulled by someone, and it was top priority to find out who did it. This is the kicker: the principal asked Donna if she thought Emma could have pulled the alarm and then hid under a desk.

"*Caroline!*" Sylvie grabs my arm and digs her nails through my clothes into my skin. "*Where the hell are you going?* Stay on your side of the road. This ain't London."

I quickly veer back onto the right side of the road and say a silent prayer that I didn't hit the oncoming car.

"Caroline—what the *hell?*"

Sylvie's eyes burn holes into the side of my face.

"Pull over, honey. I'm driving."

"Sylvie. I'm not pulling over. I'm sorry. I'm fine. I just . . . wandered for a second. I'm back on track. Trust me."

"Jesus. That scared the shit out of me. I can't believe I'm saying this, but I might actually be safer with George tonight."

"That poor girl. I feel terrible."

"Who, Emma? Yeah. It's screwed up. Seriously, don't let it ruin your night. You don't need anything more to worry about." She reaches out to touch my arm. "It's not like it's your fault."

For a weeknight, there's a good turnout for the charity dinner. Tonight's profits go directly to the High Hopes Children's Hospital.

It's a warm, starlit evening out on the Pine Terrace where

cocktails are being served. The sound of the three-piece band floats in the air like big, puffy cumulus clouds. At the edge of the terrace you can see the lawn dotted with tables dressed in white linen awaiting dinner. The silver cutlery winks back at the stars. The staff calmly scurries to have the chowder and beef medallions ready for two hundred fat wallets.

I make sure to say hello to Andy's customer and his wife and introduce them to Sylvie, who declares them the most underwhelming people she's ever met before leaving my side to stake out the party. I'm not at all hungry, but I have a few bruschetta to keep myself busy and take the last sip of my Chardonnay.

Andy and I agree it's fine to leave once we bid on a few things at the auction table, so I search for Sylvie to say good-night. She's standing in the middle of a never-ending train of giddy women spanning the ballroom. They look like little kids at an ice cream truck. Except for Sylvie, who looks out of place in this crowd. Most people find it surprising that Sylvie and George live in the suburbs. For one thing, they don't have children, and they both work in New York and carry city sophistication around like a badge of honor. My theory is that Sylvie needs to feel different from everyone else, and that's what the suburbs provide her.

"Hey, Sylvie."

"*Oh*–there you are. Come here. Get in front of me while no one's looking."

"For what? I can't. Andy and I are going. I just came to say good night."

"*What?* What do you mean? You're not having a reading?"

"What reading?"

"This is the line for Madame Troia. I told you, Caroline.

I knew you weren't listening to me. You know you've had this far-off, la-la-land look on your face the whole night. What's up with you?"

I sigh heavily. "Yes, Madame Troia, I know. No, I'm not having a reading. We're going."

"Now?! You have to leave *now?* I don't think you get who she is. I don't think you do. How do you think Jennifer found out about Brad and Angelina? Don't be a fool. Here, stand in front of me, I'll let you cut. You're not missing this."

"I'm not in the mood, Sylvie. Really."

The din of chatter from the front of the line swells and ripples back to us.

"What do you mean she's taking a break?" someone in front of us blurts out nearly inciting a riot. The crowd waiting for Madam Troia is on the verge of a coup. She's just announced she's taking a break because of a difficult reading.

"That's an outrage. I've been standing here for almost an hour," Sylvie growls to no one in particular. "Hold our spot, will you, hun," she says to the woman behind her in line. "I've gotta tinkle."

I walk with her to the bathroom, where there are a few women already on line. I get behind someone in a grey pin-stripe suit and short, cropped hair. I swear it's a man, but no one is acting strange about his/her presence. Sylvie finishes up a conversation with someone behind her, turns around, and grabs my arm with the intention, I can only assume, of removing it from its socket.

"*Jesus Christ*—look who's in front of you!"

"It's a guy, right?"

"Oh, excuse me," Sylvie says to the guy in front of me. Leave it to Sylvie to oust him. What guy would want to stand on line in a woman's bathroom, anyway? Sylvie maneuvers her way in front of me.

I catch a glimpse of myself in the floor-length mirror to my right and take in my surroundings through its reflection. Across the rose-tinted bathroom is a row of little vanity seats wearing strapless, taffeta ball gowns. The room smells of old-lady perfume; the candle-lit sconces cast a soft glow. I'm standing ankle-deep in plush pink carpeting. All of the ladies are talking in hushed tones. It's like I'm standing in someone's dream.

I look back at the mirror. The monkey is hardly recognizable. As a primate, anyway. It's down to a prune-shaped bruise in the hollow of my cheek, and the gash above my eyebrow has shrunk and scabbed over.

"This is my friend Caroline," Sylvie says as I turn my gaze away from the mirror and shake the hand that's outstretched before me.

I turn to look at my watch while saying, "Nice to meet you." I just want to go to the bathroom and get out of here. If my bladder weren't ready to burst, I would be home by now. The line is taking an eternity. Andy's probably sent out an APB already. I lift my arm to check my watch and realize Sylvie's friend has not let go of my hand. I look up now, this time with vested interest. It's the guy in the suit. But it's not a guy. He's a she. And she doesn't seem at all uncomfortable about still holding my hand. "I'm sorry I didn't get your name," I say.

"*Caroline*, what's wrong with you," Sylvie says with an embarrassed chuckle. "I'm so sorry Madame Troia—my friend is a little preoccupied." She then kicks me in the shin. My reflex to grab my aching shin is waylaid since this person still has my hand. "Caroline was just leaving, but I told her she couldn't go without meeting you. Did I tell you that you practically saved my friend's life? Patrice Summer. You warned her about her husband—*ex-husband* now—at the movie premiere at the Tribeca Film Festival. Do you remember—oh, of course, you *must*. You were right on the money with that one."

My thoughts are having a three-way tug of war: Why would a psychic choose to take a bathroom break if she "*knew*" there'd be a line; why did my so-called friend just kick me in the leg; and how exactly am I going to reclaim my right hand? I can't believe this is Madame Troia. She looks like my accountant.

"You are not staying for a readingk?" Madame Troia breaks into my internal monologue while she lassos my eyes with hers.

"No, I'm afraid I can't." She still has my hand, now sandwiched between both of hers. "I really must go—" I turn my head away from her, and this time I move my whole body to the right so she'll have to let go. She doesn't.

She leans into me and says, "Do not believe all that you read."

CHAPTER FIFTEEN

Thursday, September 28, 2006, 9:10 p.m.

What? Was she talking to me?

"Excuse me?" I say.

This prompts Sylvie to drape her arm across my back and pop her head in between us so she doesn't miss anything.

"You will be deceived," Madame Troia says matter-of-factly.

I look at Sylvie and then back at Madame T. Is she doing her thing right now, right here in the ladies' room? She remains stone-faced. She hasn't moved a hair, and it looks like she hasn't even moved her mouth.

"Soon you will discover something you have known all alongk to be true. Other things you think you know, but are wrongk."

A bathroom stall opens up, and the lady in the suit turns her back to me, walks into the stall, and closes the door. And just like that—she's gone. Not a "Do svidaniya" or even a "Good luck with that one!" Nothingk.

"Well, that was bizarre," I say out loud to myself while

trying to figure out what just happened. I smooth the skin on my arms to quiet my bristled hair.

"*Caroline*, oh my God, did you hear what she said? 'You will be deceived.' Isn't that fantastic? 'You'll find out something you always knew.' Was that it? Do you remember what she said? I mean, I didn't even know she was reading you. I thought she was just shootin' the breeze. Damn, she's good. No cards, no nothin'.'"

I hightail it out of the bathroom without peeing. There's no way I'm going to let her hold my hand again, especially on her way *out* of the bathroom. My thighs are squeezed against each other the whole way home so I don't have an accident in the car. Andy knows not to talk to me when my bladder is ready to burst. Or rather, not to expect me to talk to him. All my concentration must be funneled into not peeing in my pants.

I've never believed in psychics or mediums of any sort. Not tarot cards, wishbones, black cats, or horoscopes. Not fallen eyelashes, ladybugs, or even the Super 8 ball. Not even paper origami fortune-tellers my friends and I made when we were kids.

I don't even believe in birthday candles.

I've always believed I'm in control of my destiny. I certainly don't go around blaming my zodiac sign for my mistakes.

Friday, September 29, 2006, 7:30 a.m.

MEG CALLED LAST night to see if Lilly and Tessa were available for a play date with Delia after school today, which is perfect. I'll be home from Sullivan's in time to pick them up by 5:30 and won't have to explain my whereabouts to anyone.

Sylvie's story about the lockdown weighs heavily on my mind. As if I didn't feel guilty enough for pulling that goddamn panic inciter in the first place. It has to psychologically damage a five-year-old in the process. Now she's one of the suspects. Then, I had to deal with the hocus-pocus of Madame Crystal Ball. "You are right about some stuff, and wrong about other stuff"; gimme a break. Although as much as I'd like to block out that whole thing, it was kind of comforting to hear, "Don't believe everything you read."

I try to think back on my life when it was normal. A week ago. What did I do with myself? If not for dodging Internet accusations, petty crimes at the grocery store, racing to the emergency room, and elementary school misdemeanors, what would I do? To think I used to cut coupons.

As I drive the girls to school, I'm preoccupied with my session today with Dr. Sullivan. I didn't get the blood test he requested to check my B12 levels. I'm not going to Dr. Kriete's, that's for sure. Her office has left two messages for me already this week, but I don't care. Maybe I can find a clinic around Dr. Sullivan's office.

I pull the car up to the school and spot Gabrielle in the distance. She's walking in my direction with the smugness of someone who's got news to hawk. It's all in her shoulders. Perhaps she's already tossed her gossip grenade to a bunch of unsuspecting innocents. She could be striding out of a cloud of shrapnel right now, leaving a ballet of gaped mouths behind. She better keep her distance from me. I can't handle her when my backbone's *intact*. She couldn't be frothing with news of Sylvie's niece, could she? That little girl was in the library the entire time. Did she see me? Does she know who I am? Could she have turned me in?

I should've had my neighbor bring the girls to school today.

It's 8:35, and the bell will ring in five minutes. The crossing guard nearly has a stroke blowing her whistle at kids weaving dangerously through cars. Others zigzag across the school lawn. Horns blare. Lilly and Tessa are jabbering about the bake sale and clamoring for money. Every morning, my senses are assaulted. My body braces, on the ride over, in expectation of the onslaught. I have to get here earlier, before anyone arrives. When it's desolate and quiet, and I won't run into anyone.

Getting closer by the nanosecond, Gabrielle takes long, emphatic, cross-country-skiing strides toward my car. Anxiety bubbles under my skin. Out of the corner of my eye, another figure appears, as determined as Gabrielle, walking in my direction from the other side of the school. It's Mrs. Stanton. She zeroes in on me, and her index finger soars into the air to say *hold on there*. I've successfully dodged that finger for three days now.

My anxiety is foaming.

Mrs. Stanton swings her arms for momentum like a speed skater. The best I can hope for is that she and Gabrielle collide on their way over here to incriminate and irk me, respectively.

Breathe in. Breathe out. I thank my lucky stars for the school drop-off lane; it keeps you in a constant state of motion. You just pull up alongside the parked row of cars at the curb in front of the school entrance, your kids jump out, you close the door, and you're on your way. Virtually no interaction with anyone. No explaining, confessing, defending, apologizing. It's impossible to linger. It's against the rules. Gotta keep moving. I'll be out of here before you can say, "Arrest that woman."

If this car in front of me would just get going. In my rearview mirror there is a train of cars lining up behind me, and more filling in to the left. *Wait.* Why are they filling in to my left? *Shit.* I'm not in the drop-off lane. I'm in the park lane. Well, how the hell did that happen? And as if that's not enough, to pick like a vulture at my already tattered central nervous system, the car to my left is idling without a driver. It can only belong to the woman running across the lawn with a Batman lunchbox yelling "Kyle!"

I'm trapped. I'm fucking trapped.

I can't believe this. There's no way I'm gonna watch Gabrielle slither her Burberry-ed body over here to trap me. Or worse. Mrs. Stanton will have just enough time to alert the police of my whereabouts for a quick arrest. I'm sweating through my shirt.

So much for a painful collision; they've just joined forces, and they're approaching together. They might as well link arms. They keep shading their eyes like they can't see anything in front of them. That's a good thing. The sun is slamming my windshield. Another good thing. They might not see me sitting here. I can't believe that I haven't prepared for this. I mean certainly I had to expect someone would talk to me about that morning. There must be a way to identify the exact alarm that was pulled. They could have fingerprints, for Christ's sake. Can you plead the fifth to a principal? Would that be incriminating? I'm having really horrible thoughts right now. Really, really horrible. If I throw Sylvie's niece under the bus, I'm in worse shape than I thought I was.

I either need to abandon my car right now and run the other way, or . . . where is Kyle's mother, for God's sake?

I can't consider leaving the car because if I stand up, I will pee my pants. I have to hide. I'm in the park lane, so it won't seem odd that the car's empty when they get here.

I quickly slide my seat back as far as it will go. I adjust the cruise control so the wheel sticks out to the max. Then I slip into the little cavity under the dashboard. It's not as easy as it sounds. As I lower myself to the floor, I swaddle myself with my arms, squeeze my toes under the brake pedal, and stick my head between my knees. They will never see me.

I could really use some oxygen, but my stomach has no room to inflate. Short breaths. I definitely won't pee in this position. My bladder is somewhere under my armpit. There's a frenzied tapping at the window. Shit.

"Caroline? Caroline! Is that *you?*" Jesus. "What are you *doing* down there? Caroline? *I can see you."* *Shit.* Does she have to be so goddamn loud? "Girls, why is your mom *hiding* under the steering wheel?"

Girls?? Oh good *God, I thought they jumped out already. Jeez . . .* they're in the car? No *way . . .* for God's *sake. "Girls,"* I say in a loud whisper without turning my head, which I can't do anyway, *"are you guys still here?!" Geez,* does Gabrielle have to announce to everyone in North America that I'm hiding from her? She's making a *spectacle* of herself, and she's embarrassing the girls. Moving in millimeter increments, I lift my head. Lilly and Tessa (who is red-faced) are waiting. I whisper, "I didn't think you were still back there."

"What are you doing down there? Are you really hiding from Mrs. Callis, Mom?" Lilly asks, half-smirking.

"You told us to wait while you looked for money for the bake sale. Remember, you said, 'Let me pull over and get you some money.'"

"I thought you dropped money on the floor and crawled down there to get it," Tessa adds.

"Mom, we're late. The lines went in."

"Uh . . . yes, uh, let me . . ." I try to move my head. At least Lilly has the good sense not to remind me that I forgot to *bake* something for the bake sale. "Okay, all right, will you—I . . . is she still standing there?"

"Yeah, Mom, she's still there, and she looks sorta angry," Tessa whispers.

I slowly unknot my body from this ridiculous idea. "Just looking for my contact!"

"You wear contacts?" Gabrielle is still talking through the window. "Well, that's a new one on me. How could you find it like that?"

I work myself back up on to the seat and go through my handbag to find some guilt money for the girls.

Lilly grabs onto the front seat from behind.

Tessa asks, "Mom, do you have my lunchbox up there—I don't have it."

"I don't have mine, either."

"Oh, jeez, did I not make your lunch? *God* . . . okay, that's all right, here's some money." I look in my wallet. "Buy something big. You can have dessert for lunch, and then tonight, you'll have lunch for dinner . . . something like that . . ." I grab two bills. "Here—here's some money. I don't know what the big deal is. I used to have dessert all the time when I was a kid. Especially at school. And a lot of it."

I turn to the girls who are facing each other in what looks like an eyeball-bulging contest. Then they see the money in my hand.

"Five dollars each!" they say in unison. They look at each

other, and Lilly shrugs and says, "Works for me. You're the best mommy in the world!"

Lilly gives me a hug and asks softly, "Do you wear contacts?"

"Not really," I whisper.

"Oh, good one, Mom. Love you!"

I stretch my neck to give Tessa a kiss as she starts to back out of the car, then she closes the back door with gusto.

Gabrielle is still there.

She sticks her fingers into the slender window opening, then shifts her eyes at me, thinks better of it, and retrieves her fingers.

"*Caroline*," Gabrielle taunts through the crack in the window, "I just discovered something *very* interesting, ya know . . ."

Mrs. Stanton is nowhere in sight. She must have gone inside once the bell rang.

" . . .something *you* may want to know—"

My foot presses the gas pedal, and I pull away from the curb. Gabrielle lets out a screech that could wake the dead.

"Can't chat, Gabrielle, I'm in a terrible hurry—" I yell back at her while keeping my eyes on the road ahead. I glance in the rear view mirror. She's waving her arms frantically.

"*Are you crazy, Caroline? I was leaning on your car!! Caroline, did you hear me? I have something to tell you!*"

After I return home, I sit in the kitchen and stare at the clock above the stove. The morning moves like a boulder. I figure I should just start driving to Dr. Sullivan's office since I can't bear waiting.

No other patients will be there because he'll be coming from an outside appointment. Sullivan's receptionist has the day off to attend a funeral. I was instructed to ring the bell.

When I arrive, there's a yellow sticky note stuck to the door.

"C.S.: I'm on an important phone call. I'll be off soon. I'll come get you when I'm finished. I hope you don't mind waiting in your car. Thank you for your patience. F.S."

After about fifteen minutes, the office door opens and he hurries out to greet me. He's flustered. He's walking and talking faster than last time. He doesn't look me in the eye even once.

He hastens back to his office and jumps right in before we even sit down. As much as I admire his waste-no-time approach, I'm slightly put off by his abruptness. The honeymoon doesn't last very long around here. It wouldn't hurt him to throw me a "How ya doin'?" or "Nice shoes," or something.

"Caroline, after our last session, I took some time to review old notes and transcripts, and I've chosen a few that I think will be helpful to you in piecing together the past. If at any time it becomes overwhelming or disturbing for you to listen to the tapes and you wish me to stop them, you must let me know, otherwise I'll let them play. It's sometimes through an episode of heightened emotion, as tumultuous as it may be, that you arrive at crucial realizations. I think you know now, after your last visit, that this isn't going to be easy. Remember, we don't need to listen to these old tapes at all. There are other ways that we can proceed with your therapy."

He folds his hands together before continuing. "I'd like to leave some time at the end of our session today to talk about what you're thinking—your reaction to what you've heard. We really didn't get a chance to do that last time."

I sit not so patiently and nod; I don't interject or distract him. I just want to get to the tape.

"Caroline, before we get started, I'd like to ask you if what you heard from the tape the other day, from your mother, was news to you? Or do you have memory of those events?"

I exhale deeply and collect my thoughts. "Uh . . ." I breathe heavily again. I don't know where to start. "Well, I—I, it's—impossible to me. It doesn't make any sense. I mean, am I living in a make-believe world?" I check myself, my tone. I don't want to get emotional. "I keep thinking, 'What's happened to me?'" I shift in my seat. "There are gigantic holes in my memory. Whole parts of my life. How can that be? I don't remember being overweight. I don't." I close my eyes for a second and inhale. "I remember being teased by kids when I was young. Why they teased me, I couldn't tell you. But I know I used to always try to be ready with a comeback, you know what I mean," I look over at Dr. Sullivan. "So I wouldn't get embarrassed when they said something that hurt my feelings. It made me feel a little tougher, even though I was on the verge of tears. I remember, sometimes if I didn't have anyone to play with after school, I'd stay in my room and write down 'comeback' ideas until I came up with something really good. Something clever that would make them leave me alone. It became sort of a game. Something I could control. It protected me.

"As for my mom, I guess I always had a sense that she didn't like me very much. So that's been confirmed. But why? Is it because I was overweight and she was ashamed of me? I don't know—maybe that was part of it.

"But hearing her say that JD and I—" My thighs begin to tremble, and my teeth. I squeeze my leg muscles to force them to be still. "To hear her say we weren't twins—well, that—that can't be true. It just can't. There's no way I could have made that up. I have a memory so clear I could reach out and touch it. It's of two little girls in my kindergarten class. They were identical twins. They never left each other's side. And they wouldn't speak to anyone but each other. I thought they were the luckiest girls in the world. There were times when I was older that I thought of those girls, but I couldn't conjure an image of their faces in my mind—I didn't know if I was really remembering JD and me. I mean, of course it had to be us, right? But now, I wonder if it was two other girls. And not us at all. Or if it was really my dollhouse dolls all along."

Dr. Sullivan makes a note in my file.

"The story my mother told about my teeth, it—" A cough gets stuck in my throat. It's sharp and feels like half a toothpick is lodged in there sideways. Tears fill my eyes without warning. I didn't even feel them coming.

"It's okay, Caroline," Dr. Sullivan says, passing me the tissue box. "These emotions are not on the surface. They're coming from another place."

"It broke my heart—" The next exhale actually feels good, like everything ugly is riding on its tail. "I don't know what else to say."

Dr. Sullivan looks down to read the top of the tape he's about to place in the recorder. He jots something down.

"The strangest thing happened in the car after I left here," I say before he presses play. "I tasted blood in my mouth. The entire way home, I tasted blood."

"I know we still have some physical things to rule out regarding your memory loss, but I want to mention another explanation. It's quite possible that these are repressed memories, or memories that you have unconsciously blocked due to trauma contained in them. However, even in their absence, these memories can be affecting you on a conscious level. It's very possible to retrieve repressed memories in therapy, if that's desired. From what you've told me thus far, it seems to me repressed memory may very well be at work here. Another possibility is dissociation, which we'll talk more about at another time. If either of these two explains your loss of memory, you should be aware there's a reason you've suppressed them to begin with."

"Are you suggesting I let them be? I can't go through life like this. Wondering what's under wraps, about to be revealed. What if someone knows something about me that I don't? No, I need to know. Everything. I'll deal with the consequences."

Dr. Sullivan doesn't comment. Something shifts in his eyes. Not even his expression changes. Though he's communicated something. Only I have no idea what it is.

He pops in the tape.

> **Dr. Sullivan:** You don't think someone tried to hurt her, do you? It was an accident, right?
>
> **Caroline:** *Listen*—that's not the point—I don't want to talk about that. I want to tell you about the *tape*. And what difference does it make if it was an accident or not—what are you, Columbo all of a sudden?

My legs are crossed, and my foot is bobbing like the plastic ball at the end of a fishing line that jerks up and down when something's been caught. The tone of voice coming from the tape—coming from me—is disarming.

I put my hand up in the air to get his attention. "Dr. Sullivan, I don't understand what's going on here. What are we talking about? Are you sure that's the beginning of the tape? It sounds like I missed something. Like you started in the middle."

He looks down at the clear plastic window of the tape recorder and presses what I imagine is the rewind button. The tape whirs to a halt; he presses play. It begins at exactly the same point as before. He stops the tape.

"Caroline, I believe, if I remember correctly, you will tell me the complete story later in the session. Why don't we just listen some more and see where this goes. Okay?"

I exhale "All right."

Caroline: JD wanted me to go to our parents' house, she was living there with Lilly at the time, in the basement, in sort of an apartment they had. She wanted me to get her mail and some of her clothes to bring to the hospital where she'd been sleeping on a cot next to Lilly.

She ended up living at the hospital for two weeks. It probably would've been longer if things didn't end up the way they did. That last day she left for an hour to have coffee with someone. Everything changed that day. She asked me to stay with Lilly at the hospital while she went for coffee. Just in case anything happened.

Something did happen. But not to Lilly. JD never came back. That's the day she died.

CHAPTER SIXTEEN

Friday, September 29, 2006, 12:17 p.m.

I break my stare from the tape recorder to look over at Dr. Sullivan. I can't help but think that if I hadn't showed up at the hospital that day and JD had never gone out for coffee, she'd still be alive today.

Dr. Sullivan: How long did you sit at the hospital before you knew something was wrong?

Caroline: I sat there for hours. I tried calling her cell phone several times, but there was no answer. I finally called my mother at about six, I guess. I didn't call earlier because I thought JD was just having a good time. It was her first time out of that hospital room in weeks. I wasn't going to track her *down*. It was the least I could do.

Listen, you're not going to understand any of this unless I start from the day of Lilly's accident. And the day I went to JD's apartment a few days later. JD blamed herself for the accident, but of course it wasn't her fault. She knew who was driving the car, you know. She told me herself. She saw the car, and she saw the driver. But she wouldn't say who it was. Don't ask me why she'd want to protect the person who nearly killed her own kid. We all begged her. Even the cops. It didn't matter. Her lips were sealed. That was JD, when she got something in her head, when she made up her mind, nothing could change it.

Dr. Sullivan: Were there bystanders?

Caroline: No. Because it didn't happen out in the street. It happened in the parking area behind the shoe store where JD was buying shoes for Lilly. You had to walk through an alleyway between stores to get to it. JD said there were very few cars back there, and no one was milling around except for a worker from the diner throwing garbage in a dumpster. But he went back in the restaurant before anything happened. They wanted to put the shoes in the car and grab a sweater for Lilly before they got ice cream. You know something, if JD and Lilly had gone straight home instead of going for ice cream, the accident would've never happened.

Anyway, JD threw the shopping bag into the back seat. Lilly had her teddy bear tucked under her arm, and she was singing to a balloon she had in her hand. JD let go of Lilly's hand to get the sweater out of the car. In that split second, the balloon must have slipped from Lilly's hand, and she leapt out into the parking lot to grab it. JD didn't see what happened next—but she heard it. When she sprang from the car, she saw Lilly's body thrown in the air. JD said Lilly looked like a rag doll, her teddy bear flying in the air, too, and even though it felt like slow motion, it happened too fast for JD to do anything. Lilly fell on the roof of a parked car and then bounced on its trunk before hitting the ground. That poor little girl broke so many bones. You wouldn't believe how many surgeries she needed. Hanging by a thread. The next day the police returned her teddy bear, Cheeky, to the hospital. Both plastic eyeballs were crushed.

JD thought she was going to lose her. Lilly had barely moved on from the heart problems she had at birth, and now this. She pulled through, though, that spunky kid. Who would've predicted how this turned out? Instead, we lost JD.

Dr. Sullivan: That's awful, Caroline. How painful that must have been for all of you. You said you wanted to tell me about a tape?

Caroline: I'm getting to it. Once Lilly was admitted, JD didn't leave her side. She basically moved in with her. After a few days she asked me to get her mail and some clothes from her apartment. The apartment smelled bad. There were dirty dishes still in the sink from the day of the accident, and the garbage needed to be taken out. It would've been nice if my mother went down there to straighten up a little. Don't you think? I tidied up and packed a little bag for JD, some clothes and shampoo and stuff. A couple of Lilly's favorite toys. I grabbed the mail, and I was about to leave and head back to the hospital when I saw the red light flashing on her answering machine.

JD had about nine or ten messages, mostly from friends, one was from her boss, and then there was the last one. At first I was confused because the voice sounded familiar to me. But out of context. I had an immediate reaction to it—a flush of excitement. I hadn't heard that voice in so long, but in an instant it all came back to me, as if I was waiting for it. But the tone was different than I remembered. Angry and accusatory. He was yelling at JD. "Don't you *ever* threaten me, JD. I don't want to hear from you again. Don't be an idiot."

It was Timothy Hayes. He and I were engaged to be married a long time ago. I couldn't believe it was him. I hadn't heard his voice in years. I hadn't thought about him, either. Why would he be calling JD? They hardly knew each other. I mean, of course she knew him, from when we were together, but they didn't have any kind of relationship. In fact, she didn't even like him. I'm not sure Timothy liked JD either. That should've been a red flag for me—JD liked practically everyone, and vice versa. When Timothy and I got serious and I moved in with him—well, I thought, 'Could she be jealous?' She didn't have a boyfriend at the time. She said she didn't want one. I mean, she had boy crushes over the years, but nothing serious. She wanted to focus on school. But let's face it, that's just not normal.

Timothy and I were together for three and a half years. We got engaged the summer of our junior year. Timothy's dad loved the idea of him being with one girl. He thought dating a bunch of girls in law school would be distracting. Mr. Hayes was so happy about it that he bought Timothy an apartment in Hammond. We planned on staying there through law school, since Timothy was staying in town for his law degree. After he graduated, we'd get married.

In all that time we were together, JD hardly had any contact with him. That day in JD's apartment, when I realized the call from Timothy wasn't for me, that it was for JD, I was—I felt . . . deceived. We weren't even together anymore, but my first thought was that I caught him. Or her. Doing something. I didn't know what. I paused the tape to get my wits about me. I tried to remember the last time we were all together. As if it would provide a clue. JD told me a few times when she was in law school, after Timothy and I broke up, that she saw him at parties, even though he went to a different school.

I started the message from the beginning. When it was finished, I played it again. And again. I can practically still hear it in my head.

His voice was shaky calm. Like he was scraping together composure. Mock tough guy.

He said, "Okay, JD, you got the money—five hundred fucking thousand is more than you'll ever need." He told her not to call again. He said, "You better be the only one that knows about this—don't even think about telling your sister." Then he threatened her, like "You tell anyone, and you won't know what hit you." He said that his father would "handle her" if she told anyone, he'd "destroy her." The last thing he said was, "Keep your fucking mouth *shut*. I don't want to hear from you again. We have a deal. I kept up my side, now it's your turn."

The phone on Dr. Sullivan's desk begins to ring, and both of us jump up from our seats. He stops the tape and smooths back his bangs. "Excuse me, Caroline, I'm sorry, I have to take this . . . it may be important." He looks down at the phone and clears his throat, then answers it. "Hello, Dr. Sullivan. I see. What's her condition? Yes. Of course. You'll have to give me twenty minutes. I'll be there as soon as I can. All right then."

"Caroline—I'm so sorry to do this. Now especially. Unfortunately, I need to leave. It's an emergency, otherwise, of course, I'd never leave like this—in the middle." He fills his cheeks up with air—two taut balloons that burst in one audible surge. His pained expression is no consolation.

I drop my head and catch it with my hands. As I teeter on a tight wire, Dr. Sullivan packs up his net.

He's already out of his chair, pushing papers around in circles. "Caroline, I'll call you later. I'll get you back in right away—at your convenience, all right? I'm sorry. I must go. I'll walk you to your car." He paces behind his desk looking for something. From the floor he pulls a brown leather backpack and stuffs a folder into it; he turns to the tape recorder and pops the tape out, and puts it in his front trouser pocket. "And if you'd like to talk on the phone a bit—please—whatever works for you, we need to discuss this, what you just heard." He stops shuffling, and I sense his eyes on me. "Caroline?"

I stare at the floor, seemingly hypnotized by the shag rug. He's moving so quickly, and I can't seem to move at all.

It's time to go. He needs to leave. "Caroline?"

I sit in my car for I don't know how long. I don't understand any of this. It's too much already, and I feel so slow, like my mind is on a delay so that the truth doesn't hit me all at once.

To hear that story about Lilly. My sweet Lilly. My whole body twitches.

The part about Timothy is astounding. If he was the one to blame for the accident, the one driving the car, JD saw the car and said she knew the driver. She must've threatened to tell the police. He bribed JD to keep her mouth shut. A scandal like this would've busted a few rungs on his ladder.

But why would JD cover for him? And how could she not tell me any of this?

Maybe she did tell me. Maybe I did know.

I should be climbing out of my skin with rage. But I can't get myself there.

I have pieces of memories. I recall chunks of time. They are clear, hulking mountains in my mind. They're heavy and well grounded. But a thick, wet fog rolls in and obscures half of the hills and all of the peaks.

Driving around Dr. Sullivan's town, while struggling to knit together gossamers of memory, I unintentionally circle the same neighborhood three times. I'm perspiring through my shirt, under my arms and on my back, though there's a chill in the air. I pull over into the parking lot of a fabric store that's gone out of business and shut off the car. Timothy and I had already split up by April 2000 when the accident happened. What was he doing in Lanstonville that day? Lanstonville is not the kind of place people come to or drive through. It's at the cross section of never-been-there and never-want-to.

The newly familiar sense of dread slides down my throat and fills my gut. I pray I had nothing to do with this.

It's almost 5:30 when I arrive at Meg's to pick up the girls. She's on the phone with her mother, and I insist she not hang up on my account. I'm so happy to see the girls. Though I know I'm not acting like myself. I try to be normal, but I know I look at them differently. At times my attention is almost suffocating; other times my mind's adrift.

Who's noticed this shift in me? I'm sure not Lilly, but I'm

surprised Tessa hasn't called me out on it. Regardless, it feels good to be home.

After we eat turkey meatballs that I pull from the freezer, the three of us sit at the table, slouched, silent, still, stuffed. It's been a long week. The kitchen faucet has a leak, creating a slow, steady ping as it hits a stainless steel lid at the bottom of the sink. I look down at my daily schedule, which I left on the table this morning but failed to read or act on. Call plumber about kitchen sink; call electrician about sparking socket; call mason to cement brick back to stairs; and 1:30 haircut.

Lilly wants to get the sleeping bags from the attic so we can all camp out together in her room. I agree to this providing she clears some space on her floor.

Andy's still at work when we wiggle our weary bodies into sleeping bags, so I leave him a note in the kitchen next to his dinner. Smarty finds a crevice between Lilly and me and squeezes in. We look like caterpillars with dangling arms, holding hands. The girls fall asleep before me. Every time I lift my head to look at the clock, Smarty's head pops up too—crooked and wondering.

The house feels fragile. It's a windy night, and drafts leak through the house's pores, whistling eerily. The walls moan and push back against the wind.

Lilly's stomach rises and falls with her subtle breathing. I smooth her hair onto her pillow. Pink and yellow gingham. Her small fingers, with the softest of skin, are in my hand. No one's gonna let go this time. I promise you that, Lilly.

It's morning, and sunlight gushes through the open blinds on the little window in the corner of the room, allowing slices of light to stream through and stripe my face, jolting me out of an unsettled sleep. Everything in the room is soaked and bleached from the sun. What normally is bold is sucked pale.

The old screens in Lilly's windows billow in short snaps with the wind, which sounds different this morning. Last night it was aggressive, brusquely changing direction, wildly indecisive. This morning it just hisses. Like a snake. One long, languid sound, and then a snap of the screen. *Secrets, secrets, secrets.*

I spring off the floor. It sounds like the wind is speaking to me, and it creeps me out. I snap my fingers next to my ear to drown out the wind. Smarty scoots off the end of the sleeping bag and trots out of the room. I start the shower in the hall bathroom, jump in, and clench the loofah to scrub my skin until it's pink, gouging the underneath of my nails and the insides of my ears with a soapy washcloth in an attempt to purge the secrets in my head. I don't want to know any of these things. I thought I did. But I don't. I can't shake this perpetual feeling that my body is hosting phantom parasites. They syphon my spirit and steal my strength and breathe my oxygen and poison my soul.

If I have to, I'll dig into my skin and strip back the layers, or cut my hair until I'm bald, or brush my teeth till my gums bleed. I'll get rid of them. The razor shaves every follicle from armpit to ankle. I wash my hair three times. The first time the shampoo doesn't even lather. My hair's too long. I wish I hadn't missed that appointment. I can't think clearly with all this hair. My thoughts are getting snared and twisted in the length of it. I try to comb my fingers through. They get stuck in the knots and caught in the tangles.

At the bathroom mirror, scissors in hand, I cut my hair. I don't think about. The manicure scissors are slow, but the sound of the snip is satisfying. My heart beats hard against my chest. The long, thin mouse tails drop and lie limp at the bottom of the sink. My fingers move freely through my shortened hair; the ends just tickle the tops of my shoulders. I slip into the laundry room quietly and grab some clothes from stacks I never put away.

I check the time. Andy will be up soon. But I'll have enough time to check one thing on the computer. I'm not breaking my promise. I'm not Googling myself.

I'm Googling Timothy.

It won't surprise me if he got himself out of a hit-and-run. That is, if JD ever pressed charges. He's a pig. I'm sure he's got kids of his own by now, and if someone nearly killed one of them? I can assure you, Hayes & Hayes would crush them.

Halfway down the stairs, I am greeted by the aroma of coffee. God, I love that thing.

I can see into the kitchen from the steps. There's evidence of breakfast. The eggs and asparagus are on the island. Andy must be awake. Shoot. The television is on in the family room. The sports channel. Or it could be Game 4 of the 1996 American League playoffs—on video—which he watches with regularity. I've been told I'd understand if I were an Orioles fan.

I sidestep around the kitchen island toward the den, prepared at any moment for him to pop out of the family room for a coffee refill.

I back myself safely into the den—my footsteps are drowned out by the uproarious cheers of an eighth-inning homerun. Slowly turning the doorknob while quietly pushing the door closed, I sigh heavily and turn toward the desk.

"*Andy!*" My head jerks back and hits the door.

He jumps out of the chair and knocks his coffee over. "Caroline!" Coffee is everywhere. "You scared the crap out of me!" He's desperately grasping the keyboard and mouse. *"Hurry—get something. If it gets in the keyboard, it's toast."*

"Oh, God, no." I spin around, helpless, "Um, um . . ."

"Grab some tissues."

I run to the bookcase and stick my hand in the tissue box. "It's empty—" I tear my shirt off and throw it on the coffee spill just as he has yanked the keyboard into the air. "You think it's ruined?"

"I don't know, Caroline—jeez—" He pulls at the bottom of his T-shirt to collect the drops trickling down from the corner of the keyboard. My T-shirt is soaked. This prompts Andy to take his shirt off and wrap it around the keyboard while gently pressing his palm down to blot it. He turns to me and notices that from the waist up, I have nothing on except a sports bra.

"Caroline—" he's now grimacing, "if you really wanted to strip for me—you didn't need to trash the computer." He bounces his eyebrows. Then his eyes rest on my hair. The two little vertical lines between his brows grow deeper.

I swish my shirt around the desk, which just spreads the coffee out, so I cradle the T-shirt in my arms. "I'm gonna get rid of this and grab another shirt. You think it still works?"

"Well," he sighs, sinking back into the chair, "I don't know. Either way, it's probably not the worst thing in the world. You know we all spend too much time on this thing anyway. We're going to turn into sociopathic deviants who have forgotten how to engage with people." He hits the keys, but nothing shifts on the computer screen; then he turns the keyboard upside down again, and more coffee drips out. "Are the girls addicted to that stupid game, what's it called? They need a time limit, right? You're on it more than any of us." He spins toward me and grimaces again when he focuses on my hair. "I know you have a legitimate excuse." He holds his hand up in the air.

"Right." What's that supposed to mean?

"What's your book about, anyway? And when do I get to read some? Andy shrugs. "It doesn't have to be perfect, you know. I promise not to have a red pen in hand. Don't make me wait till you finish writing it." He smirks, then zeroes in on my hair again. "Hey, whatcha do with your hair? When did you get—that?"

"This?" I feel around for my hair, remembering its new length, while I walk toward the door. "Can you check the keyboard again? I need to get on there."

In the kitchen, Tessa's on an archeological dig in the fridge. I better forget about Timothy and reel myself into Saturday mode. Everyone's home. That means family time.

"Tess, you're up early."

"Oh, hi, Mom—what's for breakfast?" She grabs the milk and turns to face me. Her mouth springs open, and the carton slips from her hand. It falls to the floor. The pink plastic top pops off. The milk gushes. Here we go again.

"Oh, Mom, I'm sorry—" Tessa grabs the plastic handle and yanks it up, salvaging a cup or two.

I drop into a seat at the island and slide a kitchen towel across the counter so that it flies off the other end and falls to the floor. "Daddy just spilled his coffee on the keyboard. We should get Lilly down here to have a shot at the orange juice," I say, while Tessa swooshes the towel around with her foot.

"How's your lip?" I ask.

"Fine." She's staring at my head. "What happened to your hair?"

Why is everyone so uptight about my hair? "I cut it."

"You did it yourself? Oh. It's short. Short's—good." She nods her head and picks up the towel from the floor. "Should I put this in the laundry room? Mom?" She walks around the island. "Mom, do you want to give me that? You look like you peed in your pants." My wet shirt has soaked my grey leggings, leaving a dark, wet spot across my lap.

"Sure."

Her eyes drift down. "Why are you wearing a bra?"

"It's a sports bra."

Tessa's stance is fixed. She gawks at my hair, my top, my leggings, then shrugs. "Oh." She takes the wet stuff to the laundry room.

Five hundred thousand dollars is a lot of money. What did she do with it? I get up to check if Andy's made any progress.

"Where you going?" Tessa returns. "I thought you were making breakfast."

"Oh, maybe Daddy'll make French toast."

"Hey, Mom?"

"Yeah?"

"Daddy said he'd take us to the movies today, and . . ."

She probably used the money for hospital bills. Who knows if she even had insurance? I get to the den, and Andy's still at the desk. "How's it going?"

"I got it working," he says without turning around.

"Could you make some French toast, Andy? For the girls?"

"Oh, honey, could you do that, I just need a minute here."

So much for a computer strike.

He emerges from the den an hour later, at which time

he lays down the Thompson Family Computer Rules. Which includes a time limit that he's already broken about four times over.

The three of them finally, finally get their shoes on to go to the carwash and then to the movies. I decline their invitation and tell them I have shopping and straightening to do. I practically pace the kitchen, wiping the same spots on the counter, while they lace their shoes at the front door.

"'Bye, Mom!"

"'Bye, Caroline!"

The door clicks closed. I'm at the desk Googling Timothy Hayes before they've pulled out of the driveway. Andy moved the chair away from the desk but I don't have time to drag it over. I stand instead—since this will be fast. Now I won't linger.

A startling number of hits pile up. Quickly, I scan them to find something remotely close to what I'm looking for.

Timothy Byron Hayes III sentenced to 25 years.

CHAPTER SEVENTEEN

Saturday, September 30, 2006, 10:37 a.m.

Holy shit. I read the bold, underlined words three times. I grab onto the desk and knock on it twice, then smack myself on the cheek to make sure I'm awake. Before I read it again, I need to sit down. This will take more time than I thought. I lower myself into the chair, but my body doesn't hit chair when I think it should. That's because the chair is not underneath me. My arms flail and grab in vain at anything. Everything. The mouse pad, the keyboard, my desk calendar, a cup filled with pencils—which is wrapped in one of the cords. It all cascades on top of me. Except for the keyboard, which is dangling off the desk by a skinny black cord. As I splatter onto the floor, the trash basket is knocked over and gutted. I brush the pencils from my lap and reach for a chair leg to twirl the chair around. I sit stiffly. I'm alert as hell.

Twenty-five years for a hit and run?

Ring—

Not the freakin' phone. I'm not getting it. I don't care if it rings forever. I don't care if it rings *Yankee Doodle Dandy*. I'm not going anywhere until I read this. After the second ring the machine picks up—goddamn it—why can't people just hang up—now I have to return the call. It's Pastor Owens.

"Shit." I spring out of the chair and run to the kitchen.

"Oh, hi, Pastor. Sorry, I was upstairs and—"

"Hello, Caroline. Sorry to bother you." He's talking quickly. "But we couldn't find the gift baskets, and—"

Shit. The gift baskets. I forgot about the fundraiser.

"Oh my gosh—I have them. They're in my basement."

"Oh, good. That's fine. You'll be bringing them now, then? We're expecting people to arrive in less than an hour."

"Now? Uh, yes, of course you need them now." I look at the clock. "Well . . ."

Someone's in the house. I hear the front door open. Then presto, Lilly appears. She breezes through the kitchen and strides down the hall toward the den without saying a word. Without looking in my direction.

I pull the phone away from my ear for a sec. "Lilly, what are you doing here?"

"What do you mean? I live here, remember?" she says, cracking herself up. But she doesn't stop to say this; she keeps walking.

"Lilly! Where are you going?" I follow after her but only as far as the phone cord allows. "What about the movie? Where's Daddy?"

She mumbles something I can't hear.

"Lilly, I'm talking to you. *Lilly?*"

Nothing.

"Don't go in the den, Lilly! Did you hear me?!" She's

not listening to me. "*For Christ's sake—*" She's in the den. **"Timothy!"**

That she heard. She steps out of the den and looks down the hall at me. "What did you call me?"

"Lilly."

"No, you didn't. You called me Timothy. Who are you talking to?" She points to the phone, which I'm still holding.

"*Oh dear God, the Pastor*—Hello, Pastor, are you still there?"

"Is everything okay, Caroline?"

"Oh, yes, yes everything's fine, really . . . I'm sorry about that . . ." Lilly disappears into the den.

"*Lilly!* Did you hear me—I said—*do not go in the den!*" The phone now becomes a pointer, and I'm using it in a dramatic way to point at the den, which is senseless since we all know where the den is, and Lilly, in fact, is in it as I speak.

"*Mommy,*" she comes out and straddles the doorstep, pointing to something on the floor, "What is the matter with you? *I just need to get my glasses for the movie. They're in my backpack. It's right there on the floor.*" She's talking with her hands and arms.

"Pastor?" I check to make sure he's still there.

"Caroline, is this a good time?"

"Yes, no. It's not a good time." I give Lilly the stop-sign hand and a pinched face to say, "Don't you move an inch."

"Why don't I send Mrs. Cochran over to pick up the gift baskets? She's right here with me, and she's happy to help out."

"Oh, really? She can do that? I'll leave them on my back porch. That's great. I'll see you Sunday."

"Thank you for all your help, Caroline."

"Not at all. You're very welcome. Whatever I can do.

Bye-bye." I hang up the phone. "Your backpack is not in the den."

"Mom, I can see it from here. It's purple. It has a flower key chain hanging off it," she says in a sing-song, I'm-mocking-you kind of way. "Why are you so freaked out? Is there nuclear waste in there—do I need an oxygen mask?" She covers her mouth and croaks. "Houston, we have a problem." She walks into the den, grabs her backpack, and retreats. "You really need to chill, Mom."

She stops at the refrigerator and takes out an apple, and bites into it without rinsing it, and I don't say anything because I'm 'chillin'.' The phone rings again as Lilly pulls out her glasses and a white envelope from her backpack.

I grab the phone, "*Yes—*" I dispense with proper telephone etiquette.

"Is this Caroline?"

"Yes, this is Caroline."

"This is Dr. Cooper's office, you had an appointment today for a cleaning. We're wondering if you're on your way?"

Jesus, the dentist. "Oh, my gosh, that's *today?* Are you sure?" I look at the clock. "Um, yeah, I'll be there as soon as I can. Thanks for calling."

"Okay, but if you don't get here soon, you may have to wait."

I spin around in place, "Lilly, that was the dentist. I forgot my appointment." I turn around again looking for my schedule. "*Geez*—I cannot function without that thing." I fix back onto Lilly. "Where's Daddy? Is he outside waiting for you?"

"No. Daddy wanted to buy tickets before they sold out. He wants you to bring me to the movies to meet them."

"Geez. All right, let's hurry. Grab your glasses. I'm late

for the dentist. Oh, wait a second. You have to help me bring the gift baskets upstairs. We need to leave them on the back porch. Hurry."

"I forgot to give you this." Lilly holds out an envelope. I look at it suspiciously. "It's from Mrs. Stanton. She said you're hard to nail, something like that." I look down at the envelope in Lilly's hand, but don't take it. In case it's a subpoena.

Can a minor deliver a subpoena?

"Mom, *here*, it's for *you*. You can touch it. It's not poison." Sing-song again. Great. My own daughter is serving me a subpoena.

"Okay. Fine. *Whatever*." I snatch it from Lilly and drop it in my handbag. "I've got bigger fish to fry." Lilly gives me one of those are-you-from-outer-space looks, which I'm getting used to. "Come on, Lilly. Let's get those stupid gift baskets."

THERE'S A PARKING spot in front of the white Colonial that serves as both the dentist's office and dwelling. I keep the engine idling. I glide my index finger against my top teeth. I want to ask the hygienist if my teeth are implants, but I don't know if I can bring myself to do that. A schizo question like that will get around this town by dinnertime.

Isn't it strange that when people die—because maybe their heart has failed them, or their mind has failed them, or maybe some insidious cancer has poisoned them from tip to toe, and they're in the ground, six feet under, shriveled up and decomposing—their teeth remain intact.

The note from Mrs. Stanton is waiting for me on the passenger seat. I pick it up for the fourth time. This time I slide my finger under the glued flap.

Mrs. Thompson—

I've tried to get your attention outside school several times this week but to no avail. One minute I see you, the next, I don't. Anyway, I started to tell you the morning you volunteered in the library, but what a crazy day that turned into. I was very surprised to see your name when I was searching on my computer last week.

I didn't know you were a baker. An award-winning baker at that! I'm a baker, too! Well, I couldn't find my favorite apple pie recipe, so I was searching for one resembling my own when I found a newspaper article announcing you had won first prize in the Apple Pie Contest at Witmans' Farms last fall. Congratulations!

Just wanted you to know that I printed the recipe and tried it over the weekend. It's fantastic. I loved the cranberries. Very nice touch!

It's such a joy to see our parents involved in the community in such a positive way.

Sincerely,

Edith Stanton

The letter falls into my lap. As do my hands.

Apple pie contest? I won the Witmans' Farms apple pie contest last year. Me. I won it.

It's true.

I grab my phone from my handbag and call the dentist's office to tell them I can't make my appointment. Something has come up. Let's face it—compared to the rest of me—my teeth are in pretty good shape.

I pull out of the parking spot and head to the grocery store.

I'm in the mood for pie. It's not every day a Google search reveals news like this. Yes, it's time Caroline Thompson strapped on an apron and made some pies!

Instead of going home for the recipe, I'm gonna wing it—it's a pie, for heaven's sake. This is gonna be a great day!

Once I'm at the store and in the produce department, I scan the types of apples before me. All good apple pies have a variety, so there must be a combination of apples in this recipe.

The produce guy is unloading cauliflower.

"Hello, excuse me, sir. May I ask you a question?" This will only take a minute.

The produce fella looks over at me, places the last cauliflower atop the pyramid of others, and tilts his head, curls his tongue over his top teeth, and sucks down on them like he's trying to dislodge a stubborn strand of spare rib. With both hands, he grabs his brown leather belt and hoists his pants up. He's moving in slow motion.

"Sure, darlin', what can I do you for . . . ?" He talks with the same sense of urgency.

"I'm making an apple pie that calls for a combination of apples, two of each, I believe, I just forgot which ones to use." I feel tingly. I think it's excitement.

"Slow down there, you're talkin' faster than an *in*surance salesman, heh, heh, heh . . ." He places his hands on his boney hips and looks up at the ceiling. "Now, yer talking apple pie, you said—is it . . . ? First of all, you know it's a great season for apple pie, mainly 'cuz it's apple season. That's rule number one—always work with the season."

I start to jog in place to do something with my energy. I just need him to tell me the types. Then I'll be out of here.

"Whoa, you gearin' up for pie or you a lightweight? Heh, heh, heh . . ."

"I'm a little short on time—I just need to know what apples to use."

"Well, you can't rush a good pie, that ya know, but I'll tell you, I'd start with Romeo." He yanks at his belt again, this time in a seesaw way, up on one side first, than the other. Why do guys do this? Are they adjusting themselves? Do they have an itch? It's off-putting.

"Do you mean Cameo? Or do you mean Rome?" I say, jogging over to tear a bag off the roll.

"Yup. That's right."

"Yes—both?"

"Stay away from the McIntyres—they're too soft, make your pie a big mushy mess. You want it firm."

"McIntosh?" Oh dear, for Pete's sake. I start bagging some apples; I decide on Golden Delicious, Cameo, and Braeburn, mainly because they're right in front of me. I load them up in three separate bags.

"How many pies you fixin' on makin'? That there's alotta apples!"

"Four." I stop to count out loud to myself using my fingers. "No, five. Six apples for each pie, times five pies, is thirty. So I need ten of each kind. Great."

"'Course, I won't be in the kitchen witcha," he pauses to see if I'll argue that, "so you want your slices thick, a good mound, standin' up straight . . ."

"Thanks, thanks for all that."

I jog over to the aisle with the foil pans and grab a handful, and I hear the produce guy call out, "Good eatin'!" There are some red and white striped aprons hanging next to the dishtowels and oven mitts. I grab one each for Lilly and Tessa. They're going to flip out over baking pies. We're gonna have a real Thompson Family afternoon. Filled with familiness and happiness and togetherness.

On the drive home, the radio plays all my favorite songs one after another. That never happens. I take it as a cosmic sign of good news. Stars aligning. It feels good to sing at the top of my lungs *and* know the lyrics. Gosh, I'm always amazed at how good I am at drumming. I totally have rhythm. And probably no one will ever know that about me. I wish people could see some of my good qualities. I almost don't hear my phone with all my singing. A new text. At the next red light, I peek at it quickly. It's from Andy.

"Never got into movie. Sold out."

Slicing through my good cosmic aura, like a machete, comes a vision of the newspaper article on Timothy's conviction. I slam on the brakes. Some guy behind me leans on his horn and doesn't let up. Thank God he didn't hit me. "I'm sorry. I'm sorry," I say in my rearview mirror, but he can neither hear me nor read my lips. He probably thinks I'm a lousy driver, which I'm not. I'm a great driver. I'm offended by his insinuation. He's probably already put me in the all-women-are-sucky-drivers category. That really riles me.

"I'm a damn good driver!" I yell this into the rearview mirror and throw my foot on the gas. That damn article is still up on the computer. I never closed out of it. Lilly was in there last, getting her backpack. We left the house together.

It's not unlike Andy to walk into the house and go straight to the computer. With his shoes on. He could have seen it by now. He could have read about Timothy getting twenty-five years for nearly killing Lilly. He does know that Lilly is . . . *was* . . . that JD is really . . . ? Shit. I don't know what he knows. *Jesus Christ.*

Pins and needles prick my scalp. It's my fight-or-flight response; the pricks are hot, electric zaps and there are hundreds of them. I pull into our driveway. Andy's car is nowhere in sight. That's good.

But the front door is unlocked. Before I open the door, I stop. His car is in the garage. He always parks it in the garage after he gets it washed. I open the door halfway . . . slowly. I extend one foot over the threshold with contrived calm, keeping my hand on the door knob. I crane my neck around the door. Lilly's backpack is in the foyer next to the bench. There's the smell of something cooking. But the house is strangely still.

I hold the door against my body for protection like a shield, not knowing whether to stay or go. And never come back. I don't want to live like this anymore. I despise this. I want it to stop. I want it to go away. But I don't know how. My cell phone rings. Tears percolate from the back room of my eyes. Traces of feigned bravado disintegrate. I quickly answer before anyone in the house hears the phone and knows I'm home. In case I decide to bail.

"Hello," I whisper, moving back outside, pulling the door almost closed.

"Caroline, is that you? It's Andy, can you hear me? I gotta ask you something."

"Yes." I stand on the welcome mat and stutter, "Where are you? Are you home?" Something trickles down my leg.

"We have a bad connection, where are you?"

"I'm . . . I . . . I can't hear you. *Are you home?* Where are the girls?"

"We're at the diner."

I slump down onto the brick stairs, and tears barrel silently down my cheeks. "Did you go . . . straight from the theater?"

"What?"

"I said, did you go there right from the theater? Or did you stop home first?" My heart waits for an answer.

"Well, the girls were really hungry, so we stopped here first."

A squall of hot air rushes from my mouth.

"Shoot. I should've called you to join us. Listen, they already got their burgers. For some bizarre reason, things have been moving really fast here. Go figure. Anyway, I called to see if you want something. You want a veggie burger or something?"

Breathe in, breathe out. Breathe in, breathe out. I stink of body odor. My shirt is stuck to me. I pinch my shirt away from my underarms.

"Caroline? Honey?"

I use the cuff of my sleeve to mop my cheeks and under my chin.

"Are you still there? Caroline . . . ?"

Once I'm in the house, I lock the door behind me. The deadbolt and the chain. They'll need to ring.

The article about Timothy is still on the screen for all the world to see. A cold front blows through my body like a nor'easter, leaving me shivering in my clothes.

> *Timothy Byron Hayes III was sentenced yesterday to 25 years to life for first-degree murder. He was convicted of murdering Jane Dory Spencer, 28, in what*

first appeared to be a suicide but was later determined
to be arsenic poisoning. He will be eligible for parole
in 18 years.

I see the words. I string them together one at a time in the order they were written. "Murder" and "convicted" and "killed" and "arsenic." And all the other words flanking them, turning them into unfathomable statements. But my brain is frozen. It's a block of ice. Nothing's getting in. Or understood. My entire body is immobile. I sit staring at the screen.

The girls are calling, "Mommy! Mom? Mommy?" I jump from the chair and perch myself at the edge of the desk, clutching my handbag, shielding the screen. How did they get in? The back door is visible from my desk. I would have seen them. I call back.

"*Yes?*"

Silence. No one.

"*Girls?*" I stammer.

Nothing. I ease back down; my handbag's in my lap.

"*Caroline*—" Now it's Andy. I spring from the chair and stand with hands on hips—my back concealing the screen—my handbag falls to the floor.

"Yes, Andy? Is that you?" My voice cracks.

No answer. No voices, only the sounds of the house. The gurgling of the fish tank. The deep, intermittent gong of the wind chime on the back deck as it sways in a listless breeze. The almost imperceptible breathing coming from the CPU under the desk. I look down at it with disdain. I hate that fucking thing. I hate it. I kick it violently. "*I fucking hate you! You piece of ignorant shit.* " It immediately wails—a guttural groan. I drop to the floor and throw my arms around it, pressing my cheek up to the textured metal panel. "I'm sorry, I'm sorry, I'm sorry, please, *please* don't die, I need you, I . . . need . . . I have no one . . . I'm . . . sorry . . ." I grovel at this insulting, abusive, taunting, spineless fucking box. Its partner in crime, my other abductor, sits on the desk telling me everything—with its unabashed open face, it holds nothing back. It doesn't care how fragile I am, how lonely I feel, how desperate I've become.

It's Andy again, closer this time, "Caroline?" Then laughter.

"*Andy!*" I bellow at the house; I'm shriveled up under the desk. "Where are you? Stop playing with me!"

Only my echo returns. Then, silence. I sit back down in the chair. There's a reflection of my hands in the screen. They're hovering over the keyboard, trembling like a junkie in detox.

The cell phone rings in my handbag.

"Hello," ekes out of me. I hear Dr. Sullivan's voice, and I slump over and sob.

"*Is this what a nervous breakdown looks like? Huh, doctor?*" I beg him for answers without stopping to hear them. "*Tell me, is this what it looks like? Or is it worse, what I have, am I . . . crazy . . . ?*" I can't hear a word he says. He could have confirmed either one or both. Perhaps offered another diagnosis, more gruesome. I can't calm myself down. I want it to be over. I finally want it to be over.

"*Caroline*—" His voice breaks through. "Listen to me, you need to calm down—so I can talk to you. Can you hear me, Caroline?"

I knew JD didn't commit suicide. I knew she couldn't have done that. There was no way she'd kill herself and leave her daughter alone. Not JD. She was . . . centered and responsible . . . and happy. She felt right in her own skin. Peer pressure didn't exist for her. Not even in high school when the girls wore Gloria Vanderbilt jeans—she'd go to the thrift store to buy something old that no one had ever heard of. She never worried about what the other girls thought of her. She was never even curious. She'd look right through all those pretentious girls. Above them. Being admired never mattered to JD. And so the irony was that she was admired more than anyone. We were all dying to be that comfortable with ourselves. She never knew it, and she never needed to.

"Caroline? Are you still there? *Caroline?* Tell me what's going on. What are you doing right now?"

Timothy killed her because she was the only one who knew he mowed down Lilly, nearly killing her. No one thought Lilly would pull through. So he had to get rid of JD before that happened. Before she told anyone.

"*Caroline, are you there?* Please talk to me, what are you doing right now? Where are you?"

I can't believe she didn't blow the whistle on that bastard. This was her chance to cut him down. He gave her half a million dollars to keep her mouth shut.

"**Caroline**—"

"*Yes.*"

"Where are you?"

"I know about JD . . ."

"You do?"

"Yes. I . . . know . . . what *really* happened . . ."

CHAPTER EIGHTEEN

Saturday, September 30, 2006, 1:16 p.m.

I have no choice. I don't wrestle with the decision. I don't contemplate or deliberate. Or even think about it, really. I just get in the car and drive to Dr. Sullivan's at his urging. What's there to think about? It's not like anyone needs me around here. For what? To help the girls sell Girl Scout cookies? Or make lunch? Or buy them new bathing suits? I don't think so. Andy can take the girls to sell popcorn or wrapping paper or the crap du jour to raise money for whatever group of grubby hands it is this week. He can drive Smarty to the groomer—or let his hair grow. I don't care. They can order takeout. He can take the girls to swim practice or horseback riding or that kid's birthday party at that pottery place. If that party is today. If any of that's today. Screw the schedule. Was my mental breakdown on the schedule?

My family doesn't need me. All these years, what the hell have I been doing? Anyone can make turkey sandwiches.

When I arrive at Sullivan's, there are two empty parking

spaces that flank each side of the office door. Dr. Sullivan is waiting outside, wearing a baseball cap and sitting on one of those cheap folding chairs with nylon webbing woven around an aluminum frame. I remember this kind of chair from my childhood. Our neighbor, Mrs. Gemelli, had parents, older Italian folks, who visited, and they'd sit on her front lawn in those same chairs. Same color, even, except for where a new nylon strip was used to repair an old, worn-out piece of webbing. Every time they'd visit their daughter, they'd pull those beat-up chairs out of the trunk of their car. It didn't matter that their daughter had nice wooden lawn chairs with striped cushions for them to sit on. They brought their own. I once heard them argue about the chairs. Mrs. Gemelli said, "Why do you bring those ratty chairs here, all the way from home. I have nice chairs. New chairs. You have to bring those every time and embarrass me? Why do you do that?" Then her mother would yell something back in Italian, waving her arms around like an octopus; she'd sometimes rip off the apron she'd have tied around her thick waist and throw it on the ground, and the father would just sit in his green chair and read *Il Giorno*, and Mrs. Gemelli would storm into the house.

I imagine Sullivan taking this chair off his boat once the summer fishing season has ended and bringing it to his office.

I take the parking spot to his left, and he puts down the newspaper. It's folded in half and half again so he can peer over it or to the side. There's a can of Dr. Pepper on the ground next to his foot.

He stands slowly and waits for me there. When I approach, he looks curiously at my feet, so I do, too. I'm not wearing shoes. I turn back to the car and hope I have a pair in there. They're on the passenger-side floor. I slip them on. He holds out his hand as if to touch my arm, then changes his mind. He regards me closely. To get a read. His eyes are heavy and tired. His cheeks seem ruddier than usual, giving him a clown-like appearance compared to the paleness of the rest of his skin.

"I'm glad you came. Caroline. I'm very glad." He motions for me to walk ahead of him through the open door.

On the way to his desk chair, he stops at the credenza and bends over, peering into the lower cabinet.

"Would you like some water?" he asks without looking at me.

When he hands me the bottle, I gulp half of it and place it on the table beside me, keeping it in my grasp. An anchor for my hand.

"I'd like to talk about yesterday, Caroline." He stands behind his desk. "First let me please express my sincere apologies, once again, for leaving at such a critical time for you. I'm sorry it happened that way, and I appreciate your understanding."

For the first time since yesterday, I think about his other patient.

"Now then, there was a lot of information there—from the tape. Let's talk about that." He sits in his chair, and it sighs. "Did you know about Lilly's accident, or going to JD's and hearing her phone messages?" He uses his pudgy hand to sweep away the hair from his eyes.

"No."

He looks at me with concern. "How has Lilly been developing, physically? Have there been any health-related repercussions for her? Has she had any setbacks from the injuries she sustained?"

I pause to think about this. It's still hard for me to think about the little girl in the tapes getting hit by the car and belonging to JD as my Lilly. It occurs to me now that these tapes are a prequel to my life as I know it. "No, thank God, she's been good." I'm relieved to realize things could be a lot worse.

"That's great. That's really great to hear. She's very lucky. Well, then, let's talk about the day you went to JD's and heard the message from Timothy. Did you know about their communication?"

I shake my head without looking up.

"Let's step back. Tell me about Timothy . . . and your relationship with him."

"What do you want to know?"

"Anything. Anything you can remember."

If he had asked me that a week ago, it would've been a different story. But in the last seven days, any memories of Timothy have been wrapped in barbed wire. Getting to the Timothy I knew will take more than a pair of shears.

"It's hard to say, now. Maybe I never knew him. Anything I remember of our time together, well, it—he—doesn't seem like the same person. So, I can tell you what I thought of him, what I remember of him, but it may be the thoughts of a deluded schoolgirl."

"That's okay. Your relationship with him was real. Tell me about that."

"Well, I remember thinking we were a lot alike. We were drawn to each other from the start—the first weekend of my freshman year. We fell in love and stayed together almost till the end." I say this without thinking.

"End of what?"

"College. He proposed to me during the summer before

our junior year. I couldn't imagine being happier than when I was with him. We made plans for the future—lots of plans. Our honeymoon was going to be in Greece; we planned to live in Greenwich, Connecticut, have five children—we even named them." I stop and think about how easily these memories come to me. It's like unpacking an old box of Christmas ornaments that got lost in the attic. Things I haven't seen or thought about in years, but as I unwrap them from their tissue paper, I remember each one with a flood of emotion.

"What did you study in college?"

"I was an English major, Timothy, poly-sci. He had plans to go to law school and follow in his father's and grandfather's footsteps and work at the family firm in New York. He even spoke about public office someday. I remember the apartment Mr. Hayes bought for Timothy after we announced our engagement." Again, a surge of euphoria. "I was thrilled to get out of my dumpy apartment. I shared it with two girls. It cost me two-hundred dollars a month, and it was all I could afford. My mother didn't even argue with me when I moved in with Timothy. She was happy to see me out of that apartment. She was excited about the engagement.

"It was all too good to be true.

"I remember the day I realized I was the girl who'd hooked Timothy Byron Hayes. That didn't stop the other girls from trying. He was handsome—and the way he dressed, not like a typical college kid, always in collared shirts and khakis. He was charming. He always knew the right thing to say. Ultimately though, his charm did one of two things: got him in, or out, of trouble.

"You said you were together for over three years. So your relationship ended before graduation?"

"Well, I . . . Yes. I didn't graduate."

"Oh, I see. Why was that?"

"I don't know."

"You don't remember?"

"Well, I, no, I didn't remember—but I . . . recently found out."

"How did you find out?"

"I read an old newspaper article online. I didn't finish college because I had surgery at the end of my junior year."

"I see."

"It was a hysterectomy, I think."

"Caroline, I'm very sorry to hear that. What do you mean, 'you think'? Did you not remember the surgery?"

"No. I've been piecing things together. After I read the article, I had to see the doctor for my fall. She confirmed the hysterectomy."

"Why a hysterectomy, were you sick?"

"I got pregnant. I was getting an abortion . . . when . . . well . . . the guy wasn't a doctor. I almost died."

"And Timothy, was he—?"

"Yes."

"How did he handle all of this?"

"I don't know exactly, except he found the guy for me, to do the abortion."

"What happened after the surgery?"

"I don't remember ever speaking to Timothy again. I moved back in with my parents. I didn't finish school."

"And Timothy?"

"I heard he went to law school."

"That must've been very painful." He looks at me and stops talking. And I stop talking. I just sit there with my half thoughts. Maneuvering the squares of a Rubik's cube to see if colors will align.

"What did you do then, after you left school?"

I think about this before I answer. "I don't know, exactly. I'm not sure what my condition was . . . emotionally. Or physically. I have a recollection of my parents arguing a lot. My mother wanted me to see a psychologist once I got back home, but my father thought I would "snap out of it" on my own. He'd say, "As soon as she meets a new boy, she'll be fine. She just needs to get a job. They're always looking for kids at the mall. She'll meet a boy there.' I don't think he even knew what I studied in college. Or that I was the editor of my school newspaper and wrote articles for our town weekly. My mother would argue back, "She's not going to work at the mall, she's a smart girl." I'll never forget that. It was rare that my mother said anything complimentary about me. I guess I was surprised she noticed. That was the only time I felt some sort of admiration from her."

"Were you in love with Timothy?"

"Yes."

"But then you met Andy." Sullivan smiles gently.

Just as he says Andy, my phone rings in my handbag on the floor. The nerves at the back of my neck buzz, sparking like firecrackers. I don't look at the number or even the phone. I know it's Andy. I completely forgot about them. I never left him a note or a message that I was going somewhere.

"Do you want to get that, Caroline?"

"No." It rings a few more times, then stops. A moment later, a different sound indicates a message.

We sit for a minute in quiet. I can't worry about them. They're fine. I don't have the wherewithal to worry about one person, let alone four. "You stopped the tape yesterday, before it was over."

"Yes, I know. I have it cued up to where we left off. We can listen to that now unless there is anything else you'd like to talk about."

"No."

He opens the center drawer, first rolling back on his chair to clear his stomach out of the way, and reaches his hand in for the tape. He pops it into the recorder and presses play. I place both my hands on the arms of the chair and curl my fingers around the thick wood. Time for take-off.

Caroline: Then Timothy said, "I don't care if she looks like my clone, no one will ever believe you, anyway." I thought the message was over, I thought he was hanging up the phone. There was a long pause, but he started talking again like he just remembered something. He said it under his breath, almost to himself, "How many guys can say they knocked up sisters—" Then he gasped. Like he caught himself saying out loud what he really meant to be thinking, because he started to freak—knowing this was on the machine. What a jackass. The dumb asshole tried to retract. He started panicking: "I mean, I didn't mean— I didn't say—JD, listen—you erase this message. Do you hear me? If you know what's good for you. I don't want to threaten you, JD." Something like that. Then he told her to erase the message, to go buy something nice for herself, before he threatened her. "Don't make me send someone to get the tape from you. I don't want to hear from you again. Even if she dies."

And that was it.

Clone?

Knocked up sisters?

What. The. Fuck?

The tape continues. Zizzing and zizzing. My voice. Dr. Sullivan's voice. I can't discern any of it. I'm obsessed with a feeling in my throat. It feels tight. Pulled and twisted, so tight there's no channel for air, in or out. I can't get air. Where are all the windows? There are no windows in this office. The door. From which did I come? There are three. Which goes to the hall? I snatch my handbag from the floor and launch clumsily out of my chair.

"Caroline—where are you going?" Sullivan is on his feet with his hands out to the side like a farmer trying to corner a pig. "Caroline, don't go like this—we need to talk about it. That's why you're here, that's why you came to see me—"

I finally spot the door and rush toward it before he says another word. I can't bear to hear him talk. His voice is now in stereo since the tape is still playing. Actually, three people are talking. Two of him and one of me. It's like a freak house. His voice makes me sick. I grab at the doorknob and pull with all my strength, but the door doesn't open. Pressure is building inside of me. Like I'm filling with steam—it's hot and it's heavy, pressing hard against me from within. My head can't take the pressure, nor can my chest or my heart. I wring my fingers around the neck of the knob and strangle it with both hands—turning it and twisting it opposite directions. Nothing.

"You locked the goddamned door? Open this door! Open this fucking door now!" I pound my fist against it. *"Open it!"*

"Caroline." He inches his way from behind the desk toward me.

"You knew the whole time, you fucking loser. You knew who Lilly's father was. But you still had to ask me? 'Did you love Timothy? Tell me about your relationship with Timothy?'"

"Caroline—you shouldn't get in your car. You can't leave here like this. You need to calm down. Why don't you sit?"

"You open this fucking door now before I—" I'm about to threaten him with bodily harm as I give the door one more violent yank and fall through the other side. He comes after me, but I shuffle to my feet, get through the next door, and make it to the car. My key remote beeps and obeys me by unlocking the door. I shift into reverse and back out of this memory lane for the insane for the last time.

In the rearview mirror, I see Sullivan pull the office door shut and hurry to his car, his belly jostling to and fro. My eyes dart away from the mirror. I never want to see him again. For several blocks I catch glimpses of his car in my rear view mirror, following me. Every now and then another car gets between us, but sooner or later his ends up behind mine. But I can't worry about that hypocrite now. I've got other hypocrites on my mind.

No wonder JD didn't want to fill in "father's name" on Lilly's birth certificate. All the things I still have of JD's and Timothy's. Stuff I've kept all these years. I can't believe I saved all that bullshit of theirs. I hate them. They both got what they deserved. I need to clean my house and soul of everything of theirs. All their dirty, ugly, deceptive bullshit.

Andy keeps calling on the cell phone, looking for me. He and the girls are worried. Where am I, and am I all right, and when will I be home, and what am I doing. He'll put the girls to sleep, but he's waiting up for me. We'll watch a movie together. We'll spend some time together. If he doesn't hear from me, he's calling the police.

I text him back. I'm out. Don't wait up. I don't tell him where. I don't owe anybody anything.

I drive for hours. Weaving in and out of streets I don't know and will never drive again. I get lost twice, but it doesn't concern me. I'm sick of hearing my own thoughts, so I grab an apple from the bag on the floor and bite into it. The crunch becomes hypnotizing. I eat them one after the other.

Once it's late enough that I'm certain everyone is asleep, I go home. Andy is sleeping on the couch with the TV on. I go straight to the closet. To the box. To the letters. And the pressed flowers. And the promises on Hayes & Hayes letterhead.

CHAPTER NINETEEN

Sunday, October 1, 2006, 12:01 p.m.

The flesh on my arm is being kneaded like bread dough.

"Mommy, Mommy . . ." Lilly's imploring, kneeling on top of the blankets next to me on my bed.

Through narrow slits in my eyes, I see her. Before my eyes close I take her hand from my arm and kiss her palm gently. She was supposed to be mine. She may have been born out of a union of betrayal—but look at them now. He almost killed his own daughter. Instead he killed the mother of his daughter. I should feel lucky.

I should.

"Mommy—get up. *Get up.*" She lifts one dead-weight arm, and it flops back down on the bed. "Come on. Rise and shine. We gotta get ready." She scooches toward Andy's side of the bed and pulls my arm, hoping the rest of me will follow.

"Lilly, sweetie, not now, I need to sleep. Please." I cup my hands over my ears.

"You have to, Mommy. They're coming soon. Come on.

You have to get out of your jammies." She whisks away my blanket. "Mommy, why are you sleeping in your clothes? Where are your pajamas?"

"How do I look?" Tessa pirouettes into the room. Her grass skirt spins up around her waist. "Daddy said we could wear these. I'm a hula girl! Isn't it beau-ti-ful! Wah waaah wah waah . . ."

"*Please.*" I pull the blanket back up to my chin. "Close my door. Go show Daddy. I need to sleep."

"For how long? What about the party?"

"Daddy can take you."

"Take us where?"

"To the party."

"The party is here, *duh*—"

"Our party, Mom." Tessa stops spinning. "It's today."

"Everybody's gonna be here soon."

I peer over the bulge of the pillow beside me to get a look at the clock. It's noon.

"Sweetie, are you okay?" Andy suddenly appears in the doorway. "You look terrible." He walks to the bedside and puts the back of his hand on my forehead. "What happened to you yesterday? I waited up as long as I could. Where were you? What's going on?"

"I'll tell you later. I can't go to the party, I'm sorry. I can't move . . ." My eyes close.

"Oh, Caroline—are you *serious*? Come on—you need this party. This party is for you, practically. You need to have some fun. You've been so stressed lately. I'm gonna call your doctor. I've never seen you like this. You're worrying me. Are you in your *clothes?*"

"Do not call the doctor. Andy, I'm serious. Promise me.

Right now." I lift my head about an inch from the pillow, but it's too heavy to keep up there, and collapses.

"Okay. *Okay.* I promise." He holds his hands up in surrender. "If you're worried about setting up and all that stuff, I got it covered. You're a guest. All you have to do is show up with a smile. We'll do the rest. We can handle this! Right, girls?"

"Yeah, Mommy, we can handle this." Lilly flexes her biceps as Tessa braids the grass strands on her skirt.

"May I get you something to drink, Mrs. Thompson?" Lilly pretends to write on an invisible notepad.

I don't move. Smarty jumps on the bed and puts his head on my stomach.

"Maybe you just need a hot shower. Lilly—do me a favor, put the shower on for Mommy."

"*No, Andy.* I don't need a shower. I need you to leave."

This makes him take a step back.

"Let's leave Mom alone. You sleep, sweetie." He puts his arms around the girls. "You'll feel better when you wake up. The party starts in about an hour and a half. I'm not accepting no for an answer." He walks back over to my side and kisses my forehead. Walking toward the door, he whispers to the girls, "Do you know where Mommy keeps those big ice pails?"

Lilly says, "I dunno. Do you think she'll be out of bed by tomorrow? We need to get to the sculpture garden."

"I don't know, honey."

"If we don't go I won't earn that badge, and I'll have only eleven, and that means Alexandra will still have one more than me."

"It's just a stupid Girl Scout badge, Lilly."

"Shut up, Tessa."

"Sshhh. Can you two give it a rest," huffs Andy.

They close the door behind them. Lilly pops her head back in. "Oh, Mommy, Smarty caught another mouse in the back. He brought it in, but—"

"Lilly! What did I tell you?"

THE WARM AIR on my cheek is coming from Tessa, who's breathing about an inch from my face. "Mommy? Mommy, are you feeling better?" she whispers. She's sweeping the hair that's fallen across my face back onto the pillow. She places a soft kiss on my cheek, and I slowly open my eyes. She's curled up next to me under the blankets. She pops up when she sees my eyes open.

"Mommy, you're awake! It's time to change. Some people are here already." She's turned up the volume and revved up her motor. I wish I had kept my eyes closed. The smell of crab cakes and clams whacks me in the face. I used to love those smells.

"Honey . . . I can't," I mumble to Tessa. "I'm sorry."

She gets up and kneels on the bed with her arms limp at her side. Smarty is next to her, sitting in the same position. "You're not getting out of bed? You're not coming to the party?" She can't believe it. "Why?"

I shake my head.

"It won't be a party without you." Her eyes fill up with tears.

"Yes it will," I breathe.

"No it won't. If you're not going, I'm not going." She plops her head on Andy's pillow, tucks her knees up to her chin, and slips her feet back under the blankets. The grass of her skirt is bent upward and falls around her shoulders. Smarty lays his chin down and stares at me.

I can't believe she's pulling this. On *me*. I'm the mother of reverse psychology.

"Tessa." I try to muster an ounce of energy. "What are you doing? You can't stay here."

"Yes I can."

THE NEXT TIME I open my eyes, the curtains on the front windows are glowing softly. Tessa's face is in a shadow. She's looking through a telescope she's made out of her hand and is studying the ceiling intently while chewing on the Band-Aids that wrap the fingertips of her other hand. Andy appears at the foot of the bed.

"Daddy!" Tessa exclaimed.

"Sweetie, I'm begging you. Please put these on. Here," he says as he extends his arm with a pair of jeans and a white shirt. "Everyone's asking for you. Just for a little while. Besides, you need to eat something. It's two-thirty. Really. Come down. Please?"

I smell the smells of food I don't want to eat. Indistinguishable chatter comes from people I don't want to see. I have nothing to say to them. And I don't want to hear anything they have to say to me. Why do they want to see me so badly? *I* don't want to see me.

Or be me.

Andy and Tessa will not go away until I relent.

Whatever. Who gives a crap, anyway?

On the way downstairs, Lilly, with hot dog in hand, meets me halfway and hugs me with her entire being. It doesn't smell like a turkey dog; it smells like a real hot dog. To my surprise my mouth waters.

"Oh *Mommy*—come on, before you miss any more. Guess who's here? Nicole! The new girl who moved in down the street. Daddy saw her father when we were walking Smarty, and he invited the whole family! She grabs my hand and yanks me down the stairs, briefly looking back at me to ask, "Can Nicole come in our car tomorrow for the Girl Scout trip? She joined our troop!" Her eyes scrunch, "Do you want to comb your hair, Mommy?"

"Huh?"

"Oh, no." She freezes midstep; her eyes, as wide as moons, drift down my shirt. With a pained expression, she says, "I got ketchup on your shirt. I'm really sorry."

"It's okay, sweetie. Don't worry." I pat the top of her head, hoping she'll turn around and keep walking.

"You wanna change your shirt?"

"Sure . . ."

She doesn't move, so I walk around her down the stairs.

Lilly calls from behind, "Do you want to change now? I'll wait for you—"

I pause on the last step and look around the kitchen and through the sliding doors to the backyard.

"Mom, it's a pretty big stain," she says, once she catches up to me. She takes the napkin wrapped around her hot dog and rubs my shirt, creating a bigger splotch. The ketchup seeps through my shirt, making my skin cold and wet.

I pull my shirt away from her. "Don't worry. It's okay."

In the kitchen, Andy spots me first. He comes over and kisses my cheek. "I'm so glad you came down, Caroline." He smooths down the back of my hair. "Have something to eat. The food is great." He whispers in my ear, "You have a big red stain on your shirt. I didn't see that when I grabbed it from your closet, sorry 'bout that." Then he shouts across the kitchen, "Hey, Vicki, here she is. We had to tell her you wouldn't leave unless she came down." He laughs at his own joke and slaps me on the back with unintended gusto, which propels me off the step into the kitchen. Officially.

Vicki scoots over as I sit down on a stool and put my hands in my lap. "It looks like you had your way with the salsa!" She elbows me. "Caroline, great party. Boy, Andy is quite the host. You taught him well, Darlin'." She squashes down closer to me, "You okay? Andy told me you had a bad week? I called you every day, ya know."

"I'm fine." A bird outside in the distance is sitting on a tree branch, but Vicki's head is blocking my view of the branch so the bird looks like its sitting on her head.

I look back at her. She appears annoyed.

"Caroline, did you hear me?" Vicki moves her face closer. "Are you listening to me?"

"Yes."

"I said you should've called me if you weren't coming to bunko. I could've gotten a sub for you."

"What?"

"Why didn't you come to bunko on Thursday? It was at my house. I called you at like, 7:30, but you didn't answer. And you didn't return any of my calls. I'm just sayin'."

"I don't know."

"Oh, forget it. What's the matter with you? Are you on meds or something? You're totally zoned out."

She grabs the back of my stool. "Caroline. I said, do you want me to fix you a plate?"

"Am I on *meds?*"

"Are you?"

"I don't think so."

She lets go of the stool. "I'm getting you some food. Sit here. I'll fix you a plate. And a *drink*. One for you, two for me. You're weirding me out."

She spins out of sight into the backyard. My neighbor stands by the pool steps, waving me over through the sliders. Maybe she's waving someone else over. These are *our* friends? We don't have this many. They're not ours. How were they available on such short notice? Andy called them six days ago. Must be losers. Takes one to know one. I hate parties.

Everyone's mouth is moving simultaneously. No one's listening. Everyone's talking. What's everyone talking about? It's remarkable how people can sustain a conversation for so long about nothing. I hate small talk. It's such bullshit.

Heads bob up and down. Like synchronized swimmers. Fake, toothy grins. Huge guffaws. Heads thrown back. Hands over hearts. Hands over mouths. I can't imagine what's so amusing. These people are not even funny. Drinks to lips. Clinking glasses. Want another? I'm going to someone's house to get *bombed*.

They never get drunk in their own house.

On my way to the bathroom, I grab the phone by the fridge and think about the other girls in the Girl Scout troop. I'm not going to the sculpture garden. Someone else will take them. I dial Diane's number. I pull the cord as far as it will go so I can stand in the corner around the hall from the kitchen. She picks up on the first ring.

"Hi, Diane, it's Caroline."

"*Caroline? Hiya!*" she says in an overly dramatic way, like I'm a two-year-old. I hear her say to someone, "It's Caroline!"

Then a trill of laughter. "Are you purposely avoiding me?" she giggles.

"Yeah, no, that's why I'm calling, I haven't been—whatever—sorry I haven't called."

"I mean today, here—"

"Here where?"

"At your party, silly, I'm right here next to the grill. Can't you see me? I can see you. You're standing in the hall with that phone on a cord!" Another gin-and-tonic giggle.

I look out the back door. Diane is standing next to the grill, waving at me. "Yup, I see you."

"You're crazy, Caroline, why are you calling me? Why don't you just come out here? Andy—guess who I'm talking to?" Diane is laughing with him about how crazy I am. Then she agrees to take the girls. I hang up the phone while they're still yucking it up by the pool, Andy looking a bit uncomfortable.

I turn down the hall toward the dining room to take the front stairs back to my room.

"There you are. How ya doin'?" Andy must have walked the other way through the family room. His eyes drop down and check out my shirt. "Listen, we're out of ice. I can't believe the caterer only brought four bags. Now that you're here, I'm gonna to run to the store." He grabs the keys from the dish on the table by the front door. "The caterer can't spare anyone, so I'll be right back. Go talk to Meg. She's been looking for you."

I grab his forearm. "Let me go. I'll get the ice. *Please.* I need to do something." I try to extract the keys from his hand by peeling his curled fingers back one by one.

"No, Caroline. You just came down. Absolutely out of the question." He clenches his fist and takes my hand off his arm. "This party was for you—for us—the four of us to—I don't know. Caroline . . ." His head slumps forward. "All of a sudden, it seems like it was a colossally bad idea. I mean, with you hiding upstairs and now down here avoiding everyone. What's going on? Do you need to see a doctor? Or a—you know—or something. Do we? Am I supposed to be reading into something here? You gotta talk to me."

"This is a great party, Andy."

"Then why don't you go out there and enjoy it." He sweeps his hands toward the kitchen. "You deserve it, sweetie. Go talk to Meg, for God's sakes. She's really concerned. She told me she called you five times this week, and you didn't call her back."

"Please. I can't handle the chit-chat right now. Okay?"

He looks at me closely. "I don't know what that means. What does that mean, Caroline? These are your friends."

"I'm serious." I look at the floor. "I, I need . . . something to do. I'm begging you, please. It's the ice or upstairs."

He stares at me silently. Then his eyebrows do that thing where they scrunch up into a volcano over his nose. His eyes are confused. I feel sorry for him. Desperately sorry. It aches in my heart. The pains in my heart don't go away these days. The heartaches are chronic; they layer on top of each other from one day to the next, thickening, like a callus.

"All right . . .Caroline. Fine. I can't believe I'm doing this, but, all right. I'm deferring to you on this. Brother. But no lifting the ice bags. You get that guy at Siedermann's to do it. Promise me."

"Yes, okay. I won't lift anything." I put my hand out for the keys.

"And the caterer will take them out of the car. Drive carefully. Sure you're up to this?"

"I'll be right back. You won't even notice I'm gone." I leave him with his hands on his hips, shaking his head, looking defeated and uncertain.

WHEN I DRIVE up to Siedermann's, I can't tell whether they're open or closed. It looks dark through the windows. But these kinds of places always look dark. I grab my wallet from the glove compartment. The little door to the glove compartment clicks closed in such a satisfying way. I love doors. They give such an appearance of order.

If I could just find a mint, I'd feel like a million bucks. In the console between the front two seats I find a map, Band-Aids, peanut butter crackers, a coloring book, crayons . . . no mints. There's a disgusting amount of wrappers, uncapped sunscreen tubes, an audiocassette wildly tangled in its own tape, and a chewed lollipop stick. How long has this been so gross? I scoop the contents into both hands and dump it onto the passenger seat next to me. Sorting is one of my favorite things to do. It's so rewarding. Instant gratification. Garbage goes into an empty grocery bag, and good stuff goes back in the console. Maps are smoothed out and folded along their God-given creases. Juice boxes beyond their expiration date—gone. Tangerine rind hard enough to be potpourri—gone. Little scraps of paper with phone numbers and no names—gone. Party invitation for the Fourth of July—gone. Oh, this is wonderful. I'm nearly at the bottom when I see a plastic wrapper rolled up like a sleeping bag. It's an almost unidentifiable package of Sno Balls. I unroll it. There's a small, squashed sliver of a Sno Ball left inside. I take the miniature pink crescent moon from the plastic. There's no cream. Just pink, sugarcoated cake. It's crusty and hard. God only knows how old it is. I place it gently on my tongue and close my mouth to let the saliva reconstitute it, to extract its goodness and bring it back to life. I close my eyes and savor it. The sun beats through the windshield creating a terrarium within the car, warm and cozy and safe. I rest my head briefly on the soft velour of the passenger seat.

A LOUD TAPPING on the window startles me. I lift my head from the seat. My face feels odd, and I run my fingers over my cheek and lift a gas station receipt from my skin.

I look out the driver's side window. The police.

"Ma'am, excuse me. Ma'am, can I have a word with you?" He asks through the narrow opening at the top of the window.

"Yes, officer. Is everything all right?" I'm disoriented and can't remember where I am.

"I was just going to ask you the same thing. Everything okay in there? Feeling all right?"

"Yes, just fine."

"The owner of this store," he points behind him, "called the station and said you've been out here for a while. Couple of hours."

"Couple of *hours?* Is he crazy? That's not poss—" I look down at my watch, but I don't have one on. I can't remember what time I left the house.

"Why don't you step outside, ma'am, and let's see your driver's license."

"Two hours, why would—" my wallet is resting on my lap where I left it. I pull my license out while opening the door.

The cop's eyes drop down to my stomach. "You need to

go to the hospital, ma'am? Are you bleeding?" He reaches for his walkie.

"No, no–" I look down. "I'm not bleeding. This is ketchup. See, smell–" I lift the bottom of my shirt.

"Please put your shirt down ma'am," he says with both hands up.

While looking at my license, he says, "Have you been drinking, ma'am?"

"Oh, no. God, no."

"Just taking a nap?"

"Yes, that must be it. I must have fallen asleep. I've been so tired. I just needed a little sleep, I suppose. I have two little girls, and I've been exhausted. Not that I'd trade them for anything in the world. I love my girls."

He's eyeing me closely. "I'm sure you do. Anybody I can call for you?"

"Oh, no. I have my cell phone right here." I get back in the car to look for my phone. Five missed messages.

He gently closes the door behind me and slips the license through the window opening.

"Why don't you go home now and get some rest. Drive safe."

"Thank you, officer." I turn the key in the ignition and drive out of the parking lot, and make a right onto North Avenue. I look in the rearview mirror. Red lights are flashing. It's not the police car. It's a neon sign, like at the carwash. Every second I drive the lights get smaller but still hold my attention. I focus really hard to make out the sign. Siedermann's.

Crap. The ice.

I make a U-turn at the bakery, head back to Siedermann's, and park in the same spot.

There's a woman standing at the front door of Siedermann's. Thank God they're still open. I hop out of the car. She's an older, square-figured woman with a short, blond perm. Not the good kind. And Buddy Holly glasses. Next to her, there's a skinny, older gentleman in a plaid shirt with rolled-up sleeves. He's tall, but without stature, like he's missing his vertebrae. Next to Sponge Bob and Gumby is a younger guy with tattoos running up and down both forearms, greasy hair and low hanging jeans, chewing gum with his mouth open. The Siedermanns. The two guys are looking at me, and Sponge Bob is locking the door.

"Hello! Excuse me!" I shout from my car; the driver's side door is open, and I stand just behind it. "I just came for some ice. Can I just grab some ice? We're having a party, and we ran out." I try to smile.

Sponge Bob turns around. "We're closed," she snaps. The husband, standing behind her, immediately looks at his shoes and shoves his hands in his pockets. The boy crosses his arms in front of his chest and straddles his feet. He lifts his chin a little.

"Just a *bag*! I don't need to look around or anything. I don't even need to go in—you could bring it out to me. I have cash. Keep the change!"

"Honey, we're *closed*. Can ya see we're locking the door? Whatcha been doin' out there? Saw you pull in two hours ago."

Does she call this customer service?

Someone who wears teal polyester pants and a shirt covered with kittens should not be so nasty to people.

"We were open *then*."

"You listen here, little lady, you have time enough to spy on me and call the police, don't you? But you don't have the

common decency to sell me a bag of lousy ice? Shame on you!
You . . . you . . . spy! This is the last time I'm ever coming here.
Or any of my friends—which it so happens I have many of,
and they're all at my house right now—and as soon as I get
back, I'm going to tell them exactly what kind of . . . inde-
cent . . . not decent . . . people you are."

At the end of my rant, my cell phone vibrates.

"*Who is this?*"

"Caroline?"

"Oh, hi, Andy—"

"Is everything okay?"

"Well everything *would* be okay if these devil-people from
Siedermann's . . ."

"You're still at *Siedermann's?* Do you know how long
it's been?"

"Yes, of course I know how long it's been!"

"What have you been doing? Caroline . . . Caroline, are
you still there?"

"Yes. Yes I'm still here. . . . I fell asleep."

"*What?* Behind the *wheel?!*"

"No, Andy, I was parked. At Siedermann's. I just put my
head down for a second, and—"

"I sent George out looking for you. He didn't see my
car there—"

"What?! *Why would you*—? Well, he's right. Because I
drove the minivan."

"I was just about to call the police. You didn't return my
calls, and—"

"The police?! They have better things to do than . . ."

"I should have gone for the ice. I hope you're happy,
Caroline, people are leaving, you missed everything . . ."

"Well, if the party's over—we don't need *ice*."

He blows out a gust of frustration. Then he says, "Just bring one bag."

"Fine. I'll be home in ten minutes."

The parking lot has completely cleared out. The rude Siedermanns have gone. My minivan and I are an island on a concrete sea.

I drive to the grocery store for ice.

ANDY IS CROSS armed, leaning up against the kitchen sink across from the island, when I get home. "It's over. You missed the whole entire party. Congratulations. I hope you're happy. Nice job."

The girls are watching a movie in the family room. The caterer is packing up. Two burned hot dogs sit on a sunflower paper plate. The dishwasher is purring.

He begins pacing the width of the kitchen, taking a sponge to the counter around the sink, the island, the stovetop.

He stops at the sink, rests up against it again, his shoulders hunched. "I don't know what to say. Really I don't. I tried so hard. To do something for all of us—but especially for you. Just to show you—" His voice cracks. He stops.

My eyes search the floor. I can't bear to look at him. My heartache throbs. "It was a really nice party . . ."

"*A really nice party?* Is that a joke? I mean, what's with you, Caroline? Do you care to tell me? You stay in bed all morning—all week, practically. Except for when you're out, God knows where, and sneaking into our house late at night, at God knows what time." His arms are flailing all over the place, and he can't spit the words out fast enough. "To say you're not acting like yourself is an understatement. You say you don't feel well. But you forbid me to call your doctor. You've got a bruise on your face, a gash on your forehead. You've been wearing the same clothes all week, even to bed! Except for what you have on today, which looks like it was on the losing side of a food fight at McDonald's, and your hair, well—I don't know what to say about that, did you have an appointment with our lawn mower?" He paces with angry arms— once in a while he shoots me a scared look or maybe he's just making sure I'm still here. "Then, you insist on picking up the ice. So I let you. And you fall asleep in the car and return three hours later?" He looks up at the kitchen clock. "No—*three hours and twenty-five minutes.*" He throws the sponge in the sink, a good six feet away.

"Oh, but you feel okay to go out last night past midnight? Somewhere? Oh my God!" He stops and faces me. "Are you having an affair?"

"An affair?" I choke. "Of course not. Jeez, Andy."

"Well, how do I know?" Arms in the air. "That's how these things happen, right? I don't know! Great—so you're not having an affair. Whew. Well, that's good." He pulls out a stool and perches at the end of it. "Then what's going on, please tell me, I want to know. Go ahead, I'm all ears." He doesn't know whether to be scared or angry or worried or furious. He crosses his arms and then uncrosses them, leaving them hanging at his side.

I am surprisingly calm. Like the air before a storm. Still. Yes, this is the right thing to do. It's time to tell him everything.

CHAPTER TWENTY

Sunday, October 1, 2006, 6:37 p.m.

OVER ANDY'S SHOULDER, in the backyard, I see the Fosters, our empty-nest neighbors, having a beer by the pool. They're always the last to leave. They don't even care if the hosts are around or even home.

I pick up the bag of ice and heave it onto the island. The bag is wet and heavy; it pirouettes several times before the end with the crimped staple gives out, hurling an ice chunk across the counter, through the air, pelting Andy in the chest.

He doesn't flinch, not even to pick up the cubes that have crashed to the floor or the ones that are now afloat in puddles of ice water streaming off the top of the island, running rivers around a huge bowl of apples.

"Okay." I'm still calm. "If you're sure. I know you think you wanna know." My cheeks stretch to fill with air until they hurt; a second later they're flat. "Okay. Fine." My shoulders slump forward. "I can't bear it anymore, anyway. I'm not the kind of person I thought I was. What made me think I could handle this myself? And what's worse, I'm not the kind of person you thought I was." Andy's back stiffens. He looks alarmed. He stands up. The energy shifts.

"What are you talking about? I thought you were sick. You have the flu or something, right? It's worse?" He tilts his head to the side and grabs one of his eyebrows, yanking the hair.

"Andy, I been thinking a lot lately about . . . a bunch of things. I don't know why. But like, well, how we met . . ."

"How we met?" His body caves. He shakes his head. "Why? Why are you bringing that up, Caroline? What's going on?" He pulls his shirt out of his jeans. "I thought we had a deal. Neither one of us would've planned it like that. But look at us now. Right? It wasn't out of convenience. We love each other." His eyes look defeated. "I mean, thank God you knew Debbie. Right? If you weren't at her wake, we wouldn't be here right now. In *our* kitchen. With *our* family. I mean if you really think about it, Debbie brought us together. She was our guardian angel."

Oh my God. He thinks I knew her.

The back door slides open too fast and slams against the door frame with a thud—rattling my bones. I pray that when my body settles, everything will shift into its proper place.

"*Caroline—there* you are!" Delores Foster sticks her head in the kitchen. "We've been looking for you all day. If I didn't know better, I'd think you were avoiding us."

She's now completely in the kitchen. I can't deal with her right now. Or her husband. Or my husband. If only I could vacuum up the words that just came out of me. I need to get out of here. I need to think before I speak.

Delores's husband, Howard, waves from the patio. "I just

love what you've done with the backyard. Did you put in all new landscaping? I did see the landscaper here. It must have been every day for two weeks, right?" She slides onto a stool and teeters a bit before grabbing the edge of the counter for dear life. "Boy, those landscapers with all those motors zazzin' away. Lotsa noise, but it sure does look good. Anyhoozle— what's you been up to?" She slips off the stool, then quickly gets solid again.

"Um . . ."

She reaches for a napkin and knocks her Heineken over. It spins around a few times on the wet surface, whisking a few ice cubes across the island.

"Oh, dear, did I do that?"

"No problem." Andy picks up the bottle and throws it in the recycling bin by the door and smiles awkwardly at our guest. He stands by the door anxiously, with his hand on the lever. I take a step back toward the stairs.

"Thanks for getting that, hun," Delores offers. She looks at Andy and me, one at a time. She swooshes around a napkin.

"Is Howard still out there? Let me go get him, I know he'd love to see you, Caroline. You too, Andy. Let me get him in here." She totters toward the door through tense air, smothering a good Heineken buzz in the process.

"Let me get that for you, Delores." Andy grabs the lever and yanks it open. He raises his hand in greeting to Howard, who's still drinking by the pool.

While I cower out of the kitchen.

I grab two sleeping pills from the medicine cabinet and fall heavily onto my bed.

I DON'T KNOW how much time has passed. I drift into a medicated sleep; my thoughts are slow and outside of my head, floating around the room; my body is heavy, making deep depressions in the bed. I have a faint sense that the bedroom door opens, and I think it's Andy. I think I hear him whisper, "*Caroline?*"

Tuesday, October 3, 2006, 7:30 a.m.

MY CELL PHONE alarm is set to the happy, carefree banter of chirping birds. I used to love that sound. I realize now how ridiculous it is. No one's that happy.

There's no schedule on my nightstand. Thank God. That means one of two things. I have nothing to do today . . . or I don't give a crap about any of it. If I didn't need to get the girls ready for school, there's nothing that would get me out of bed.

My palm touches the crest of Andy's pillow. Cold. I think of what's become of us in one short week. I'm bobbing and weaving his every move. He's demonstrated every emotion on the mood meter. Most of them I've never seen before. I'm sure he'd say the same about me. There's no use trying to shake this sense of dread that's lodged in me these days, as if I carry a chromosome for it.

In the bathroom, there's a note on the mirror. "We need to talk. Let's make some time tonight after the girls go to sleep. I hope you feel like your old self today. I love you so much, Andy."

At least now I can prepare for it. It's time. Andy's a good man. He deserves to know. And what am I ashamed about? I'm a good person. With a troubled past. But that's because

I've been let down by people. And I've buried some memories. He may be shocked at first, but he'll come around.

The girls go with the neighbors to school, and I float in and out of rooms, trying to be productive. I do some laundry, the dishes. I put the television on so I won't be so lonely. I sit on the couch and look into space and think about what I'll say to him.

The sound of my cell phone wakes me. Time has passed. I try to get my bearings. What time is it? I grab the phone from the coffee table.

"Hello?"

"Caroline, is that you?"

"Who is this?"

"It's Dr. Sullivan—

Click.

I'm not talking to that phony son of a bitch. He has some nerve calling me. He can burn in hell for all I care.

When the phone rings again seconds later, I let it go to voice mail. I erase the message before listening to that windbag and promise myself never to listen to another thing he has to say. To think I ever thought he'd help me. I don't need him. No wonder I've been a problem solver all my life. How can I depend on people? So that's what I do: I depend on myself to figure stuff out. No one lets you down that way. God, that feels great, knowing that about myself. It feels right, actually. Like I'm meeting myself for the first time. That's who I am. Self-reliant. And come to think of it, no wonder I forgot all this stuff. Who'd want to remember any of it, anyway?

What if I never know all of it?

Maybe that's a good thing.

It's 4:00, and I'm still in my pajamas. I go upstairs to

change; I need to pick up the girls from Diane's house soon. I grab some sweats from my closet. In the bathroom, I brush my teeth.

I can almost swear I hear Andy calling my name. How can that be? He never comes home this early.

I open the bathroom door. "Andy?"

"Caroline?" He's calling from the stairs.

It's definitely him. He's in the house. I pull off my pajama top and hurry to get dressed. I grab a hooded sweater.

"There you are. How ya doin'?" He walks into the bathroom and gives me a hug. He rests his hand on my pajamas, which are in a ball on top of the hamper. "You just getting dressed?" He pulls away from the hug and looks at me.

"I've gotta pick up the girls from Diane's house. She took a bunch of them on a Girl Scout thing." I turn to brush my hair at the mirror, moving quickly. "You're home early."

He looks at his watch. "Oh, yeah. Good. I'll be able to say good-bye to them."

"Good-bye?" I stop and look at him through the mirror.

"Yeah, I tried calling you a few times today. You haven't answered your phone, huh?"

I walk past him to get my cell from my dresser while he continues.

"I've got to go to Frankfurt. It's an emergency. Total PR disaster. Charles was supposed to go. They called me yesterday during the party. I told them I couldn't go. I said no. I didn't want to go out of town with all of us . . . like we are."

I have three missed calls from Andy. Two missed calls from Dr. Sullivan's office. Two from Meg. Three from Vicki and one from Diane.

"Caroline, I guess you didn't listen to my message. I've got

to go. And it feels like the worst time. It seems like you're—
I don't know what to call it. We've got to figure this out.
Together."

I fidget with my phone some more to keep my eyes off of
him. I can't do anything for him.

"But now I have to go to Frankfurt. Charles's brother died
last night. He was sick. But still, Charles didn't think it was
imminent. Anyway. I have no choice now. I'm leaving this
afternoon. The car is coming to pick me up. I need to pack
right now. Honey?"

"Okay." I don't know what to feel anymore.

"Okay, what?"

"I understand. You have to go. Okay." I grab some socks
from my dresser. "Maybe it's better that he's going. It'll give
me time."

"It'll give you time for what?" His face is like a road map
to Crazy Town.

"What?"

"You just said, 'It's better that he's going, it'll give me
time.'" he sits at the edge of the bed and pulls me to sit next
to him. "Time for what, why is it good I'm going? Caroline,
you're really upsetting me."

I pop back up and check the time. "Andy, I didn't say that,
I didn't mean that."

"Caroline, what's happening to us? To you?" He leaps up.
"I admit it. I'm scared!" He throws his hands in the air.

Now I look at him. My behavior is torturing him, and it's
not fair. "It's all my fault. I know now, I need to just tell you."

"What? Tell me what?"

"We'll talk when you get home. It's gonna be okay. It

really will." As I say that, I actually feel it's true. We're gonna get through this.

The doorbell rings, and he runs to the bedroom window.

"Crap. The car's here." He turns from the window and looks at me. "Jeez, this sucks." He rubs his cheek with the back of his hand. Is he crying?

I try to smile. I don't want him to leave like this. "It's all right, Andy, trust me. Everything's gonna be okay. I have to get the girls now." I kiss his cheek. "Have a good trip. When you get back, I will be my old self. You'll see." I hug him tightly. And just as I hug him, I smell his scent and feel something odd on my chin. I rub my chin, but the feeling doesn't go away. It feels itchy, like it's touching something scratchy, but it's resting on Andy's suit jacket. In a flash, a memory crosses my mind of the day I met him. I hugged him at his wife's wake. I told him I was Debbie's friend, and I cried real tears. Only they weren't real because I never met her. He cried, too. Could that be the last time I saw him cry? At the wake, his suit jacket was itchy when I rested my chin there. I remember that. And I can remember the smell of that place. The funeral home, like dead air and mothballs. And his arms hugging me back; his jacket was on, and I felt the stiff crinkle of the suit fabric around my waist, as I do now. Only then, I wasn't mourning the loss of a friend; I was on a mission. To find a father and sister for Lilly. But not just any kind of sister . . . *the perfect twin.*

Thursday, October 5, 2006, 9:13 a.m.

THE DAYS JUST morph into each other. With the blinds kept closed, if not for the girls' presence, it's hard to tell the time of day. Sullivan's tenacity is really annoying. Now he tries to call before the girls leave for school. I just answer it without saying hello. And hang up.

What's in it for him? Considering my last three visits, there's nothing in it for me. Why can't he just let me go like he did the first time?

Speculating his motives starts to bug me. I don't want to be thinking about that fat phony, but something nags at me. Like a mosquito in the kitchen—impossible to catch, impossible to ignore. I need to give up because I'm not going to talk to him. No more digging or sifting or mining. There's no gold there. I'm not opening myself up anymore.

But something else bothers me. There's no way Timothy would be stupid enough to kill JD for fear she'd call him out on the hit-and-run. He gave her the money. No, he's not that stupid. There's something else. Something I don't know. I feel it in my bones.

When my cell rings, it startles me, and before I'm conscious of it, I answer it.

It's Sullivan.

"Stop calling me. This is harassment now. I call the police and you're busted. I've got phone records." I threaten Sullivan on what must be his seventeenth call.

"I wouldn't do that, Caroline."

"Then leave me alone." I pull the venetian-blind cord open and closed. "You sprinkled your devil dust all over the goddamned place, and everything is back. Only worse." He starts to talk, but I don't let him. "How am I better—can you answer that? How am I a better person? Is this what *cured* looks like? I thought I could move on. Live my life, whatever I could piece together. But what is my life? I'm like a jigsaw puzzle with half the pieces missing. I'm living in a private hell. I don't know who I am. Everything's . . . nothing's . . ."

"Caroline—"

"She didn't kill herself. I knew JD could never kill herself. It was Timothy. He killed her. He almost killed his own daughter, but instead he killed JD. The mother of his daughter."

I never listened to JD. Every time she warned me about him. Always, "You decide for yourself, Caroline," she would say, and "Do you really love him, Caroline?" But now I'll never know if it was because she knew he was evil, or because she wanted him for herself. Look where that got her. I never figured Timothy for a murderer. He might look like a peacock, but he's got the backbone of a chicken. With the balls of a vulture.

"Caroline, I know you don't want to see me anymore. Think what you must about me. But I told you it'd be difficult. It's so painful for you. I don't really blame you if you can't hear anymore. I understand how half of you wants to know everything but the other half doesn't. If that makes any sense. But there's another tape. It's something you need to hear. You don't know the whole truth."

Thursday, October 5, 2006, 11:35 a.m.

LAST NIGHT, TESSA told me there was a special place dedicated to meditation in the sculpture garden they visited. A docent brought them there and taught the girls how to meditate. She told them that one way was to close their eyes and think about things they're grateful for. She explained that this simple act helps to make them more positive, especially on days of disappointment or frustration. On the drive to Dr. Sullivan's office, I try just that. I attempt to think of things I'm grateful for. I search my heart, but it feels like reaching beyond the teeth of a shark to get there. Instead, I find myself praying. First: that after this last tape, no matter what it contains, I'll be able to resume a happy life with Andy and the girls. Even if I need to work at it. I'm ready for that. I'll work as hard as it takes. I'm a natural problem solver. I make things work. I don't run from problems. I meet them head-on and roll up my sleeves. I'm the architect of my own destiny. I've always believed that. Second: I keep thinking about my parents' deaths. They happened right around JD's. I'm praying Timothy had nothing to do with that. "You don't know the whole truth" sticks in my brain like a rusty nail.

I sit in my usual spot across the desk from Dr. Sullivan, and pull the lapels of my sweater closer and tighten its belt. I don't look at him. I simply sit there, my arms crossed in front of my chest to cushion the blows. He's flitting around as if I busted in on him naked. Not that I need that visual to calm me down. I'm as calm as a corpse. I wait forever for him to get the tape recorder set up. He looks over at me and opens his mouth to say something, but thinks better of it and instead presses the play button.

Caroline: Did I tell you who was driving the car that hit Lilly?

Dr. Sullivan: No. Do you know who it was?

Caroline: JD knew who it was. She saw the driver's face, and she recognized the car immediately. She told me she knew beyond a shadow of a doubt. But she said, "If I tell the cops, no good will come of it." She told the cops it happened too quickly. I couldn't figure out who'd she'd want to protect that badly. I mean Lilly's life was hanging by a thread. Did I tell you she was in a coma for a few days? The doctors gave us little hope. We thought we were going to lose her, with all the internal injuries. Somehow, by the grace of God she pulled through. But, JD never got to see that.

I shouldn't have let JD go that day. It's my fault. I blame myself for her death.

Dr. Sullivan: Why would you blame yourself, Caroline? There's nothing you could've done. This had nothing to do with you.

Caroline: I could've kept her at the hospital. She'd be alive today.

Dr. Sullivan: You don't know that. She could've died the next day. Or the following week.

Caroline: The day JD died was the day she told me who the driver was. I don't know why she told me that day. I know she was feeling vulnerable. It would be her first day out of the hospital in over three weeks. It was almost as if she knew it was her last chance to tell someone. She swore me to silence. It was Mrs. Withers. She was still driving at ninety-three. In the old light-blue Dodge Dart she owned forever. JD said there was no mistaking that car.

Though Mrs. Withers was always proud, we knew she lived with heartache. Her husband of fifty-three years had died a while back, and all her friends were gone, too. She and Mr. Withers never raised any children. It's funny, she used to look after her house and her things like they were her children. Her house was always kept up. If something fell apart, she fixed it right away.

Just because she never had children, she wasn't the kind who hated kids. She loved Lilly. Mrs. Withers used to sit on her front porch and wait for Lilly to visit. Once a week, they'd have a tea party together. Lemonade and Social Tea Biscuits. JD moved into my parents' basement when Lilly was born, so Mrs. Withers was like a surrogate grandmother to her. That probably sounds crazy since Lilly's real grandmother, my *mother*, was living in the same house with her. But my mother was too busy for tea parties. She had Hummels to dust.

JD didn't tell the police because she thought Mrs. Withers was already suffering from what she did. JD thought Mrs. Withers' guilty conscience would end up killing her. In fact, Mrs. Withers died about a month after the accident. Only two weeks after JD died. They never spoke about it.

When I went to Mrs. Withers' funeral, she was laid out wearing a fancy pale-blue dress and her signature pink lipstick. She wore the same necklace she'd worn every day of her life. A small gold locket. Only this time it rested open on her neck. In it were two tiny photos of a baby. I knew Mrs. Withers for all those years growing up right next door, but I never knew she had a daughter. Her niece told me at her funeral. The baby died when she was three months old.

Dr. Sullivan: That's why your sister didn't want to press charges.

Caroline: That's quintessential JD for you. No matter her own personal pain, she wasn't going to take someone else down, especially if she thought it was senseless. An eye for an eye wasn't her way of thinking. I think that's a demented way to go through life. I couldn't turn my cheek if my life depended on it. No one's going to get over on me. JD thought some things were meant to be. That's lazy thinking. She would ask me, "Caroline, do you think you can control everything?" Of course you can. I pity people who don't realize that. Those are excellent values. I'm the architect of my destiny.

Some people are just too goddamn passive, and they rationalize their ineptitude by saying lame things like, "Things happen for a reason," or "It's not meant to be."

That might be the one fundamental thing that differentiated me and JD. I'm okay with that now, discovering that we had our differences. Even twins diverge in some way.

Dr. Sullivan: What do you mean "twins"?

Caroline: Me and JD. Even twins as close as we were—we still had distinct traits.

Dr. Sullivan: I see.

Caroline: What's the sense in turning your cheek? I'm not a floormat for other people's dirty boots. That's one thing my mother always said about me: "No one's gonna pull the wool over Caroline's eyes."

Dr. Sullivan: And in this case . . .

Caroline: Where would you like to start? You want to start with my fiancé abandoning me in college? Of course, I'll never know if it was because I got pregnant with his baby at the wrong time, or because after the abortion and hysterectomy, I'd never be able to have his children. Talk about the circle of death.

What about that phone message on my sister's machine

the day I found out that they were screwing behind my back? The sister that wanted to be her own person, march to her own drummer. Couldn't find her own guy? Has to sleep with my fiancé? Strange behavior for someone who was *"saving herself."* Don't you think? Talk about a change in tune. JD even got pregnant. To really stick it to me. Unfortunately for her, it was my baby.

Dr. Sullivan: What do you mean?

Caroline: Isn't it obvious? Lilly was supposed to be mine. Mine and Timothy's. Anyone could see that. We were engaged. He made promises to me. I told you that—go back to your notes. Are you listening to me, or am I wasting my breath here?

Dr. Sullivan: I remember you told me that you and Timothy were planning your future together, where you'd live and how many children you'd have. I believe you even said you came up with names for the children.

Caroline: That's right, and I can tell you Lilliana wasn't one of them. I don't know what JD expected a girl to do with a name like that. Maybe pick her teeth with hay and do-si-do in her spare time.

Dr. Sullivan: Did you ever think that not having a life with Timothy or a family with him might actually be a positive outcome?

Caroline: That's the stupidest thing I've ever heard. I can't believe I actually pay you.

Dr. Sullivan: JD decided to keep the baby. Do you think she knew she'd be on her own?

Caroline: I don't know what Timothy led her to believe— but one thing was always clear with Timothy. He was going to finish law school and become partner at Hayes & Hayes and go into politics. He wanted to be somebody someday. At least, that's what his father wanted. And when his father had his mind set on something, nothing stood in his way. Certainly not an illegitimate grandkid.

No one could ever tell JD what to do anyway. When she had the baby, she made me swear to never ask her about who the father was. I was devastated that she didn't trust me enough to tell me. Now I know why. She most assuredly did not believe in abortion. She didn't even believe in pre-marital sex. Or so she said. Of course being antiabortion is always easier when you're not in the position to need one. But I think after my horrific experience, she decided not to go down that road. There was nothing Timothy could do to stop her. He did the only thing he could: threaten her and pay her off.

You know where the police found the money?

Dr. Sullivan: You told me they found it in your sister's freezer.

Caroline: That's right. All hundreds. All of it was there when the cops found the bag. Timothy put the money in a NYAA bag. Just like his father and his grandfather, he was a member of the New York Athletic Association. Stupid asshole put the money in a NYAA plastic bag that's used for dirty workout clothes—so they can be washed and folded neatly in your locker, waiting for your next workout. So you don't have to cart home your smelly, sweaty clothes like some poor asshole. At the NYAA, once you take those soiled clothes off, you never have to touch them again until they're soft and dry and clean. I guess that's what money smells like.

He wrapped the money in a towel from the locker room and put a pair of white socks on top. Clever. That would really dupe someone looking for 5,000 crisp one hundred dollar bills. Wouldn't it? What an idiot.

Oh, and the note—sitting on top of the towel—said, *Disappear.* His handwriting. Wrote it himself. Clever as a fox.

I found the tape. But you already know that. I'm just pointing out that without me the police wouldn't have had a case.

Dr. Sullivan: How so?

Caroline: I gave them the tape. Don't forget what it contained. The threats and the admission to a half-million-dollar bribe. All they had to do was find the money. I wasn't going to do everything.

Dr. Sullivan: But bribes and threats do not a murderer make. There must've been other evidence.

Caroline: What about the fight they had at the Red Horse Tavern—there were witnesses. Including the hostess. In fact, she was a witness at the trial. Remember JD said she was meeting a friend the day she left the hospital? It was Timothy.

Dr. Sullivan: She told you she was going to meet Timothy?

Caroline: No.

Dr. Sullivan: How could you have known? Didn't she die that afternoon?

Caroline: Because I was the one who arranged it.

CHAPTER TWENTY ONE

Thursday, October 5, 2006, 2:17 p.m.

Dr. Sullivan presses a button on the tape recorder and the tape comes to an abrupt stop.

"What? What's going on? That's it? That's the end?" I'm at the edge of my seat.

He looks over at me. "No. Caroline. It continues on the other side." He turns it over, and my voice on the tape resumes.

Caroline: You heard what Timothy said on JD's answering machine. I told you how angry he was—he threatened her. Do you think he would've agreed to meet her in public? Where so many people would see them together? He couldn't risk being linked to her. This had to be handled with care.

Dr. Sullivan: Did you want to get JD and Timothy together for the sake of the child?

Caroline: What?

Dr. Sullivan: Were you thinking of Lilly? Was this a gesture out of love and concern for your sister and her child?

Caroline: I gotta tell you—you say the most fucked-up stuff. Do you actually think this shit? Is this what they teach in psychology school? It's fucking scary. Love for my sister? Are you serious? Where was the love for *me?!* Did she think about *me* when she was *screwing my fiancé?*

I despise hypocrites.

Let's be honest. I'm gonna spell it out for you since you seem to be a little thick upstairs. Lilly is *my* daughter. Not JD's. I don't give a shit who pushed her out. That's simply a technicality. That'd never hold up in a million years. Any decent-minded human being would agree. As for Timothy—she could have him. I certainly didn't want that scumbag anymore. I wanted Lilly. The other two could rot in hell for all I cared. All I needed was Lilly and a twin for her. But I knew I could find one easily enough. Every girl needs a twin. Oh, and a proper father. We weren't going to be a broken family. I wasn't looking for pity. First, I had to deal with the two of them. There was no room for JD in this scenario. And Timothy, well, I had to be clever with that one. It wouldn't be good enough to just get rid of him. He needed to be humiliated, like he humiliated me. Killing him wouldn't have caused him any pain. He'd have to suffer. His father would have to eat crow over this, too.

Dr. Sullivan: How did you arrange for them to meet?

Caroline: I'm so glad you asked. I've been dying to tell someone. And, as it happens, you're the only one I can tell.

Getting them together was pretty easy, actually. To get JD at the restaurant, I sent a note to her from Timothy on Hayes & Hayes stationery. I still have lots of letters Timothy sent me tucked away in a box. In fact, I recently got a new letter from Timothy—from jail. I must say I was surprised. But not interested enough to open it.

Dr. Sullivan: You didn't read it?

Caroline: No, I didn't read it. And I'm not going to. I just threw it in the box with the others. I don't have to listen to him anymore. He can send me a letter a day till he croaks. The conversation is over. Anyway, where was I? Oh, yeah, the notes he used to send me when we were in college were all on Hayes & Hayes stationery. Even though he was in school, he loved pretending he was a big shot. Sometimes he would send me flowers pressed into the letterhead. So romantic. I saved everything. The sheets of stationery that held the pressed flowers were blank. That's what I used for the letter to JD. I mailed it from New York City so it would have the proper postmark. It said:

JD—I need to speak to you about the girl. I know she's not doing well. I've been thinking about the possibility of never meeting her. I don't think I want that. Please meet me. Before something happens. I'll be at Red Horse Tavern on April 21st at 2:30. It's in Bellowsfield. Please come. T.H.

The note I sent to Timothy from JD, in an envelope marked *Private and Confidential*, was sent to his office. I knew his secretary sorted his mail and that she wouldn't open a letter marked *Private and Confidential*, but she might look at the return address and sender. The note to Timothy said:

Timothy—I thought twice before sending you this note because of our agreement. But I need to share some news with you. You'll want to know about this. Before others do. I would have put it in this note, but knew you wouldn't want a paper trail. If you don't meet me, I'll tell someone else. Maybe the *New York Observer* would be interested. With a name like Hayes, the papers can't resist. Nor the police. I'll be at Red Horse Tavern in Bellowsfield on April 21st at 3:00. JD

I wanted JD there by herself for a while so she'd be forced to order something. Before she left the hospital that day, I removed the cash from her purse so she'd have to use her credit card. I left her some coin change in case she needed it for a parking meter. She hated parking tickets—I knew that would really upset her.

At about two, right before JD left, I borrowed her phone from her handbag and went down the hall to make a call to Timothy's office. Unless he decided not to meet JD, he would have already left. I told his secretary that I was JD Spencer. That I was meeting Timothy at Red Horse Tavern in Bellowsfield at three, but I was running late. I told her his cell phone mailbox was full. I asked her to relay this message to him if he called the office, or maybe she knew the phone number of the restaurant since Timothy probably told her he was going there. I asked her if she'd be kind enough to call there and ask them to pass the message onto Timothy. I knew if Timothy showed up at the restaurant and they handed him a message from his office, he would have a stroke. His secretary couldn't have been more obliging. In fact, she went above and beyond. She actually left a message for Timothy with the restaurant hostess with the additional information that his evening meeting in New York City had been cancelled.

Dr. Sullivan: How do you know she called the restaurant?

Caroline: The hostess took the witness stand at the trial. She gave the details of what happened that day. I couldn't have done better myself, really.

She said Timothy walked into the restaurant like a guy who was meeting his bookie or his mistress. She said she could spot a guy up to no good in a second. He was wearing a baseball cap and a suit, and he walked through the restaurant with his head down, and his eyes ping-ponged, like he was looking for something or trying to avoid it. She asked him if she could help him, and he snapped at her. He walked into the dining area himself and found JD, who had been waiting a half an hour, maybe longer. The hostess said that JD got up a couple of times to use the bathroom, and that the busboy said she walked very unsteadily. He thought she was drunk. Apparently she bumped into a customer who nearly fell to the floor.

The hostess said she approached the table Timothy was standing at. He didn't sit. She said when she asked him if he was Timothy Hayes, it was like "time froze." The only thing that moved was anger, flashing across his face. She didn't want to wait for his answer. He was making her uncomfortable. So she just said, "Your secretary called and said your dinner meeting in the city is cancelled and your cell phone voice mail is full." Then she darted away. She heard Timothy say, seething, "How did my secretary know I was here?" She looked back at him and said he looked like a time bomb ready to blow. He grabbed JD's arm and got up close to her face. A half-filled ginger ale sat on the table in front of her. Before Timothy left the restaurant, he jerked at her arm so hard that her head buckled forward.

The hostess sent the manager over to the table because she was afraid things would escalate. As the manager approached, he saw Timothy jab his finger in JD's face and heard him say "I warned you, you stupid shit . . . you just sank your own ship," something like that. The manager asked him to leave, which he quickly did. The hostess didn't see him again until that day in the courtroom.

At the restaurant the next day, they heard news that there had been an accident on Route 206. A girl was found dead in her car. The hostess said she immediately thought it was the girl who'd ordered the ginger ale.

Of course, while the hostess was giving her testimony, Timothy's lawyer was objecting all over the goddamn place. Thankfully, she was able to say what needed to be said.

Do you want to know how she died?

Dr. Sullivan: Do you mean—yes, why don't you tell me.

Caroline: The police thought it was the accident that killed her, at first. You know, the impact of the crash. Her car was found wrapped around a tree. It happened about fifteen miles from the Red Horse Tavern. That's a winding country road that doesn't get much traffic. Who knows how long the car was there until someone found her.

Sometime in the early evening, a lady driving by saw the car and pulled over to the side of the road. She said it looked like an accordion. The hood was crushed back all the way to the windshield. But there was no sign of the driver. She was too nervous to get out and look around herself, so she called the police.

When the police arrived on the scene, they looked in the window and saw JD's body slumped onto the passenger seat. They opened the driver-side door, hoping she was still alive, and were knocked out by the smell. JD's face was in a pool of vomit. There was vomit everywhere, the steering wheel, the dashboard, the face of the speedometer. JD's pants were soiled. The heat that had built up in the car from sitting in the sun had intensified the stench. Thank God JD will never know she was found that way—it would horrify her.

The police report described her complexion as jaundiced. Her body was taken to Danielston Hospital and examined by a coroner. Once the autopsy was done, the coroner concluded she'd experienced severe gastric distress, which caused the uncontrollable vomiting and diarrhea, and that it was her convulsions that caused her to drive off the road. And collide with a tree. A pathologist was brought in to advise on possible chemical substances in her body. He found traces of arsenic in her digestive track. Some Nancy Drew-type in the police department leaked an unauthorized, preliminary report to the local news saying it was a suicide. You know, because it's all the rage to commit suicide with arsenic. Huge embarrassment for the Bellowsfield Police Department. They confiscated everything in the car, including the water bottle with the arsenic. Which had the fingerprints.

Dr. Sullivan: Whose fingerprints?

Caroline: Obviously I never wanted it to look like a suicide. Where would that leave Timothy? I have to admit, when I read that it was a suicide, I thought I'd have to hunt down that inept moron who fucked up the investigation and get rid of her, too. Total loser. After all that work.

It took some effort getting Timothy's fingerprints on the water bottle. And because Bellowsfield is Podunkville, it took forever for them to reverse the cause of death to murder.

I don't know what took them so long. The day after the accident, I gave the police a sealed envelope. I told them JD wanted me to turn it over to them in the event anything ever happened to her. It contained the answering machine tape. Which, of course, JD knew nothing about. I told the police that JD left the hospital that day to meet someone. That she was very nervous but never told me who she was meeting.

Dr. Sullivan: You started to say you got Timothy's fingerprints on the bottle.

Caroline: To tell you the truth, I probably have a hundred things with his fingerprints on them—letters, photos, books, a razor, toothbrush, his mouth guard. But nothing that could help me. I wasn't really sure at the time what I was looking for. The only concrete idea I had was to immerse myself in his routine.

I found his office easily enough in New York City. It was in the same building Hayes & Hayes has always been.

Every day for almost two weeks, I went to New York and stood outside his office building. It was easy to blend in—so many people walk up and down Park Avenue, especially during rush hour. Hundreds of people pour out of Grand Central Station and walk north on Park Avenue, walking past his building just two blocks up from the train station.

I followed him whenever he left his building—from across the street, of course—for lunch or for meetings, for the gym, or at the end of the day for dinner, or to his apartment on the Upper East Side. He was incredibly predictable. Before the tenth day of following him, I could tell you what he'd wear, where he'd eat lunch, what side of the street he'd walk, what kind of vodka he favored, and what time, roughly, he'd get up the nerve to sing at the karaoke bar. "My Way," of course.

But it was his morning routine that would pay off for me. He traveled to and from work, actually everywhere, by car service. Exec Town Cars. In the morning, usually by nine-thirty, a shiny black car would pull up to the curb in front of the revolving doors to his building. The driver would get out of the car and walk around the back of it to the right passenger door, open it, bid Timothy a good day, close the door, and walk around the back of the car to the driver's seat and leave. After about four days of this, I noticed that when the driver opened Timothy's door, he'd pause to wait for Timothy to gather his things and whatnot. The driver would fidget as he waited. He'd straighten the knot of his tie, brush off both arms of his suit, and button the top button of his jacket. Every day the same thing.

Timothy certainly took his time getting out. I couldn't see what he was doing in there, but when he got out he always did the same thing: guzzle what was left of his water and toss the empty bottle onto the seat before he walked away.

Slob. No shame even. I hate litterbugs.

The last day I followed him, I wore my gray interview suit and pearls. I knew this would be the day. A spritz of jasmine water, makeup and heels, and I was ready. I hadn't dressed like that in a long time; my job at the Philadelphia Post never required anything smarter than jeans.

I knew it wouldn't take me long to get what I needed. By the time Timothy was sitting at his desk taking the first sip of his morning coffee his fate would be sealed. The water he drank in the car that morning would change his life forever. I love moments like that, life-changing ones.

I waited until he was through the revolving doors, in the building, out of sight. I was hoping there'd be a few double-parked cars, dispensing blowhards of their own, to block Timothy's car. This would give me a little more time. But there were none. I didn't panic because I knew that it would take the driver time to get back to the wheel. As soon as I saw the driver walk around the back of the car, I slid into the back seat. Right where Timothy sat a moment before. The seat was still warm, and the air smelled like him, masculine. Pine and leather. It felt good sitting there. I felt good. Like an executive. Important. I felt like a some-body. Having a hired driver who opens the door for you and says, "Have a good day, miss" could really get to your head.

I had a tissue ready in my hand to grab the bottle of Poland Spring. But it made the grip too slippery, and the bottle spit out of my hand, landing on the floor of the car. The driver sat heavily into his seat, making the car rock. He shifted into drive and pulled into the moving traffic heading north on Park Avenue when I saw the shock in his eyes. His bushy eyebrows popped up in his rearview mirror. "Eighty-second and Madison," I said without look-ing at him. From the seat next to me, I pulled Timothy's newspaper onto my lap and lowered my head into it. The driver quickly veered toward the curb.

He looked at me in the rearview mirror and said, "Miss, I don't take hailers. You gotta call if you want a car."

I ducked to the floor to grab the neck of the water bottle through the tissue.

He shifted into park at the curb and turned around. "Sorry, miss. Gotta let you out. I got somebody waiting." He thrust his arm over the top of the front seat, revealing a thick gold chain around his wrist. "Here's a card with the number. Call ahead."

With the bottle safely in my bag and the newspaper folded and tucked under my left arm, I said, "I'm sorry. I didn't know I needed to call. I'm from out of town." I grabbed the door handle, my hand still lined in tissue. I strode over the puddle and turned back to the car to take in the moment, but it had already pulled back into traffic heading north.

Dr. Sullivan: So you took Timothy's water bottle and newspaper with you.

Caroline: It wasn't very hard. Once I got home, I wasted no time. I helped myself to Mrs. Withers' garden shed. That shed was like a time capsule. Iron garden tools from the fifties, a push mower from the sixties, galvanized pails, fertilizers and weed killers that could grow you a thick blanket of chest hair or cause you to go bald, and an old box of rat poisoning—the old kind—with arsenic. As kids, JD and I made up scary stories about the things that were in that shed and what would happen if one of us got trapped in there. Mr. Withers told us about the rat poisoning. He saw us look in the window of the shed sometimes, and he put the fear of God in us over that stuff. One day he told us if we so much as looked at it, we would die. I was scared to death of that box. Mr. Withers used silver duct tape to wrap the box from top to bottom and up and around again and again until the entire thing was sealed. When he needed to use it, he slit through the tape at the top with a pocketknife and then taped it up all over again when he was finished. He even showed us a dead rat once. We never went anywhere near that shed again. I thought there'd be a good chance that box was still in the shed. I wasn't disappointed.

I knew JD would never be suspicious of a water bottle in her car. She always had one in the car. I replaced the bottle she had in her cup holder with Timothy's after filling it with a mixture of water and rat poison. I knew she'd drink it at some point that day, possibly even the entire bottle by the time she got to the restaurant. She must've had at least some of it on her way to meet Timothy, based on what the hostess said about how JD behaved.

The rest of the story you can probably figure out on your own. The letter from Timothy was in JD's purse, and so was the cell phone I used to call Timothy's office. It didn't take them long to find the money in her freezer.

Dr. Sullivan: So Timothy didn't kill JD.

Caroline: Well, no, but to his credit, I couldn't have done it without him. The bribe, the note, the public argument, the water bottle—he was practically an accomplice! Hayes & Hayes could never save his sorry ass. Even his own secretary testified against him.

I'll never forget the look on Mr. Hayes's face the day they announced the verdict. It was priceless. Whenever I need a pick-me-up, I think about it. Of course, that was the end of Hayes & Hayes. Can't get many new clients when you send your own son to jail.

Dr. Sullivan: How could you be sure you'd end up with Lilly?

Caroline: JD appointed me as Lilly's custodian when she was born, in the event she'd ever need one. It was documented in her will. All legal-shmegal. I agreed to be the custodian long before I knew who Lilly's father was. Before I knew Lilly was really *mine*.

So maybe some things do happen for a reason.

I would have died for JD. Instead she died for me. That's what twins are for.

SILENCE FILLS THE room. The voices on the tape have stopped, but the message clings to the air like carbon monoxide. The mechanical whirring abruptly ends when the tape runs out with a snap. The small gray box speaks no more.

There's nothing more to hear.

I let go of the wooden arms and put my hands up over my mouth. I try to stop anything more from coming out. But it's too late. I feel disconnected from my body. Like I'm floating outside it, observing myself. I shut my eyes so tight that the flesh on my lids pleat. I suck my lips in to seal my mouth closed and hold my breath. The world seems to fall away.

My first thought is, *How could she do it?* As if she's someone else, not me. Because she feels like someone I don't know, someone I've never met. But the problem is, I'm her.

Did Sullivan think I'd give myself in? Knowing this?

I'll do myself in before I give myself in.

Wednesday, October 11, 2006, 3:13 p.m.

IT'S BEEN SIX days since I've been out of my house.

The despair has settled in my heart like wet cement. Dr. Sullivan still calls. Waiting. For what, I don't know.

Andy comes home tonight from Frankfurt, and I'm prepared to tell him everything. I mean show him. Among other things, I'm a coward, too. I can't sit in front of this decent, loving man, look him in the face, and tell him who I really am. I'll leave it for him to read in black and white. I've printed everything I could from the Google searches; I've culled sins from my memory box; and anything I learned from the tapes at Sullivan's, I've documented. It's all there, every sordid detail of my inconceivable past, for Andy to read and decide for himself what to do. It's time I tell him who I really am—though I dread it more than death, thank God it's finally here.

PART II

Saturday, April 21, 2007, 9:03 a.m.

S ecrets are likes knives. Aren't they? While some are dull, others can do quite a bit of damage.

An innocent secret is not really meant to be kept quiet. It's shared around the dinner table like a butter knife. Passed from sister to brother, shoulder to shoulder, mother to father. Spreading the truth, thick or thin.

Then there's a different sort. The dark kind. Like cleavers, they aren't passed to anyone. They're buried deep—silenced— but forever deadly.

My secret was buried for years. In the bowels of a brain and a box. And now, a book.

Yes, my book is finished! It's called *The Memory Box*. And it's all true. Well, except for the part about "Caroline" losing her memory. Of course, *that* didn't happen. I can assure you I remember every minute and always have. I just thought the story could use a little Hollywood: "Control freak stay-at-home mom living in the privileged suburbs Googles herself and unearths dark secrets from her past that she can't remember." More gripping, right?

Truthfully, I had never planned to write the events of my life into a book. But then I got to thinking about terrorists. Why, after executing horrific acts of carnage and destruction, did they always want to claim responsibility for their actions? The reason finally occurred to me: they wanted credit. Of course. They'd pulled off the unimaginable, and they wanted their pride and cunning to be known. They weren't ashamed. Or repentant.

I don't condone the work of terrorists. They kill people they've never met—killing for the sake of killing. While I'm a softie for retaliation and revenge, the work of terrorists is cowardly and random—who are they targeting? A bunch of people on a street corner? That's insane. I must admit, however, the amount of effort it takes to terrorize does not get lost on me. The planning, the sacrifice. That, I appreciate. But more to the point, I don't care much for the word "kill," with its negative implications. The word even sounds violent, whereas sometimes it's not violent in the least. In fact, it's often a quiet solution to a problem. Like if a gardener of heirloom roses discovered one summer that aphids were growing under her prize-winning variety causing the plant to become diseased and die prematurely, she'd spray the leaves with a pesticide to kill the aphids, thereby saving the rose bush. She would not be vilified by townspeople or implicated by police. She was simply problem-solving.

One of the challenges with secrets is that they need disguises, which manifest as lies. Tinkering with the truth is an art form and, when done masterfully, can paint exquisite stories. A few well-designed fibs can render the most beautiful portrait of the ugliest subject. Critics see lying as a character flaw. And the repeated liar as pathological. Nothing could be further from the truth. The practiced fabricator is crafty and clever. The two C's must be woven into her skill set. Even if she wears the guise of an absentminded, murky mommy who'd even lose the kitchen phone if it wasn't connected to the wall!

Seriously though, for me, relocating to Farhaven and becoming an insta-Mommy of two and blending in with these people couldn't have been easier. The hardest thing about it was learning to be late for school pickups, over-exercising, eating fewer trans fats, and drinking too much. I already had the "being fake" thing down cold. Learning to be late was a bit vexing—but really, how hard was it to be like these women?

Becoming a masterful liar, like any expertise, necessitated practice. I started at a young age and, if I may boast, was quite good early on. It still amazed me no one knew *I* was the one who sent those awful letters to Suzie, the sporty girl who nearly stole JD from me in first grade, accusing her of being a boy. I signed JD's name to the letters, and she and my parents were called to meet with the principal, along with Suzie's parents. I never meant to get JD in trouble. Obviously, I didn't think it out very well; I was seven. That's what I mean about practice. Nevertheless, the results were stellar. Those two avoided each other like Baldwin and Basinger from then on.

All this is by way of explaining why I wrote *The Memory Box*. In the absence of being found out, how would anyone know how clever I was? Does that make me a narcissist? If so, blame my mother for that. Elaine could have taught a Ph.D. program on narcissism. Apart from my heretofore success, writing the book was one of my greatest accomplishments.

Believe me, it wasn't effortless. Even if I was acutely aware of the plot points.

The world will never know *The Memory Box* was based on a true story disclosed through the lens of repressed memory. (Who'd forget she can mix a perfect arsenic cocktail!) I was realistic enough to recognize that some people would think the things I did to get where I am today were wrong. My solution: disguise the story with a little forgetfulness-cum-nervous breakdown—people love that stuff anyway. And the setting could not have benefitted more from the juicy fodder Farhaven freely offered.

The irony of moving to Farhaven and becoming a super-mommy was that while it saved me—by hiding me in the cellulite of the suburbs—it nearly killed me. Stripping every ounce of my true self was excruciating. Would no one ever know how creative and resourceful I could be? *The Memory Box* was the only solution. I wrote the book so I could remain alive somewhere. On those pages. God, it felt amazing.

Unless Dr. Sullivan ever read it, no one would know Caroline was really me. Only he knows the truth. It was thrilling to be able to tell *someone.* Especially someone who was compelled to keep it a secret. Do I feel sorry for him? Having to carry this around? No. He knew it was the right thing to do. He knew Lilly was always meant to be mine. I wasn't going to live a life of self-pity; no one rewards a sap. I always ask my girls, "Do you want to be pitied or envied?" In Dr. Sullivan's heart of hearts, he knew he'd be out of business if everyone were as motivated as I was. Losers keep his practice alive.

I promised Andrew that he'd be the first to read it, know-ing I'd need to change our names before I gave it to anyone else. But I couldn't resist giving him a copy with all our names intact. The morning after I left him the manuscript on the kitchen table, it was still there—looked-over and placed face down—no longer tidy with its corners lined up. I knew he'd finished reading it. I imagined him pulling an all-nighter, as he'd done with other books. This time, the book was mine. I thought he might take it into the den to read, but it was right there where I'd left it. I'll never forget that day.

As I stood in the kitchen, staring at the manuscript, the oddest sensation seized me that morning. At first it was subtle, nearly imperceptible, like the onset of a rolling fog. It crept over me with quiet, unsettling determination. I tried to shake it. But the feeling only grew stronger. It permeated my joyful veneer until it snuffed the thrill from my core. I'd never felt anything like it.

Things weren't going as planned. I didn't expect to feel doubt the day after I handed him my manuscript. I anticipated pride and celebration, joy. It was a triumph, for God's sake.

No. On second thought, it wasn't doubt that wormed its way into my giddy fever. It was something else entirely.

As a warm breeze leaked through the screened window over the sink, I shivered. And grappled with this feeling. It was foreign.

It was fear.

Fear. My *God*, it had gripped me and shoved its ugly face in mine. Why had it taken me until that moment to recognize how insane this was? It was pure madness to hand over the details of a not-so-Hallmark life story to one's husband. The very secrets that had been hidden from him, and from everyone, for years. Now, in black and white. Was it naiveté or ignorance? Or *audacity?* It was reckless, for sure. I was

overconfident. Not about me, about Andrew. I had been certain he was too boneheaded to figure it out. I don't mean that
in a disparaging way; it's one of the reasons I married him. I
used our names in this version of *The Memory Box* as a test. A
game I thought would be fun. Yes, it was dangerous—but that
was the thrill. He'd never connect the dots. I told him I made
it up, that I drew on our real life in some parts, but that's what
a writer does. It wasn't like him to be suspicious. He wasn't
even typically curious. Not in a million years would he deduce
that he was "Andy." I know—pathetic. It used to amuse me,
how trusting and gullible he is. Then it just became sad. And
a joke you can't share with anyone is only so funny.

What if the game backfired? The longer I stood by myself
in the kitchen, the more paranoid I got. Could the story have
instigated the tiniest fissure in his skull? At that very moment,
he could've been at the computer, looking stuff up.

He must have just left the kitchen, because the scent of
his shaving cream lingered in the air. There was no other evidence he'd been there, nothing in the sink or on the counter-
tops. No sign of him in the house. The only sounds breaking
the quiet came through the open window—birdsong and the
girls' laughter floating from the garage.

The cherry tree outside the kitchen window had already
shot out some new growth, and the branches, not yet with
leaves, scraped the window, making a sound that gave me
chicken skin. I filled the teakettle with fresh water and
clicked on the front burner. Smarty Pants came trotting into
the kitchen and nuzzled my leg as I opened a cabinet door. I
picked him up and kissed his head while staring into the cabinet, wondering what I wanted from it. I lifted one of Smarty's

ears and whispered, "Who's my best friend?" He confirmed what I already knew.

I took a step closer to the table with Smarty in my arms, and keeping some distance from the stack of pages, I checked to see if Andrew had written anything, but he hadn't. Metal-winged butterflies flickered in my stomach. I glanced out the window again; the lawn mower rested against the grill. I strained my neck over the sink, but he was nowhere in sight.

THE KETTLE WHISTLED. I let Smarty tumble to the floor as I turned back to the stove. Andrew was standing there. For how long? He was leaning on the kitchen table with both hands flanking the manuscript. Staring at me, waiting for me to notice him. Smarty sat and looked at him. He waited for Andrew to say something. So did I. We stood in silence for what seemed like an eternity.

"Caroline," he said without any noticeable expression whatsoever, breathing in deeply through his nose.

My heart did a triple-axel.

"Yes." I blinked back tears I was surprised were gathering.

"It's great."

"Great?"

"Okay, crazy. Crazy great. I couldn't put it down."

"Really?"

"Really, I mean it. How would I be able to read it so fast? It was unputdownable." He threw his hands in the air.

"*Unputdownable?*"

"I don't know how you came up with it—the idea, I mean." He shook his head. "You know, in the end, it was just—so—so—whacked. Very sad."

"I know, wasn't it sad? Do you really think so? Sad? *Whacked*?"

"Jeez, that was one sick chick." He picked up the manuscript and tamped the pages against the table to align them into a neat pile. "I mean, she killed her own *sister* . . . after being obsessed with her for all those years."

"Obsessed?" I shook my head. "No, she wasn't obsessed. That's not right, Andrew." My hands and arms couldn't make up their mind; they moved from my hips to cross at my chest and back again.

"Okay. You're the writer, *but* . . ." He put his hands up to surrender. "Anyone who could smack her teeth out with a hammer trying to chip a tooth to match her sister's is my definition of obsessed. And demented."

"*Demented?*" That nearly choked the breath right out of me. *And* it hurt. Maybe this hadn't been a good idea after all.

He looked at me with sparkling eyes and laughed, "She killed her sister, for Christ's sake!"

"Her sister betrayed her!"

He laughed even harder, "I know you're supposed to love your characters, but really, you're scaring me a little, Caroline." He walked to a cabinet and pulled out a bowl and added, "Oh wait, *then* she frames her ex-boyfriend . . ."

"*Fiancé—*"

"Fiancé, whatever. Let's agree she was mental."

Mental?

"Andrew, she persevered and triumphed—in the face of *adversity*."

"Triumphed? What chapter was that? She ended up having a breakdown. How did she triumph? She went cuckoo.

This is not a feel-good story about human achievement. Unless I missed something."

He walked back to fix his breakfast. I had to check my tone. I needed to keep some distance. He was right, after all: the triumphant Caroline stood before him in the kitchen. I didn't write about that part. That's for the forever-unwritten sequel.

"But you liked it?"

He grabbed a box of Shredded Wheat and poured some. "Oh yeah, I really got sucked in. It definitely made me uncomfortable. A lot."

"Really?"

"Jeez, a lot of times. That's what you wanted, obviously, right? Like when she started choking, or thought she was choking and then fell on top of her daughter and broke her collar bone . . ." He stuck his head in the fridge looking for the milk.

"Oh, I made that up!"

With the refrigerator door between us, he popped his head over to look at me, "Uh *yeah*, you made it *all* up, right?" He winked at me, then took out the milk and orange juice. "You made up the part about how 'Caroline' went looking for a husband, right? 'Cause that one hit close to home. I mean, I guess the way we met is unorthodox, but the obituary search really freaked me out." He shook his head. "You got a crazy imagination."

While chewing, he raised his hand as if he'd just remembered something. "*But*—before you start sending it anywhere, we need to discuss something."

"Yeah?" I picked up Smarty and stroked his ears. I needed

something to do with my hands. Smarty Pants would absorb my anxiety.

"Now Caroline, don't take this the wrong way, okay? Don't bum out on me. I'm super proud of you, writing this book—I know how hard it was, how long it took. It's great. I've already told you that. I mean, I could never come up with something like that in a million years."

"Yeah?" I pulled out a chair and sat down; Smarty sat in my lap.

"Listen, it's . . . *interesting,* I guess, that you used our names. But seriously, it's creepy. Okay, I know, it's not like anyone's ever gonna think it's us, that 'Caroline' is you, but still."

Well, there you have it. Give a guy a mile and he drives in reverse. But that's why I love him!

"Oh, no, wait. You called the husband 'Andy.' Not 'Andrew.'"

I knew it. I said he'd never connect the dots.

"Oh, come on. 'Andrew' is too uptight," I said without thinking.

"Uptight? *Thanks.*" His face dropped.

"No, what am I saying?" I yanked myself back into the moment. "No, I mean," I poured juice in his glass, splashing it everywhere. "I *love* 'Andrew.' It's very . . . refined."

"Great. Anything else you want to tell me?"

"Whaddaya mean?" I used a napkin to wipe the table without looking at him.

"Well, since you're coming clean."

"What's that supposed to mean?" I spun around to face him. That was a strange thing to say. He was freaking me out.

Would he be so calm . . . if he suspected? That would be devious. And that would require intelligence.

I walked over to the sink and sponged around the drain.

Without looking at him I said, "No, I—no—"

"Caroline, seriously, I don't want to harp on it. You don't want people to think it's a true story, right? You have to change the names. It's non-negotiable."

"Oh . . ." I sighed, "yeah. That's not a bad idea. I just thought the girls—"

"The *girls?* They're not going to read this book. Not until maybe they're . . . thirty. Honestly, Caroline, there's stuff in there that's upsetting—some of it's really familiar. I'm not going to judge you for that. I know all about 'drawing on true experiences for writing that resonates' or whatever those headlines say on your writing magazines. So I'm not going to tell you to yank it. Just change the names. Win-win." He dusted off his hands.

"How do you think Lilly would feel about reading that the character named 'Caroline' is really not the biological mother of the character named 'Lilly'? That 'Caroline' actually killed 'Lilly's' real mom? She's not mature enough to know it's a sick, made-up story to which you attached our names with a sprinkling of factual references. I get it—but *they're* not going to."

No, Andrew, you don't get it. And it doesn't look like you're *ever* going to.

"I'll admit," he continued, "there were times I had to stop and scratch my head—wondering where the nonfiction ended and the fiction began." He forced a chuckle. "If I didn't know you better, Caroline . . . I mean a husband less secure might be a little worried after reading that." He let out a clumsy heehaw. "This much I do know: you have a crazy imagination, *and* I can't possibly be as clueless as the Andy in your book. He's a good guy. But I don't want a sap like that associated with my name, thank you very much."

Secure? If secure is the new stupid.

He stood up to put his bowl in the sink.

I walked over and put my arms around him from behind, resting my cheek on his back, and said, "He's also handsome and charming, and a great kisser . . ."

"I didn't read anything about him being a great kisser."

As we stood there, all I could think about was the day I met him at his wife's wake. As smoothly as it's all played out, there've been times I've wanted to shake him by the shoulders and tell him the whole truth, just to see his reaction.

He was quiet as he rinsed his bowl, then he turned around to face me, putting his arms around my waist. "Listen, Caroline. I'd be lying if I didn't tell you I know what this is about." His eyes were serious.

The hair on the back of my neck sprung like porcupine quills. My mouth couldn't form a single, intelligible word. Since I couldn't trust what emotion they'd carry, that was fortunate.

"I know about tragic loss, too. Hell, that's what brought us together. But you lost more than your husband. You lost your parents and your sister. And I know how hard JD's death was, and *has been,* for you. It doesn't matter that she drowned when the two of you were kids."

I wasn't prepared for this. My brain cells tripped over themselves, shoving each other, fighting over how to advise my mouth. I dropped my head so he wouldn't see the confusion in my eyes.

"How old were you again? When JD died?" Was he grinning—or did I imagine it?

"Whaddaya mean? You know how old I was. Why are you asking me that?"

This conversation was becoming unnerving. I needed a Sno Ball so badly; I would've eaten it right in front of him.

Instead, I turned away and picked a spoon out of the sink. I stuck it in the sugar bowl by the coffeemaker, then shoved it in my mouth.

"Caroline. What are you doing?"

"Waa?" I let the sugar pool on my tongue. Let it slide down my throat slowly as it dissolved.

"Did you just eat a spoon of sugar?"

"Noh."

"I *saw* you." His face scrunched into a question mark.

"JD was five."

"*Five years old?* Can you imagine if our girls experienced that kind of trauma at five? Do you see what I mean?"

I couldn't follow him. No, I didn't know what he meant. Was he outing me? Was he patronizing me? Was he empathizing? If I weren't so scared, it would be funny—*I* was having trouble keeping up with *him*. He hugged me and lowered his voice. He became gentle, but I couldn't relax.

"Sweetie, sometimes people react to tragedies with anger. And that's obviously how you dealt with it. I'd never ask you to change that. If you need to write about some chick murdering her sister, so be it. I won't criticize you. Did I think it was going to be a different kind of book? Yes. Was I expecting it to be so disturbing? No. But maybe it was important for you. To move on or whatever. I don't know. I'm not a shrink. Maybe your next one will be a bit more cheery?"

He kissed me on the forehead and turned to the sink. "Makes for a great read, though."

"*Daddy*—"Tessa called from outside, "*what are you doing?*"

"I told the girls I'd take them on a bike ride. Then, I've got to mow the lawn." He wiped his hands on a kitchen towel.

I held onto the counter.

"You wanna come?"

"I need some breakfast. You guys go. I didn't even have my tea yet. Anyway, I have to bake something for the block party. A pie or something."

Andrew squeezed my shoulders and kissed me. "I'm really proud of you, Caroline. I always knew you had it in you."

"*Dad*," Lilly popped her head in the back door, "are you coming? Hi, Mom."

"Hi, sweetie."

"I'm coming, I'm coming . . . I had to finish your mother's book." He slipped his sneakers on without unlacing them. "Hey, I thought the Google thing was really clever. I've never done that—Googled myself. I oughta try that," he said before closing the door behind him.

I LOOKED AT them through the window and let out a gust of breath I didn't realize I was holding. It was behind me now. The day I'd waited for wasn't in my future anymore; it was in my past. Now, the rest of my life. A smile filled my entire body. Instinctively, my hands rested on my heart. I had everything I'd ever wanted.

Tessa and Lilly put on their matching helmets. They both were wearing their *Girls Rock* T-shirts. A girl at their school made fun of them for dressing alike. I told them to ignore that nasty girl. She's just jealous because she doesn't have a sister. Mean girls always get the punishment they deserve.

"Caroline—" Andrew snuck his head through the kitchen door.

I jumped and knocked over a juice glass.

"I just remembered what I wanted to ask you. About your book."

"Yes?" I crossed my legs and drummed my fingers on the stack of pages.

"How did she forget all that stuff that happened? How come she didn't remember?"

Silence filled the kitchen, as though it seeped out of the walls and up through the floor. He stood there, half in and half out. His hand rested on the doorknob as he hunched over, waiting for a quick answer. But I didn't have a quick answer. I never actually thought about an explanation for that. "She" didn't *lose* her memory, but no one knew that but me.

"Caroline?"

"Yes?"

"What was it? You never really said what it was. Did the shrink figure it out? I was just curious."

I forced myself to keep in mind who was asking this question. I had to be careful not to mangle a clever person's thoughts with his. All this agitated me. It was a book, for Christ's sake. Suspension of disbelief! I was agitated.

"Daddy—what are you doing in here?" The girls were now in the kitchen. They had slipped in from the front hall. With their shoes on.

"Are you coming or not?" Lilly stuck her hands on her hips.

"Yes, I'm coming. Sorry. I wanted to ask Mommy something about her book." He looked back at me, "It doesn't matter, Caroline," he shrugged. "It's still awesome." He stepped into the kitchen and smiled. "Just thought I missed something. It's better to keep people wondering."

When he smiled again, it erased my concern. I realized my own paranoia was at work. He wasn't prodding me. He was genuinely happy for me. How did I find someone like him?

"Mommy, congratulations! You finally finished it!" Tessa dove at me and hugged me tightly, squashing her head up against my stomach.

"Yeah, Mom, way to go. I'll read it later, okay?" asked Lilly.

"Someday, kiddo," said Andrew, looking back at me with exaggerated eyes.

"Am I in it?" Lilly asked.

"Am I in it, too?" Tessa chimed in.

"Very funny, girls," he grabbed both their arms and pulled them backward toward the kitchen door, kissing the top of my head as he walked by. "Let Mommy have her breakfast. I thought you guys wanted to go on a bike ride?"

"Love you, Mom."

"Yeah, love you! Now we have two smarty pants in the house!" said Tessa as the back screen door swung shut. A minute later, Andrew was on his bike, and the girls were running up the driveway to get their bikes from the front of the house.

It was quiet again. My body buzzed with excitement and love and happiness. I don't know if I'd ever felt that way before. I closed my eyes to take a mental snapshot so I could always remember that scene and that feeling.

Smarty made it difficult to bask in the warm and fuzzies. He stood in the kitchen doorway barking like a lunatic. With every bark, his body popped off the floor.

"Smarty, quiet down." He stomped into the room and stood at the base of the table, yapping like mad, insistent. The bark was strangely hostile.

"What's the matter, Smarty? Sweetie, you've got to settle down. What is it? Did you catch something?" I smiled to lighten things up. That was a mistake; he growled as if he thought I was mocking him.

"Okay, Smarty—" I reached out to calm him. He was standing on something. As my hand approached his head, he snatched it from the floor, gripping it in his teeth. A piece of paper. I tried to take it from him, and he snarled. I jumped back. He was officially scaring me. What was the paper in his mouth? I stood tall to show him who was bigger. Then I hunched down to grab the corner of it and pulled.

He wouldn't let go, and yanked back and forth to shake me off. Something we usually did for fun with his stuffed cat. I released it and stepped back. I'd never seen him like this. He took off and ran out of the kitchen, nearly flying through the air. That's when I saw what he had in his mouth. An envelope.

The sound of his nails grazing the wood floor made it easy to follow him. Upstairs he bolted, passing a toy mouse on the stairs. "What is it, Smarty?" I called out to him, thinking about how people with pets don't see the absurdity in asking them questions. When he got to my bedroom he started yapping again, quick, sharp barks. When I arrived ten seconds later, I saw him at my closet. The door was open—leaving it in plain view. My memory box. Knocked over on its side. I was horrified. Its contents spilled out, littering the floor. Toy mice mixed up with my things. My cherished possessions.

"*Smarty!*" How did his toys get in there? Jesus, the girls. How could I leave that door *unlocked?*

My blood pressure was soaring.

He lowered his bottom onto a pile of letters and newspaper clippings, and stared at me defiantly.

He had a strange look about him. Accusatory. His ears were taut. His face grotesque.

"What did you *do*, Smarty?!" Crazy with rage, I dropped to the floor and swept my private things with both arms into a big pile. JD's hairbrush, Timothy's eyeglasses. My dollhouse dolls—the twins—their hair wet from Smarty's drool. Nearly *ruined*. "Shame on you. What's gotten into you, *wretched* dog." As soon as I said that, he sprang and yelped. He was inches away and frightening. There was no way this ball of runt hair was going to expose *me*. This goddamned, pint-size mutt knew what? Not half of it. He was gonna bully *me? Seriously?*

I didn't recognize him. And he didn't recognize me.

The envelope he had in his mouth was on the floor. I snatched it and recoiled before he could react. Before he could bite me. Then I slid backward, toward the back of the closet and farther away from him.

The envelope was wet from his slobber. It was sealed shut from the dried blood that once soaked the paper towel inside it. I knew instantly what it was. I carefully flaked the cracked pieces of crusty paper towel that, after years of being stuck to the envelope, took on the shape of its corner. They were still in there, exactly as I remembered them. Gauzy red fibers of paper towel clung to the two broken teeth and the shards of a third.

I lunged at Smarty. "*Get out!* This is none of your fucking business!" What if he had swallowed them, or hid them somewhere? Or left them for someone to find. "These things are *mine*. How could you do this to me?" My cheeks were wet, but I didn't mean to cry. I wanted to pick him up and throw him out, but I was afraid he'd bite me. Instead, I thrust my foot at his butt, and as he flew through the air, I slammed the door shut.

Smarty was still in the room. He barked without pause, that I-don't-need-air bark, just outside the closet door. The razor-sharp barks mutated into an eerie howl. He wouldn't relent. I didn't care. I was safe now. With my things. I didn't care if he barked himself out of oxygen.

I held those teeth in the palm of my hand and wrapped my fingers around them. "I would've done anything for you," I said to her. I would've knocked every tooth out of my head.

Up on bended knee, I collected the strewn papers and objects, stacking the pages of my life back together, bringing order to the chaos. With reverence, I placed everything in the box. The envelope had fallen apart, wet from Smarty's saliva. So instead I wrapped the teeth in a tie-dyed bandana I found in the box, the one JD wore when she was in high school. I held it up to my nose and detected the faintest smell of her still on it.

I hadn't seen these things in years.

A photo of two young girls in bathing suits, we were about nine or ten, our arms pretzel-locked, hair long and wet, skin glowing brown, both wearing a one-piece navy bathing suit, hers with a yellow stripe around the waist, mine with a yellow hair ribbon tied like a belt. Or a stripe. Happy vacation grins. On the back, my mother's handwriting: *Summer 1978—Cape Cod—Caroline and JD at the beach*. I held that photo for a long time; we always loved each other on vacation. I closed my eyes. "I miss you so much . . ." I whispered, wishing she could hear me. "You made a terrible mistake, JD. A terrible, unforgivable mistake. You know that now."

When I put the flap down to close the box, it wouldn't sit flush. The flap stuck up. I lifted it to move things around and settle the contents. A bunch of letters, cinched with a rubber band, were snug against the inside wall of the box, their corners pointing upward, keeping the flap from closing. I peeled them away from the side and placed them on top, then lowered the flaps again. Before closing the box, the letter on top caught my eye; it appeared, from the back, to be sealed—unopened. I picked up the bunch and flicked at their corners like a deck of cards. Just the top one was sealed. The return address on the back read *State Penitentiary I.D. #7849382.*

I ripped off the rubber band and the letters scattered to the floor, fluttering like the wings of release doves. They were from Timothy. Love letters. The ones I saved from college. All of them opened but one. It was addressed to me. *Caroline Schwarzenbauer.* It wasn't like the ones he left in my dorm room. It had a stamp. He sent it to my house in Pennsylvania. The postmark read *November 2000.* Before I married Andrew. Before I moved to Farhaven. I never opened it. I never intended to. Reading it would've given him the last word. That was out of the question.

It didn't matter anymore. I won. Andrew's reaction to my book proved that. I had everything. And he had nothing. It wasn't supposed to turn out that way—we were supposed to have each other—but he fucked that up. And I was resilient. Good things don't come to those who wait. Good things come to those who shift gears.

I picked up the unopened letter from the floor. My Lanstonville, PA, address was written in Timothy's handwriting. Letters so small you could hardly make out the words, in a scratchy hand, like they were etched in stone, no curves, just pointy, sharp corners, like scissor blades. Still kneeling, I tore the back flap open with no regard for the envelope's original configuration. I felt flustered as a rush of emotion took over. It was so familiar. Like I was in college and just found a letter from him on my dorm-room dresser. He'd stop by when I was in class to leave me love notes all the time. They were all in this box.

I sat down on my heels and unfolded the letter. My entire body was still, except for my heart. I was twenty all over again.

It was remarkably easy to slide back into the world of Timothy. That's how it always felt to me. He was more than my boyfriend or fiancé; he was an entire world of being. That morning, in the closet, I slipped into that nostalgic place so deeply I didn't notice Smarty was jumping onto the door, pawing at the louvers, snapping interminably. I pretended he wasn't there.

Dear Caroline—

I've got some news for you.

First, I want to tell you about the night I fucked your sister—since she didn't tell you, did she? I just wanted to have some fun, but she didn't see it that way. That bitch bit me and I've got a scar on my face to prove it. She was surprisingly feisty for being shit faced. I asked her about you that night but she wasn't very chatty. Probably because I had to grab her from under the chin so she wouldn't bite me again.

For years I thought she was too wasted to remember that night. Especially since she didn't like me very much. Then one day I heard from her, when she needed money for her kid's hospital bills. She said if I didn't come through with the money, she'd go to the police about that night.

She was wise not to take her law degree too seriously and throw accusations around that would never hold up in court. Smart not to take on Hayes & Hayes over an innocent roll in the hay. Who'd believe her anyway? I could get any girl I wanted.

Funny how life works. I had both *Schwarzenbauer* sisters, and you both had me. JD hustled me for half a million dollars and made me think I was the kid's father. You thought the same thing, right? Well, I'm not. The kid's not mine.

At law school, your sister had quite a reputation. No one could get past second base with her. I'll never know how that was a turn-on for my frat brother, Paul Lilliana—but he was in love with her. I thought she was a bitch for not throwing the guy a bone before he died. Looks like I was wrong. At least he got some after all. The brain tumor killed him a week after graduation. But you probably know all that. Nice family they would've made. At least those lovebirds are together now.

I'll admit, I thought the kid was mine. That's why my brilliant "lawyer" didn't want me taking a paternity test. But when you're in jail, you have a lot of time on your hands. I got to thinking that maybe she wasn't. A friend of mine took care of what we needed for the test. I'll spare you the details. Let's just say you're not the only resourceful one.

Your stupid sister didn't want you to know I fucked her. All to protect your feelings? I bet she never knew who the kid's father was, either. Doesn't matter now.

So that leaves you, Caroline, and the girl. Is that why you killed JD, for the girl? You're a fucking psycho, Caroline. Thank God I got rid of you when I did. Even though my father couldn't prove it—I know it was you. Yours is coming. I'm not going away. I have a new lawyer now.

Timothy

My mouth dropped open. I let go of the letter. It zig-zagged through the air until it landed on the floor next to the others, taking forever to get there. My heart changed its tune. It knocked like a gavel on a steel drum. I gasped aloud and sprang to my feet. That ignited Smarty again outside the closet.

"*No!*" I boomed. No, he did *not!* Jesus, JD! What the *fuck?!*

I used a scarf to pick up the letter so my flesh wouldn't touch its unfathomable contents. I did the same with the rest of them.

Why, JD? Why didn't you tell me? How could you let him get away with it?

I shoveled the letters with the scarf in my hands, dropped them into the box and kicked the flaps closed. I spit on my hands, then rubbed them on the sleeve of a denim jacket hanging behind me. I stepped back from the box. My heart knocked hard against my chest. Or was it my brain against my skull? Or was someone at the door? I couldn't discern sounds. Thoughts. I stood alone in the closet with my mutant reality. For how long had I been living this fucking mirage? I swirled around and felt the wall for the light switch. If only I could turn the spotlight off this horrifying show. I was desperate for darkness. My hands swished big circles on the wall until I found the switch. Off. Dim slices of light from the bedroom slipped through the louvers and striped the floor. I turned to the box and kicked it again and again until my foot throbbed and the box gave way.

JD's old, beat-up wallet was on the floor behind the box. Damn. I ripped open the flap for the last time to bury the wallet. But instead, I dropped to my knees, snatched it from the floor, and tried to smooth the scratches in the leather with my thumb. I tore through it. Why? What was I looking for? The soft leather in my hands made me think of JD in the summer, her golden skin. A dump of memories fell on me. JD and her easy smile. Our secret language. I searched the wallet for anything JD. I wanted to see her so badly. Loose change and her Social Security card. I needed to see her face. I needed to find forgiveness in her eyes. Her law school ID, driver's license and phone numbers written on torn pieces of paper nestled in with the coins. Oh my God, the photos. Each one a knife in my heart. The tears came. Would she ever forgive me? A silent sob warped into pain.

"*Lilliana,*" I cried out loud. *Lilliana. Oh my God.* My body shriveled into itself. My head tipped over and met the floor. I wish I could have sunk through the floor and kept going. How could this have happened? How could I not have known? *Paul Lilliana? Why didn't you tell me? Why didn't you trust me? Weren't we better than that?*

I would've done anything for her.

I wanted the wallet out of my hands; I threw it, and it smacked against the box. It splayed open. The photos fanned out. It was JD and me at our high school graduation. Arms slinked around waists. Proud sister smiles. Caps and gowns.

"Sweetie!" Andrew was in the hall right outside our room. Oh my God. Andrew. I turned to face the louver door. Could he see me through the slats? I bit down on my hand to silence my chattering teeth. My body rattled.

"Caroline?" He walked into our room. His voice was light and airy—like angel food cake. It came from the opposite side, by his closet. I hugged my knees and rocked myself.

"*Caroline*, are you in here?" I could hear a grin on his face. He opened the door to our bathroom. My body jerked in the air from the sound of the knob.

I stiffened as he walked to my side of the room and stood in front of my closet, on the other side of the door, inches away from me. If the door wasn't there, I could reach out and grab his leg. Or he mine. "Whoa, Smarty, what's with all the noise? You find a rat this time? Calm down. There's nothing in there." I saw Andrew pick up the dog and pet him. Smarty growled in my direction. "Lilly, come up here, will you?" he called into the hall. "Take Smarty out. He's going crackers. He thinks there's something in the closet."

My body coiled into a mangled knot of skin and bones and nerves.

Lilly walked in. "Smarty, you quiet down," she said, wagging her finger.

"Take him, will you?" Andrew handed the dog over to her. "Where's Mommy?"

"I dunno. At the computer?" Lilly's voice trailed off as she left the room, "Shush, Smarty. That's your outside voice."

Andrew turned to leave and called into the hall, "Caroline, you in the attic? You wanna do that Google thing?" My body froze.

"Honey—where are you?" His voice drifted away, clinging to the air. "Caroline, let's Google ourselves. It'll be fun . . ."

ACKNOWLEDGMENTS

THE ROAD TO publication is a pothole-filled journey. If you're a writer, you know there are one million chances you could hit a bump in the road, fall out of your car, get bruised pretty badly and decide driving is not for you. Then end up walking everywhere you go for the rest of your life. There are infinite potential detours. Red lights that never turn green. Drivers who swerve into your lane and crush your car to smithereens. Sometimes you'll think you know where you're going when you set out, only to get lost along the way. Or maybe you simply run out of gas. There are as many opportunities to sabotage your success as there are days in your creative life, or even hours. To not listen to those cynical voices, whether they are external or internal, in order to get to this day—the day your flicker of an idea becomes a book— is close to a miracle.

There were many people whose encouragement, both big and small, kept me going. Thank you for cheering me on, holding my hand or paving the way for me to go the distance. To you, I bow my head in appreciation.

When *The Memory Box* was a preemie, there were early enthusiasts. This supportive network buoyed my resolve. I am so grateful to Sidney Offit for his generosity, his exuberance and encouraging me to "run home" and finish writing, but mostly, for believing I could. Sally Harrison and Joel Harrison for your persistence on my behalf and for being legit movers and shakers. Sue Temkin for calling in a favor for an unknown, Kathy Neumann for tackling a literary conundrum, Sheila Valenti, for being my first real fan. Lillie Bryen, for exceeding every definition of *best friend*. Rosanne Kurstedt for helping me slog through in my darkest hours and always seeing things with fresh eyes, even for the hundredth time. Westfield Writers Group, Cheryl Paden, Lillian Duggan, and Ann Ormsby to whom I could always bring my draftiest draft. For your personal magic and for seeing things I was blind to: Emma Schwartz, Marisa Mangione, Kathy Maughn. To my editor, Candace Johnson, whose enthusiasm, savvy, and collaboration were invaluable.

A special thanks for words or deeds: Chris Tomasino, Emily Rapoport, Laura Studwell, John Biguenet, Wendy Loggia, Yoonsun Lee, Mary Caye Swingle, Lois Walter, Mary Pat McCourt, Kim Manning, Brigid Robertshaw, Marci Bandelli, Robert Foley, Hannah Tinti, Dani Shapiro, Arielle Eckstut, and David Henry Sterry.

To my mom, dad and grandparents who taught me the virtues of hard work. To Stephen, Luke and Anne Lesko who think highly of me at exactly the right time.

To Peggy Natiello, for your effortless affirmation and for showing, not telling, that the first step to doing something is simply making the decision. To Bob Natiello for being my biggest cheerleader and for keeping me on my literary toes—who needs Strunk and White when you have Bob Natiello in the family?

For being the truest believers and everything to me, Margaux, Mark and Joe.

Readers Guide and Book Club questions for The Memory Box by Eva Lesko Natiello.

In order to provide discussion topics for reading groups and book clubs, important plot points are revealed. You may wish to explore these questions only after finishing
The Memory Box.

1. THROUGHOUT MUCH OF *The Memory Box*, we witness Caroline's panic as she discovers her inability to remember important events from her past. Do you empathize with her? Have you ever experienced something similar? In order to aid your memory, have you relied on outside sources? Did you ever discover that a memory from your childhood was something you fabricated from pieces of things?

2. THE AUTHOR RELIES on several "memory boxes" in the story. Discuss how some of the memory box devices are subjective and others are objective.

3. WE FIND OUT a great deal about Caroline and her childhood from listening to the audio tape of Elaine's session with Dr. Sullivan. Discuss what we learn about young Caroline and her relationship with JD.

4. CAROLINE HAD A heightened interest in twins. Discuss Caroline's insistence that she and JD were twins. Why do you think that's so important to Caroline and do you believe it's true?

5. WHAT ARE YOUR thoughts about Andy? Do you think Caroline has underestimated him? What do you think about Caroline's relationship with Lilly and Tessa?

6. FACADES PLAY AN important role in *The Memory Box*. Discuss the different facades at play and what they present and what they conceal.

7. IF IT IS a universal human quality to be concerned with what others think of us, discuss how each of the characters' concern manifests in different ways.

8. COMPARE THE RELATIONSHIP Caroline had with Timothy to the one she has with Andy.

9. HOW DOES THE setting affect the story?

10. DO YOU AGREE or disagree with Dr. Sullivan's decision to uphold the confidentiality agreement he has as Caroline's psychologist?

11. WHAT ARE YOUR thoughts about Caroline? Do you think it's possible for a person to be both good and evil?

12. WHY DO YOU think JD never told Caroline who Lilly's father was? Or about what happened at the party with Timothy?

13. HOW DOES THE book explore the concepts of perception and reality?

14. SOME PEOPLE MIGHT consider Caroline to be the ultimate control freak. Discuss the theme of control in the story.

15. THE TERM "GOOGLE Effect" is described as the habit of forgetting information that can be found easily by using Google or other search engines. Have you noticed a decline in your memory since the emergence of internet search engines and your use of them?

16. WERE YOU SATISFIED with the book's ending? What do you think will happen next?

ABOUT THE AUTHOR

EVA LESKO NATIELLO is an award winning author who lives in the New Jersey suburbs with her husband and two children. *The Memory Box* is her debut novel and a recipient of Houston Writers Guild 2014 Manuscript award. She is currently writing her next novel.

CPSIA information can be obtained at www.ICGtesting.com
Printed in the USA
LVOW08s2354061016

507769LV00001B/138/P